RAINE FALLING

HELLS SAINTS MOTORCYCLE CLUB

2014

Angela —
thanks for
taking this journey
with me —
Paula
XOO

RAINE FALLING

HELLS SAINTS MOTORCYCLE CLUB

PAULA MARINARO

Montlake Romance

Text copyright © 2014 Paula Marinaro
All rights reserved.

Published by Montlake Romance, Seattle

www.apub.com

Amazon, the Amazon logo, and Montlake Romance are trademarks of Amazon.com, Inc., or its affiliates.

ISBN-13: 9781477825686
ISBN-10: 1477825681

Cover design by Mumtaz Mustafa

Library of Congress Control Number: 2014908876

Printed in the United States of America

*Dedicated to the memory of my mother, Georgia Pomakis,
who saved up some of her brave just for me.*

CHAPTER 1

I heard screaming, begging, and crying. I saw them huddled against the wall. Pleading.

That's what was waiting for me at the end of the long, battered hallway of the apartment that my sister and her addict boyfriend, Jamie, shared. As I passed their bedroom, I could see a razor, coke residue, a rolled-up bill, and a small mirror sitting on the floor. I knew if I looked further that I would see a syringe and a heavy elastic band. When Jamie's sleeve was rolled up, his arms looked like a road map that said: Next Stop Heroin. This Way Please.

Jamie's drug of choice was H, and my sister's drug of choice for the past year had been Jamie. More recently, though, I knew she had been doing coke and not just a little bit. I had stopped giving Claire cash about a month ago, after I realized that most of it was either going up her nose or into his arm. I still came by once a week when I knew Jamie wouldn't be there. I bought my sister groceries and cleaned the house. Sometimes she would even go out with me.

Those were the good days, and I would like to be able to say they were just like old times. But I can't say that because my kid sis and I never really had the kind of upbringing that could draw on "remember the good old days" scenarios. One thing you can say about a shitty childhood is that it can do a lot to bond two little souls together.

Even in the worst of it, I had always reassured my sweet little sister that she and I were destined to live long, happy lives. I knew the chances were pretty good that there really were no happy endings and no rewards for surviving. But I would be damned if she was going to draw her last breath in fear, huddled on a dirty floor with a junkie's arms around her. Wondering how the hell I was going to get us out of this one, I walked towards her screams.

They had seen me anyway. I recognized the rockers on the cuts and knew instantly who I was dealing with. Not good, but it could have been worse. These guys were one percenters, no question. I had learned early though, that nobody was all bad or all good. One of the kindest men I ever had known had worn these colors.

CHAPTER 2

My dad's best friend had been one of the founders of the Hells Saints Motorcycle Club. They met while serving time in county. Spending two years together in a five-by-nine cell, you learn a lot about a man. In the hours of swapping stories, they had discovered that aside from having a long and unpleasant relationship with the United States criminal justice system, they had a lot in common.

My dad and Prosper had both grown up in foster care. They had served their country by joining the service. My dad had been Army and Prosper had been Marines. Jack and Prosper had each completed two tours in Vietnam. They both loved bikes, tequila, and dark-eyed women. Prosper was released a month after my dad. The two of them took to the road that very day, riding across the country, sharing everything. And that everything, eventually, had included loving the same woman.

My mother was Lakota Sioux. She was living in desperate poverty in the Badlands of South Dakota and selling little earrings by the side of the road. My dad liked to say that while she had easily been the most beautiful thing he had ever seen, it was her gentleness that had shone through like a beacon. It took him three days to convince her to ride out with him. Her name was Magaskawee and she was eighteen years old. My dad called her Maggie.

Maggie, Prosper, and Jack spent the next six months on the road together. My mother was pregnant before her nineteenth birthday. When Prosper heard the news, he rode out that same afternoon. I couldn't say for sure, but my guess is that being around her every day and not having her was something he had learned to live with. But watching her grow ripe and beautiful with the seed of his best friend growing deep inside her was just too much. So Prosper had left. Soon after that, he had started a family of his own. That family was the Hells Saints MC.

Prosper came back into their lives a few years later. By then, I was a little girl. I had been a shy, observant child living in a land of ordered chaos. I learned early on that there was a lot to be said about sitting quietly and watching. I watched for secrets. I found out Prosper's secret when I watched him watch my mom. Then I watched my dad watch Prosper watching my mom. My mom spent all of her time watching us, so it all worked out okay.

She was nineteen when I was born and eight years later she was gone. She gave us as much as she could in the time we had with her. She taught us the Lakota ways. She would often sing lullabies to us in rich, Native American language. She loved us. And we knew she loved us. I always knew we were safe with her. I didn't always know that about our father. I knew he would never hurt us, but there were times when I knew he didn't see us. Sometimes when Claire would laugh or cry or demand attention in her sweet baby way, he would look at her as if surprised she was still there or even there at all.

Our mother never forgot. And she was soft. Her skin was soft and her long hair was soft. Her eyes were a soft, deep brown color. They were fringed with thick, soft eyelashes. When she spoke, it was in soft tones. She never raised her voice. If we were out in the yard playing, she wasn't the sort of woman who would stand on the porch and yell for her children. She would walk to us and put her hand gently on us. Then she would guide us home. She was our world. It seemed as if she had no other family. We never had any grandparents or aunts or uncles visit us. Once I heard her talking on the phone to someone called Tanka. She was in the bedroom with the door closed, but I could hear her crying in between the words. I asked my mom about it, but she just shook her head and went sad for two days. I never brought it up again.

So Maggie made her family where she could. Although I know sometimes they made her uneasy, she welcomed my father's rough, wild friends with gentleness and grace. And they seemed gentler around her, those big, muscled, hardened men. Men that the town folk would give a wide berth to would turn sweet around her. My dad had an open-door policy when it came to his friends. Everyone was welcome at any meal. There was never ever not enough. From macaroni and cheese to roast beef. No one left that table hungry.

My mom had a way of making everyone feel like an honored guest. Whether the guest had just been released after doing five to ten or whether he was one of the "shadow people" who had been thrown out by his latest old lady and needed a hot meal, a shower, and a woman's advice. My mother treated them like kings. Because of this, these rough and tumble men were around a lot. When they sat at Maggie's table to break bread, they found their manners. They found their pleases and thank-yous. They found their ability to keep their elbows off the table and their napkins at the ready. They kept their mouths closed when they chewed. They kept their voices low and their conversation mainstream. They complimented the food and drank their beer from a glass. They offered to help with the dishes.

One thing they didn't do was ever find themselves too close to Maggie. Not in the kitchen, not in the dining room, not at the table. Our father had been known for his crazy jealous nature. His love for his boys only extended as far as it didn't interfere with the love of his life. Prosper was the only one who got close to her. Jack only allowed that because when Maggie had a choice to make, she had chosen him over Prosper. He also put up with it because Maggie would have it no other way. Our mother had put her foot down on two things in her whole life. One was that she made each and every important decision regarding her babies. The other was that wherever was home for Maggie and Jack was also home for Prosper.

But they were all gone now. Cancer took my mom early on. After losing her, my dad drank himself to death. I hadn't seen Prosper in many years.

Prosper had been a hard, handsome man. He had dark brown eyes and light brown hair that was streaked through with caramel and honey sun-kissed highlights. When he picked up the small girl that was me, I felt like I was sitting atop a redwood. He had a deep, gravelly voice and sang a mean Bob Seger. In the summertime, there would often be a warm crackling fire in the smoke pit of our backyard. He and my dad would play soft music and sing in deep harmony. Claire and I would fall asleep to those tunes in our mother's arms. I grew up knowing all the words. Sometimes I heard my mom humming Prosper's music softly to herself when she thought she was alone.

Other times there would be different people in our backyard. On those nights there would be no music, just loud men and women with letters on their jackets just like Prosper's. I didn't need to watch them to know that their secrets came from dark places. On those nights, I would keep Claire upstairs with me, tucking her in close. Keeping her safe from the dark shadows that they cast upon the bedroom walls.

On my eighth birthday, Prosper bought me a beautiful silver harmonica. As much as I had loved the wonderful little music maker, the best gift of all was the time we spent together. He talked to me about how the harmonica was a magic instrument because it was so small. So small that you could carry the gift of music with you wherever you went. He said that if you had music, you were never alone.

Prosper taught me how to hold it so that the low notes were on the right and what those notes meant. I learned that if I blew into one little hole it sounded one way, and if I sucked the air in it sounded another way. I learned how to isolate those sounds. He taught me to breathe from the diaphragm. He tutored me on the fine art of overblows and how to choke them. Prosper said that while the standard lip lock was a cool way to go, you really needed to do it a different way to play the blues. He taught me how to make rich, soulful sounds by bending notes. I practiced so much I was in a permanent state of cramped hands and swollen lips.

My mother was pretty sick by then. Prosper and I would spend hours sitting by her bedside singing and playing for her. Mom's favorite was Bob Seger's "Turn the Page." She made us play it over and over again. To her unending delight, Prosper learned to replace the long, soulful sax with a beautiful riff on his mouth harp. When he taught me how to sing in harmony, my childish voice was clear, strong, and fearless. I loved him because he shared her with me. In quiet moments while I sat playing on the floor, they talked softly to each other. I watched my mother then, and I saw what I had missed before. My mother had a secret too.

The love my father had for my mother filled his heart so completely that there wasn't much room left over for us. Her illness broke wide apart a deep hurt in his soul that only being loved by her could heal. She changed him, and when a woman changes a man that way, that man would rather die than go back to the place without her. My dad's secret wasn't that he couldn't live without our mother, but that he didn't want to.

He was disappearing before my eyes, and I took to following him around everywhere. I knew my mother would soon be gone, and I was petrified to lose him too. I waited and I watched. He never seemed to notice, but Prosper did. One morning we woke up to find Prosper gently snoring on the couch with Claire's little body tucked safely under his arm. He was there every night after that until my mom died two weeks later. Prosper was the one who arranged all the things for the service. He held our little hands in his through the whole thing. My dad was too deep in his own grief to tend to ours.

After my mom was gone Prosper would still come and visit, but there were no more magic nights filled with sweet music and firelight. When I watched him then, there seemed to be a darkness growing within him. I knew all his new secrets came from bad places, and that had made me sad.

Eventually he started to bring a woman around. She had the unlikely name of Pinky and she was fascinating. She was round in all the right places and had big blond hair that hung in soft curls down her back. She wore bracelets with little gold bells that chimed when she moved. She had a wide mouth and a big laugh. She smoked endlessly and when she hugged us, she smelled of tobacco and lilacs. I remember she used to bring us cookies, and one time she even cleaned the house. Prosper smiled when he was with her. The first time I heard my father laugh again was because of something she had said.

Prosper, Pinky, and Jack were the family we were left with. Because I was a watcher, I knew that by many standards, Prosper was not a good man. But he was always good to us and that wasn't only enough, it was everything.

Then came the night when the good in Prosper stepped up to change the crash course that had become our little lives.

CHAPTER 3

Two big men filled the dirty, little kitchen. One had a gun closely trained on my sister and Jamie.

"You here why?" A third man I hadn't noticed pulled himself away from the filthy kitchen counter and walked towards me.

"My name is Raine," I stammered. "Claire is my sister."

My palms were sweating and the fragile hold I had on the paper grocery bag started to slip. The bag broke, and the groceries fell heavily on the floor. Apples were rolling everywhere. I followed them with my eyes, trying to gain composure.

The man standing in front of me was the biggest man I had ever seen. Everything about him was frightening. He stood well over six feet tall and had massive arms covered with big tribal tattoos. His skin was the color of sun-kissed copper, and he had jet-black, tousled hair. He had a long, straight nose. His perfect white teeth looked like they were ready to bite me. His eyes were so dark, I couldn't see his pupils. The outlaw was dressed all in black. Three little silver hoops dangled from his right ear.

He continued to walk slowly towards me with his big arms crossed against his chest. When he examined me from the top of my head to the bottom of my feet, I felt myself shrinking back. I couldn't bring myself to look at him for very long. I forced myself to look past him into the dark night, and I saw myself in the reflection.

From the top of my ponytailed head to the bottom of my running shoes, I looked small and scared in my too-big scrubs. I had just finished my last class of nursing school. As of that very minute, I was a licensed practical nurse specializing in pediatrics. The ceremony itself would be in two weeks. But really I was done, and I had wanted to celebrate early with Claire.

I broke out of my trance and pulled myself back when I felt him reach out and grab my arms. He roughly turned my palms up and stretched out each arm looking for marks. Not finding any, he pushed me away from him and snorted.

"You're clean," he said.

Not sure if this was a question or not I nodded *yes.*

"Why are you here?" I asked him.

He turned to look at my sister, who was still hysterical on the floor.

"Ask her."

"What have you done?" My hands were at my sides now and balled up so tight I could feel my nails cutting into the palms of my hands. My sister's eyes were glazed over with fright, and I saw that the absolute piece of shit had a tight hold on her.

"None of your fucking business, bitch." That was Jamie.

I ignored him and walked quickly to put myself between the gun and my sister. I knelt down beside her and smoothed the sweaty matted hair off her face.

"Claire, please *please* tell me. What have you done?"

She wouldn't look at me. When I looked up, I saw three really big badass bikers staring down at the cleavage left open by my over-sized scrubs. A giant of a man reached over and hauled me up.

"Your sister and her jacked-up boyfriend have a real problem, sugar."

The hold he had on me tightened. I glanced down quickly at the panther tattoo that ran the length of his arm. The front of his hair was pulled back into a ponytail, while the rest fell loosely on his shoulders. He had bright white teeth, a tanned face, and a two-day stubble.

I took a deep breath and nodded. Maybe this could be fixed.

"How much?"

"Thirty large." He smiled.

I felt the legs go out from under me. Not because I couldn't fix this, but because I could. I had saved every single dime I had ever been given or earned since the age of ten years old. I had exactly thirty-one thousand dollars saved. A small fortune to me. It was everything we hadn't done. It was everything we hadn't had. It had always fallen on me, and I had always stepped up. I lived in a tiny house that we had inherited. I never went out. I drove a crappy car and spent next to nothing on myself. I kept a close watch on that money, all the while planning on it going towards something better for the two of us. If saving Claire's life was the "something better," I was good with that.

"I'm good for it." I looked him in the eye.

I heard someone snort in the background and amber eyes skimmed my body. Then he reached out with his hand and *touched me.* Two fingers trailed a slow path from the hollow of my throat, over my scrubs, and in between my breasts to my belly button. I held my breath and watched him as his eyes followed the path he made and then below.

He looked up and smirked. "Darlin', there's no doubt in my mind that *you're good for it.*"

I pulled my arm out of his death grip and said, "I can get you that money."

Then I did a mental calculation in my head. Today was Monday.

"I need five days, and you'll have your money."

"Banks are open tomorrow, darling," said a voice so close to me it made me jump. It was the badass in black.

I looked him straight in the eye. "It's not in the bank."

He arched his eyebrow.

I hurriedly added, "It's my money. I'm not doing anything illegal to get it. Don't worry."

I heard some chuckles and looked around the room to a sea of black leather and grins.

"Darlin'." Badass grinned. Then he pulled his hand through his hair, cocked his eyebrow at me, and continued, "I don't care if you do blow jobs at a thousand a head to get it."

That was accompanied by a lot of hoots and hollers. Then it started.

"I would be in a grand for that. Look at that sweet mouth."

"Fifteen here, if you include anal."

"Hell, I'll give her five hundred bucks right now just to show me her tits."

I ignored them and reminded myself that I was my mother's daughter. I looked Badass right in the eye. He waited until the hilarity died down.

"Why can't you get it now?" He wasn't smiling any longer.

I took a deep breath because I didn't like thinking about Gino.

"Because it's hidden in a strong box in my ex's garage along with a lot of other stuff that I left when I *left*."

"You left thirty grand in your ex's garage?"

I nodded. "I had to leave everything. He doesn't know it's there."

"How long ago?"

"About four months."

"How do you know he hasn't found it yet?"

"Because he would have found me and killed me for hiding it from him." That was what a horror Gino had become. It was the straight-up truth.

His eyebrow went up.

"But it's your money? Not that I give a shit. Just trying to sort this out."

"Yeah, it's my money."

"Go get the shit now, Diego?" asked a man from the sidelines.

So the man in black was Diego.

I shook my head. I was seriously afraid of that lunatic Gino.

"No!" Claire called out. Everyone turned their eyes to my little sister.

"No?" said Diego.

Claire turned her big, beautiful blue eyes to him and said, "Then he'll find out where she is, and when you're gone, he'll come back and hurt her."

"What do you mean, hurt her?" Diego was staring at Claire.

I stood very still watching Claire.

"He broke her nose before, and . . ."

"And?" Diego was looking at both of us now.

I held my breath and shook my head slightly in warning to Claire.

"And . . ." Claire had paled looking at my face.

"Yeah and what?"

I pulled my arms tight around me. Praying to sweet Jesus she wouldn't finish that sentence.

". . . some other bad stuff," she ended weakly with her eyes on me.

I closed my own eyes and began to breathe again.

"He took a really rough turn on the bitch," Jamie croaked out gleefully. He was a guy who never missed an opportunity to capitalize on shame.

Diego's eyes squinted and I felt them on me.

"He raped you? That sonofabitch *raped* you?"

All eyes on me then. I felt myself flush and go dizzy. Faces started swirling around in a haze. My head pounded and my lungs hurt. I had stopped breathing.

"Did he?" Diego was moving towards me.

I couldn't seem to catch my breath.

"Did he rape you?" He was closing in on me.

Breathe, Raine. Just breathe, I told myself. Inhale. Exhale. One . . . two . . . three . . .

"Raine, did he?" Diego was still moving in.

Suddenly a burst of air escaped my lungs in a giant whoosh, and I had to steady myself with the force.

"No! Of course not." All that air, and all I could manage was a squeak.

All eyes still on me. I thought I might throw up and briefly wondered how Diego's badass biker boots would look with puke all over them. The thought made my stomach turn one more time.

I desperately wanted this conversation to move on. But not in the direction it took.

Jamie chimed in from his throne on the floor, "Why would I say it if it ain't true?" He was sniveling from his place in the corner.

"Because you're a desperate jacked-up ass who would say anything and do anything." I made myself busy looking for my pocketbook and found it on the counter. I had recovered my ability to inhale and exhale and was taking full advantage of the moment.

Feeling those eyes still upon me, I was fighting against a full-blown anxiety attack. I needed to calm down if I wanted to get us out of this one. And I needed to get us out of there fast. I dug into my pocketbook and my hand came out shaking.

I handed Diego my license and said, "This is where I live. You come by Friday night and I'll have your money. Or you can tell me where and I'll bring it to you."

He looked at me like I was from another planet. "Seriously?"

I realized how absurd that was.

"At least you know I'm not going to be hiding from you. My sister and I will both be there. If we don't come up with the money, you can kill us then." I said it more casually than I felt. I took my license back from him and put it in my bag.

"Killing ain't the first thing I'd have in mind." He was staring at my breasts. And he was doing it to make me uncomfortable. Then he grinned. Asshole.

I was a long way from smiling. "If I don't have your money, you do whatever you want to me. But my sister leaves with me now."

I held out my hand. "Agreed?"

He took my cold hand. He held it too tightly in his man paw and said, "Agreed. We recoup our green and it's all good. That's unless we find the little missus and her man are in it up to their ears. Then the thirty grand won't mean jack. If that happens, we'll be looking for a payment of a different color. You get what I'm sayin', Babe?"

My eyes turned to Claire.

My sister struggled from where Jamie was holding her. "Raine, I swear to Jesus, there's nothing else. And he can get it. Jamie *has* that money." She pleaded with him, "Don't bring my sister into this."

Jamie tightened his hold on my sweet baby sister and said, "Bitch, shut up. Let the cunt pay, so we can get these assholes off our backs."

I heard a sharp intake of breath from behind me and Diego took a step towards Jamie. Claire tried to pull away from him and elbowed Jamie deep, catching his ribs.

"What the fuck? I'll hurt you, bitch" Jamie reached out and grabbed my sister's hair. Then he snapped her neck so far back, for a minute I thought that he had killed her.

All hell broke loose. Gunner and I both moved in on Jamie. Diego yanked me back quickly and held me so close against him that I could smell leather and clean soap. I pulled away from him just as fast. My eyes were glued to my sister. I watched as the blond biker put his hand against the junkie's throat and squeezed.

"Let her fucking go. Right. Fucking. Now."

"Fuck you, Gunner!" Jamie managed to squeak out. Then he did the unthinkable. He spat in the biker's face.

Gunner roared and let go of Jamie's throat. He pulled back fast and hit him once hard in the face. Jamie lost his death grip on Claire. With a sob she got up and ran to me. I struggled to be free of the iron armband holding me, and Diego let me go. I opened my arms to my sister, pulling her close. The Hells Saints were all over Jamie, and I could hear the sickening crunch of breaking bones. Gunner picked him up and threw him across the kitchen, splintering a row of cabinets. When Claire opened her mouth to scream, I clamped my hand over it. We heard sirens sounding in the distance. Another vicious kick to the ribs and someone said, "We gotta get the fuck outta here."

Diego grabbed my arm and growled, "You got five days to make this right."

Then he pulled me close and whispered against my hair, "You got no green, you gone. You take your shit, and you leave tonight. Get me, Babe? You lying about this shit, you find a way to disappear. Your sister lying about this shit, she's dead."

"I wasn't lying," I whispered.

Diego took one long last look at me and headed for the door.

"How will I find you?" I called softly to him.

Diego turned around and looked at me.

"Got that," he said and was gone.

Claire and I ran to my car and, after the third try, the engine turned. We pulled out of the parking lot exit just as the police were taking the off-ramp to the complex. I pulled onto the highway and reduced my speed to legal. Claire had begun moaning in the seat. Her nose was bleeding. I made a split-second decision and turned off the exit that led to the hospital. The strangulation marks on my sister's throat stood out in sharp relief against her pale skin. She was holding her head to one side, cradling her neck in her hand. I was beginning to think that Jamie might have done some serious damage.

16

Claire was also jonesing from the coke, and I knew the nose-bleed had something to do with that. I was familiar with a lot of the staff at the hospital, and I knew they wouldn't question it if I told them my sister had been mugged. From the hospital, I was pretty sure that I could get Claire into rehab for the blow. I wasn't sure how Point General Hospital would feel about employing a nurse with an addict sister. I guessed we would just have to wait and see on that one.

It took me an hour in the parking lot to convince a sobbing, terrified, strung-out little sister to go along with the plan. She wanted to get clean, and I knew that wouldn't be a problem with Jamie out of the picture. I also knew that if things went bad, I couldn't have her anywhere near me or that house on Friday. Claire was the only thing I had left that I loved. I wouldn't lose her. If it came down to it, I would give my life for hers. No question.

It took me the better part of the night to get Claire settled into the hospital and to arrange for a subsequent bed in rehab. We had to file a (falsified) police report, and I was exhausted from the fear and the lies and the worry.

CHAPTER 4

To say I thought a lot about that night would be a lie. To say I thought of nothing else would be much closer to the truth. I jumped at every sound and locked every window despite the heat of the evening. I jammed a chair against the bathroom door while I bathed and against the bedroom door when I slept. I fretted and worried constantly. I had a permanent headache and my eyes hurt. I wanted this to be over. I had no idea what had happened to Jamie. I didn't want to know. If my head was clear, I might have worried about him coming after us. But my head was full of other really, really bad things.

About a year earlier, I had moved in with Gino Abbiati. He managed a club next to the hospital that served cheap drinks and pub food. Best of all, the staff never made you feel rushed or complained when a study group of ten took up a table for a few hours during the busy time. Appreciating this, we always ordered the cheapest thing on the menu to be able to tip big for the privilege of sitting there.

Gino was beautiful, charming, and persuasive. He smiled, flirted, and asked me out every single time I was in the place. He never charged me for my drinks, and on the odd occasion I ordered a burger, he would pick up the tab for that too. He was genuinely interested in everything I had to say and took every opportunity to converse with me. I held him off for a while, but not long enough to really get to know him.

He showed up for our first date with the biggest bouquet of flowers I had ever seen. Since no one had ever given me flowers, it could have been one rose and it would have had the same effect. He showered me with just enough and just the right kind of attention. He took me out when he sensed I needed that release, and when the class work became overwhelming, he sat up with me all night and tested me on my flashcards. One time when I complained that my hand was cramped from taking such copious notes, he showed up with a little handheld tape recorder so I could record my lessons. No one had ever done anything like that for me. No one had ever treated me that well. No one had ever paid enough attention to my life to know about the things that would make it easier. He not only paid attention, he made an effort to make it easier.

I fell hard and he wanted me to move in immediately. He hounded me about it day and night until finally, six months into it, I accepted. The agreement was that I would stay at his place but still keep my grandmother's house. He had wanted me to put the house on the market, but that was where I drew a hard line. Gino didn't even attempt to cross it, and we lived happily ever after for a while. The sex was great and we actually had fun together when he wasn't drinking. He had a nasty streak that came out when he drank, but he had never hit me. I had been dealing with drunks in one way or another most of my life, so while I wasn't okay with the nasty drunk side of Gino, I could put up with it.

I put up with it right until I caught him in bed with our sixteen-year-old neighbor. When she saw me, she had run out screaming. Disgusted, I turned to walk out the door. From the look on her face it appeared that she was happy to be escaping and not just from me. But Gino wasn't happy at all. In fact, he was so enraged that he came charging at me. The first punch he landed broke my nose.

Then he took payment from me for the sex I guess he thought he was missing.

I always knew I had to go back and get that money. But I also knew that the money would be safe there. Gino never went into the second bay of the two-car garage. The thought of what he might do if he found me there made me sick. I was straight-up terrified of him. Gino Abbiati had raped me while I was barely conscious, and my nose was gushing blood. That made him an animal in my mind. All the good forgotten.

Maybe I had made some mistakes in judgment in my life *but I wasn't that girl.* And I was never ever going to be that girl. The one who forgot and forgave when a man beat her and raped her. That girl was not me. The only way I had escaped from him was because he was so strung out that he passed out right after. I had no thoughts of giving him another chance at hurting me again. A drunk Gino was annoying. A jacked-up Gino was deadly. I wished with all my heart that I didn't have to go get that money. It loomed over me like a big, black doomsday cloud.

Waiting around the house until the time rolled around was just too much. I jumped at every noise. I paced. I couldn't eat or sleep. I decided to see what I could do about getting to that money sooner. I sat outside Gino's house in different spots, at different times, for the next two days. Finally, I saw Gino and his Lexus leave with a pretty, flaxen-haired blonde riding shotgun.

Now or never.

I slipped around to the backyard and carefully turned the door to the garage. It gave way immediately. I saw a newly installed alarm system to my right and figured it was to the main house. Who would alarm a garage? But I hurried anyway.

The cardboard box I had hidden the money in was at the very top of the shelf. I grabbed a ladder to retrieve it. I had it! I hurried down the ladder and was heading out when the automatic garage door came flying open. Gino was standing in the driveway with the Lexus still running behind him. I looked quickly at the alarm to see the sequence of lights going crazy. I must have set it off. I was shaking so hard at seeing him that I almost wet myself.

Gino was standing in front of me shouting. His hands were clenched in outrage. The next thing I knew he was straddling me while alternately choking and hitting me. I felt the fury of his fists pound into my face. Gino had my head caged firmly in his hands and was getting ready to smash the back of my skull in. I fought and screamed like a wildcat. Then I heard a gunshot and felt plaster raining on my face.

"Get off her now, you woman-beating sonofabitch!"

Gino let go of my skull just long enough to turn around and scream at the pissed-off blonde.

"Shut up, cunt, or you'll be next!"

I felt Gino slump on me then. I pushed him off and looked up to see the blonde heaving with the exertion that came from clocking Gino with the butt of the gun. That coming after shooting the hell out of the ceiling.

She extended her hand to pull me up and said, "The guy is pure bastard. Now get your sweet ass out of here and never come back."

Gino started moaning. The blonde and I looked at each other and ran like hell.

CHAPTER 5

I wasn't sure if I could make it home. My head was pounding and my cheek felt slick with blood. I wondered if I would need stitches on my face. I was sick with the knowledge that Gino would come after me now and vaguely wondered if I needed to worry about Jamie as well.

My hands were trembling so hard I could barely drive. I decided to pull up to the back of my house and go through the cellar as a precaution. My eyes welled up with tears. I wasn't a crier. Self-indulgent tears had been one of the luxuries I wouldn't allow myself. I had learned early to keep my feelings bottled up until the emotion passed. The few times I had allowed myself tears, I had cried for so long and hard that I couldn't stop for hours. Opening those floodgates was a bad idea for me. But it had been a really shitty few days.

I fumbled with the keys as I felt huge drops of water begin to form in the corners of my eyes and flow freely down my cheeks. I looked down as the tears began to drop on my white tank and wondered briefly why they were pink. How much was I bleeding? My mouth was starting to swell, and I had been tasting blood all the way home. I took the edge of my shirt and spit blood into it on my way to the bathroom. This was not good.

I looked in the mirror. My blue eyes were so dark they looked purple. The side of my face was beginning to swell. Still sobbing, I washed my face carefully and threw my bloodied clothes into the laundry basket. Then I changed my mind and threw them out in the trash. I wanted no reminders of this night. I picked up the cardboard box that had nearly cost me my life and painfully made my way up the stairs.

It was a full moon and I jumped at every long shadow cast by my wornout furniture. Still afraid to turn on any lights, I cried my way into the kitchen. I needed a shot of booze for my nerves and a bag of ice for my face. Mostly I needed to get a damn hold of myself and stop crying, but I just couldn't seem to manage it.

Carrying the box towards the table, I stopped when I saw him.

The stuff of nightmares.

There was someone very big and scary shadowed against the outline of my kitchen cabinet. He saw me at the same time I saw him. The badass biker who wanted my thirty grand or wanted me dead, and he was two days early. I let out a shriek. He moved fast but I was faster. I turned and ran down the hallway, knocking things in his path as I went. I heard him swear loudly behind me as a chair came crashing down in front of him. I felt something swipe at me and miss. I was glad I didn't have much on because it meant that he couldn't grab my shirt to pull me back. I was almost at the door when he got me.

With steel arms, he pulled me tight against him. I went crazy. I bucked and kicked and bit and scratched. He just held on tighter, avoiding my kicks and blows. I knew I wasn't doing much damage. However, with all that fighting, my bra had somehow managed to work itself towards my neck. I felt his hands move to my breasts, squeezing.

That struck a terror of a different kind in me, and I suddenly went still. My back against a solid wall of muscle and my breasts being firmly kneaded by big warm hands. I moved my hands to cover his in an attempt to pry them off. When I felt each one tweak a nipple I felt a rush of wet go straight through to my panties. I was so humiliated that I wanted to die.

"Please," I whispered.

"Please what, baby?" He whispered against my hair, still holding on to me.

"Please let me go."

"Please let me go, *Diego*," he said against my hair.

"Diego?"

"Yeah, baby."

"Please, Diego. Let me go."

Suddenly I felt my lace bra fall back onto my bruised breasts. Diego turned me around to look at him. His face went from mild amusement to instant shock. I heard his sharp intake of breath.

"Who?" he roared and it felt like an accusation.

I jerked my face out of his big hands and looked into his black eyes.

That was a good question. Who really had done this to me?

The answer made me sad, and I smiled slightly at the irony. I looked him in the eye and said, "I did this to myself."

Then I walked straight past him to get the money.

I needed to put some clothes on, but more than anything, I really just needed this day to be over. I decided to forego the extra two seconds it might have taken me to go and throw on a pair of sweats. Plainly speaking, I just didn't give a shit. Besides the bastard had already seen everything I was showing anyway. I stood with my back towards him as I unlocked the metal box containing the envelope that held the money. My outstretched arm was shaking so much that I thought the cash was going to jump right out of the envelope onto the floor. But it didn't.

Diego was standing against the doorjamb with his arms crossed against his massive chest, staring at my face. He didn't make a move towards the money, so I jabbed at him again with the envelope. My head was throbbing, I was bone tired and on the verge of tears again. I wanted him to take the damn money and leave. I really didn't want to vomit in front of this man, but it was dangerously close to happening.

I headed towards him all bloody and bruised. I was wearing nothing but bloodstained pink lace. My hair was matted with gore and draped around me like a weird cape. I was woozy from my headache, making it impossible to walk a straight line. Waves of nausea kept swirling around me. I fought with everything I had to maintain some sort of dignity.

I was the undead.

He watched me carefully as I approached him. Unfolding his arms, he let his hands rest casually on his hips. His black eyes never left my face. Avoiding his gaze, I reached down and grabbed his hand. He gave it up willingly. I pressed the envelope deep into his big paw and then looked right into his eyes.

"This is finished."

With as much dignity as I could muster, I wobbled past him down the hallway. Once in my bedroom, I gave the cheap lock a satisfied twist. Then I sat on the edge of my bed to take stock. I trusted that having gotten what he came for and two fucking days early to boot, Diego could find his own way out. I forced myself to relax. Taking a deep breath I summoned what was left of my courage and gently began to examine my face. With infinite care I pushed determinedly past the tenderness searching for fractures on my cheeks, jaw, and nose. Thankfully, I found none. Thanks to one mean-ass, quick-thinking sistah, I wasn't sporting a split skull.

Because of my extreme nausea, I went through a quick checklist. I wasn't disoriented, definitely had no memory loss, hadn't lost consciousness, and my speech was fine. I hadn't eaten since supper last night, and I supposed that was where the nausea was coming from. I tore off my underwear, pulled on a pair of pajama shorts and a tank top. Then I started to crawl into bed. That's when the first wave of nausea hit me full force. I ran to the bathroom and proceeded to dry-heave my way into what I hoped would be oblivion.

CHAPTER 6

Diego pulled himself away from the wall and watched Raine make her way to the bedroom. The envelope of cash was still in his hand. *Friday.* She was supposed to go get this on Friday. What the fuck had happened? He had worked this to keep her safe, and it fucking all blew up.

Twenty minutes after the cops left in disgust with Jamie refusing to go to the hospital or file any charges, Gunner was back. And he had brought a few of his brothers with him. All it took was seeing them to make Jamie give it all up. The *all* being the mother lode.

There had been about five hundred grand in cash, four nines, a good amount of uncut coke, and a shitload of H hidden in that shit hole. As to who he had fucked over to acquire that tit stock, Jamie sang that tune like a sweet canary. That took about fifteen minutes to put together. The rest of the hour was spent teaching Jamie exactly what it meant to hold out and then spit in the face of a Hells Saint. No one bothered to check if he was still breathing when they left.

Given the amount and variety of the recovered stash, it had taken a couple of days to sort out. Wars had been started over less. Because it was suspected that at least some of the green had come from his territory, Diego had been sent up to investigate. The drugs belonged to Los Diablos Rojos, but the green was something that the Saints definitely had a stake in.

Today at church, they had discussed Raine and Claire. Not sure how deeply they were involved in this whole shit storm, Diego had Gunner put out some feelers. When he reported out, the general consensus was that Claire wasn't a bag bitch, but just another stupid little piece that got caught up with the wrong guy.

They knew from their people that Raine had driven Claire to the hospital right after she had taken her from the junkie's shit hole. They knew about the bogus police report and that Claire was in rehab. They knew that Raine lived in a shitty little shanty on the outside of town that had belonged to her grandmother, and that there was no extra floating around. They knew where she shopped for groceries, and that her car was thirteen years old. They knew she was a pediatric nursing student who had just finished up with honors. They knew she didn't fuck with the drugs she had legal access to. They knew she was clean.

The vote was taken and the shit with Claire and her junkie boyfriend was considered a settled issue. The only thing that remained was to let Raine know. When Diego said he would "take care of that," the members of the Hells Saints smirked, thinking they knew exactly what that meant.

On his part, Diego couldn't get Raine out of his mind. He got hard every time he thought of her. Unbelievably gorgeous. Every guy in that fucking kitchen held his breath when they saw her. Brave too. Christ, just walking into that room took some guts. Then as cool as anything, she had put herself between her sister and a loaded gun. Tight little body when he held her against him. Plenty of long dark hair, smooth tanned skin, and deep blue eyes. Her little sister not bad either, as Gunner had pointed out several times. He had called them exotic little pieces. Diego had to agree.

There was some other information that Diego had gone after but that was personal. He had paid a lot for the file, and it had Gino Abiatti's name on it. As soon as Jamie let it out that the piece of shit holding Raine's money had beaten and raped her, Abiatti was a dead man. Knowing that Friday night Raine was going to be putting herself in the path of that psycho, Diego had put a plan in place. But Raine going there early had fucked up his plan. And Gino had hurt her again. Abiatti had a lot to look forward to. Diego was gonna make sure he spent a whole lot of fucking time dying.

He picked up his cell.

CHAPTER 7

I laid my head on the cool tile after some totally nonproductive retching. My ass was up, my head was under the toilet, and I was clutching my stomach. Between the throbbing in my head, the hurt in my face, and the pain in my stomach, I thought I was going to die. The next wave of nausea hit me. I was clutching the sides of the toilet dry-heaving my innards out, when I felt a blessedly cool cloth on my forehead. For one insane desperate moment, I let my head lean against it and memories of my mom came washing over me.

"Here, drink this," said a voice that was definitely not my mom.

A glass of something cold was gently pressed against my lips. Thickly shaved ice and water coated my throat. It tasted like heaven. I knew who was standing next to me, but I was too exhausted to give a shit or even wonder at the absurdity of it.

Shakily I handed the glass back to him. When he reached down to fold me in his arms and carry me to my bed, I went with it. He gently covered my hot, dry body with the cool sheet. Then he held out a small white pill that I recognized as a Valium.

"This will help you sleep."

I so wanted to end this day. Knowing that the little white pill would help that to happen, I took it and closed my eyes.

I woke several hours later to a moonlit room feeling something warm touch my stomach. It was light and feathery. Just enough to wake me up, but not enough to keep me awake. I started to drift back to sleep. Sudden realization hit me. I shrank against the wall. My scream came out like a whimper, and I realized distantly that I was still punchy from the drug I had taken.

He put his two fingers gently to my mouth and said, "Shhh. Easy, baby."

My whole body stiffened, and I put my hands out to stop him. He pulled me fast against him and wound his hand in my hair.

"Relax. If I was gonna do you, it would have already happened." Then he paused and added, "Many, many times over."

I stopped breathing and willed my mind to bring me somewhere else.

"Look at me, Raine." He tightened his hold on my hair and pulled my face towards him. His black eyes smiled down at me. There were two dimples denting the light scruff on his face.

I got very still. Reaching back into the defenses of my mind, I did as I was told. I watched him watch me. His eyes touching every corner of my face. He took his thumb and ran it gently across my lips. When I instinctively ran the tip of my tongue across it, his eyes grew dark. He moved in closer. His eyes moved to my mouth, and then his lips slowly followed. He rained soft little kisses on the sides of my mouth, and that I didn't mind at all. I began to respond to the gentleness. He began to make gentle circles on my stomach with his hand. I arched slightly against him, and he moved over me, pressing his lips deep against mine, opening me to him. I felt an instant burst of sharp pain and pulled away hard.

"What is it?" He had stopped the kiss dead in its tracks.

"My lip," I whispered.

"Show me," he whispered back.

I reached up and rolled down my bottom lip, gently exposing the ragged cut that I knew was there. I released my lip and watched. He watched too. He watched to make sure I didn't pull back when his big body moved over mine. He reached for something from the bedside. Then he rolled back over on his side, one hand on my waist and the other hand moving to my mouth. I felt it before I saw it. The cold clean sensation of the sliver of ice sliding up and down the sore place on the inside of my lip felt so wonderful that I sighed against it. The remainder of the Valium worked its way back into my system.

"That's it, baby. Let it work its magic. Close your eyes. Nothing else is going to hurt you tonight." He was speaking from somewhere far away . . .

I closed my eyes and breathed deeply. So nice . . . so nice of him . . . so nice . . .

My thoughts began to drift together as I fell into a soft, gentle sleep. But not before reaching for his hand and holding it lightly in mine.

"Thank you," I whispered through the haze.

Diego pulled me close. "Sleep, baby."

And I did.

CHAPTER 8

When he heard her breath grow even and felt her body mold into his, he pulled her even closer. He felt her warm and soft against his chest. He had smoothed her hair. She smelled like spring. Her scent was clean and fresh. She felt even better. He wondered what it would be like to be loved by a woman like this.

Diego had seen the damage up close. He had winced at the torn lip, the swollen eye, and the bruises covering her chin, chest, and neck. She had taken a pretty bad beating. It was because of him that monster had whaled on her. He had put her in harm's way.

If that wasn't enough, Diego had broken into her house, waited for her in the dark, chased her, fondled her, and had taken all her money. He had scared her and not just a little. He knew terror. He had seen it in her eyes when she first saw his shadow, and then later when she had woken to him. He had caused the fast beating of her heart. And not in a good way.

Diego had watched Raine retreat and go perfectly still. She had wrapped her arms around herself and pulled them in tight. Her eyes had grown dark with fear, and something undefinable when she thought he was going to hurt her. Then she had responded so fully when he showed her gentleness and kindness that he wondered how little of it she had known. He was curious about her. He wondered what kind of woman she was. Then instantly he knew. If he wasn't

real careful, she was the kind of woman a man could get lost in . . .
for as long as they both shall live. Raine was that kind of woman.

Diego held her and watched her sleep through the night. She
slept fitfully, sighing and murmuring, alternately pressing against
him and pulling away from him. He shifted her a couple of times
to watch her face and had felt the soft skin of her belly warm the
palm of his hand. The Valium had cast its spell and she slept deeply.
He wondered at the demons that invaded her dreams, and he found
that he didn't want to leave her to them. As dawn began to break,
the first rays of light touched her face, revealing the deepening pur-
ples, reds, blacks, and blues of the beating she had taken. The one
he hadn't stopped.

Diego had to go meet with his brothers to discuss the shit with
Jamie. There was a lot that had gone down with that deal, including
the intel on the H and coke. Shit that had to be revealed and bound-
aries that had to be redrawn because of it. Club business was fully
on his mind when he left her sleeping. It wasn't until two days later
that Diego realized he had forgotten to tell Raine that she could
consider all debts to the Hells Saints MC paid in full. And by then
it was too late.

CHAPTER 9

I woke up alone with a fuzzy head and too many aches and pains to count. I ran the shower, and stiffened when the hard sprays of water hit my skin. I noticed the beginnings of several more deep blue bruises where that bastard Gino had pummeled me. I wondered again if I had to worry about the junkie and the bastard tag-teaming me one night in some dark parking lot. Then decided I was too fucking tired of it all to care.

I got out of the shower and wiped the steam from the mirror to peruse the damage. I looked at the inside of my mouth first because I was still worried about loose teeth. Blushing, I said to myself, *Don't think about him.* Diego had too much of an effect on me to be safe.

This time my nose was okay, but there was a swollen purple bruise under my left eye. I had streaks of red running through the whites of that same eye where several blood vessels must have broken. My bottom lip was swollen and keeping with the color of the day, it was blood red. There was a big patch of blue sitting like a soft plum on my chin. I had a deep gash on my hairline where the ring he was wearing caught me on that second slap. But all in all I was okay. Not bad. I had seen worse. And thanks to Gino, I had seen worse on me.

After the shower, I made my way slowly to the kitchen. I needed coffee. I was still shaky. The first time around I spilled the grounds all over the counter. I got all weepy again. So I figured what the hell and decided to give way to a full-fledged pity party. I figured I had earned it. Instead of making my bed or doing the laundry or engaging in the other millions of household things that needed doing, I headed to the garden.

Teary eyed, I eased myself into the deep Adirondack chair. I let the wind dry my hair and the sun shine on my face. It took a couple of hours, but I was able to calm myself. Finally, finally I began to lose that numbing sick feeling. I reached into my pocket and found the silver harmonica that was never far from my side. I played a long mournful tune.

My thoughts wrapped around me like they always did when I played my harp. They took me back to a time when everything that was wrong had turned out right. At least for a while.

CHAPTER 10

I was sitting on the dirty floor of our living room trying to untangle Claire's hair. It was early evening, and our father hadn't been home in two days. I heard a loud bang as someone came busting through our back door.

I looked up to see Prosper walking quickly through the house, stopping only when his eyes fell on us. He ran to me and wrapped his big hands around my face. He stood me up and turned me around twice, looking me over. I watched as he did the same to Claire. He nodded at us and gave me a look that was trying to be a smile. Then he turned, taking to the stairs three at a time. We heard banging and doors slamming. He was back again and holding our two little backpacks overflowing with clothes. Prosper bent down close and folded both of us in his big, strong arms. Without even bothering to close the door behind us, he took my baby sister and me out of there.

We rode in that van for a long time. He drove and drove and all that time he never said a word. I held Claire's little hand tightly in mine, but really, we were not afraid. Dusk had turned into night when we finally turned off the highway onto a dirt road. Claire had fallen into a deep sleep. I shifted her to lie on my lap, the warmth of her little body comforting me. At the end of the road stood a big, rustic cabin with lights shining brightly from every window. The door slammed behind Pinky, and she was in the driveway even before Prosper came to a complete stop. She fell on him the minute he was out of the van. I couldn't hear what he was saying, but whatever it was calmed her. Then I watched as they both approached the van.

Prosper opened the heavy van door, and Pinky stuck her head in slowly. She looked at Claire asleep in my lap, and something that looked like pain crossed her face.

She smiled at me gently. "Hey, Little Darlin'. Claire looks mighty sleepy. Can I take her and put her inside? We have a nice big warm bed just for her. One for you too. I made cookies. I've been waiting for you, and I'm so happy you're here, honey." She had her arms outstretched ready for Claire.

I looked past her to Prosper and he nodded. I had long known that Pinky had secrets too. She had more than Prosper and more than my dad. But unlike Prosper, I knew that the darkest of Pinky's secrets were about things that had been done to her and not about things she had done to others. I reached past Claire to find the small, dirty, pink bunny that she dragged with her everywhere. I said solemnly, "She's going to need this."

Pinky turned to Prosper and unloaded the precious bundle into his big arms. She turned back to me.

"Raine, do you know why you're here, honey? Why Prosper came and got you?"

I nodded wisely. "It's because our daddy doesn't come home or take care of Claire anymore."

"That's right, sweetheart. And Claire needs someone to take care of her, doesn't she? So until your daddy can do that again, Prosper and I thought we would do that for her, and maybe you might let us take care of you too."

All the fear and utter despondency that had sat heavy on my little heart for too long washed away and was replaced with an anger so deep that it filled me.

"I take care of Claire. I do that. I wash her and make her eat. I try to comb her hair but she runs from me. I take care of Claire!" I shouted.

"I do that! We don't need Daddy to do that ever, ever again! And you! You do not get to do that!"

That was it. I was done. I felt my heart break. The big, dark lie took its place inside my soul where it would dwell and feed and soon become bigger than all the good things. Because now I had a dark secret too, and that secret was that I needed my daddy to do that more than I needed to breathe. And try as I might, I could not make that happen. That was the darkest secret of all. I pulled my arms around me to keep the hard, jagged truth in tight, so it wouldn't shred me to pieces on the way up. I drew myself in and held on tight.

Prosper saw me wrap myself around and he knew.

He knew.

He pulled Pinky gently out of the way and handed Claire to her. He nodded her towards the house. With a look of great sadness and infinite understanding, Pinky left us, taking Claire and Pink Bunny into the cabin.

My little chest was heaving, and my throat was balled up so hard with unshed tears that it hurt to breathe. Prosper slid into the seat next to me, not too close but not too far away either. He looked out the window away from me for a time. He casually started unwrapping a candy bar that had been in his pocket. He broke off a piece and popped it into his mouth. He offered the rest to me. I hesitated, then accepted the peace offering. We sat that way for a while, listening to the sounds of a country night and tasting the smooth, creamy chocolate on our tongues.

"You still playing that little harp I gave you?" he said not looking at me.

"Every day," I said, not looking at him.

He nodded. More silence.

"You know, don't you, Little Darlin', that you're just about the smartest, most courageous friend that I ever had?"

"I'm not brave, Prosper," I whispered miserably. "I'm scared all the time."

"That true, Raine?" He turned to look at me then and raised an eyebrow. I looked up at him and nodded the sad truth.

"Well, I know something about being brave, Little Darlin'. I learned it in Vietnam. Shit, I even have a medal called a Purple Heart in a box right on top of my brown dresser in that cabin over there. If you want, I can show it to you some time."

"They give medals for that?" I asked.

"They sure do, honey. The thing I learned most about courage is that it's something brave people call upon when they are so scared to do a thing they can barely breathe, but they do it anyway because it's just the right thing to do."

"Does anyone ever get tired of being brave, Prosper?" I put my tiny hand in his.

He squeezed it gently and said, " Sure they do, Little Darlin'. People get tired of being brave all the time."

"What happens then, Prosper?" I was looking at him, the weight of the world on my shoulders.

I heard something catch in the back of his throat. He had to clear it before he went on. "Why, they call on someone who has some brave left over. That's what they do, honey."

"Prosper?"

"Yes, Raine?"

"Do you have any brave left over?"

"Little Darlin', just so happens that I been saving up a bunch of brave just for you."

I thought about this for a while.

"So, Prosper?"

"Yeah, Raine?"

"You got this?"

He brought the back of his hand up to his eye.

"Yeah, Darlin'. I got this."

I'm not sure how long we stayed at the cabin by the lake with Prosper and Pinky because little ones measure time differently. But I knew it was good time. Claire and I flourished. We had plenty to eat and there were always homemade cookies. Sometimes there were people wearing the leather letter jackets, same as before. Same as before, I would sleep tight with Claire next to me, keeping her safe from the shadows thrown on the wall.

Prosper bought me several harmonicas in different keys and continued my earlier lessons on the art of playing the harp. The best part of all was, sometimes at night, I would sit curled up at his feet, and he would teach me to sing harmony.

Our father had first come to see us about two weeks after we were there. Prosper met him at the end of the driveway, and they talked for a long time before he came up. Claire ran to his arms, and he held her tight. I stayed back, watching. When he reached for me, I put my little hand into Prosper's. In that moment I saw a look of such unbearable pain cross my father's face, I knew that he loved me. He started coming more often after that, and the dark shadows started to leave his face. When I watched my father watch Claire, I knew that he saw her.

Right after that first visit, Prosper took me by the hand and led me to a wooden bench in the back of the yard. He sat real close to me with his hands planted on his thighs. His eyes looked into mine.

"Raine, what I have to say here is pretty important. Fair to say, it will be the most important thing you're ever going to hear. So I need you to listen to me real close and to remember. Now I'm going to help you do that, but you have to help too. Can you do that for me, Raine? Can you listen real close and remember what I tell you?"

"Yes, Prosper. I do solemnly swear it."

He smiled at that.

"Raine, I'm gonna help your daddy get where he needs to be. Me and him, why, we had a long talk and we're going to do whatever that takes. That's our job. When he does that and when I think . . . when

I know *he is ready to be the daddy that you and Claire deserve, you'll be going back home with him. When you're back home, he is with you, cooking and cleaning and doing all those things that the good daddies do. That's his job. You good with that, Raine?"*

"I'm good with that, Prosper."

"Now in the beginning and a long time after that, I'm going to be checking and making sure that everything happens the way it should be happening. But I won't be doing it in a way you can see."

He took my small hands in his and held them tight.

"That won't be me not wanting to see you and Claire. That will be me stepping back and letting your daddy be the man I know he is. It's important to me that you understand that, Raine."

"I understand."

His hands were getting sweaty. He let go of mine to reach into his pocket.

"Can you read this, Raine?" He handed me a small piece of paper.

"Yes, I can." And I could.

"We're going to read this every day until you memorize it."

"My job, Prosper?"

"A very important part of your job, Little Darlin', but not the whole of it. You and I, we're going to read this so much that no matter what happens or where you are, you'll be able to bring it to mind."

"What is it, Prosper?"

"It's the whereabouts of a place where you can always find me. Today, tomorrow, twenty years from now. You there, I'm there. And if I'm not there right then, there will always, always, be someone there who can find me. You're gonna walk right into that place, and you're going to go up to the bar and tell whoever is behind it that you're Raine and you're looking for Prosper."

"Prosper?"

"Yes, Little Darlin'?"

"What if there's nobody behind the bar?"

"Well, you see, honey, that's a real good question. If you don't see anybody behind the bar, you just use the lungs that the good Lord gave you. You belt out a yell asking who it is that's supposed to be behind the bar. Then you tell that man what I just told you. If the day comes when I'm not around, I've made arrangements for that too. What that means is that you and Claire will have a safe place. Always."

"Like magic," I whispered. "But better because it's real."

"Just like that, Raine. The other part of your job is to know when you're going to need to go to that place. That place is not because you miss ole Prosper, or your dad won't let you eat ice cream for supper. That place is for a time when things are so dark that you cannot see the light coming through. That place is what we call a game changer, sweetheart. That means if there comes a time when you need that place, everything about your life will have to change because you know it just is not safe for you and Claire to be in it anymore. If and when that happens, you come find me."

"Like when you came and got me and Claire this time, Prosper? Because my daddy didn't come home, and we didn't have food. And it felt like it was dark all the time, even when it wasn't?"

"You got it, sweetheart."

And I did.

CHAPTER 11

The sweet obscure sounds of Eva Cassidy played out from my iPod, and I was singing along in perfect harmony. The subtle tones of my young voice had grown into something sweet, strong, and sultry. Music gave me such pleasure and transported me to a place far from the ties that bound me. I had taught myself to play the guitar and would often sing and play long into the night. It had helped to keep away the loneliness. In those formative years when lifelong friendships were being forged, neither Claire nor I had the kind of lives that invited other people in.

I was feeling okay, and I was singing in the sunshine. Every so often, I would lift up my chin and let the healing light shine down on my battered face. I stayed out there most of the day. I let the wind take my hair and the grass tickle my toes. I drank lemonade. Then I had myself a couple of beers. I worked in the little garden until my back ached. Occasionally, I would find myself glancing at the back entry. In my mind it was no longer just a screen door but a dark threshold that would lead me out of my warm, sunny space and into a world of worry.

I was glad that the drop was over and the MC had their money. Past experiences notwithstanding, I knew it was much better to be off their radar. The Diego thing. I decided to not even go there. I still worried about why he was in my house last night. But the Saints were all paid up now, and it was all good. Diego was a complication I couldn't afford, period. So what if he smelled like clean soap, and when he held me in his arms I had felt safe and protected. He hadn't stuck around for the light of day. My mom would have said that was him being a "Walk-away Joe."

"Real men are the ones who go to sleep next to you at night, wake up next to you in the morning, and hold you in their hearts all the hours in between. You make sure when it's your time to choose that you pick a man like that."

Yeah, I thought wryly. *Good luck with that.*

The sun was low in the sky when I finally walked into the kitchen to make myself a sandwich. It had been a good day. I had started the day off thinking my life was a train wreck. By the end of the day, I was comparing it to more of a derailment. My life hadn't crashed and burned, it had simply gotten off track.

I pulled the screen door open wide ready to face the next thing. When I walked into the kitchen the next thing hit me like a bullet. How could I have missed that? The envelope bag was sitting on the table and must have been there all day. Or had it been? I walked towards it praying to sweet, sweet Jesus that it was empty. Hoping against hope that Diego had grabbed the cash out of it. Why would he want a stupid bulky bag anyway, right? He wouldn't. Nothing to worry about. Nothing to worry about. Nothing to worry about. Don't worry. Nothing to worry about. At all.

When I picked it up and saw the cash sitting like a heavy stone still in the bag, I sank to the floor. This couldn't make sense in any way that was good. Diego hadn't taken the money. Which meant . . . what? Or after having taken it, had he come back while I was outside singing it up in the garden thinking the worst was over?

Shit, they had even sent him to come two days early for it. Why leave it without a word? Unless maybe he forgot it. Oh, of course that was it. How dumb of me to worry. He had been so hypnotized

CHAPTER 12

Minutes after Diego left Raine, he hit the road. He had business that needed to be taken care of. Besides, he needed some time and distance to sort this out. He had held her in his arms half the night, for fuck's sake. Really. He shook his head and tried to clear it.

He could still smell her. Everything about her smelled clean and good. He loved the feel of her thick dark hair. It had been unexpectedly soft and full when he buried his hands in it. None of that sticky hairspray shit for her. Her eyes were a deep blue except when she was afraid or in pain, then they had turned almost violet. She was all woman, that was for sure. Soft and warm with long, slim legs and full breasts. She was a fucking beauty. When a woman like Raine entered a room, conversation stopped.

Not Diego's usual type. He liked his women on the trashy side. He liked them in tight pants and tall heels. Hair teased out to *there*. He liked them with lots of tits, lots of ass, and lots of attitude. The kind of woman that you "rode hard and put away wet." The kind that gave as good as she got. The MC called the kind of women Diego took to his bed "band-aids." They were cheap, came in all sizes and shapes, got the job done, and were disposable.

He had been hitting a fine little band-aid at his home chapter. Her name was Ellie, and there wasn't a soft thing about her. He wasn't big into sharing, so when he was around for a while, she was his. He had no idea who she was doing when he wasn't around, and he didn't give a shit. She worked every angle, any time she could, to corral him in. Because they were not that and never would be, Diego didn't put up with her trying to claim him. When she pulled that jealous bullshit once, she hadn't been invited back into his bed for a very long time. Diego knew the other women didn't like her much, and with good reason. For them being invited into Diego's bed was a win-win. First part being obvious, second causing Ellie to go crazy green with jealousy.

But she had a willing mouth and could go all night. She was just the right amount of sass. Diego knew she had a crazy mean streak, but he really didn't give a shit. Ellie would be waiting for him at the club when he got there. She was always good for a mindless go at it, and that's exactly what he needed. Maybe some good mind-numbing slamming would help to get his head out of his ass about Raine. Because the farther away he rode, the more he realized that getting involved with her would be a mistake. Men like Diego didn't become involved with women like Raine. Women like Raine scared the fuck out of men like Diego. Women like that required an all-in kind of loving. Women like that were worth it.

He took his time going south and enjoyed the ride. He thought best when he was on the road. He certainly had a lot to think about. His brothers were glad to see him when he finally arrived. After getting down to MC business, Diego had a good night. Both the news and the green he delivered were well received and cause to party big. Diego worked hard to drink Raine away. Ellie, sensing his mind was elsewhere, worked to keep Diego's attention on her. Knowing what it took to keep him sated and satisfied, Ellie gave Diego hours and hours of mind-blowing, very dirty sex. She could sense something was different. Although she knew he didn't like it, she couldn't stop herself from holding on tight to him the next day. Diego didn't seem to mind. That should have made her happy, but instead warning bells were going off in her head.

Later, Diego felt Ellie's tits push against his arm as he drew a card from the deck. Normally, it wouldn't be happening. He had strict rules about that PDA shit from her. But he figured he owed her. She had literally fucked him raw. He was feeling pretty content. He had a pocket full of green, a belly full of some kickass chili, a cold beer on the table, and he was winning at poker. *Hell*, he thought to himself, *I got this*. He had almost convinced himself he had forgotten what Raine even looked like.

Diego had just drawn a royal flush. Yeah, things were definitely starting to look up. It felt good. Simple. Domestic beer, uncomplicated pussy, and a friendly card game with his brothers. He took a long swallow from the cold bottle. Amidst good-natured groans, Diego pulled the winning chips towards him. He grinned as he started to deal out the next hand. As he casually glanced towards the door, the cards froze in his hand, and a look of total disbelief crossed his face.

Raine Winston had just walked through the clubhouse door of the South County Chapter of the Hells Saints MC.

CHAPTER 13

It had taken me a lifetime to get to where I was going. I lost count of how many times I almost turned around. I measured the distance by remembering the milestones of my life. The good and the bad. I missed Claire and I wished she were with me. No one else would ever truly understand what a "long strange trip" it had been. I was glad that she was safe and getting the help she needed, but I had never felt so alone in my life and I needed her.

The thing was that I had held on to the *safe place* for so long, it had taken on mythical proportions in my mind. No matter how bad things got, knowing that there was an out option for me had made me brave. Now I was heading straight into *it*. What if *it* no longer existed or never had? What if my journey's end brought me to an empty lot? What if it brought me to a place where something that once was, was no longer? With all the passing years, I had not doubted for a moment Prosper's promise. But on that long lonely road, I was losing faith. Prosper had never lied to me though. I couldn't imagine him starting with something that had been so important. There would be something at the end of this road. I made myself be sure of that. I owed him that faith. I drove on.

CHAPTER 14

Iparked in front of a long, low building with a flat roof and no windows. Half a dozen Harleys, a van, and a couple of trucks were all parked in front. Painted on the side of the building was a large broken winged angel, the emblem of the Hells Saints MC. So it was here. The safe place was an MC clubhouse. *Of course it was.* This wasn't good. Not good at all. I wasn't sure what I had expected, but stupid me hadn't expected this. My safe place was the home plate of the shadow people of my childhood. Things had just gotten worse and my brave was almost on empty.

Quickly I pulled myself together and got out of the car. I headed towards the door.

It took a minute for my eyes to adjust to the dim lights. When they did, I felt the impact of several feral eyes boring into me. The lamb who had just walked uninvited and alone into the lion's den. The room was one long, massive rectangle. It had a scarred oak bar that ran the length of it. There were a few pool tables in the back end of the room. Several worn couches lined the walls. In the middle of the room sat various heavy wooden chairs and tables. Some round, some rectangle, some square. Most of them occupied. There were a few card games being played. There were lots and lots of women whose choice of clothing screamed barely there, draped on the men playing those games.

I felt sick inside. I didn't want to be here. Instantly I knew I had made a mistake. This was no one's safe place. The adrenaline screaming through my body set me in a fight-or-flight response mode. But I was tired of running, so I figured I had better pony up and fight for Claire and me.

I looked straight ahead to the bar. Holy shit. Now what? Taking a deep breath, I walked towards it like I had a right to. Even though there was no one currently behind it, I thought that it would be a good place to start.

I heard it.

Then it pounced.

The stuff of my nightmares. The thing that I had packed up all my earthly belongings to escape. My sister's would-be killer was barrel-assing it towards me with hell to pay in his eyes. I was going to have to hightail it out of my safe place. Thanks a lot, Prosper.

"What the fuck, Raine?" Diego was on me before I had gone three steps. "You follow me here? You crazy? What the fuck? Private property, Babe! This is not cool!" His fingers were digging into my arm. He was dragging me to the door.

I pulled away from him. Sweet Jesus. I had just driven all day trying to escape him, and here he was. If I let him take me out of that door, it was going to be over for Claire and me.

"Get off of me!" I yanked back. Then I pushed him. Then I kicked at him.

He looked at me horrified and released his grip for a split second. I ran from him and instinctively looked for the biggest guy in the room to help me. I stood right in front of that guy.

"I'm looking for the man who's behind the bar today." My voice strong and clear. My body shaking.

Everyone just stared at me. It was awful. The stuff of nightmares. I tried again.

"I need to find the guy who is working the bar today," I repeated desperately.

Diego came up behind me, and I could feel his breath on my neck. He grabbed my arm *again* and started to yank *again*. The big guy put his hand up in a stop gesture to Diego.

"This your woman, D?"

"No! I am not his woman. I need to talk to the guy who's behind the bar today." I was near hysteria.

No one answered. Not one person responded. Those were my magic Ali Baba Open Sesame words. I had played this scene over and over again in my mind. They were the words that held the key that unlocked the door to the safe place. And no one was answering.

God help me.

Diego started dragging me towards the door.

"You got business with me, darling?" A voice came from the back. I couldn't see him, but thank you Jesus I could hear him.

"I got this, Jules." Diego still dragging me. Me still trying to scratch his eyes out.

"Woman's got something to say." The voice was getting closer, but I still couldn't see.

"Woman's got something to say, she's going to say it to me. Outside," Diego said.

"No, Brother, ain't happening. She's not your woman. She came here looking for the man in charge, and today that man is me. Taking into consideration that her face looks like somebody used it for a punching bag, and *again,* she asked for me, I'm going to hear the lady out. Because you know me fifteen years, Brother, you're going to be okay with that. Because I know you fifteen years, I'm gonna assume you got nothing to do with the black and blue that she's sporting."

Diego stopped dragging me to the door, but to make up for it his fingers were a vise grip on my arm. The man belonging to the voice stepped out of the shadows. He was six feet five inches easy. He had on a clean, white wife-beater under his cut. A black-and-silver belt was holding up his low-riding, loose-fitting jeans. He had muscles on top of muscles with a few muscles thrown in for good measure. His hair was blond, long and loose around his face. A thin scar ran from the outer corner of his left eye to his mouth. He looked like a Viking God.

"That fifteen years, us knowing each other, just bought me not sticking a knife in your belly for that remark. You know me to ever hit a woman, Jules?" Diego grew hard and tense beside me.

"That's why you got the assuming part, friend." Jules's eyes were steely blue. "Now, little lady," he turned to me, "What can I do for you?"

This was it. Make or break it. This was the game-changing moment that it all depended on, and I was running out of brave.

"I'm Raine and I'm looking for Prosper," I said like it meant something.

Quiet but not just quiet. Absolute dead silence.

Then "Holy fuck" from someone at a table.

"Say again, sweetheart?" Jules stepped closer.

"My name is Raine and I need Prosper." Voice trembling. My brave spilling on the floor.

Diego still clutching my arm. Quiet and furious.

Jules's eyes were locked on mine. He broke away a millisecond to nod almost unperceptively towards the door. Then he was back on me.

"You're gonna want to step back, Diego."

"No fucking way, Jules."

"She belongs to Prosper, and you are going to step the fuck away." Jules crossed his arms in front of his chest.

"Prosper's? You telling me that Raine is Prosper's old lady, Jules?" Diego held his ground.

"No, Diego. I'm telling you that Raine is Prosper's *family*. You going to make me keep telling you to get that vise grip off, Brother?" Jules looked him in the eye.

"Prosper here?" Diego asked and I held my breath waiting for the answer.

Jules nodded once.

Diego didn't let go, but he visibly loosened the death grip. I tried to yank myself away from him.

He looked at Jules. "This doesn't make sense, man. Are you telling me that Raine is family, as in daughter?"

"Not sure myself, Brother. But there's been a note hanging behind that bar for as long as I've been in the MC, and from what I hear longer than that. As far as anyone knows, it has been there a good twenty. That light outside? Shines all night long. Prosper pays that."

"What's the note say? Exactly?" Diego was looking at me.

My eyes were glued to Jules. Holding my breath.

"Note reads that if a chick named Raine ever comes in that door looking for Prosper, it means she needs safe. And she gets safe. If Prosper's not here, he's found. No matter where. No matter when. No matter what. Brother minding the store takes care of that. Prosper not around permanently, whoever's minding the store takes care then too," Jules replied, looking at Diego's hand still on my arm.

"Look, D, I see you got some kind of stake in this. But the way I see it, twenty years the brother has kept a light burning, and the chick has not used that out. Now she shows up with a face that looks like a punching bag, and you looking like you got something to do with it. I know you. I like you and I respect you. Just step the fuck back before this gets ugly, Diego."

"You come here to be safe, Raine?" Diego's eyes were on me, furious. "You come here because you feeling you're not safe? Me coming to your house and fucking tending to your wounds. That shit was me keeping you safe. Me arranging it with the club so it's settled. You keep the green, and Claire gets a pass. You tell me you don't think that's me keeping you safe?"

Then.

"You setting me up, Babe?" He dropped the hold on my arm.

I took a step away from him and reached into my pocket. My anxiety was so bad that my whole body was a mass of hard shaky movements. I shoved the money at him.

"You left this on the table."

He looked at me like I was crazy. "Yeah, my point."

"You brought it *back*. I got it for you. I got the shit beaten out of me to give it to you to keep my sister safe." I was heaving, my chest ready to explode. I was confused and scared and my brain was still all *what the fuck was the man I was running from doing in my safe place?*

"Yeah." Diego was watching me.

"It was over. *It was over.* Then I go into my kitchen and there it was. All of it. You came two days early and waited in the dark. Then you left it. Like it was no good. Not enough."

Big heaves now.

"You said that if the MC ever found out that Claire's involvement was more than what she told you, then the money wouldn't be good enough anymore. You never told me different. You never told me anything had changed. You never said *safe*. You never said *settled*. You never said *pass*."

I went on with my heart beating in my chest. But I was getting some of my brave back.

"You were waiting for us in the dark two days early! You came after me when I ran. You took that money. You took it then you left without *saying a word* about bringing it back. Then it was back. *It was back. And Jamie was in the papers. Jamie was beaten to death, and you left the money. You told* me. You said it goes wrong, you would be looking for a different color payment."

I was breathing hard now trying to get it all in.

"So that color to me means red. And red is the color of blood. So if the green was not enough, you were coming back for the red. *You said that.* You said it and you never told me anything different. So don't sit here in *my safe place* making it seem like I'm out of my fucking mind. I came to the only place I know that might stop the 'killing my sister' thing from happening. *So yeah, damn right this is me not feeling safe.*"

Goddammit. I had started to cry. Damn him.

"Un-fucking-believable. *Un-fucking-believable.*" Diego was running his hands through his hair.

Looking at Jules, he said, "That MC shit I came down here to settle."

"Got that," Jules answered. He was looking at me.

No one moved. In the whole place. The Hells Saints clubhouse was rocking a silence so loud it was deafening. Diego was shaking his head. Jules was by my side and I was looking towards the bar. There was *a note.* There was a *light on.* My heart was so full it was close to bursting with the gladness of it. The spell was broken when some slut (yeah, my first thought) came up to Diego. She made sure I watched as she stretched in her six-inch stilettos to press against him and whisper something in his ear. She linked her arm through his and pulled him away from me.

He shook his head and muttered, "Jesus, Raine." Then Diego walked away with her.

All tits and short tight *everything,* the woman did a hair toss. She flashed a look back at me that clearly said, *You're out of your league here.*

She was not wrong.

"We're gonna get you something strong, doll." Jules put his arm around me and steered me to the bar. He sat me down on a stool. He put down two double shot glasses, splashed something amber into them, and poured out two glasses of beer. Handing one glass to me, he lifted the other. We tipped them back. He splashed some more and we tipped back again. The heat hit my belly and my eyes teared up. The second one was a killer.

"Drink the beer, honey." Jules said to me, "It'll wash away the burn."

"There's a note." I looked at him.

He nodded.

"And a light." I grinned at him.

"Sure is, honey." He smirked.

Because there was *a note and a light* and because the Viking God and I were having a moment, I did my own version of a hair toss. I did it, because even though I hardly ever worked it, I knew how much I could really rock the whole tossing-the-hair thing. And I did it because the light and the note and the Viking God standing next to me were all making me feel that maybe I was not out of my league.

Not even a little bit. Not even at all. So I shook out my long hair, and I smiled a smile so wide that I almost split my torn lip open again. And Jules smiled right back.

CHAPTER 15

Diego had gone back to the card game with Ellie leading the way. He played a couple of hands badly. His eyes never off Raine for long. He saw the hair toss. He *definitely* saw the hair toss. Then goddammit, she smiled at something Jules said and he leaned into her. When Diego saw Jules put his hands on Raine to brush the hair away from her face, he was halfway out of his seat. He saw that Jules was looking carefully at something near her hairline, and he forced himself to relax. Jules had been a medic in the Marine Corps, and he knew his shit. Better he see if something was seriously wrong there. But Diego felt the jealousy curl in his belly like a serpent.

Ellie watched Diego watch Raine. Ellie didn't like this. Not one fucking bit. She had done her time waiting for Diego to get how good they were together. The bitch better stay away from her man.

CHAPTER 16

Yeah. Right here. Got that. Right." Jules had answered on the first ring.

Silence.

"Not too long." Jules was looking at me. "Definitely been through some shit. Yeah. Later, boss."

"Need the room," he yelled out to the club. Everyone started moving out. No questions.

But not Diego. Diego came right up by my side. Crowding me. Not looking at me.

"Prosper?" Diego to Jules.

I held my breath.

"Yeah, man. Boss is on his way and he wants the room clear. Totally, Brother."

"Ain't happening," Diego challenged.

"With that." Jules sighed.

Jules poured three more shots. One for me, one for him, and one for Diego. He left my shot on the counter. He grabbed the other two in his big hand. He handed Diego the bottle. He nodded once to the back of the room, and Diego started walking.

Jules looked at me and winked.

"It's going to be fine, honey." He followed Diego to a table in the back of the room.

Diego just kept walking past me. I took a deep breath and turned to the bar to pour the fire down my belly and wait. A few minutes later, I heard the door fly open. I heard the footsteps that stopped right inside that door. I heard them come from behind me.

"Raine."

A voice that sounded sweetly familiar. A voice that sounded like firelight, long blended notes on a silver harp, and summer nights on a lake. A voice that sounded like my mother, my father, and everything that family meant rolled into one. A voice that sounded like home. And although I knew he was coming and I had prayed for him to be waiting for me, I couldn't look at him. The shame and the fear and the feeling of defeat overwhelmed me. I was that little girl in that van again. All those years ago. Because even though I had tried my hardest to keep it all together, I had failed. All the sacrifice and the hard work and the saving every dime had still brought me to this. To a place I needed to be rescued from. No matter how hard I tried, I had failed. That was the darkest secret of all.

So I turned and stood with my back against the bar. My arms wrapped around me, holding down tight. My face turned away from Prosper. *And he knew.* I could hear the sharp growl when he saw the damage. He looked in the direction of Diego and Jules.

"The cocksucking sonofabitch who did this," Prosper snarled.

Diego nodded and confirmed from his table at the end of the room. "Dead man, Brother."

Prosper's attention was back then. I felt his eyes on me, and I wanted more than anything to run into his arms. But I knew that if I unwrapped mine, the bad would come shooting up and rip me apart.

He moved slowly towards me and I tensed. My eyes burned brightly with their refusal to cry. Then he was next to me. He was looking at his shoe. I was looking at the spot on the wall.

He knew.

Damn if he didn't reach into his pocket and pull out a bar of chocolate. He unwrapped it and popped a piece into his mouth. He handed the rest to me.

I reached across the years and took it from him. We sat in silence for a while, relishing the sweet taste of time gone by on our tongues.

"You still play that little harp I gave you?"

Him not looking at me.

"Every day."

Me not looking at him.

I put my hand in his and my head on his shoulder.

"Prosper?"

"Yes, Little Darlin'?"

"I've run clear out of brave," I whispered.

"Just so happens I got some brave saved up just for you, Raine," he said against my hair.

More silence.

"So, Prosper?" I dropped my chin to his shoulder.

"Yes, Little Darlin'?" His voice shaky now.

"You got this?" My voice shaky now too.

"I got this."

I turned into his arms. I was not a little girl anymore, but just the same I held on to him the way a daughter hangs on to her father. He held me tight, the way only a father knows how to do. We stayed that way for a long, long time. I didn't see Jules and Diego leave. But I know they must have because when I thought to look for them much, much later, they were both gone.

CHAPTER 17

When the call had come telling him that Raine had just walked into the MC, Prosper had let out a deep sigh. His first go-to was complete and selfish joy. Pure unabashed happiness. He was going to be seeing his Little Darlin' again. He knew that if she remembered after all this time, it meant that she had never forgotten. There wasn't a day that went by that he hadn't thought about Claire and her.

The second go-to was anger because, on his watch, the bad had come around and found her. He wasn't sure what the bad was, but Prosper knew that Raine had known some hard times. He also knew that she had always found her way around them. Whatever brought her to a place where she felt she needed safe haven must be bad. Really fucking bad.

Prosper had kept a close watch on them for a very long time. Years. Last time he knew, Raine was in nursing school and Claire had been working at a bank. Things seemed good and Prosper was satisfied. Time had moved on for him and life happened as it does. Thinking the girls were in a good place, Prosper had eased up on those reins.

Now after all these years it was with mixed feelings that he pushed through that door. She had her back to him. That was enough to stop him cold. That long, dark, silky hair that hung to the small of her back. Her slim body and those long legs. So much like her mom. His Maggie. The love of his life. Twenty years her being gone and still. Still the love of his life.

Raine and her sister were all he had left of Maggie. He honestly thought that he'd never see them again. Now here his Little Darlin' stood. Coming to him for help and counsel. Maybe even for a home. It took everything he had to call out her name. He had no idea what to expect when she turned around. Not knowing how he would handle it if he saw Maggie's face in hers. Not knowing how he would handle it if, worse, he didn't.

Then she turned slightly to him. He could see her battered face, and it looked bad. Really bad. Dark fury clouded his vision. He looked to his boys to make sure this would be dealt with. Prosper looked back at Raine. At first glance only seeing the beating life had showered on her. Then looking past that and seeing his Little Darlin'.

Just enough of her mother in her to mark her as Maggie's daughter. She had the high, proud cheekbones, full mouth, and the beautiful tawny skin of a Lakota woman. That hair was all Maggie's. The deep blue eyes that hid nothing and said volumes, those were Jack's eyes. The long thin nose, that was Jack's too. Prosper saw his old friend in her. She was her father's daughter for sure.

But the sad, "barely holding it together for the greater good" look, that was all Raine. It was a look he remembered seeing on her too often. When her mother was dying. When she was following that fool bastard of a father around for days hoping he would notice her. When he found her in that shit hole of a house, sitting on the floor trying to untangle her baby sister's hair when she was no more than a baby herself.

Prosper had never forgotten the look on her face when he and Pinky had taken Claire from the van and had tried to reason with an eight-year-old Raine. The sadness bleeding out of her. The anguish on her little face. That way she had of drawing into herself, arms holding tight against her waist and eyes pulled away. It had broken his heart, watching her retreat into a place where he couldn't find her. He'd hoped never to see it again. Seeing it now on her made him want to kill.

And once all the facts were in, someone was definitely going to die for this. That was for sure. But for now, he was going to take care of the closest thing he would ever have to a daughter.

CHAPTER 18

Diego couldn't fucking believe it when she walked into the MC. Could Not Fucking Believe It. He had just spent the day drinking and sexing her off his mind. He had spent the better part of two days clearing that shit up with his club. He was even feeling it enough to put up with Ellie hanging all over him. Yeah, he was golden.

Then the door opened and Raine walked through it.

Last person he ever fucking expected to see in this shit-hole den of thieves.

Seeing Raine had hit him so hard in the chest it had pummelled him backward. His first thought was to get to her and to get her the fuck out of there. Then she kicked at him, pushed at him, and walked up to Cage. Cage being easily the biggest badass in a room of very big badasses and said some shit about needing to see the guy behind the bar. Who everyone in the room knows is the go-to guy.

Jules tells *him* to back off. Back the fuck off?? He had to be shitting. Had to be. Then the shit about Prosper and her lighting into him.

Making no sense.

Then making all the sense in the world.

Diego could definitely see where Raine got the money thing. He had gone to explain it, but he had gotten so caught up seeing her beaten like that, honest to fuck, it had dropped from his mind. He got caught up with her in a different way. No shit, that the message didn't get relayed. So she had gotten a different message. And it had scared the shit right out of her. Then she was raging at him.

Raging. At. Him.

Then Raine had started crying.

Diego watched as his brother, Jules, had made her a drink and made her smile. He watched as Jules put his hand in her hair and leaned in close.

Really close.

Too fucking close.

Then seeing her with Prosper. Raine not being able to look at him. She had looked so fucking beautiful and broken pulling herself in like that. It moved Diego right off the chair. If it hadn't been for Jules pulling him back, it would have been him holding her. Not Prosper. It would have been him. Whether she wanted it or not, it would have been him.

CHAPTER 19

The Hells Saints compound consisted of a few buildings and a large clearing. There was the main clubhouse where Prosper and I sat talking into the night and half the next day. The room that had been "cleared" was a large room that housed a long, fully stocked bar, several tables and chairs, a couple of pool tables, and a variety of big worn couches and deep, soft seats. To the right of the main area lay a set of heavy wooden double doors that had the Hells Saints insignia carved into them. They led to a meeting area.

There were two other long buildings. One was a warehouse. I wasn't sure what was in that. The other was a dormitory-style building. It was similar in size to the clubhouse, but it held a large kitchen with several industrial-size appliances. It had one very long table down the middle and several other small tables and chairs. Off the kitchen were two long hallways built shotgun-style with rooms off the main corridor to the left and a back entrance. Those belonged to the brothers and were for their private use. Whatever that meant.

Just to the back of the buildings was a large outside gathering area. There were several picnic tables, Adirondack chairs, grills, and a big fire pit. A huge stack of wooden pallets and logs covered with a tarp was not too far from the pit. There was also a concrete slab with some more picnic tables that was covered by an open porch and wired for electricity.

The whole compound was surrounded by woodlands. If it were not for my GPS getting me close to it, I would never have found my way.

Prosper and I talked and talked and talked. I could not stop. Once that door was open, the words came flooding in. He wanted to know everything about Claire and me. Everything I had to say, he was interested in hearing.

So I shared and watched. I watched, taking my lead from the expressions on his face. When his eyes grew soft and his mouth curved into a small smile, I continued. When something I said made his eyes grow dark and hard, I hurried past that to the next thing. After a while he sensed that, and kept his face open and neutral, which made it both harder and easier to share. But I told him everything there was to tell. Letting him in, keeping nothing back. Eventually all that talk brought me to the events of the past week. Claire, Jamie, Gino, the fragile-looking blonde who saved my skull from being cracked like an egg, and finally Diego's part in it all. I saw his eyes go hard at that last part for one instant. Then it was gone.

Prosper also shared with me. But not everything. That wasn't his way. But he shared the important things and the things that would matter to me. He talked about the MC and how he had helped it to grow and expand into several thriving businesses. I secretly wondered how many of those businesses were on the books. Of course, I didn't ask.

He talked about how a "break of faith" had taken him outside the MC for a short while. He left to get his head cleared, and he spoke of the places he had traveled to. Eventually, his meandering brought him back to the Hells Saints. The place where he had begun and the only family, save mine, that he had ever known.

To my delight, he told me that his restless travels had also brought a new understanding of committed love. That understanding came in the form of a small blonde with a big laugh who made the best cookies east of the Mississippi. Pinky. They had stayed together through it all and had gotten married last spring. I was happy for both of them and couldn't wait to see her.

It was nice and familiar and safe being with Prosper. I had no doubt in my mind that I had done the right thing by coming to him. The only doubt I had in my mind was why I hadn't done it sooner. Because sooner may have made all the rest so much easier. But as they say, hindsight is 20/20.

The brothers had given us the time we needed to work it through. The clubhouse had stayed cleared without so much as a knock on the door. Prosper and I walked out arm in arm into a cloudy early afternoon. I was exhausted and I think Prosper was too. Diego, however, looked wide awake and was leaning back against the wall of the warehouse, watching the door, waiting for us to come out. He pulled himself away from the door and walked towards us.

In a straight line. Right towards us.

He totally ignored me and chin-nodded Prosper.

"You and me."

Prosper looked at him and nodded.

"Then me and her." Diego shot that out like a bullet. I took *her* to mean *me,* but since he was still not looking at me, I couldn't be sure.

"Respect that you bided your time and gave us that to sort it out. But you going there with Raine, we see how it lands with me first, Brother. I'm feeling it, then it goes to her. I'm not feeling it, it stays." Prosper's tone was mild but his eyes were hard.

"Let's do this." Diego started towards the clubhouse, then turned around and looked right at me.

"Don't wander, Babe. This will not take long." He looked at me long and hard.

Prosper and I had been on our way to the kitchen house for some lunch when Diego had put himself in front of that path. Prosper told me to go on and that someone would be there to help me find things and get settled. He had a suite of rooms in the house, and they were to be at my disposal. He had already told one of the recruits to go in there, change the sheets, bring my stuff from the car, and put some shower stuff in the bathroom for me. Prosper really only kept the rooms out of old habit. He and Pinky owned a house not far from the compound.

Forget the lunch, I hadn't showered or slept in two days. If I counted the night of worry, make that about three. I was going to take a really long, hot shower. Then eat, if I could make it that long without falling dead on my feet.

I wasn't even thinking about dealing with Diego.

Prosper had that. And I was going to leave them to it.

~

Prosper and Diego had their sit-down. Because Prosper had been dealing with some Saints' business a couple of states away for the past month, he had to be brought up to speed with the whole mess. The Hells Saints didn't deal in drugs but had been on the radar of Los Diablos Rojos MC because of a missing cache of cocaine and heroin. Business and relations between the Saints and Los Diablos were shaky at best. The Saints' involvement with Jamie came on the money-lending part of things. Jamie had his own agenda. He was borrowing money from the Saints and fronting dope from Los Diablos with the intent of hijacking both the cash and the drugs.

Essentially, he had intended on building a small fortune then disappearing. In order to clear the way for that, he was playing the MCs against each other. Prosper's chapter bordered the Diablos' territory so when it all came down, it all became clear. Diego had come down to sort things out. The sort-out had gone well, and both sides left church that day satisfied. The tenuous alliance the Diablos and Saints shared was back on track.

The only thing that had been left to sort out was Claire's involvement in the dealing and the deception. In order to clear this up, there had to be no loose ends or stones left unturned. Serious bloodshed could and had been spilled over that much green and that much dope. Jamie had just been beginning and they were not sure how wide his shit had spread. When they found out Claire was just a stupid little piece (yeah, he said it) that got hooked up with the wrong guy, they had decided to let it alone. The MC had no way of knowing that Claire or her sister, Raine, had any ties to Prosper. Nor did they share that.

Diego told Prosper that he solidly, solidly regretted putting Raine in the path of that psycho. He shared with him his intent to deal with Gino before Raine went to him and how he had pushed MC discussion along to make that happen. He told him about the file and the phone call making sure that Gino was going to pay for the hurt he had put on Raine. He explained how when his wrecking crew got to Gino's house, he was gone. The house had been tossed and nothing had been found. Diego had Gunner on the house and so far nothing had turned up. However, they would find him and when they did . . . well, when they did.

Prosper listened to it all. Intently. Because this was his club, he knew most of the story but had needed some of the details filled in. He also wanted to hear what his brother had to say. Diego had Prosper's respect and had from the time he was a recruit. Prosper accepted what he said and gave props to Diego for sorting it all out in the way he had. He asked a few more questions. They shared a beer and then a couple more.

Prosper liked him. Diego was a solid, clear-thinking, tough motherfucker of a man. But that didn't necessarily mean he wanted him sniffing around his Little Darlin'.

"So you and Raine," Prosper asked casually.

There it was. Diego wasn't fooled at all by the casual tone of Prosper's voice. He was going to meet this head on.

"Yeah. Me and Raine." Diego took a long pull on his beer. "But she don't know that yet."

He put the beer down and looked Prosper in the eye. "You good with that?"

"Not sure, Brother," Prosper replied honestly.

"You know me," Diego said. "I know you and understanding what she means to you, the respect I have for you, you know I wouldn't go there and fuck her up."

"Worry is, Brother, that life has fucked her up. So a man wouldn't have far to go, all good intentions aside, to cause more pain. Truth is, I would like to see a brother get in there, take care of my girl, keep that shit away from her. Raine needs someone who would lay it down for her. She deserves it. Her mother deserved it. Claire deserves it." He was looking into his empty glass now. Prosper grabbed the bottle. He filled Diego's glass and then his own.

He drank it and muttered, "Damn Winston women keep picking the wrong fucking men."

Then he looked at Diego.

"D, looking out for a brother here. Seriously, don't know if you want to go there. Women like Raine and her mother. Beautiful inside and out. So fucking heartbreakingly beautiful that they get in there and stay in there. Even when they are not yours, even when they are fighting for their last breath. Even after they have passed from this life to the next. Women like that are so achingly soft and good and so fucking special. You get all of it, you're the luckiest man on the face of God's green earth. You get a part of it, you take it and thank the Lord for the small bit you get. Every fucking day. You thank the Lord."

Diego looked at Prosper, and he knew it wasn't the booze talking. The only woman Diego had ever seen Prosper with was Pinky. They had a good thing. He treated her well, and as far as Diego knew, he didn't fuck around on her. Prosper was getting on in years now, but no doubt he was still a good-looking guy. Tall, all lean, hard muscle, and although gray now peppered his light brown hair, he still had all of it. The lines on his face made him look like a badass with experience. The chicks really seemed to dig that. But no, Diego never knew Prosper to step out. You just had to take one look at Pinky to know she adored her man.

But listening to him now, Diego came to realize the ties that bound Prosper to Raine went deep. Raine's mother had evidently been Prosper's one true love. And as badass and tough and dark as Diego could be, he absolutely positively believed in the whole "one true love" thing. He knew what having that would mean to a man like Prosper. He knew, long ago, what it had meant to him.

"Raine's been through some shit." Prosper was looking at Diego. "Shit that happened in what they call the formative years. Shit that happens when you're that young sets a course for the rest of it."

Prosper was looking right into Diego's eyes.

"Shit that she keeps buried deep. So deep she has to wrap her arms around herself to keep it in. Because if she don't, she's afraid that, on the way out, it will tear her up so bad inside that it will kill her. Stuff she keeps down. Stuff she thinks no one knows or can see or can touch but her. She carries that for her and for Claire. She doesn't share that. She carries it."

"That's where you're wrong, Boss. She gave it to you last night. I saw it. I heard it. She gives it sometime." *And she will give it to me*, Diego thought but didn't say.

❧

Prosper looked hard at Diego. He could see the poor bastard was already over the fucking moon for his Little Darlin'. *Good luck with that*, Prosper thought but didn't say.

"Twice, Diego. Twice in a lifetime of carrying it. She trusted me with her shit twice. Last night and when she was a tiny little thing of eight years old. She only gave it to me then because she was dog tired and worn out from being left alone to care for her baby sister for two fucking days just one month after her mother had died. That's what it took then. Her sister in danger of being killed and a beating that left her face battered is what it took this time. I cannot even begin to imagine what she has dealt with on her own for the last twenty years, if this is what it took."

Diego was getting it.

Prosper pulled his hand through his hair, then slapped it hard on Diego's shoulder, giving him a little grin.

"Brother, you just don't know. She will complicate your life. You'll have to fight to get in, and sometimes it will take everything you got just to hang in there. These women define complicated. But once you're in, there's nothing sweeter in life than a woman like my Maggie was. Guy who gets a shot at her daughter, guy willing to go the distance, is one lucky sonofabitch. Guy like that, tough road ahead but paradise at the end of it. Eternal fucking paradise. But the getting there, the shit you don't know. You might want to think about it. Loving and being loved by a complicated woman like that is hard work, Brother."

"You see any part of me that spells weak, Boss?"

Prosper grinned.

"You got a story to tell me, then I got a story to hear." Diego was ready. He wasn't smiling.

Prosper looked at him for a long minute and he wasn't smiling either. So he began.

"Once upon a fucking time . . ."

CHAPTER 20

The tub was huge. The water was hot and there was a lot of it. There were big fluffy towels and shampoo, sweet berry body wash, and lotion. I changed my mind and took a bath. I did the thing where you fill the tub halfway, get in, and turn on the water every five minutes so you get the hottest part of it. Oh, yes I did! I stretched and let the hot, soapy, silky water slide over me. I washed myself gently, over and over again. Trying to wash away the worries, I guess. Maybe trying to make myself new again. The room was a den of steam when I was done, and everything smelled good, including me. I stepped out and towel-dried my hair until it was tousled and damp. I spread lotion all over my warm body and the open pores cried out in ecstasy.

I dug in my bag and pulled out a pretty kimono. I had gotten it for really cheap at a little store in Chinatown. It was powder blue and had matching silver dragons on the front of it. When you wrapped it around with the thin belt, it looked like the dragons were intertwined. Very cool. The silk felt good against me. I was feeling great until the steam wore away from the mirror, and I was reminded of the deep bruising on my face. It would be a while before the colors faded, but at least the swelling was gone. The blue did bring out my eyes, I grinned wryly at myself.

Being with Prosper, my father in every way that mattered, had put the smile on my face and had lifted some of that crushing weight off me. I forgot how good it felt to give worries away. It wasn't just that. It was just good being with family. He looked good too. The years had been kind and I knew part of that was Pinky taking good care of him. He was still strong and lean. His face was lined now, and he had beautiful streaks of gray running through his hair. When I knew him, he had been rocking a goatee and a little soul patch. Now he was clean-shaven. He wore a plain silver wedding band on his left hand where before he'd had lots of chunky man rings. He was still hard and from habit I had watched him while he talked. All the secrets Prosper had now were old ones. Nothing new was dark. I was happy for that.

I wondered what he and Diego were talking about. I thought I would find out soon enough. I thought about the fact that Diego was here at all and what that meant. I thought about the fact that Diego had stood outside staring at the door for hours waiting for us to come out. That meant something. I thought about how he had told me not to wander. I thought about how I was safe now. Well, maybe it wouldn't be so bad, him not wanting me to wander. In the tub I had thought about his hands on me that night, and how his mouth had felt against mine. I thought about the kiss that had ended in pain, and how he had worked to stop that pain. Yeah, I gave some time to thinking about Diego.

I picked up the towels in the bathroom, tied the belt of my robe loosely, gave my hair one more fluff, and walked out of the room ready to slip into some clean sheets. And I would have done just that if Diego hadn't been leaning deep in the armchair, legs crossed at the ankles, looking totally relaxed and as if he owned the place.

I stopped dead a few feet away from him, right outside the bathroom door. He stood up. I took a small step back. He moved a small step closer. He took the towels and clothes from me. He walked over to the hamper near the bed and tossed them in. He came back and stood in front of me. Him looking at me. Me looking at him.

He took his hand and brought it up to my hair. He traced it lightly with his index finger from the top of my head, down the side of my face, past my neck, over my breast, and to where it fell down near my waist. He held the strands loosely in his fingers and watched it as the damp silky mass slid through his hand. I was watching him, but because his eyes were downcast, couldn't see his secrets. He was close, very close. Too close. I took a small step back. He looked up, still holding my hair, and took a small step forward. His eyes on me. My eyes on him. He leaned his head in and I leaned my head back. My head hit the back of the door frame, my back flat against the wall. He stepped in and the side of his body fell flush against the front of mine.

Diego dipped his head close to my ear and whispered, "Nowhere left to run, Raine."

Oh my God! This wasn't good. And it wasn't good in a scary way. I pulled my arms around me.

For Diego's part, he felt that and realized his mistake immediately. He put his hand around my head and pulled it close. "Don't be afraid, Raine, not of me. Not ever afraid of me. It's done. I talked to Prosper. He talked to me. You're safe. Claire is safe. And I swear to Christ I'm sorry for the shit I put you through. Everything. I'm sorry, baby."

I stood stock-still and processed that. He stood where he was, not moving, and waited. I unwrapped my arms from my waist and put them up between us. My palms on his chest. He was warm and rock solid. He moved to have one of his hands cover mine and the other past me, resting on the door frame, trapping me in close to him. I was staring at his chest.

I looked up at him. "You talked to Prosper and it's over?"

He nodded. "Yeah, honey. I'll tell you all about it after."

"After what?"

He raised one eyebrow. Then his eyes left mine and they burned a path down my body and up again. His eyes were sparkling and warm and he stepped in a little closer. I felt him go hard against my belly. My legs turned to jelly. I pulled on his shirt to keep myself from falling.

"Your hair is so fucking soft, baby." He was holding the locks of my hair up to his face now, working it slowly between his hands. His eyes hot on me. He grinned. I felt the heat rising everywhere, and I knew my whole body was blushing.

"It's wet," I murmured lamely.

He grinned wildly and leaned in to whisper, "I like wet."

I blushed from my head to my toes.

"Never had a woman who blushed before." His smile was getting bigger. "Honey, you're all pink and hot and we haven't even started yet. I like that."

If it was possible, I blushed deeper. I was hot all over. All my girlie parts on red alert.

His mouth moved against mine, softly teasing. His mouth moved to the side of mine, and his hand slipped to the small of my back to pull me even closer. "Relax, Raine."

I opened my mouth slightly to respond and there it was. His tongue in my mouth. Sweet, gentle, like he knew what he was doing. It was nice. It was so nice. I loved the way his tongue was dancing in my mouth, shooting sparks that went clear to my panties. I kissed him back. Boy, oh boy, oh boy, did I kiss him back.

He bent down and picked me up, just like in the movies. He came down on the bed with me on my back and him on his side. He broke off long enough to look at me. His hands touching my hair, his knuckles brushing the line of my jawbone. His mouth on mine and on my neck and on the deep Y of my kimono. His hands all over me now. His mouth brushing the kimono open. He was kissing me in the deep cleft of my breasts. His mouth working magic softly on my skin. He brought his mouth up to mine, kissing me deeply.

Lots of deep, gentle kisses. Then back again, this time his mouth worked its way down the silk to my hard, jetting nipple and captured it and pulled lightly. Up to this point, it had been nice. Hot and nice. A high school heavy-petting session. But the whole nipple thing was starting it in a different direction. Something that every woman knows from experience would escalate quickly from the nipple thing to the panty-dropping thing.

This was happening too fast. I wasn't a casual-sex kind of person. I knew if I went there with Diego, it would definitely mean something different to him than it would to me. In the fifteen seconds that these thoughts were going through my mind, I was also thinking of the hair-tossing, stiletto-wearing, "you're out of your league" smiling woman who had slithered up to claim this man just yesterday.

Diego felt the shift immediately and stopped. I put my hands between us and pulled the edges of the dragons closer. He rolled away from me onto his side but kept his hand on my stomach. His other hand holding up his head. I made myself busy by fixing my robe and smoothing my hair. I felt his eyes on me.

"Raine." He was watching me.

My fault. I had opened that door and he had walked through it. Diego was going to think I was a . . .

I felt myself go hot and pink again thinking of the word Gino had used when he did something that made me want to stop . . . *cock teaser.* An ugly word that I hated. In this case it was probably true.

This was uncomfortable for me, and I pulled my arms around myself.

"Hey, you in there." His voice was light and teasing.

"I'm sorry." Me not looking at him.

"Too much?" Him looking right at me.

I nodded. Really nice that he got that.

His hand was still on my stomach, inches away from where I was holding myself together. He put his big hands on my clasped smaller ones.

"Shit, honey. I'm the one who's sorry, Raine. Should not have gone there. Next time you want me there, you find a way to let me know. Otherwise we stop at what's not too much. You liked me kissing you." His tone was teasing.

He had me there. And because he was being so incredibly sweet about this, it was all really nice again.

I smiled at him and nodded.

"And when I played with your hair. I think that was okay too." His fingers were back to lifting small strands of hair and wrapping the long locks gently in his hand.

"That was okay too." I colored a little.

"Hmmmm, let me think . . ." His eyes were on the pieces of hair that he was gently thumbing.

"When you kissed my neck," I said too quickly.

His eyes were on mine in a flash. His smile brighter than sunshine now.

I turned crimson. Then started smiling too.

He kissed me once in all the places that were not too much, tucked me in, turned out the light, and was gone. For my part, I fell into a long, heavy sleep and dreamt I was able to fly.

CHAPTER 21

Holy fuck. If Raine had known how close he had come to throwing her down, tearing off her clothes, and pushing himself deep inside her whether it was too much for her or not, she would be halfway across the country right now. He had never met a more skittish piece of pure woman in his life. He felt like he was in goddamn high school again. No. Not true. He got laid in high school all the time. *All the time.*

Diego wasn't a man who generally took his time. Oh yeah, he saw the job got done and he made sure he got them off. But he never ever let them decide. That was his job, his right. Women wanting in his bed played by his rules. He didn't get any complaints. Wouldn't have given two shits if they did complain. Women could be on their way if they didn't like his play. But this one was leading him around by the balls and she wasn't even trying.

Raine hadn't had it easy. He had learned all about her . . . what the fuck did Prosper call them? Her formative years. No white picket fence there. Dead mother and drunk for a father. No other family. Practically raised herself and her sister. She had put herself through school. Kept to herself, then didn't, and picked the wrong asshole. Gino Abiatti had raped and beaten her. *Raped and beaten her.* A sweet thing like Raine. Jesus. Bastard was gonna pay. Diego just hadn't had a chance to finish up with that. But oh, he would.

How could a man do that to a woman? Diego just never got that shit. Sure he liked what he liked in bed. He could and had been turning nos into yeses since he started bedding the bitches. But he had never ever forced himself on someone who didn't want him. The hard-on came from turning it around. That's what made a man a man in Diego's book. Trick was and always had been finding a woman who was worth the effort. He had found that once a long time ago and thought never to have it again. Fucking biker whores like Ellie had been good enough for him for a long time.

Raine. She turned herself inside out whenever he looked at her or moved in too close to her. When he kissed her he wasn't sure she knew exactly what she was doing. Oh, it was hot all right. Her tongue moved with his in all the right places. There was just something so sweet and naive about the way she hesitated. And she whimpered. Fuck him if she didn't make these little mewing sounds when he was turning her on. It made him so hard he was going out of his mind. For the first time in a very long time, he wanted to take his time with a woman.

And damn it if she didn't make him work for it. Gonna be a full-fucking-time job getting laid by Raine Winston. This "stop and go" shit had to stop. Had to stop. This little cat-and-mouse gig she had going on with him that he was convinced she didn't even know she was playing.

Just like Prosper said. Complicated.

Part little girl, all woman when it came down to it. Damaged and brave and beautiful and scarred and scared and tough and so fucking complicated.

She was made for him. Now he was just going to make sure she knew it. And if it took him stopping when the only thing he wanted to do was keep going . . . then he was going to stop. For now.

CHAPTER 22

I woke the next morning to a bright, sunny day. I went from fast asleep to wide awake and felt my heart beating hard in my chest. Something had jarred me awake. For just a second I didn't remember where I was. Two seconds after that came a hard knock at the door.

"Raine, Little Darlin'? You up?" It was Prosper and then I remembered.

I looked at the clock and it was almost noon.

"Coming!" I shouted.

I ran to the door and opened it wide. Still sleepy with tousled bed head and sleepy eyes.

"Yeah, sorry, Prosper." I was a little breathy from having woken up literally a minute ago and running to the door.

Prosper took one look at me and cleared his throat. Jules was behind him grinning madly. He was looking at me slowly from head to toe. By the time his eyes returned to my face, that grin had turned into the closest thing I had ever seen to pure lust *ever*.

"Do you need something?" I asked Prosper.

"Oh yeah," Jules muttered behind him.

Prosper turned to look at Jules and growled. Yes. He. Did.

He reached past me to close the door and said, "Sorry, honey. It can wait. Get dressed and come get something to eat when you're ready." Then the door closed on me.

"Okay," I said to the door. I threw my hair up on top of my head and went to take a quick hot shower. I really didn't want to delay being in the room. Prosper and Jules must have needed to get something. I was determined to be of no trouble whatsoever.

Besides, I had washed my hair just last night or really just a few hours ago. The hair thing brought back some other memories and I pushed them aside. I noticed in the mirror I was pink again. Sweet Jesus, I had to stop blushing at the mere thought of that man. I lathered on some more of that great berry lotion, then threw on a fresh pair of clean and really worn button-fly jeans. My lucky jeans. I added a soft-pink, light V-neck tee. I redid my hair, pulling it together and wrapping it around to form a loose bun at the nape of my neck. Then I quickly applied some pink lip gloss, soft black eyeliner, and mascara. Pretty silver dangling hoops and the same pair of low biker boots completed the look. I was out the door in twenty.

Diego was at me before I fully closed the door. The smile I greeted him with died on my lips when he grabbed me close to him and snarled, "Raine, you're not in some cottage at the end of the woods anymore."

"I know that." His tone made my stomach hurt.

"There are thirty rooms in this bunk and at any time they're filled with bikers. Sometimes those men are alone. Sometimes with their women. Sometimes with their whores. Depending on who. Depending on when. Sometimes brothers. Sometimes guys visiting. You hearing me, Raine?" His eyes were hard and he wasn't talking quietly.

I nodded.

"You hearing me, Raine?" He was getting louder.

"Yes." He was making me feel horrible.

"So now you know this, you never *ever* open that door again without having some fucking clothes on!" He was furious.

I swallowed hard. I had clothes on, but I was getting that my pretty light-blue kimono with the silver dragons on the front maybe didn't count.

"What do you never ever do, Raine?" He was acting like a total asshole.

I glared at him and he glared back.

"Open the door without being fully clothed," I said softly. I was humiliated, and all the sweetness from the night before had been pushed right out of me. I felt the sting of tears burn behind my eyes.

I pulled away from him and walked to the kitchen area where there were about a dozen guys sitting there, all of whom suddenly had somewhere else to look. It was dead quiet. They had heard everything. I felt sick.

Jules looked right at me and winked.

"You want some eggs, Raine?" He set a cup of coffee down on the table and pulled a chair out for me.

"No, thanks." My lip quivered.

"Yeah, she does. Two over easy. Throw some bacon and toast on that plate." Damn Diego again. Sitting his big bad self three seats down and across the table. Then he turned his back to me and started talking to the guy next to him. I glared at his back for a second, wishing him dead.

I looked helplessly at Prosper, who was just folding the morning paper. He had these little half-moon glasses on. Despite my growing humiliation at being treated like an infant, I noticed them as another testimony to the passing years.

Prosper was looking at me. "When was the last time you ate, Raine?"

No help there. Seems Prosper was in league with Diego the Devil.

I thought for a second and honestly couldn't remember. I waved my hand away. I wasn't real happy with him at that moment either. I went to wrap my arms around me. Prosper casually and not unkindly stopped me. He grabbed my hand and held it with his own at the table. Then he began introductions.

All the guys in the kitchen house were Hells Saints. Most, but not all, from this chapter. Some nodded, some smiled, and a couple actually unfolded themselves from their chairs and said their hellos close up. Two shook my hand and one kissed it in a sweet attempt at being charming. I blushed hot at that one. Pipe was the one who had kissed my hand. Reno gave me a chin nod.

Next I met Crow.

Crow was the poster boy for badass gorgeous. He wasn't as big as Jules and Diego. He probably stood just about six foot. His skin was a beautiful light brown with subtle undertones of copper, not unlike my own. He had a wide bandana on his forehead and the rest of his hair hung loose way past his shoulders. It was a rich, deep sable. His nose was straight and his nostrils flared. He had a wide mouth and high cheekbones. His green eyes were like shards of emeralds, hard and sharp.

"*Yaa' ta' sai*," Crow said to me in clear Apache. *You're welcome here.*

"*Aheeiyeh.*" I bowed my head, using the formal thank-you reserved for those deserving of great respect. His greeting had meant a lot to me and I wanted him to know that.

He met my eyes and honest to goodness it took my breath away. I felt Diego turn and tense across the table, and I couldn't have cared less.

"You're Apache," I said to Crow.

"And you're Lakota Sioux," he said back at me.

I looked over at Prosper and Prosper shrugged. "He asked."

"You asked if I was Native?" I smiled at Crow. I loved having the chance to lay claim to my mother's heritage. I always felt complimented when it happened.

"No, I asked if you were taken."

Wow.

His eyes left mine then and did a slow, long sweep down my body. Everywhere his eyes touched burned me. No one had ever looked at me like that, ever. I finally knew the meaning of that over-used quote in romance books that said, "He raped me with his eyes."

Wow. Wow. Oh. Wow.

Diego was halfway out of his seat. Crow looked at him, clapped a hand on his shoulder and said, "That door ever opens, Brother." Then without sparing me another glance he was gone.

I was still sitting in stunned silence. I felt Diego's eyes on me, but purposefully avoided them. Jules slapped a plate down in front of me. All of a sudden I had a huge appetite and it was all really delicious. Jules smirked when he saw that I had cleaned my plate. When he asked me if it was good, I told him that he had just given me the absolute best I ever had.

Diego looked my way again and growled.

Jules burst out laughing and reached out to kiss the top of my head. He replied, "Doll, you ain't seen nothing yet."

Diego looked exasperated, but this time he was looking right at Prosper. Prosper's eyes were full of mirth. He mouthed something to him that looked like it might have been the word *complicated,* but I couldn't imagine why he would have said that.

CHAPTER 23

Fucking Crow. Goddamn him to hell, that Apache bastard.

For the second time in less than a couple of days Diego had half risen out of his seat to take a brother on over Raine. Never in his life had he fought over a woman. Now at fucking thirty-eight years old, he was gonna start? No fucking way.

He had been making his way down the hallway when he saw her fling open that door with nothing but that hip-length Chinese silk shit on. Christ, that belt barely held the thing together. He could see half her left tit and the bottom opened almost to her V. And there she stood totally unaware of it. Smiling and sleepy-eyed with those big blue eyes and soft pink mouth issuing an invitation to every fucking brother in the place. How was it possible that she didn't know that? But fuck him, if she hadn't looked hurt and embarrassed when he called her on it.

Jesus. It was going to be a full-time job keeping Raine safe. Safe from his brothers, from him, and from her goddamn self. He was going to have to make it clear who she belonged to, if just to keep her from harm's way.

But first he had to get his woman away from all his up-in-your-face, horny, blueballed brothers. He was going to do something he had never done before. Never had to do to get a woman to share his bed.

He was gonna get Raine on the back of his bike and take her out on a fucking date.

CHAPTER 24

Prosper and I took off after breakfast. We talked about ordinary things, trying to find our way back there, I guess. Or really establish a new ordinary. There was still a lot to be settled, but we had done a hell of a lot of that already and we both needed to put that away for a while. As we walked arm in arm, I remembered how much I loved being with Prosper. That hadn't changed and as the day wore on, it cemented itself in. He made me laugh remembering little things about Claire and me . . . And about my mom and dad. Funny little things that not another living soul knew about us. Family things.

It was a perfect day. Blue skies and white, fluffy clouds. We sat down on a big boulder in the sun. Prosper took out two beers he had brought along in a backpack. As a surprise, he had also packed some of the cookies that Pinky had made before she left to see her family. I was still full, but we had been hiking a couple of miles. The beer and cookies went down easy. The cookies tasted like that summer at the lake. I brought my head down to Prosper's shoulder, remembering. We sat like that in the warm sunshine. My head on his shoulder and his arm around me.

I wanted to give him something, so I took out my little harp. The look of pleasure in his eyes when he saw it made my heart sing. I played a few little tunes for him, shy at first. When he clapped and cheered with suspiciously bright eyes after the first round, I really started to show off. Like he had taught me to do, he carried his own music wherever he went. He reached into his pocket, and we played together. I had never been prouder when there came a moment, on that perfect sun-filled blue-sky day, that the student became the teacher. I taught Prosper a couple of new harmonies to some old songs I knew had been his favorites. The strong, clear joining of our voices singing in perfect harmony filled me with the most perfect bit of contentment that I had ever known. For the first time in a long time, I was really happy.

It was late afternoon when we walked back into the compound. Diego was sitting with a bunch of the guys in the yard. When he saw Prosper and me walk in from the woods, he raised his head and watched us approach. It had been a wonderful afternoon filled with good memories, homemade cookies, perfectly sung music, and well, love. A perfect day. Because I was still feeling that, and I was sick of being at the receiving end of Diego's petal-pulling game of "I love her and I love her not," I met Diego's eyes from across the field and smiled big, wide, and happily at him.

Let's see what he does with that, I thought wickedly.

The response lifted him off his chair. I just couldn't figure him out. But just then I wanted to be happy, so I let myself be.

Diego nodded to Prosper. He put his arm around me. "Good day, Babe?" He pulled me close.

"The best," I answered because I was still feeling it and because he was being nice again and I wanted to go with that.

Prosper did a backhand wave as he walked away from us.

"You up for a ride?" Diego was asking me.

I nodded happily because this was definitely going to be my day. I loved motorcycles and the thought of being on the back of Diego's excited me. He took my hand and led me to the bike. He passed me the helmet. I tried to put it on, but the heavy bun in back of my head was in the way. So I unpinned my hair and shook it out. I dipped my head back and ran my fingers through it. I pulled the heavy strands all to the side and began to weave it into a braid. I dipped my fingers into my pocket and pulled out the cloth-covered rubber band that I always kept on me for hair emergencies. I heard the sound of someone clearing his throat and looked to the picnic area where the eight guys that Diego had just left were all sitting in absolute silence staring at me.

I looked at Diego. To my surprise, he just looked at me and smirked.

"Damn fucking wet dream," he murmured. Then he said, "You good, Raine?"

I nodded and pulled my leg over the bike and adjusted the helmet. I wrapped my arms around him.

We roared out of there and I held on tight. The beautiful day was turning into an equally beautiful dusk with red and deep-blue streaks shooting across the sky. The wind was fresh and cool against my skin. Diego was a great driver and I was an experienced rider, so our bodies dipped and straightened. Weight shifting in harmony. It felt like a dance. Along the way, he would slow down and point out little things that he thought might interest me.

Eventually we pulled into a little cantina. He took my hand and pulled me along behind him. Once inside he pushed me in front of him, his hand guiding me by the small of my back. A pretty, obviously pregnant woman smiled when she saw him. He said something to her in Spanish that made her blush and place a hand on her stomach. Her eyes were warm when she smiled at me.

She seated us at a table at the end of the room, and I noticed that Diego seated himself with his back against the wall. The woman put her hand on his shoulder. Diego grabbed it, turned it palm out, and planted a kiss right in the middle of it. The woman laughed and hit him with a towel. Her dark eyes shining.

"Ah! Diego, when are you going to get a woman of your own and stop making my wife blush?" A smiling man had come upon us quickly. He put his hand protectively and more than a little proudly over his wife's baby bump and stated, "All this excitement is not good for my son."

He had a long dark ponytail, a rosary hanging around his neck, a silver wedding ring on his left hand, and a detailed scripted tattoo on his neck that read *Alejandra*. The pretty pregnant woman, whom I assumed was Alejandra, looked lovingly into her husband's eyes. She nodded at me. She said something softly in Spanish. Her husband turned to me in an exaggerated display of surprise. I knew he had noticed me and was up for giving Diego a hard time.

"Well, well, well! Who do we have here?" He smiled at me.

I extended my hand and introduced myself. "My name is Raine. Nice to meet you. I'm a friend of Diego's."

At "friend" Diego lost a little of the mirth that danced behind his eyes, but just a little.

Alejandra's husband took my hand, then turned it palm *down* and placed a kiss upon it. His wife shook her head, smiling, and Diego actually rolled his eyes. Someone called him from the kitchen. He winked at me and said, "Unfortunately, duty calls. But I'm very pleased to meet the new *friend* of Diego Montesalto."

He turned to Diego. "Anything you want, Brother."

He slapped him on the shoulder and they did a thing where they shook each other's hand, but they extended themselves way up so they were grasping each other's arms. That thing that guys do.

Diego ordered for us. The food was cheesy, spicy, and perfect. I had a margarita and Diego had a Dos Equis. Diego Montesalto, the most interesting man in the world. I smiled into my margarita thinking of the ad for beer. Diego was relaxed and entertaining. He told me how he had met Alejandra and her husband, Rafe. It was a good story and made me laugh.

It was late when we started back and the night had turned really cool. Diego reached into the leather bag on the bike and took out a big thick sweatshirt. He stood close and raised my hands over my head. He slipped the sweatshirt on and pulled my braid out. He bent down and touched his lips to mine briefly, then full-on kissed me. I pulled away when I heard a shrill whistle coming from the cantina and turned to see Rafe standing in the shadows smoking a cigarette and wagging his finger. Diego good-naturedly flipped him the bird, and we were off.

When we pulled into the MC compound there was music playing, loud conversation, and firelight. The Hells Saints were gathered around the fire pit with their women. They were casting long shadows, and it made me uneasy. *Something wicked this way comes.* I hadn't liked these gatherings as a child, and I still didn't like them. I wanted to go inside. I turned away from Diego to undo my helmet and saw her. The woman who had flashed me the superior smile and had plastered herself against Diego when I first arrived. Had that only been a couple of nights ago? It seemed like a lifetime.

She was staring at me and not looking happy. At all. She looked mean. Crazy and mean. I stared back, a chill running up my spine. I had had enough of crazy to last a lifetime. I knew this kind of crazy and where it was coming from. If she thought she had a claim on Diego, so be it. I barely knew him, and if it came down to that, that's what I would say. *Have. At. It.*

I wasn't the kind of woman who fought over men. I never got that. There were so many other things you had to fight to keep in this life, a man should not be one of them. But I knew there were some that didn't see it that way. This woman full-on worried me. I pulled my arms around me and held on tight. Diego had been talking to Reno. When he turned and looked at me, a frown crossed his brow. He looked past me and his eyes skirted the wooded edge. By then she was gone.

"Raine."

I looked at him.

"You okay, Babe?"

I managed a smile. "Yeah, thanks for a nice night. I'm going to head in now."

Diego shook his head. "No, Babe, you're not. Prosper got his groove on the harp. You seriously gonna miss that?"

"What time is it?" Something had just occurred to me. All of a sudden, the time had become very important.

He looked at his phone. "11:05. Why?"

I had only fifty-five minutes left to end a day that had been just about perfect. I honestly could not ever remember having that before. Ever. And it was something I had aspired to. One day of not worrying about anything. *One whole day.* I really didn't want anything to mess that up for me. But Diego had grabbed my hand and was pulling me along. What could possibly happen in fifty-five minutes? Then the wind tugged at my hair, loosening a tendril and whispering in my ear. *Something wicked this way comes.*

The air was electric in the way I remembered it as a kid. But now I forced myself to look at the scene before me with adult eyes, and damn if I didn't feel that same shiver go up my spine. It wasn't the good kind of shiver. It was the kind of shiver that came from being a lifelong watcher and knowing that the secrets that lay deep within these shadow people were dangerous ones. They were the kind of secrets that knowing about could hurt you. Even get you killed. These might be Prosper's people and Diego's people, but they were not my people. These were the kind of people that scared me.

As I walked through the sea of badass outlaws and their women, I felt cold inside. No matter who my dad was or who my Prosper was or who the man I was on the arm of was, I wasn't a part of this. A bunch of bikers and their women. Their women. Some of them were old ladies, some were girlfriends, and some were honest-to-goodness whores. They were definitely a type. They were fat and skinny, short and tall, blondes, brunettes, and redheads. Some were older, some younger, but definitely a type. Big hair, lots of makeup, and lots of tit showing. Whether those tits were large or small, they were on display. They smelled of cheap perfume, cheap booze, and desperation. They were hard women. Hard-loving, hard-living, hard-hearted women. Dangerous women wanting to be owned by dangerous men. Willing to do anything to make that happen. The men knowing that and taking that on. The air crackled with it.

I looked past all that to Prosper. Prosper definitely had his groove on. He was jamming with Crow, and they were both playing some mean guitar. I recognized some of the riffs and my fingers were itching to blow them on my harp. Prosper looked at me and crooked his finger. Oh no! No . . . no . . . nope! There was no way I was going to make a display of myself in front of a bunch of bikers. It was one thing belting out a tune in my own backyard or this afternoon with Prosper alone and soaking in the sunshine. But sharing my music with the people of the shadows seemed wrong.

Then Prosper was on me and pulling me with him. When he sat me down next to him and called out to the night, "This one is for Maggie," I came undone. How could I refuse to sing along to a song dedicated to my mom? He had me there. Crow began to strum out the beginning chords of Bob Seger's "Turn the Page." I took the harp out of my back pocket and replaced the soulful sax with some sweet harmonica. I had been playing this for years by myself, and honestly playing with Prosper was a dream come true. Prosper and I sang Seger in perfect harmony, taking twists and turns that, while not in the original version, worked well for us. This had been my mother's swan song. I was going to sing the shit out of it. And I did.

When it was over, Crow, Prosper, and I were grinning the hell out of each other, and the shadows were going wild with applause. Almost against my will, I turned my eyes to look for Diego. I saw him walking with Ellie away from me and towards the porch area. I felt a burst of jealousy that I pushed down. I turned my attention to Prosper when I realized he had been saying something. The something was that Pinky's sister had gotten into a pretty serious car accident, and Prosper was flying down that night to be with Pinky while she sat with her sister. He had just been waiting for me so he could tell me, and the playing, I think, had taken his mind off it for a moment. I was grateful he had given me that moment and hoped with all my heart that Pinky's sister would be okay. He thought no longer than a week and that I should stay at the compound.

I didn't want him to go. And if he had to go, I wanted to go with him. I didn't want to stay with people I didn't know. Now I was really starting to miss Claire. We had never been apart this long, and I knew she missed me as much as I missed her.

But if he had to leave me, I wanted Prosper to go with a clear state of mind. So I smiled, kissed him on the cheek, and told him that I would be fine. And I would be. Because this was my perfectly happy day. He got on his bike and left for the airport. It was 11:45.

I was tired and started heading away from the crowd and back to my room. I felt Jules fall in step with me. I was glad because I didn't want to walk alone in the dark. I also didn't want to run into Ellie and Diego doing whatever the hell they were doing. I couldn't help it. I wanted to help it but I couldn't. As I walked by, my eyes searched for them. And bingo. There they were. Ellie was plastered against him *again,* but this time Diego had his hands in her hair and his mouth was moving against hers. Just great. While I watched I saw him pull her head away from him. He had a scowl on his face, and she was smiling up at him. My heart hurt. Before I could look away, he saw me.

"Raine." He frowned, still holding her away from him. He dropped his grip on her and moved towards me.

Ellie pulled at him and he growled at her, "Get off me!"

I took a step back, feeling broken. Damn. I wished it hadn't hurt seeing them together like that. But it did and not just a little bit. Especially after the time we had just shared. What was going on? Was it really that easy for Diego to go from me to Ellie and then back again? I knew what I needed to do. I needed to keep walking and let tonight be forgotten.

Walk-away Joe.

Diego stood in my path. Big arms crossed, feet wide apart. Blocking my way and blotting out my view of the she-devil he had just seconds ago been wrapped around.

Ellie wasn't going to be forgotten that easily. She moved quickly to put herself in front of Diego and way too close to me.

"Yeah, that's right, Pocahontas," she sneered.

Oh no, she didn't.

"Me and Diego. Bitch. For two years now." She did one of those head-bob things.

"Shut up, Ellie." Diego, face dark and body tense. Watching me.

"Really, honey, she should know." Ellie looked back at him, smiled brilliantly, and tossed her hair.

Then she was back on me at full attention and she wasn't smiling.

"Yeah, that's right, *Raine*." She spat my name out as though it tasted bad on her tongue.

"Diego took you for a ride on his bike tonight, but it's me that he has been riding *in his bed*. You were sitting on his bike, I was sitting on his face."

Oh my God! Who says that?

"Come to think of it, I was wearing that same sweatshirt the last time I went down on him. Yeah, on my knees for my man with nothing on but his sweatshirt. Is that why she's wearing it, baby? Because you like the smell of me on her?"

Her words hit me like they meant to and pierced a spray of heavy artillery right through me. My stomach cramped, and my fingers were so tight at my sides I broke skin. I felt that shot everywhere. It filled me with such a deep ache that it didn't even leave any room for me to go into. So I had to just stand there all-out and take it. Then I wrapped my arms so tight around me that my ribs hurt.

Jules flew into action and wrapped his fingers around Ellie's throat, almost lifting her off the ground. Diego and I were locked in an eye battle. He almost looked as shocked as I felt. Almost.

"Shut up, you fucking skank," Jules roared.

Ellie wasn't done. She still wasn't done.

How could she not be done?

"Let me go, Jules!" she spat out. She twisted violently. Her eyes were on me with hate. She was heaving and there was spittle at the edges of her mouth.

Jules let go of her neck but wrapped his big arms around her middle, trying to drag her away from me. She was so angry she was convulsing.

"How stupid are you, bitch? You think for a minute he is going to choose a beat-up, beat-down, dirty little Indian whore over me? You think you're special? You think he's into you? You're just the flavor of the month, bitch."

Then she sneered, "*You're being used.* And if you don't believe me, just wait and see. Wait long enough, you'll even get used to it. Christ, half your body is black and blue. You're used to it already." Ellie's voice cracked. "You feeling me, bitch?"

I heard something in her fall apart, and I *watched* Ellie then. Under all that venom and teased hair and heavy makeup, Ellie was young. And desperate. And hurt. And fighting for something she felt slipping away from her. We were not dissimilar in that way. But life had twisted Ellie in a way that I had worked hard to keep from happening to me. And to Claire. Ellie was spiteful and mean and dangerous. Ellie was poison. And Ellie was wrong.

I was all over it then and cat-spitting mad.

"You done? You done now, Ellie?"

Then I took a step closer and leaned into *her*.

"I get that you're not happy seeing me with Diego. I get that you don't like me being anywhere near him. I get that he has had you . . . let me see if I've got this right . . . in his bed, on his face, and what was that last one? Oh yeah, *blowing him*, for the past two years. I get that you're his regular fuck buddy, and to you that means he's your man. Am I feeling you so far, Ellie?"

Jules was holding on to the finally subdued Ellie. Diego hadn't taken his eyes off me the entire time. His eyes dark with fury and his mouth grim. I couldn't even look at him. My eyes were hard on Ellie and hers were harder on me. I had her full attention, and she was certainly feeling me.

"I get because of your fuck-buddy status that you don't appreciate a . . . hmmm, what was that again? Oh yeah, a beaten-up, beaten-down, dirty little Pocahontas coming in to threaten that. I get that you think I'm too stupid to understand that I'm nothing more than a flavor of the month. I get that you think beaten-up whores like me should be used to life's little disappointments."

Oh yes, I did. And I wasn't done yet.

"I'm definitely feeling you, Ellie. Now listen up, because this is you feeling me.

"Pocahontas, just to be clear, was the daughter of Powhatan. He was the chief of the Algonquian Indians. She was an honest-to-Christ real Native American princess. I'm not her. My name is Raine, Ellie. You got issues with *me*, you call me by my goddamn name."

She was watching me and I was *watching* her. None of the crazy was gone from her eyes, but she was listening.

"I met *your man* a week ago. In that time, I've been threatened by him, rescued by him, and judged by him. I've had dinner with him and been for a ride with him. What I've not been is fooled by him or used by him. Or, and hear this clearly, *fucked by him*. So you don't get to call me a whore. The Diego trophy is still all yours, girl-friend, and it certainly sounds like you have earned it."

I paused for a minute to let that sink in. Then I full-on started again.

Oh yes, I did.

Because really? *Really?*

"You're right about one thing, Ellie. That black and blue you see on me is from a man. He hit me and I left. The reason I went back wasn't because I needed him, but because I needed something he had that was mine. He found me and he beat me again. That's not something I plan on ever getting used to. There's no reason for me to ever go back there again. The hope I had of him loving me died with that first punch. If he ever comes back to get me, I'll not go back to him. I'll kill him. You still feeling me, Ellie?"

Ellie's eyes were on me, brittle with hate, but also just a glim-mer of understanding.

And I had more.

"I don't fight over men. I don't respond to threats made by women who want to fight over men. Whatever there is between you and Diego is none of my business. And honestly, despite the crazy you're wearing, I get this is what it costs you to love him. I get it, and I'm sorry for the part I might have played in making you feel this."

And I honestly was. No woman should be made to feel that much pain over loving a man. I didn't like being part of what caused that.

But because Ellie was too far gone, she wouldn't take the out I had just given her.

"Bitch, you don't even know what it takes to love a man like him." She just couldn't quit.

I took a step back then. There are some women who will just never get it.

I was talking to Ellie, but I was looking straight at Diego.

"I do know. I know exactly what it takes. It takes everything. It takes it all. And every time, every single time you dare to hope it's gone for good, it sneaks right back in, and then it takes some more."

It was 12:01.

CHAPTER 25

Crow had seen that crazy chick approaching Raine and was on it. When Jules moved in on her throat, he was only half a step ahead of Crow. Jesus, what was Diego thinking? You don't go from a woman like Ellie to a woman like Raine without doing some serious damage control first. He had left her out there. Again. When Diego moved to go after Raine, Crow stood in front of him.

"Brother, you need to clean this up first." And he nodded right at Ellie. Diego knew Crow was right, but had to make one thing clear.

"Me taking a minute to do that should not be mistaken as me opening that door. You feel me, Brother?"

Crow walked away thinking that's exactly what that meant.

CHAPTER 26

Diego had headed Ellie off when she went for Raine the first time. She had thrown herself at him when he had tried to tell her it was over. What Raine had seen was Ellie's last-ditch attempt to persuade Diego another way. But she had turned her fury onto Raine. The twisted look on her face, the spittle foaming at her mouth, she had gone full-on crazy. A full-on assault. Holy fuck, Ellie wouldn't shut up. Ellie had Raine on the ropes and kept slugging.

Diego knew Ellie had it in her, but honestly, he was shocked at the venom that came spewing from her mouth. He knew that anything he said would just make it worse. So he watched, ready to pick up Raine and physically remove her if it came to that. But it didn't come to that.

Because his girl had handled it.

While Ellie continued her battery, Raine had gone perfectly still. Her hands fell to her sides, and she was listening. She absorbed each blow. Ellie pressed her advantage, backing Raine against the ropes. Raine took in all the shit that Ellie was handing her.

Until she didn't.

Then she had come out swinging.

CHAPTER 27

Diego banged on my very locked door much later that night. I ignored him and his ridiculous pounding. He had stood on the other side of that door yelling my name and threatening to "kick in this fucking door right now." I had to pull the pillow tight around my head to drown out his voice. Eventually he went away. Actually, eventually, I heard someone come and drag him away.

I had stood my ground with Ellie, but it had taken a toll on me.

Two years. Ellie and Diego for *two years.* I didn't know how to feel about that. I didn't know what to think of a guy who would spend *two years* with a woman like that. Two years and he had never taken her on his bike. That seemed to be the core of what set Ellie off. I hadn't one clue, not one insight into this whole MC thing. I didn't think I wanted to.

But I sure as hell knew Crazy. I had spent my life avoiding Crazy. I certainly would never willingly start a thing with Crazy's man. I wasn't about to open my bedroom door in the wee hours of the morning to let that man in. Not at dawn or twilight either. Opening that door would bring me nothing but trouble. And heartache.

The trouble I could handle.

The heartache would kill me.

Just seeing her with him wrapped in his arms proved that. For just a little while last night at dinner, I had let myself imagine what it would be like to be loved by Diego. I imagined it all to be wonderful. A little house with a fireplace and flowerpots in the window. Wind chimes and stained glass. And babies. Lots of brown-eyed, soft-skinned, chubby little happy souls. I would love them and the man who gave them to me. *As long as we both shall live.*

Then it all came crashing down on me. I felt like such an idiot. Ellie had called me Pocahontas and beaten-up. She had made me feel humiliated and pathetic. I swear to God, I was ready to just turn and run. I wanted to run and run and run as far as I could away from her, from him.

But then her voice cracked and I *saw her.* And when I saw her, I saw myself, or what I could have become if I hadn't been fighting to keep that down for my whole life. So I had tried. I tried to explain and apologize and bring her into the Sisterhood of Lost Souls. But Ellie was too far gone. I didn't know what happened between Diego and Ellie after I left, but I hoped I would never see either one of them again.

CHAPTER 28

I got up and got dressed. I wanted to be out of there before anyone saw me. I felt like I needed to put more than a few hours between my total humiliation and those who had witnessed it.

But that was not going to happen. Jules was manning the kitchen and must have heard my shower running because there was a hot cup of coffee and some cinnamon toast waiting for me. When I tried to wave off his offer of coffee and head for the door, he took pity on my nervous glance around. He told me that Diego had "apparently cleaned up the Ellie mess and they reached a mutual agreement" (whatever that meant), and "he had got rid of her" (holy shit, whatever that meant).

Then Jules explained that the "getting rid of" meant that Diego had given Ellie the transport to catch a plane, train, or bus. Her choice, as long as she was gone by that morning. That meant Diego would be gone at least most of the day. Then he was going to do some MC business that might take a couple of days. Crow was out doing a restock at one of the bars that the Saints owned downtown.

Good news and good news.

The day was already looking up.

Too bad Diego wasn't taking that plane, train, or bus with Ellie. I was singularly unimpressed with the "shipping her off" thing. Crazy finds its way back. It always does. I wasn't ready to face Diego, and I was thinking that the "not ready" thing may turn into a "never, ever ready" thing. Pure self-preservation. He wasn't the man for me. Besides that, this whole mess had hurt me a lot. I honestly didn't think I could be with a man who could be with a woman like that.

So I had my cup of joe with Jules and munched on some toast. I told him that I planned to take Prosper's car out for the day and get some errands done. I wasn't familiar with the area, but was hoping there was a branch of my bank around and maybe a mall. Now that I had my life savings back, I could take a moment to do some retail therapy and take time away from the compound to think about my future. I couldn't stay holed up here forever. I needed a job.

My nursing school graduation was imminent. However, I had decided to wait for the diploma in the mail. I didn't have the heart to don the cap and gown. Honestly, I wasn't even sure I wanted to be a nurse anymore. I had taken the course of study because of how well it paid, and I knew I could probably get a job just about anywhere Claire and I decided to go. I thought it would fill my life with purpose to help the sick little children and their families, but really it had just made me sad. I hadn't liked the windowless corridors of the hospitals or the arrogance of the doctors. Having the support of Prosper made me feel like I had family. That felt secure to me. Maybe I could start thinking in a different direction now. After all, education is something that never goes away and I would have that nursing degree forever.

Jules had his head bent and was cursing over some numbers. I smiled at the top of his head. I knew that Jules was a badass. He was a big, scarred biker dude with huge hands and tribal tattoos. But to me, he was a gentle giant and a hero of sorts. He was the first one who had come to my rescue when I called out for help on that strange and fateful day. He made me breakfast and had almost choked Ellie last night on my behalf. Jules was my friend.

I brought my head close to his and looked at what he was struggling with. It was some kind of inventory sheet. A few pages' worth and, by the looks of it, it was a mess. I was a numbers girl. As a kid in school I had always loved math. I loved the unshaken reliability of it. Two plus two always made four. No matter what. It was logical and sequential and fixed. Yeah, I loved math.

After a brief discussion with Jules, I found out that the Hells Saints actually owned three saloon-type bars and were in the process of opening up a fourth. Their bookkeeper was going through some "transition time" (which I think was probably better termed "prison time") and the bookkeeping task had fallen to Jules. He was having a fuck of a time with it. His words, not mine. I looked it over, subtracted a few things where he had added, moved a couple of columns over, and then checked the total. Jules looked at me like I was Houdini and gave me a big bear hug. He made me laugh and I smiled. Then he offered me a job doing the books for the newest bar, a place called Ruby Reds. I accepted on the spot, and he told me there was even a real office to work in. I wasn't sure if this was a true and serious offer for employment, but Jules assured me it was. I couldn't have been more thrilled.

I took Prosper's car for the day. It was a five-speed black Saab. It was fun to drive and had a kickass stereo system and a built-in navigation system. I plugged in some destinations and was on my way. The area was really pretty and had these little caches of small towns that surrounded an urban hub. I stayed away from the major city, but enjoyed driving through the small towns. Two of the towns had branches of my bank, so I was able to deposit my money again. Snap! I felt that relief in the tips of my toes. I kept some out though. I stopped at a cool little store and bought Claire a cute card. I sent her the max cash she was allowed.

Then I treated myself to a day that I hadn't had since . . . well, ever. I totally enjoyed the whole retail therapy experience. The only thing that was missing was a friend to share it all with. Or a sister. I missed Claire. But I still managed to do it up. Honestly, I had a blast.

I treated myself to a Cobb salad and two glasses of wine at a little bistro nestled in the foothills. They had a great pastry section, and I spent a small fortune on scones, cinnamon buns, fruit tarts, turnovers, and muffins to bring back to the kitchen house so that Jules could get a break on breakfast duty in the morning. I also treated myself to a manicure and a pedicure. I found an organic cosmetic store and spent too much on black velvet mascara, eyeliner, shampoo, and conditioner. I bought body wash, lotion, and spray all in the same fragrance so I could layer the scents. I bought new underwear.

I bought two pairs of outrageously expensive jeans that made my ass look great and three soft sweaters in neutral colors. When the clerk told me that the navy-blue pencil skirt and the off-the-shoulder white blouse looked fab on me, I added them to the pile. I decided on four thin V-neck tee shirts in black, light pink, baby blue, and bright white. I tried on and purchased a tiny black backless dress that the sales person convinced me looked classy and not at all trashy. I threw in the silver strappy sandals to go with it. I finished off the trip with a butter-soft, black leather jacket, biker boots, pajama pants, and camisole tops. I bought a lacy nightgown in black, then I bought it in white.

I bought and I bought and I bought. Oh yes, I did.

Later I took myself out to dinner. After that, I took myself to a movie. Finally, I drove myself home to the Hells Saints compound where I had to make three trips out to the car to bring in all my packages. Some of the brothers were out in the yard area. I could see a small fire burning, but otherwise it was pretty quiet. I laid the pastries out on the counter with a note to Jules. I went to my room to unwrap and delight in my purchases. That night I had the flying dream again.

CHAPTER 29

I had a good night's sleep. I woke up rested and in a good mood. I had decided that I was going to test the seriousness of Jules's offer to take over those books. I showered and put on all my new stuff. I thought I looked pretty good in the pink tee shirt and the jeans. They were something that I would probably live in. They felt that good and they looked even better. Yep, I was going to give that one to myself.

When I walked out into the main kitchen area, I was met with applause from the dozen or so bikers who were hanging around drinking coffee and eating the great stuff I bought the night before. It felt nice to be appreciated and I blushed and smiled. Still no Diego. Thank God. But it didn't escape my own notice that he was the first one that I looked for. I felt like a coward. The more time that passed, the more I dreaded seeing him again. I had stood up to Ellie. Oh, I certainly had. But that wasn't me. I hadn't wanted to respond in kind to the crude words that came spewing from her mouth. But I had and with a vengeance. Diego was just bad news for me, for my temper, and for my heart.

Diego was gone for now. But Crow was back.

He was having a cup of coffee with Jules. I couldn't help but notice he took it black and hadn't touched any of the pastries. He had on a white V-neck tee shirt under his cut and a worn pair of

Levi's that fit low on his hips. He had a beautifully beaded black-and-silver belt on, and his glossy black hair was in a long black pony-tail that went halfway down his back. The fact that he was a truly beautiful man wasn't lost on me. When he turned his eyes on me, he took my breath away.

"Raine." He chin-nodded me.

"Crow." I smiled a little at seeing him again.

He didn't smile back. Crow, come to think of it, didn't smile a lot. He was one of those guys who didn't easily give away his thoughts. He was intense, even stoic, in the few dealings I had had with him so far. Except when we were playing music. I remember he was smiling at the end of it. But, then again, we had done some kickass harmonies.

His eyes softened when he looked at me though, and he leaned in towards me. His tanned hands curled around his coffee mug through the handle. He smelled like dark roast and Polo. I thought I could get used to waking up and smelling that. I felt the heat rise to my cheeks, and I was sure I was blushing. Crow raised an eyebrow.

"Jules was just telling me you're gonna be takin' over the books for Ruby Reds."

I looked at Jules, who was pouring me a cup of coffee. He gave me a wink.

"She worked some magic yesterday, Crow. Man, I've got to tell you, I cannot wait to get rid of that bullshit. Prosper won't hire any-one outside the club, and half these clowns can't add two and two. Man, no fuckin' shame in this game. Two plus two is about as far as I go."

"That's not true, Jules," I said softly because I hated to hear the big man selling himself short.

Crow looked at me. "Thought you were a nurse?"

"I am. Formally, I will be after next week," I said in way of explanation.

"What's next week?"

"It's the graduation. But I'm not going to the ceremony," I added quickly. "I'll get my degree in the mail. It's just that I'm not sure it's what I want to do anymore. I thought I could do some good. Maybe give back a little, being a pediatric nurse. But, honestly, it just made me feel sad and helpless."

It was the first time I had ever voiced the concerns I had out loud about my chosen career. I wondered if Crow would think that I was being foolish and self-centered.

"I get it," he said, taking a sip from his coffee mug, his eyes on me. "I've got two years towards a degree in architectural design myself."

"You do?" I asked, my eyes wide.

"Yeah. I do," he said in a tone that told me this was all the information I was going to get.

"So you ready to take on Ruby Reds? There's three of them, you know."

Jules stepped in. "I'm gonna have her break her economics cherry slowly. Brother, let's not scare the chick off before she gets the first bite in."

Then to me. "I'll keep on keeping on with the other two. They aren't as busy as Reds. Let's see how you do with that one. You like it, we talk about you taking over all three."

Jules was mopping up the counter with a bar cloth. "I have a couple of things to do this morning but I was thinking maybe later on you and I could take a look-see at those inventory sheets. Smalley was starting to plug all the numbers into some computer program. I think I've got the password somewhere. I find it and we're in business. I should be all set to give you some time about three. You gonna be around?"

I nodded and checked the time. It was only ten a.m. and I didn't have a clue what I was going to do the rest of the day.

"You up for a ride?" Crow was looking at me.

I processed real fast about the whole "back of the bike proprietary" thing and where that had gotten me last time.

"I was heading down to Reds this morning to check on some stuff."

Jules interrupted by way of explanation, "Crow is our order guy."

"Thought you might want to check the place out yourself to get a feel for it. Not sure where you'll want to set up. I know Smalley used the back office. But I also know there's a good chance he left it a shit hole. Jules works out of the back room. My guess is you might be feeling a little claustrophobic around here. So thought you might want to pick your poison." Then he shrugged. "Up to you."

"Let me grab my pocketbook," I said just that quickly. Then to Jules: "I'll see you this afternoon?"

"You got it, sugar." Jules winked.

I liked being on the back of Crow's bike. I tried not to think about Diego on the ride to Ruby Reds. It was another beautiful day and I was looking forward to seeing what my new job would be.

Crow didn't talk to me on the way. I remembered how Diego had grabbed my leg and pointed things out to me on the ride. The thought of him messed me up. I needed to stop making comparisons. I chastised myself. That night with Diego, I had harbored a small secret hope it would be the beginning of something. That something died a few hours later. This was a ride to work. I concentrated on how nice it was having my arms around Crow. He was also tight and hard in all the right places. When my arms wrapped around him I felt solid steel. I pressed against him, my soft breasts hitting leather-encased back muscle. He leaned back into me and reaching back he moved his hand lazily up and down my thigh.

We pulled up in front of a bar and it wasn't anything like what I had anticipated. I had expected a small biker bar, maybe down some alley or wedged between a few other bars. What I got was a newly constructed building at the end of a short private road. It was red brick with some cool trim and double-hung black wooden doors in the front. Next to them was a tasteful plaque that read simply "Ruby Reds."

The door opened and an attractive woman about fifty years old came towards us with a smile. She wore her auburn hair in a dramatic up-do and had a Hells Saints support tee shirt on. A Rolling Stones tongue tattoo sat on the top of her left breast. Crow introduced her as Dolly. She explained to me that she had been overseeing the cleaning and maintenance of the bar since its beginning. She welcomed me immediately and gave me a big bear hug. She told me she was Reno's mom and Pinky's sister-in-law. Dolly was the widow of Pinky's brother. The friendly redhead said she knew all about me. She said she remembered me as a little itty-bitty thing from that time we spent at the lake and called me "sugar." She grabbed my face in her soft hands and told me I was a beauty. I liked Dolly. A lot.

Apparently Prosper had called right after we left the kitchen house. The message was that Pinky's sister wasn't doing as well as they had hoped. It would be a while longer before they would be back. Jules told Prosper about my prospective new role in the business. He was all for it.

"You sticking around for a while, Crow? I've got some questions on the inventory, and I need some more bar supplies. I'm gonna show this little sugar around for a minute. Then maybe you can spare some time?" Dolly had looped her arms around mine.

"I'll be here most of the afternoon doing my thing and helping out Raine," Crow answered. The three of us then headed into my new place of employment.

The twin black heavy wooden doors opened to, what I later learned, was one of the premium tequila bars in the area. It was big inside, both wide and deep. The color scheme was all red and black with a bar that ran half the length of the room. There were red-leather nail-studded bar chairs, and the bar itself was black granite. The whole room was backlit in crimson. A huge gas fireplace stood in the center of the room. The various booths were all ebony or red leather. There was a wrought-iron gate separating the tables from the booths. The lamps dropped low over the tables and glowed with bloodshot stained glass. There were a couple of Goth-inspired candelabras and some strategically placed gargoyles in the corner of the room. The whole atmosphere was Bela Lugosi creepy. It was all very old Hollywood without being tacky or silly. It was a great room. I honestly didn't feel I had the significant cool quotient to be a part of it.

"Wow," I breathed.

"Crow designed it. Ain't it something?" Dolly chimed in proudly.

I looked at Crow in awe.

"Wow, this is your baby?" I asked him.

"Nah," he said. "Thinking some long-legged, brown-eyed, *wiwasteka* is gonna be my baby."

His eyes danced at me. "This," he shrugged, "is just a bar."

I didn't know how to respond to that. When I looked at Dolly she was fanning herself, grinning.

Then she grabbed me and headed off with me, whispering, "I thought you and Diego . . . ?"

I sighed. It seemed the gossip mill was running rampant in the Hells Saints MC.

When Dolly opened the door to Smalley's office, I was enchanted. Wall-to-ceiling shelves and a file cabinet lined one wall. A brocade-covered Victorian couch sat in the corner. Of course, it was filled with what I could only assume were Smalley's clothes. The office had its own bathroom, which was filled with man stuff. I wondered if Smalley had spent more than a couple of nights sleeping in this office. There was also a desktop computer and it looked new. Crow told me he had all of the passwords to the business programs that Smalley had used. I was familiar with most of them and my fingers were itching to get started.

Crow told me I could "throw all that shit out." I took him at his word. I pulled my hair into a ponytail and pinned it on top of my head. I grabbed some plastic gloves, an apron, and other cleaning supplies from Dolly. She showed me how to turn on the built-in stereo system. The office had one of those half doors where you could close the bottom half but leave the top half open, and that's what I did as I set to work. Dolly and Crow had their heads huddled together over some inventory and maintenance stuff. I was throwing out "shit" and disinfecting the office within an inch of its life. I started with the bathroom because I knew that would be the most unpleasant. And oh boy, was it! I just closed my eyes and wiped the place clean until my eyes stung from the disinfectant.

When Dolly came in to get me for a coffee break, she told me that they had a "person" for that. I should have waited. I smiled at her and dragged her in to show all I had done. She smiled right back and contributed some nice scented red candles, which I lit immediately. By the time I got back from my coffee break, the whole office smelled like a cross between musk and cinnamon and the bathroom was sparkling. I felt the satisfaction of a job well done.

I still had a lot left to do to get the office in check, but it was getting late. Crow indicated that it was time to get going. This he did by wrapping his arms around me and pointing at his watch. His forearms laid soft on the sides of my breasts, and he moved them slowly. It was the first time he had actually ever gotten that close to me, and he led with that.

Geez.

I pulled away, and Crow pulled me back against him and whispered in my ear, "Fuck, baby, you feel good." He turned me around and pulled me in close. We were locked in tight, breast to chest, hips, crotch, and legs. His unbelievable deep emerald eyes held mine. Then he bent and kissed me.

Holy shit. There are kisses and there are kisses. And that kiss made me hear bells. They weren't the loud clangs of heart-stopping bells that I felt when Diego had touched his mouth to mine, but I heard bells nonetheless. Soft sweet chimes that tingled my lips, hardened my nipples, and wet my panties. Tingles that sent a thrill right through to my toes. I knew that starting something, anything, with Crow, when things were so up in the air with Diego was probably a really bad idea.

But sometimes bad ideas feel really good.

CHAPTER 30

Crow and I spent the whole next week pretty much together. He drove me to Reds each morning and we did our thing. Dolly was there most mornings as well. It was nice. I had cleaned up the entire office, and Jules and I had looked over the books together. With Crow's and Jules's help I was able to get into the computer records. They were actually in pretty good shape, but it was Smalley's system and not mine. I switched things so they made sense to me and better sense for the business. I liked the work and was good at it.

Prosper was still with Pinky and the news was still uncertain regarding her sister. She seemed to rally a little, only to develop a dangerous blood clot that had to be removed surgically and some kind of filter put in. I understood a little of the procedure but not much. I had Crow take me to the florist one day on the way home from Reds and sent two huge bouquets of flowers, one to the family home where Pinky and Prosper were staying and one to the hospital for Pinky's sister. Her name was Lilah. I was really hoping for the best for them.

Diego was still gone and I knew he was checking in with Jules. He left a number where I could reach him. But I never used it. He also called me every day on my cell. I deleted the messages before I listened to them. He was supposed to be coming back soon. Honestly, I anticipated it with really mixed feelings. He definitely stirred something up in me. I just wasn't sure if that something was bad or something *really* bad because I knew it wasn't something that could be good for me. That something was definitely unique to Diego and me. It wasn't something I had ever felt with anyone else. Not even with Crow, although things had started to heat up between us. There had been more really hot tongue-exchanging sessions between us; it had never progressed much further than that.

Honestly, it wasn't because I wasn't willing. I was so willing I felt a dull ache between my legs every time I looked at him. After one particularly hot make-out session, Crow planted me on his bike right afterward. All that vibrating and bumping and holding on to that beautiful bad man caused me to have a major orgasm on the way home from work, riding on the back of Crow's bike.

Soon after that, Crow became a little distant and that had started an ache in the pit of my stomach of a different kind. I was starting to feel like that "passed around and leave her" kind of girl in a high school kind of way. Which was ridiculous because no one had passed me around and no one had left me. But the two romantic interludes I had in the recent past still felt like they had ended in rejection. I was just feeling fragile, I guess. Something was definitely up with Crow and it wasn't my imagination. He wasn't exactly avoiding me since the last marathon make-out session, but he didn't seem anxious to repeat it either. He drove me into work every day, and I started taking extra care with my appearance. I know he noticed because Jules did and so did Dolly. It wasn't anything over the top, but maybe a few extra sweeps of mascara and some extra care with my hair. And all my new clothes all in one week. Like that.

I guess if the extra effort had worked, I wouldn't have felt so . . . desperate. But it hadn't. Crow remained pretty detached. It sucked because apart from all the other mixed-up, messed-up feelings that went along with my encounters with Crow, I had really begun to count on him as a friend. And as hot-and-heavy and all-around feel-incredibly-good, curl-your-toes, take-a-cold-shower kisser Crow was, if I had known going there with him would make me lose a friend, I wouldn't have done it. I wanted to ask him what was putting us in this new place. But I couldn't bring myself to do it.

So even though I was doing well in my new role as an employee of Reds, I was feeling out of sorts. I still couldn't call Claire. Prosper was gone. I had left a career and a life behind. Honestly, I didn't know if Gino was looking for Claire and me. Sooner or later I was going to have to face those demons again, and it looked like I was going to have to do it alone. It kind of made me sad. I looked at Crow heading towards me, and that made me sad too. I was tired of wanting what I couldn't have.

"Raine?" Crow was handing me a helmet.

I looked at him, feeling melancholy.

He saw it.

"Put on your helmet, honey. And let's go get some Thai food. You in?"

I was in.

We sat down over Thai food and beer.

"You want to tell me what's making those beautiful blue eyes so sad, honey?"

What I wanted to say was why did you stop wanting me?

But what I said was, "I guess I'm just feeling a little lost. I walked away from my life, Crow. Even if it wasn't a great life. It was mine and I had a plan. I feel kind of like a failure and I feel alone." There it was.

Crow looked at me. "I know something about walking away, Raine. Sometimes it feels right, but it never feels good. And the bitch of it is the unfinished part is always waiting. Before you move forward you have to clear that shit up. But you're not alone, honey."

"I'm afraid of what's waiting, Crow. I'm tired. Really I'm alone in all the ways that matter." I slumped.

Crow reached across the table and put his hand on mine. "Then rest, baby. Rest up, take the calm, take a breath, and take a minute to figure it out. I don't know about all of what you have been through, Raine, but I can see some of it. And it looks bad. Prosper is keeping your shit close and Diego, well, he wants in. Up to you if you let him. But in the meantime, baby, you take the time."

"Me and Diego. That Ellie thing . . ." I waved the thought away.

"She didn't mean jack to him. He's my brother so I got his back. But he should have cleaned that shit up before he went there with you."

"Yeah." I was starting to get uncomfortable talking about Diego with Crow.

"It's not just about Diego, Crow. You and me and then . . ." I was totally humiliated to have to ask this but I had to know.

"Babe." Crow was looking at me.

I was peeling the label off the bottle of my beer. The heat rising on my face. He covered my hand with his.

"Raine, you think I wasn't paying attention to how good my mouth felt on yours? You think I don't get hard every time, every single fucking time I look at you and think about how you felt when I held you?"

"Then why . . . ?" I had to know. My wounded pride needed to know. My heart needed to know.

"I got some shit of my own that's preventing me from starting this with you right now. Baby, it's just not a good idea."

I pulled my hand away and he let me.

"Crow. Please. You don't have to explain. Actually, I think we should probably get going." I grabbed my purse.

"Raine." He had moved from his side of the booth to mine and was barring my escape. I really just wanted to leave.

"Raine, baby, you got to believe me when I say you don't want to go there with me right now. Won't be good for you till I clear

124

some shit up. I got a woman. Shit, babe, I got a wife. I know that most of the brothers don't give two fucks about juggling shit like that, but that just ain't me. And more than that, that just ain't you." He was very close but wasn't touching me.

There it was. His opening farewell.

He was watching me, and I nodded. "The life you had?"

"The life we both walked away from."

"How long ago?" I asked softly.

"Little over a year."

That wasn't long enough. Not long enough by a long shot.

"That's not a long time, Crow. You can still turn it around." I didn't know what else to say.

He pulled his hands through his hair.

"Thirteen months, Raine. I've not tapped into any of the pussy at the club. Haven't even looked at that until you walked in that door." Then he laughed mirthlessly and rubbed the back of his neck.

"I want you to know that. If I was clear of her, there would be nothing stopping me from starting us. I would even have that fucking talk with D. But I'm still not sure where that's going. She asked me to wait, and I'm giving her that time. We're talking."

"Okay." I reached for my purse.

"Okay?" He seemed surprised. "That's it?"

"That's it." I made an attempt to move out of the booth.

"Raine, it's important to me that you understand." He wasn't moving.

I honestly couldn't have cared less what was important to him at that moment.

"I understand, Crow, I do. Not a good time for you right now."

My eyes were bright and I hated myself for that.

"You're married, and you're talking with your wife about working it out. Knowing that, you held me and kissed me and have spent almost every waking moment with me for the past week. I thought maybe it was the start of something nice. At the very least, I believed I had a friend. I needed that most of all. But friends don't mess with your feelings like that."

It all just felt like a lie now. It hurt in the place that was still raw from the Ellie train wreck. I needed to get as far from these beautiful bad men as I could.

"Is that really all you just heard?" His mouth was tight.

"It's all I heard that matters, Crow."

He moved out of my way and took me home.

CHAPTER 31

We pulled up in front of the compound and there were lights on everywhere. The wind had picked up and the evening sky was a stormy shade of gray. I sensed it before I heard it. *Something wicked this way comes.*

Crow sensed it too and moved his hand to the small of my back as we walked towards the kitchen house. I moved forward quickly, wanting to be rid of that touch. *Just another Walk-away Joe*, my mom's words came whispering unkindly through the wind. Something was brewing, and it was waiting for me. I was back to being all alone. Well, at least that was a place I was familiar with.

I had this.

I wasn't prepared to see Dolly red-eyed and shooting down a shot of tequila when I walked in. Reno was with her and Jules was too. A lot of the other guys were standing or sitting around. Bottles and shot glasses littered the tables and the vibe was subdued. Jesus, I had just left Dolly a couple of hours ago. What could have possibly happened in that short of a time to bring her and lots of others here with her? The quiet drinking was unnerving. This was a rabble-rousing, tear-assed crowd when they drank.

I moved to Dolly and held the hand that wasn't wrapped around a shot glass.

"Tell me." I held my breath.

"Oh, honey. It's Lilah. There were some complications." Dolly was having a hard time getting the words out.

I felt a wave of sadness roll over me like a storm. I held on tight and felt my heart break for Pinky and Prosper. This was bad. Reno wrapped his arm around his mom. He looked at me.

"Prosper called a little while ago. Pinky is taking it really hard, her only sister. Services will be this week. You, me, and Mom are flying out first thing in the morning. You cool with that?"

I was cool with that. Very cool with that because it meant I was considered family. And to a girl like me, that meant everything.

"Pack funeral shit. We'll pick you up at six a.m. Be ready," Reno said roughly to me. Then he took the shot glass out of his mother's hand and walked her out.

The bikers resumed their drinking. Someone was starting a card game in the back. Crow moved towards me and I walked right past him. Done is done.

I took a long hot shower, took extra time doing my hair, and packed a few things. Thanking heaven that I had splurged on the navy-blue pencil skirt and pretty white blouse. It wasn't something black, but it would have to do. I threw in a pair of new heels I hadn't gotten a chance to wear yet, one pair of jeans, one pair of black trousers (that were not new but looked it), one sweater, and three tees. I had no idea how long we would be gone, but figured I could buy anything else I needed.

For the plane trip, I wanted to be comfortable but presentable. I wore a pair of my new jeans with some pretty strappy sandals. After changing three times, I settled on a baby-blue cami and tissue-weight sweater combination. Then because I still had hours to wait, I took some time and put my hair into a really rad crown braid. I took way too long picking out some silver jewelry and took even longer putting on my makeup in a way that looked like it hadn't taken an honest-to-God half hour to do. The cut on my hairline was still scabbed over and would leave a scar, but the extreme bruising on my face had started to fade. I could cover it with the heavier makeup I had just purchased. I was looking much better, I told myself. I was all ready to go by five a.m. and was waiting by the window enjoying a third cup of coffee when they pulled up.

Dolly told me I looked beautiful. Reno gave me a chin nod when he took in my hair. It occurred to me that I had never heard Reno say more than a couple of words at a time. However, I had noticed that when he took the time to do that, people took the time to listen. They both had taken some effort with their appearance too. Dolly had on a pretty butter-yellow top (Rolling Stones tattoo completely covered) with white silk pants. Dolly's natural auburn curls were artfully arranged, and her makeup was subtle and flawless. I had been with her every day for the past week, but I never really noticed what a truly natural beauty she was. Dolly cleaned up good.

Reno was another beautiful man. He had a darker version of his mother's hair. The coppery-colored locks were streaked in shades of warm caramel from the sun. He was bronze and lean. He had light brown eyes with fine sunburst lines radiating outward in his face from the years of riding and working outside. He was about six feet tall and had a big Celtic knot tattoo on his bicep. He was wearing a white button-down shirt with the sleeves turned up and black jeans that rode low on his hips. He had on expensive-looking biker boots and a very cool black belt with a hammered silver buckle. He was sporting aviator glasses and a man bun. He looked dark and dangerous and grim.

We rode in relative silence to the airport. Each in our own thoughts. Reno had taken care of our tickets and had checked in and printed our e-tickets via the Internet. He parked in the airport parking garage, and we made it to our gate with only minutes to spare. Then we were off.

CHAPTER 32

I sat next to Dolly on the plane. She had more than a few drinks, but she could sure hold her liquor. I got treated to Dolly's life story, Pinky's story, and some of the missing parts to my story as well. I don't know what the airline tickets cost, but for me the ride proved priceless.

Dolly and Pinky had been friends since they were both sixteen years old. Pinky had introduced Dolly to her brother, Petey. For Dolly, at least, it had been love at first sight. Because Petey was fourteen years older, it took some convincing on Dolly's part but eventually her total love (her words) for him won out. They were married the day she turned eighteen. Petey had been the love of Dolly's life. For her there would never be anyone else. She still missed him every single day. Reno had been the light of his life, Dolly said. She saw Petey in Reno every time he smiled. Since I never remembered seeing Reno smile, I couldn't imagine it.

Pinky and Dolly, once best friends, now sisters-in-law, were closer than ever. Pinky and Prosper tried, but were never able to have children. Reno was their godson. When Petey died in that car accident, Pinky and Prosper took Dolly and Reno in until they found their way. That was a long time ago. When Reno was old enough to decide which way the cat jumped, he decided that it jumped in the MC's direction. His Uncle Prosper had guided him through the prospect phase of initiation. Reno was now a brother. Prosper and Reno were tight. Dolly and Pinky were tight. And now Claire and I were a part of that. I liked it.

Evidently, Pinky and Petey's younger sister Lilah had always been a hell-raiser and a half. From the time she was a teenager Lilah had made all the wrong choices. The bad boys had led to the bad men, which in turn had led to three bad marriages. She was an alcoholic by the time she was twenty-five years old with a number of DUIs under her belt and some jail time. Pinky had tried. Lordy, lordy, how she had tried. But Lilah had been hell-bent on destruction.

The strange thing was that when she had wrapped herself around that tree, she had eighteen months sober. The tragic thing was that she wrapped herself around that tree trying to avoid a head-on collision with a car driven by a drunk driver. The guy missed her but ran himself right off a steep embankment and died anyway. Dolly leaned in to me and whispered, "It's a damn good thing too. What Prosper and the brothers had planned for that drunken bastard would have been a lot more painful and a lot less quick."

By that point, she had begun slightly slurring her words. I hoped it was the booze talking retaliation, but in my heart, I knew it probably wasn't.

Dolly talked then about the summer that Pinky and Prosper had taken us in. She said she remembered it like it was yesterday.

Prosper had lost his mind when he found out that we had been left alone. He had sent some of the brothers out to find our father while he went to get us. Pinky had been frantically waiting because she had been afraid that Prosper had killed Jack in his attempt to get at us. So the look that I remembered seeing clearly on her face that night had been both gratitude that we were safe and relief that Prosper hadn't killed our father. No, Prosper hadn't killed Jack. What he did do was send a very clear message that Jack had two weeks to clean his act up *totally* or he would never see his daughters again, ever.

I was mesmerized. Dolly went on and on, mellowed from the booze and nostalgia. I had lived my life thinking one thing, now I was hearing something that was so much more than that. Mostly that Claire and I had never really been alone in our misery, in our mourning, in the sad story that had defined our lives. It was disquieting, validating, and a host of other indescribable things to hear all of this from a perspective that wasn't ours. We had been seen. We had been wanted and loved. Someone had fought for us.

Pinky had come into our lives after our mother's death so I had always assumed that she had met Prosper after my mother died. Through Dolly I learned that hadn't been the case. I had never even considered that Prosper and Pinky were involved while my mother was alive. Never. From what I remembered, he was with us, with *her,* all the time in the months leading up to her death. I honestly never remembered him not being there. But evidently there had been times when he hadn't been.

It had started quickly between them, Dolly told me. In a very odd twist of fate it was actually Petey, Pinky's brother, who had led her to him. Evidently Pinky had been stuck on the road with her car one night and had called her brother to help her out. Because Petey had been about three sheets to the wind, Prosper had volunteered to go. Pinky invited him in for coffee and that coffee turned into a couple of beers and that was followed by a couple of really great days of *hot.* Just like that. Dolly laid it out for me. Just like that. She remembered it clearly. Dolly, God bless her, spared me nothing. At one point, I wasn't even sure she was talking to me anymore. She just seemed lost in the years.

Apparently Pinky had openly confided in her girl, Dolly, about the enigma that had been Prosper. Pinky had known there was *something,* possibly and very probably *someone,* who was getting in the way of her moving forward with Prosper. But when she tried to find her way to it, he would clam up. Woman's intuition winning out,

Pinky grew surer than ever that there was a woman. She enlisted Dolly's help to find out who that woman was and the story that went with her.

Because the brothers played it close to the vest, Petey was tight-lipped about Prosper's personal life. The only thing Dolly could get out of him for sure was that Prosper was wrapped up in some pretty heavy shit. And that shit was reaping a world of hurt on him. Apparently it involved a woman. A good woman.

Dolly had been like a dog with a bone and wouldn't let up on Petey. Petey held out as long as he could. But because he had a hard time denying Dolly anything and truly didn't want to see his sister hurt, he finally opened up. By that time our mother had been in the most debilitating stages of her illness. When Dolly heard the whole sad story, she sat at the table and wept. Then Dolly had called her girl.

Petey had warned Pinky off, but also told her that if Prosper could get on the other side of the shit he was carrying, he was a man worth having. Dolly saw things differently. She thought the hurt was too heavy a burden. She wanted Pinky to get rid of Prosper. But Pinky had fallen hard and fast. So Pinky hung in there, asking nothing and giving all. Dolly recalled the phone call she got from Pinky the day that Prosper had come clean.

According to Dolly, Pinky had been seeing less and less of Prosper. And when he did come to her, she was never sure any longer what it meant. Sometimes he was silent and angry and almost rough with her. Other times he was tender and gentle, but so distant she knew that even though he was with her, he was somewhere else. Prosper was slowly breaking Pinky's heart. It all had come to a head the morning after an incredibly earnest session of all-night love-making. A night where Prosper had been so sweet and so distant that Pinky lay awake long after Prosper had fallen into a fitful sleep. When Prosper woke the next morning, he saw the pain etched all over Pinky's face. He pulled her close then and sat for a while with his arms tight around her.

"I don't want to hurt you, honey. I know I can be a selfish bastard. I've not given a thought to what my coming to your bed like this could be doing to you. I just know that when it gets bad, the only thing that eases that pain is feeling you all soft and warm and wanting me. I don't know what this is. I just know I need it. If you don't want me to come back, I get that. I respect that and I swear to God you tell me to leave and I'm gone. None of it falls back on you. You take some time and you think about that. But before you make that decision, before I'm inside you again, you need to know."

Then he had pulled himself away from her. He had wanted to see her face when he told her the rest.

"Her name is Maggie. I've loved her since the minute I saw her. He claims her, but she's mine. Always has been. Always will be. She's not just sick, she's fucking dying. And it hurts so goddamn much to think of a life without her in it that sometimes I can't breathe." Prosper's voice had been ragged with emotion.

Pinky had tried to move towards him, but he held her away. Then he said, "I look at her and I see the only woman I'll ever love."

My heart filled with sadness at the thought of how painful those words must have been to hear.

"Now mind you," Dolly was saying, "By that time Pinky had known about your mom. Petey and I had laid it out weeks before. Pinky knew that Maggie was sick. She knew that Prosper was coming to her only after days and days of being with Maggie. Only coming to her when the sadness was so overwhelming he couldn't bear it. She even knew that, at times, it was Maggie he was seeing when he made love to her. She knew all this and had never said a word. She had been loving him through it all. Prosper had no clue what she knew and what it was costing her. It was the first time that Prosper had uttered one word to Pinky that there was someone else. And he led with that. Yes he did."

"What did Pinky tell him?" I was on my third little airplane drink by that time myself.

"I'll tell you what she told him, honey. And I'll tell you, when I heard it I was never prouder of my girl in my life. She did it quietly and gently, which is her way, but she sure told him." Dolly's eyes were on mine.

"She told him that she loved him. That it hurt her to see him so full of pain. She told him that if she could trade places with Maggie to spare him that pain she would do it. But, of course, she couldn't do that. She told him the other thing she couldn't do was to be a substitute for Maggie. That Prosper coming to her for that was cheating all of them. She told him that she was willing to do just about anything for him, but she couldn't do that. She couldn't be that. She told him that after Maggie was gone and he found he had some left, whatever he had left, she would be willing to take. She would even cherish it. No matter how much, no matter how little. Until and unless that day came, he wasn't welcome in her home. Not in her bed or in her heart either. She walked him to the door and locked it behind him so he heard."

"Wow." I breathed and shot back the rest of my drink. Wow.

"Yep." Maggie drained her drink too.

"It took a while, but he found his way back to her. And when he did, he found his way back to his two little sweethearts too," Dolly finished.

"Was that hard for her?" I asked softly.

Dolly looked up quickly then. "Was what hard, honey?"

"Us. Me and Claire. *Her* children. Was it ever hard for Pinky to be around us?" I wrapped my arms around me, waiting for the answer.

"Hard, honey? Oh no. Oh no, never ever hard. What was hard for her was to give you up. She thought you and little Claire hung the moon. She wanted you."

Dolly then told me that after everything went down that summer, Pinky had begged Jack to let them keep us. She had done this behind Prosper's back and without his consent. Prosper had wanted us too, Dolly was quick to add. But both Prosper and Jack had made a promise to Maggie. Her dying wish was that her children wouldn't ever be separated from each other or from Jack. Maggie had grown up without her father, and she didn't want that for her children.

While my mother had loved my father deeply, she hadn't loved him beyond reason. She knew he was an imperfect man. She also knew that it would be Prosper who would have to make sure our family survived a life without her. Maggie had left this life loving and being loved by two men. In the end, Prosper couldn't deny her. Anything. Even if it meant giving us up and inviting a world of worry into his life.

"Pinky took to bed for a week after you two left to go to live with your dad. Prosper was so worried about her that he called me in to take care of her. I cannot even tell you how many times she and I plotted to go get you and Claire. But she knew she couldn't go against Prosper and his promise to your mother." She smiled at me then.

"Pinky was just ecstatic when Prosper told her you had found your way back. Seeing you'll do her a world of good just about now, honey." She patted my hand and leaned back on her seat and snored lightly for the remainder of the flight.

When I looked out the window, I saw that we were flying over the Grand Canyon.

CHAPTER 33

When we got off the plane, Dolly and I used the ladies and Reno was working his cell. We had brought carry-ons so gathering luggage wasn't a problem. We had miraculously beat the restroom line so we got right in and did our business. We spent some time adjusting, readjusting, combing, spraying, and refreshing our makeup. Like that.

We were waiting at the pickup when a black SUV with tinted windows pulled up to the curb. The driver parked and came quickly around to our side of the car. I was busy organizing and pushing the handle down on my carry-on when it was taken from me. I glanced up to see a pair of dark brown eyes looking at me.

It was Diego. Damn if it wasn't.

He gave me a chin nod and moved on to Dolly. He gave her a great big hug and told her how happy he was to see her. Then he did the arm shake thing with Reno, called him brother, and helped him get the bags in. Me, he pretty much ignored.

Reno sat in the front with Diego. Dolly and I sat in the back. The talking was easy between the three of them, and Diego filled them in. Apparently I was the only one who was surprised to see him in Nevada. Diego didn't address any of the conversation to me, but his eyes met mine a lot in that rearview mirror. So much so I was squirming in my seat trying to find a way to get out of his vision. Short of literally ducking my head there wasn't a thing I could do; I took to looking out the window.

Shit. Shit. Shit. Because seeing Pinky for the first time in twenty years at the funeral of her only sister wasn't stressful enough, let's add a little Diego to the mix.

CHAPTER 34

Pinky, Petey, and Lilah had grown up in an old farmhouse near Carson City. Diego explained that although there were enough bedrooms for all of us, there was only one bathroom. Prosper thought we would probably be more comfortable in the hotel a couple of miles up the road. That's where Diego brought us. The plan was that we should do what we needed to do to feel human again after the plane trip. Diego would be waiting to bring us to Pinky and Prosper, where we would eat the potluck that well-meaning family and friends had foisted upon them.

We checked in. I went to grab my bag from Diego, but he already had it in his hand along with the key to my room. He simply looked at me when I made a move for both of them.

He said, "Room 33. Elevator. Third floor. Move."

Diego grabbed my arm and steered me in that direction. I craned my neck back to see if Dolly and Reno were following. Dolly was busy organizing something in her purse, and Reno was back on his cell. No help there. Diego didn't look at me while we waited for the elevator, not when we were in the elevator, and not while we were out of the elevator and heading towards the room. He didn't look at me. He didn't let go of me either. I kept sneaking little peeks at him, and what I saw was scary.

We got to the room. He put the suitcase down for a millisecond, slid the key card quickly through the lock, and pushed the door open hard when the light flashed green. I hesitated, pulling back and worried about going into that room with him. He felt it. Although he didn't hurt me, he tugged me hard towards him. Once inside, he kicked the door shut with his foot, threw the suitcase on the bed, and pressed me hard against the back of the door.

"Your fingers broken, Raine?" He growled at me, his face three inches away from mine. His body pressed against me.

Major asshole.

"Move back, Diego," I breathed at him.

"You broke your fingers. Both hands. Hearing gone too. Voice ditto. Only explanation." His hand moved to the back of my neck.

"Stop it." I twisted my head away. He held on tight.

"You don't pick up your cell. You don't take my calls at the clubhouse. You don't open your door for me. You ignoring me, Raine? You fucking ignoring me? 'Cause let me tell you right goddamn fucking now, I'm not the kind of guy you want to ignore." His dark eyes glittered like shards of black diamonds.

"Get your hands off me." I pushed at him.

"The fuck I will, Raine." He stepped in and now he was even closer. Great. Just great.

"I don't want to do this now." And I didn't. So I pushed at him again to drive my point home. He wasn't going to bully me.

"You don't want to do this now? Really, Raine? Is now not a good time for this?" He roared at me.

"You know when *would* have been a good time for this? Over a week ago when I almost banged down your door would have been a good time. But with the shit she said I figured I would give you that. Every day that I called the clubhouse or your cell would have been a good time. But you wouldn't take my calls. You wouldn't return my messages. So maybe it's not a good time for you, but it's a fucking great time for me." His eyes flashed.

I wasn't liking this. Not one bit. But the alternative was to fight a battle I couldn't win. I thought I might as well get this bullshit over with him once and for all.

"Okay," I said to the top of his chest.

He let out a breath then and I felt the air around him change. He took a small step away from me. He moved his hand to my hair and gently pulled my face up to meet his eyes.

"Okay." His eyes softened just a little. Mine didn't.

We did the eye standoff thing for a few moments, which I thought I might be winning. Then his eyes moved to my mouth, and his hand shifted in my hair. This wasn't good. Not good at all. This wasn't me winning.

I hissed at him, "She *overshared,* Diego. And when she was done oversharing, she called me a dirty little Indian whore. She gave that to me. All of it. She threw it at me. I had no clue it was coming, and she threw that at me. And *you.* You didn't do a thing to stop it! You knew what you had with her, and you let her throw that at me." I was heaving.

"Always knew she could be a raving bitch but didn't know how deep that shit went with her. Woman like that in a place like that, safer to find out where her head was. Even if it meant you having to catch some of it," Diego gave as way of explanation.

He was still way too close to me. He also had his head up his ass. Way up his ass.

"What you're referring to as shit, Diego? That was love to her. That's how deep that went for her. Two years? Two years and you didn't know that was love to her?"

"Bullshit, Raine. Jesus, that was never even close to what that was. I knew it. She knew it. I made that clear. We both knew what that was."

I just shook my head. Really?

So I tried to help him get his head out of that ass by saying this:

"There's no making that clear to a woman who you have been . . ."
I was searching for the words and didn't want to use her words.

"A woman I've been . . . ?" Diego prompted.

"A woman you have been *having relations* with for two years,"
I finished lamely.

He chortled. No, really. He did. He chortled.

"Relations?" He smirked. "Is that what we're calling it now?
Relations?" His eyes were dancing.

"For two years, whatever you want to call it, for a woman that
means something." I was not finding the humor.

Any woman knows that. And really, most men do too. How he
missed that I didn't know.

"Shit." He pulled his hand through his hair. "She said just about
the same thing but not in the same way."

Yeah, I had a taste of what Ellie's word choices were.

"Two years and she thought it was going one way and when it
didn't she fought for it the only way she knew how," I said.

"Would you have done that, baby?" The way he said that, the
way he looked at me when he said that, the way he moved closer to
me when he said that, made my girlie parts tingle.

"Done what?" I told my girlie parts to calm down.

"Fought for it?" His tone was light, and his hand was working
its way through my hair while his other hand was on the side of my
face. He leaned in.

He was being all sexy and flirty and light. But in my mind it
wasn't the time to be sexy and flirty and light. A heart had been
broken. Albeit a skanky, slutty, misguided heart. A heart that hadn't
anything like a vow, or a ring, or even a nod in the Happily Ever
After or "your feelings are being returned" direction. Not even a

heart I cared overly much about, but a heart nonetheless and that should not be taken lightly.

"I said it once, I'll say it again. I don't fight over men. I'm not that kind of woman." I looked at him and made my eyes hard. Girlie parts at ease.

He took a step back then and gave me the once-over. Slowly. From head to toe. "No, you aren't that kind of woman. You're the kind of woman men fight over, not the woman who fights over men."

Wow. I didn't know what to do with that. I didn't want men fighting over me and never knew a man who had.

"No, Diego. I'm not her either." I took the opportunity to walk away from the wall and out of his space.

"Yeah, Babe. You are." Diego was standing away from me with his arms crossed over his chest. Tattooed biceps bulging, face watching me.

"Stop it." He was making me uncomfortable.

"Babe, you walk into a room and conversation stops." He pressed his point.

"You're crazy," I said softly.

"Not crazy, honey. You walked into that junkie's kitchen and every brother in there including me was ready to give you anything you needed to make it right for your sister. Later on when you walked into the clubhouse looking all lost and scared and beautiful, all eyes turned in your direction. Then you tossed your hair and smiled, and every, *every*, single dick in that place got hard. Trust me on that."

I shook my head in denial. He was whacked. And if he wasn't whacked, this wasn't something I wanted to hear. It wasn't a comfortable thought to think *that dicks were getting hard at me back at the clubhouse.*

He continued.

"Jules practically falls over himself every morning watching for you to come out so he can feed you. Crow, who I've never seen even look at any of the talent hanging at the MC, threw down for you."

"Crow threw down for me? What does that mean?" I might have asked that too quickly.

Diego's eyes got hard and a muscle jumped in his jaw. "What does what mean?" he repeated.

"You said Crow threw down for me," I murmured.

"Means he made his interest known," he answered carefully.

"He's married." I felt the heat rising to my face, remembering the conversation.

"How do you know that, Raine?" Diego's mouth got tight.

"He told me." I moved away from him.

"Told you what?" He got closer to me again. Mouth tighter. Voice getting louder.

"Told me he was married." My voice got louder too.

"You been spending time with Crow?" He had a hold of my arm.

"Yes, Diego. Crow gave me a ride to work at Ruby Reds." I pulled away. He held on.

"How?" He growled.

"How what?" I looked him.

"Raine, how did he give you a ride to work?" His eyes were hard.

"What do you mean?" I honestly was getting nervous and really confused.

"HOW DID HE GET YOU TO WORK?" He roared at me.

"ON HIS BIKE," I roared back.

All the air went out of the room. "You have got to be shitting me right now, Raine."

I didn't say a word.

"What else?" he said, deadly quiet.

Uh-oh. Big giant uh-oh.

I took a minute. Because here we were again. Diego and me. We didn't have conversations, we had verbal boxing bouts. Sometimes gloves on, sometimes gloves off. But there always seemed to have to be the knockout round, and he always seemed to be the one eager to deliver it. He had me on the ropes again.

"What else what?" I took a breath.

"Raine," he growled.

"Not much else, geez." I attempted to pry my arm from him. "And by the way, where is Ellie?"

"Fucking damn it, Raine, already told you that shit." He was starting to breathe fire.

"What else?" He stepped in. Dragon fully awake.

"None of your . . ." I began.

"WHAT ELSE HAPPENED WHILE CROW HAD YOU ON THE BACK OF HIS BIKE?" he roared.

"WHERE IS ELLIE?" I shouted back.

Because really?

Really??

I hadn't asked for any of this. His crazy bitch had started this whole thing and now he was yelling at me. No way. No fucking way. I was done with this. He could thump and stomp and roar all he wanted. This was on him. Not on me.

He scrubbed his hand over his face and visibly looked like he was trying not to put his fist through the wall.

"Ellie is fucking gone, Raine. Packed her shit into a Greyhound bus and told her not to come back. Now answer my fucking question. RIGHT! FUCKING! NOW!" He punctuated that with a fist bang to the door by the side of my head and I jumped.

This wasn't good, and I was getting scared.

"Diego, stop this," I said with the small semblance of calm I had left.

He was having none of it. As a matter of fact, my calm just seemed to infuriate him more.

"Raine, you don't want to mess with me on this. You. Do. Not. Now you got about ten goddamn fucking seconds to answer my question, or I'm pushing you aside, getting on my bike, and riding straight to that clubhouse and putting a bullet in my brother for fucking with shit I already laid claim to. Unless you have something different to tell me in ten FUCKING SECONDS."

Oh for Christ's sake.

"NINE," he roared.

"Diego," I began.

"EIGHT." Another fist to the door by the side of my head.

"Stop this!" I yelled back.

"SEVEN." His face was shouting in mine.

"Humph." I was starting to shake. Something he already laid claim to?

"SIX." He had his hands on my shoulders, getting ready to move me away from the door.

"FIVE."

Oh, sweet Jesus. He wasn't even close to kidding about this. His eyes were dark and the veins were popping out of his neck. His whole body was leaning into me and was rigid with anger. His biceps were pumped through with testosterone and primed to punch a hole through something.

"He kissed me," I said quickly, and before I ran out of brave I added, "and I kissed him back."

Diego let go of me like I burned him. Then he took a step away. Then he took a deep breath. Then he took a minute. When the minute was over, he asked carefully, "What else?"

Something important was happening, and I wasn't stupid enough to miss that. I decided that a lot depended on what I said next. I knew Diego was seeing red, and I didn't want any bloodshed between brothers over an innocent kiss. And it *had* been innocent in all the ways that mattered.

He had laid claim to me. Diego had laid claimed to me.

I looked him straight in the eye and moved towards him slowly. I stood in front of him and put my hands out palms up in a gesture of surrender. I swirled the words around in my head a few times before I found the way to deliver them so they would make sense to this madman standing before me.

"Nothing else, Diego. Not in the way you mean. What happened was that I found a friend. Or I thought I had found a friend, and I had needed one. Prosper was gone, Claire was gone, and you were gone. You left without saying a word. You left with Ellie and it hurt. I don't know who she is to you. I only know who she thinks she is to you. I don't know what you think she is to you."

And I don't know who I am to you.

Then I continued as honestly as I could. My shoulders slumped. I was all of a sudden very tired.

"I didn't ignore your calls, Diego. I didn't ignore your messages. I was too afraid to take them. Too afraid I would fall apart when I heard your voice. I'm so tired of feeling that. So tired of feeling something only to have it taken away from me before I even begin to understand what it is. Before it even has a chance to grow into something I can recognize."

He wasn't moving, but some of the anger had left his eyes. I thought that might be a good sign.

"I needed a friend. You went with Ellie. I still don't know where you went or where you brought her or if she's coming back. I don't know how you feel about what she said."

"You don't know because you wouldn't pick up the goddamn fucking phone, Raine." His eyes were hard on me again.

He wasn't wrong, so I nodded in a way that he could take as agreement. "Crow and I share a heritage. We come from the same place in a lot of ways. I needed that, and he gave it to me. Then he took it away. And that's all that happened."

And because I wanted to be very clear, and I wanted to be very sure Diego understood, I said, "I swear it. I swear nothing else happened between Crow and me."

I waited then. I pulled my hands around me and held on tight. I felt like I might be losing something important that I never even had. It didn't make sense, but that didn't stop it from aching.

"What do you mean, he took it away?" He was watching my arms. The air shifted around him again and not in a completely bad way. But not in a completely good way either.

Oh geez.

"Diego, I don't know. Do you really want to hear this?" I looked at him. He didn't look insanely angry anymore. While I knew honesty was the best policy, I didn't want to go there with him.

"Raine, I really want to hear this." His eyes went to my face, then to my arms, then back up to my face again.

I colored a deep red. I know I did because I felt hot from the inside out. This was humiliating. Holding on so tight my sides began to ache, I searched around in my mind and came up with the words before I gave them.

"We were friends, Diego. I'm guessing by your *extreme* reaction"—I looked pointedly at him—"that me riding on his bike must mean something different to you than it did to me. But honestly, it was fun. It was nice. He took me to Reds and he worked and Dolly worked and I worked. It felt normal and busy in a good way. I've not had normal and busy in a good way in a very long time. We got into a rhythm and that felt good."

He was watching me hold on to myself in the way he had started doing.

"But, after that kiss, I think he kind of regretted it. He told me he was married and not done with that. I think he wanted to take the kiss back. He couldn't so instead he took back the friendship. That made me sad. And that's all of it."

Diego looked at me and nodded. He moved towards me and wrapped his hands around the back of my head gently. He looked me in the eye and said, "He didn't regret it, baby. No one could have that from you and regret it."

Uh-oh.

Diego leaned in and went to put his mouth against mine. When he did, my lips clamped together. As much as I wanted this, I should not want this. This wouldn't be good for me. This could prove my undoing. This was something that if it started again and stopped again, I didn't know if I could recover from it. This could hurt. Big time.

So I turned my head and clamped my lips shut.

"Raine." He was nuzzling against my jaw.

I shook my head and put my hands up to push him away. But, oh my God, I wanted him too. His lips on my neck made me tremble all over. I loved his smell. I breathed in deep, felt my nipples get hard and my legs get weak. I felt aching deep inside my belly and below. And it was building. I was trying my best to resist him. I really was. But I wanted him.

He looked at me and tucked his two fingers under my chin.

He said softly, "Not this shit again with you, Raine. Give me your mouth, damn it. Last time I'm gonna ask. Last time I'm going to be fucking nice about it. In about one minute you give it to me or not, I'm going to take it, and it will not just be my tongue that I'll be putting down your throat, Babe." His mouth so close to mine I could almost feel his lips brushing against mine.

"Jesus, Diego. Could you be any more disgusting?" I pushed at him.

But really, I wanted his tongue down my throat. I wanted his hands in my hair. I wanted to feel his warm, hard body covering me. Oh yes, I did.

And by the hungry look in my eyes, my guess is he knew.

CHAPTER 35

It had taken every ounce of restraint for Diego to stop himself from putting his fist through the door. He was going to fucking kill Crow. And he was not too happy with Raine either.

But when he saw her go all soft and dewy, her eyes bright with tears, it took everything he had not to rip every stitch of clothing off her beautiful silky skin and bury himself so deep inside of her that she would have no fucking doubt who she belonged to.

Fucking Crow going there. He would deal with that shit when he got back. Thank fucking everything holy that Crow didn't get his shit up in his woman. He owned that sweetness, and that asswipe fucking knew it. Whatever stopped him from making his play for Raine was a damn good thing. Crow would be pissing in a bag for the rest of his life, Diego ever caught him up in Raine again. Yeah, he was going to have a fuckin' man-to-man with his brother Crow.

But, for now, he was going to focus on her. He had her up against the door, her heavy tits heaving, her nipples peeking out of that shirt like someone was calling their goddamn name. He felt the heat radiating from her so damn hot that he knew her pretty little panties must be drenched right through. And this was all for him. He owned that. All of it. Whether or not she wanted it to be that way, he owned every inch of that soft wet pulsing honey.

Time to get down to business. Time to let all that honey know where she belonged.

"Yeah, baby," he said. "I actually can. I can be a lot more disgusting. As a matter of fact, I'm reining in a whole fucking shitload of disgusting. Been reining it in since the day you and those big beautiful eyes walked into that shit hole of an apartment looking so scared and lost and brave that I had to fight to stop myself from taking you right there in front of my brothers and your sister and her jacked-up fucking boyfriend. I been wanting to be balls deep in you since I first laid fucking eyes on you, baby. Now you're telling me that fucking Crow almost beat me to that? I'm fighting with everything I've got to rein in disgusting."

~

Oh boy.

"He didn't almost beat you to it, Diego," I whispered. Because I had absolutely no pride where this man was concerned, I laid it out there.

"No?" He was moving his mouth along my jawline.

"No." I was breathing heavy now and to tell the God's honest truth my panties were absolutely positively so wet, I was afraid they were leaving a stain on my jeans.

"Diego?" I loved the feel of his name on my tongue. I felt my nipples get even harder.

"Yeah, baby?" His mouth moving to the corner of mine.

"I'm still not sure this is such a . . ." I gasped. Diego had slipped his hand down the front of my pants and was moving his fingers up and down the outside of my panties.

"Yeah, that's my girl," he said against my mouth. "That's my good, little baby girl."

And as he thrust his tongue gently into my mouth, he put a finger in my honey pot, then two, then three. And he moved those fingers in me slowly. In and out, in and out. Slipping and gliding and tugging against my wetness until I started to spasm. And as his fingers fucked me, his tongue swirled, plundered, and danced in my mouth.

~

And he was in.

Thank God she had opened to him, because in about five more seconds it wouldn't have mattered. He had never forced a woman, but he had never ever wanted a woman the way he wanted Raine. He was so rock-hard for her he had cum backed up to his spine. Damn fucking damn. The minute he took her mouth, his hand was heading hell-bent to her pussy. Slipped right in. Oh yes, he fucking did. When he felt how wet her little silky panties were he almost shot his load in his pants. God, this woman turned him into a goddamn horny teenager.

And she was tight and wet and willing. And she gave it up to him. Her tight little V grinding against his big rough hand. He slipped one, then two, then three fingers in her. Then he moved his thumb to her clit and she climbed up on him like she was a dying woman. She wrapped those long beautiful legs around him, her back against the door and she gave it to him. She pushed hard against that hand, soaking him.

She was ready. So fucking ready. She swung her head back then forward, beautiful big bouncing tit hanging out from the way her shirt had slipped off her shoulder and from his free hand working that magnificent half-dollar-sized nipple. All that long dark hair spilling free from that goddamn braid she had coiled it up in. She met his eyes and held them. He worked her, sliding his fingers in and out, in and out. She fucked his hand hard. Like he liked it. She was being a good girl. His good girl. His fucking incredible very good girl.

~

I came hard against Diego's hand.

And I mean hard.

And I wanted more.

Every part of my body was on high alert. I came against his hand while he had me trapped against a door. I rode that hand like my life depended on it. Wanton and shameless and burning with a raw naked need.

CHAPTER 36

Oh. My. God.

It had been hours. Hours and hours and hours of incredible mind-blowing sex. *Mind blowing.* Diego was tender and loving, then rough and forceful, then tender again. I couldn't get enough of him, and my body responded to him in kind. I was shy, then shameless, then hesitant again. He had me up against the wall, then on the floor, then on my back with my legs spread open hitched on his shoulders while his mouth laid claim to me. *Mind blowing.*

Dolly had come knocking at the door.

Then Reno had come knocking at the door.

Diego had roared a giant, "What the fuck?"

And Reno had yelled just as loud, "What the fuck?" back.

Then Diego had opened the door, threw him the keys to the SUV, and told him to tell Prosper that we would be there soon. He slammed the door in his brother's face and came back to me. Then he showed me some more good time.

By the time I got to the shower, my girlie parts were sore in a very good way. My mouth was swollen, and I had a pink burn on my face and various other parts of my body where Diego had rubbed his three-day-old five-o'clock shadow against me.

Sweet Jesus. I looked exactly like a walking ad for hours of very thorough, very mind-blowing sex. My face was in the final stages of healing, and most of the color had muted to quiet yellows, blues, and soft blacks. Now I was adding a deep pink to the mix. Honestly, I looked ridiculous. I looked like I had just gone seven rounds. And I guess, in a way, I had.

I'll not even get started on the rats' nest that was my hair. The crown braid that I had been so proud of had been torn from the pins early in the game. What was left was a screaming mass of tangles from where Diego had pulled and buried and twisted my hair in his big beautiful hands.

The hot spray of the shower was steaming up the room, and I lost sight of my reflection in the mirror. What I found in that steam were two big hands kneading my ass again and dragging me into the shower where my opponent held me against the ropes. The beautiful man proceeded to score a knockout in the final bout. I went down smiling.

CHAPTER 37

While I was putting the final touches on my makeup, I heard Diego on the phone with Prosper making our delay all good. Prosper was sending a brother from the Nevada Chapter of the Saints for us.

I got busy straightening up the room partly because it needed it, and mostly because after hours of hot sex with Diego, I was having trouble meeting his eyes. I snuck a peek at him from under my lashes. His hair was still damp from the shower, and he had shaved. He smelled of clean soap and warm sex. I turned pink from inside out remembering. I had to get a hold of myself.

"Babe, if you're going to turn yourself inside out every time you're out of my bed, that's gonna give me all the more reason to keep you in it."

I looked up quickly at him, and he was grinning. I threw a pillow at him. Then he started laughing. I had seen the many faces of the moods of Diego Montesalto, but I had never seen him laugh. And it was a thing of beauty. The crinkles around the corners of his eyes stood out, and the dimple on his right cheek deepened. His dark eyes glittered like diamonds, and his beautiful mouth curved in a perfect U-shape.

Damn him.

He reached for me, and I ran from him. He caught me and held me close to him. He kissed me long and hard, and I melted against him.

"Hmmmmm," he whispered against my ear. "My baby is ready again."

He was not wrong.

His cell rang and I was saved by the bell. Our ride was here. Diego introduced me to Justice, the sergeant at arms for the Nevada Hells Saints Chapter. Apparently, anyone with the title *sergeant at arms* never did this "chauffeur shit" and Diego was really honored that Justice had made sure he was the one to bring us back to the house. They did the man-hug thing. The two of them shared a flask of something and a pack of smokes on the way to the farmhouse. After that first brief introduction, I was all but forgotten in the back seat. That was fine by me. I had plenty to occupy my mind.

At one point, I tried to listen in on the conversation. It was a montage of curse words. Every other word was *fucking* or *pussy* or *prick* and those were peppered with phrases like *goddamn straight,* and *you fucking feeling me,* or *cocksucking asswipe can't find his own dick with a navigation system.* The rest of the words seemed to be spoken in some kind of profane code. The two of them together were pretty bad. I had grown up around that, and my ears were still burning. I tuned them out and went to my happy place.

Because my happy place involved recent memories of tongue and hands and deep hour-long orgasmic pleasure, I heated up and turned that wonderful shade of pink all over again. My girlie parts started to tingle at the recall, and I squirmed in my seat.

Diego caught the movement in his visor mirror.

"Babe." He smiled at me. And then he winked.

I scowled at him and looked out the window.

He grinned and offered me a hit off the mystery flask, which I gladly accepted.

While I sputtered and coughed and wiped the tears from my eyes as the horrible stuff hit my belly, the two hyenas in the front seat had a good time laughing at my expense. But when the coughing fit was over, Diego leaned into the back seat and pulled me close to him. Then he touched his lips to my forehead.

"My baby is a lightweight," he muttered against my hair.

When he released me I caught Justice's eyes in the rearview appraising me.

"So she's yours, D?" Justice had turned to him.

I held my breath waiting for the answer. The last time Diego had been asked this I had screamed out a resounding "No!" This time I held my breath. Diego took a minute, maybe remembering that time too. Maybe he was giving me that out. I didn't know, but it seemed like he took a while to answer. Justice took his eyes off the road and glanced at Diego.

"Yours, D? 'Cause if that sweet thing ain't owned, I . . ." Justice began.

"Don't even fucking think about it, Brother. She's mine. All mine. All the time." Diego was looking at him.

"You lucky sonofabitch." Justice grinned and passed Diego the booze.

"Got that right, Brother." Diego took a pull on the flask, found me in the visor mirror, and his eyes went soft.

I colored. Of course I did.

He smiled a slow, soft smile and held my eyes until I looked away.

My toes were curling in my boots and girlie parts on red alert. Oh boy.

CHAPTER 38

We pulled up in front of a white, old plank-board farmhouse. There were probably about a dozen Harleys parked outside. The house was big and could have used a fresh coat of paint, but it had an honest-to-goodness perfect wraparound porch complete with two porch swings. There was pretty gingerbread lattice on the eaves, and the windows were large and clean. A brick pathway leading up to it was lined with blue stone and some pretty perennial plants that I didn't know the names of. The house was at the end of a long, dirt driveway and stood alone with plenty of space all around it.

People were milling around the porch. By people, I mean big mean-looking men with Hells Saints Nevada cuts on them. And their women. I would never get used to this, and I still didn't know why those cuts and those women made me so uneasy. I searched back in the corners of my mind to bring forth something bad that might have happened as a result of being with the shadow people of my childhood, and honestly there wasn't anything specific there. But there was an uneasiness that would never quite go away.

Now here I was once again, heading towards the source of that unease. My seat planted in the thick of it. If the entrance into the club a few weeks ago hadn't sealed it, then the last few hours with Diego probably had. If I wanted him, that meant I had to deal with them. They were his family. His choice. If I stayed with him, with

Prosper, with my job at Reds, they would eventually become my family too. Maybe.

We hit the front steps. There were chin nods at Diego and looks of curiosity at me. I kept my eyes on the prize of the screen door. Diego felt me tense beside him, and he wrapped his arms around my shoulders. I felt more curious stares. And those mostly came from the women. I wondered briefly how many more "Ellies" there were in Diego's recent and not-so-recent past. Conversation for another day. Maybe.

The screen door opened to us, and I found myself wrapped in Prosper's big arms. I didn't know if I was ever going to get used to the feeling of being swept back to being a little girl every time I heard Prosper's voice, or looked into his eyes, or found myself in his arms. Aside from Claire, Prosper was the only family I had left. And the difference between him and Claire was that Prosper had always taken care of me, and I had always taken care of Claire. With Prosper, I had felt safe. *That's what the good daddies do.*

"Hey, Little Darlin'. Thanks for making the trip. A man needs his family around at a time like this. Gonna make all the difference in the world to Pinky, you being here." He kissed the top of my head.

A man needs his family around at a time like this. And there it was. My heart lifted a little and opened a little. This could be where I belonged. Maybe.

I entered the house and saw a whole lot more people inside. Diego left me and moved to a small bunch of bikers in the corner of the room. More man hugs all around. Prosper led me toward the kitchen gently with his hand on the back of my neck. It was a large country kitchen with a white porcelain double sink, a cracked and faded cheap linoleum floor, and chintz curtains on the windows. A large rectangular butcher-block table stood in the middle of the room with a half-dozen mismatched chairs pushed in around it. Every countertop was filled with a covered dish.

There were lots of blondes (and not one that was naturally born to it) in that kitchen. Every body type. Skinny, curvy, toned, and saggy. *All* sporting serious cleavage and tight bottoms. Whether those bottoms were skirts, jeans, or shorts, they were all body-hugging. The hair was big, the jewelry was fake, and the tats were real. Except for Dolly and three other redheads of various shades that I spied out of the corner of my eye on the way through, it was safe to say that I was the only non-blonde in a crowd of at least twenty-five women.

She was standing with Dolly, her back towards me, but I recognized Pinky nonetheless. Knowing what I knew now about the history between Prosper, my mom, and Pinky, I was suddenly very unsure that I should be here. I knew that Pinky had wanted me to come and had even requested my presence. But I wondered, in the seconds I had left before she turned to me, if in her mind's eye she was expecting the child I had been all those years ago. I wondered if she had taken into account that who would stand before her was the woman I had become. The woman who, by all accounts, bore a striking resemblance to my mother. The dying woman who had owned Prosper's heart.

As a matter of fact, until that very moment I hadn't realized that I was about the same age my mother had been when we lost her. I stumbled back and fell against the hard wall of Prosper's chest.

He put both hands on my shoulders, giving them a squeeze, and called out, "Pinky, our baby girl is home!"

Conversation halted and all eyes fell on me. Pinky turned from the sink, wiping her hands on a dish cloth.

Time had been good to her. The years had taken all the sharp parts of her body and rounded them into a beautiful hourglass figure. Her hair was still blond (of course it was), and she wore it in an up-do with soft curls falling around her face. Her makeup was biker-babe chic, which meant heavier than the average woman but not over the top (which would have made it biker-babe cheap). She had on a pair of lightweight black pants and a white lace shirt that was sheer in the back. On her wrist were the gold bracelets with the little tiny bells that I remembered from my childhood.

Her eyes met mine and widened. She stood stock-still and looked at me. From head to toe her eyes seemed to miss nothing. I held my breath. I felt Prosper do the same. Pinky's eyes were suddenly bright, and she turned to the counter, giving us her back.

Pinky had turned her back on me.

I felt my heart stop, and Prosper's hands fall heavier on my shoulders. I felt him step in closer to me. Those few seconds felt like hours. One more second and I knew that both my heart and Prosper's would lay shattered on the floor. It had all come down to this moment.

Then she turned around to me again.

She had given us her back just long enough to toss the dish towel on the counter. Pinky looked to Dolly and whispered, "My baby girl is home, Dolly." Dolly grabbed her hands and smiled into her eyes.

Then Pinky put her arms out to me. She spanned the distance between us in three steps. She grabbed hold of my arms and held me away from her.

"You look just like your mamma did at your age, Sweet Pea. And from what I know of her, there weren't a sweeter, more beautiful woman that ever walked this earth. Here you stand before me looking just as pretty as a picture; I just know you're just as sweet as the baby girl Prosper and I looked after all those years ago. Now, you gonna give your ole Pinky some sugar?"

I fell into her arms. She smelled like lavender and tobacco just like I remembered. I held onto her tight, determined not to be the first one to let go.

Then I whispered in her ear, "I tried, Pinky. I really, really tried."

She hugged me tighter and whispered, "I know, baby girl. And you did real good too."

She pulled away from me and said loud enough for the whole room to hear, "Welcome home to my sweet baby girl!"

Dolly called out, "Thank sweet Jesus! That light bill was getting ridiculous."

The whole room erupted in laughter. Even though I'm pretty sure no one but us got the inside joke, it served to break the tension. Prosper left me and wrapped his big arms around his woman. He hugged Pinky so tight he picked her clear off the floor. When he whispered into her ear, she blushed and swatted at his tattooed arms, laughing. He gave her a big, soft kiss on the mouth. He put her down and held her close with one arm and pulled me closer to him with the other. The three of us were grinning like fools.

The afternoon passed quickly and turned easily into night. Slowly the masses left. I had the opportunity to peek at the cuts of the many men that filled the house, and they were from the various West Coast chapters. Diego explained to me that like a family they had come to show support. They did the same with any kind of crisis or big celebration. Like a family. I didn't really know what that had meant as a kid, but I was getting a taste of it now. And it didn't seem so bad. Maybe.

Mostly everyone had left, save a skeleton crew of cleanup biker babes and their men. The blondes worked the kitchen. Dolly, Pinky, and I were served a fresh pot of coffee in the front sitting room. Diego, Prosper, Reno, and the men who belonged to the cleanup crew were out on the front porch smoking, drinking, and congratulating themselves on being kings of the universe. Testosterone was seeping through the walls.

Every so often Diego would lean towards the window, and his eyes would find me. They held me with an intensity that spoke volumes and made me tingle from head to toe. Then he went back to the fist pumping and the slapping each other on the back and talking about whatever badass bikers discuss.

Pinky dragged out a big box of pictures. We were to pick some to make a montage for Lilah's services. Even though I was mindful of the circumstances, I couldn't help the warmth of the feelings coursing through my veins at seeing old family photos. Claire and I had no photos of ourselves as children. None of our mother, none of our father. No photos of us sitting on Santa's knee or hunting for Easter eggs or blowing out birthday candles. Nada. Zip. Zilch. I thought I remembered my mom having a book like that somewhere. Well, maybe kind of like that, but somehow it had gotten lost along the way.

Pinky's photos of her sister were funny and sweet. She had a story to go with each one. There were a few of Prosper as I remembered him. There were some of the lake house where we spent that summer. I was a little disappointed that there were none of Claire and me. I knew I had no right to feel that. So I pushed those feelings aside and enjoyed the pictures for what they were.

Lilah had been beautiful once. Young and pretty with light brown hair and freckles. Unfortunately, you could see the steady decline in the photos. The first tattoo, then the second, then the full sleeve. The first piercing, then the second, then the third. Pictures with the first bad man, then the second bad man, then the last. Finally, Lilah beginning to look better again. The most recent was with Lilah in a bikini holding up a large trout that she had caught with Pinky and Prosper at the lake house. Three months later, Lilah would be dead.

We put together a beautiful mosaic of the Kodak moments of Lilah's life. It came out great. I know that Pinky was pleased. The cleanup crew had gone by that time, their men taking them away in a roar of engines. Diego, Prosper, and Reno had moved into the house with us and they were admiring our handiwork. Reno and Prosper added some great memories to the ones that Pinky and Dolly had already provided. Leaning back into Diego's arm, I felt it again. The warm feeling that being with family provides. Maybe.

I caught a look pass between Prosper and Pinky. While I wasn't sure what the look meant, I had the feeling it was about me. Prosper got up and left. I closed my eyes and got lost for a moment at the feeling of Diego running his fingers through the strands of my hair that hung near my waist. He was always doing that. He seemed to love playing with my hair. I loved him doing it. I felt Diego move away from me and looked up lazily to see Prosper take his place next to me. I smiled at him and he smiled back. He nodded at something he had in his hand. I looked down and gasped. I lost it. Lost. It. Totally.

There, sitting in Prosper's lap, was the book. The photo book that I remembered from my childhood. I looked at him, then at Pinky, then at him again. I placed my trembling hands on it. I did the thing I seldom allowed myself to do in private and almost never did in public. I burst out crying.

And I didn't stop for a long time.

CHAPTER 39

Jesus. She was beautiful. In bed and out of bed. Goddamn crying her eyes out. She was so fucking beautiful he wanted to bury himself deep inside of her and never come out. And Diego owned Raine. She was his. He made that clear a whole lot of times in that hotel room. She had been hot for him. Willing and hungry. Soft in all the right places.

He had been watching her all afternoon. Every time she moved, he moved. Like some crazy stalker. He couldn't help it. Everything about her fascinated him. The way she hung back from conversations until she was invited in. The way she listened, really listened, to what people said to her. The way she searched the room for him. Eyes touching but never landing on all the other dudes in the room until they landed on him. Then she would smile. And that smile went straight to his dick, but on the way down, it touched his heart.

Now she was sleeping next to him. After she had finished the adorable crying marathon where she had held on to Prosper like she was drowning. That flood of tears had soaked his shirt straight through. Diego had felt a surge of jealousy run through his bones so deep he felt something crack. Pinky moved him into the kitchen, and together they shared some reefer and what was left of the tequila. Pinky shared some more of Raine's history, and Diego listened to every word.

Then they heard Prosper yell, "Coast is clear." They also heard Raine giggle and knew that the crying jag was over.

Raine was pretty quiet on the way to the hotel, but once they hit the room she never stopped talking. She was so excited about that old photo book that he swore she was practically orgasmic. She showed him pictures and told him stories. She spoke more to him in the next hour than she had done the whole time he had known her, which he admitted wasn't very long.

While he loved hearing the stories, his thoughts were mostly about getting into her pants. Every time she leaned in to point at something and her tits brushed his arm, he had instant wood. Her hair brushed against his forearm. He had to clench his jaw to keep himself reined in. He knew she was sharing something important, but having her was so new he couldn't wait to have her again. And again.

So after the fourth page of pictures, he made his move. He took the book from her excited hands and excited her in a different way. Because she was so happy she was different this time when he took her. While she was willing before, this time she was eager. She undressed him and kissed him all over. All. Over. She stroked him and nuzzled him. She tugged at him and put her mouth on him. She climbed on top of him and rode him. First, slowly with a control that had him in awe. Then harder and harder. Her heavy tits bouncing while he came hot and hard inside her.

Then he flipped her over and took her again. Then over one more time. She felt his mouth on her and she opened wide for him. And he took his time. Tasting her honey, his tongue sliding over her clit and pushing its way deep inside her. God, she tasted sweet and clean and new. He fingered her and watched her face as she started building. Her eyes on his the whole time. Just when she was almost there, he took his fingers away. She shuddered and looked at him with those beautiful big blue eyes, pleading with him to finish her. He moved his big body over her smaller one and pulled her to him. He slung her legs over his shoulders and drove himself home.

CHAPTER 40

We were back at the farmhouse with Pinky and Prosper getting ready to head out to the services for Lilah. All I could think about was the incredible night, middle of the night, and very, very hot morning I had spent with Diego. Under him, on top of him, clasped tight to him, and every other way imaginable.

Wow.

I was dressed in my new blue pencil skirt, my new white blouse, and some seriously high heels. Diego had told me (yep, *told* me) to leave my hair down and I had. Minimum makeup, large silver hoops, and I was done. Diego had a new button-down white shirt under his cut and black leather pants that laced up in the front. He looked beautiful.

And I felt beautiful standing next to him.

The services were lovely. Pinky and Prosper had decided to combine the viewing with the church services and the church was packed. The church was progressive and allowed Pinky and Prosper to do as they saw fit to honor Lilah. There was a slide show, a number of eulogies, and the ceremony ended with Prosper and me playing guitar to one of Lilah's favorite songs. "Hallelujah" by Leonard Cohen. I thought the last verse was particularly relevant. When we hit the chorus it surprised me to hear the congregation (such that it was, a sea of blond and leather) sing along.

CHAPTER 41

Prosper, Diego, and Reno headed home two days after the services. Pinky had asked me to stay behind with her and Dolly to get things settled. I was happy to do that. Despite the tragedy of it all, those were some of the best days I had ever spent. Later on I would draw on these memories as a source of solace and strength. Glad to have had that time.

Pinky and Dolly brought me right into the fold. We had long mornings sitting at the coffee table poring over the treasure book of photographs that Prosper had rescued from my childhood. Some of the pictures were events I remembered, some I didn't. There were pictures of my mom and my dad and Claire and me as babies. Candid shots. Claire and me in a bathtub, Claire sleeping in Dad's arms, my mom pregnant with Claire and holding my hand and smiling that sweet, sad smile that I remembered so well. If the pictures and the memories made Pinky uncomfortable, she didn't let on. I loved her so much for that, my heart was near to bursting. What a gift they had given me. Claire and I had mattered; we had been seen. We had been loved. I couldn't wait to share them with my little sister.

Pinky decided to put the family home up for sale. We helped her do that. The three of us drove into town and met with a realtor. The realtor came out, assessed the property, and told us what we needed to do to get a fair and quick sale on the house. We did those things.

Pinky hired some painters and had the kitchen floor replaced. We spent the week packing and cleaning and threw a lot of stuff out. A lot. There didn't seem to be much that Pinky wanted to keep as reminders of her childhood. I completely got that.

Once I walked in to find Pinky sobbing in Dolly's arms. When Dolly's eyes met mine it was with mutual understanding. Not one of the three of us had had an easy life. Packing up the remnants of that kind of life could dredge up a whole lot of muck. That week poor Pinky was knee-deep in it. That's why, Dolly explained to me later that day, Pinky had needed her girls with her at this time. Dolly thanked me for being there.

Her girls. Thanked me.

I wondered how it could be possible that these two brave, generous, loving women didn't know what a gift their acceptance and love meant to me.

Over the week I spent with Dolly and Pinky, we shared a lot of our history. It didn't happen all at once, and there was no pity party. It happened in between moments of laughter and tears. Between morning coffee and late-night margaritas. Pinky shared some hilarious moments with Prosper. I laughed until I cried. Dolly, not to be outdone, also shared stories about her man. Big badass biker stories in their testosterone fits and macho moments. They also shared their tender, most loving memories and that had made me cry in a different way. I wondered for the millionth time what it would be like to have a man love me, really love me, the way these women had been loved.

CHAPTER 42

When I returned to the compound with Dolly and Pinky, things began to take on a sort of rhythm that felt good. I continued to live in Prosper's rooms and continued to work at Ruby Reds. Pinky and Prosper still owned the lake house, which was about twenty minutes away in the direction of Reds. Prosper explained to me "in the days when he was whoring and drinking" that he spent a lot of nights at the clubhouse, but now he mostly wanted to be where Pinky was.

He went on to say that while I could consider those rooms mine, he figured eventually I would want to have more of a place to stay. He wanted me to know that I could consider the lake house my home if that was something I wanted. Wow. I wanted that. I *so* wanted that. But that was something Claire and I had to decide together. My little sister was never far from my mind and always, *always* in my heart.

My days were filled with Reds and the rest of the time I was at the compound. It became easy for me to be there. I was getting to know the brothers and their women and they were getting to know me. Slowly. I still kept to myself a lot, but eventually felt myself being drawn in. Prosper and I played music together in the evenings a lot and gradually I became a part of the firelight and laughter that

I had feared as a child. Sometimes I would help Jules cook. Pinky and I decided to start a garden. Nice.

Things were good. However, there was much I had left unsettled back in Willows Point. I knew that I would have to face it eventually. Claire and I were going to plan what came next. It had always been Claire and me. We planned what came next and this brief parting made no difference.

So my life was in a holding pattern.

Diego. He was gone on some MC business when I had gotten back. He called me every day and just checked in.

So our calls basically went like this.

"Hey, Babe."

"Hey."

"How's it going?"

"Pretty good. You?"

"Pretty good is not an answer, Babe."

"Oh."

"So, I'm gonna ask you again. How's it going?"

"Not bad."

"Babe."

He'd ask me a few questions about my day. He never divulged much himself, so at times the conversation felt stilted and forced. I tried not to think too much of it. Really, our relationship thus far had been based on sex and arguing. Or so it seemed. I wasn't sure where Diego fit in my life or *if* he fit in my life or *if* I fit in his.

And I gave Ellie some thought.

I did.

I thought a lot about Diego's relationship with her. I had been around the club long enough to know the difference between the old ladies, the girlfriends, and the whores. Most times the guys would have all three. Some even had the added fourth, which meant a wife at home with kids. Fidelity was not in the Badass Biker Dictionary. Except maybe for Crow, and who knew what that was about.

I stayed away from the girl posse. Despite everything, or maybe because of everything, I was still a watcher. When it came right down to it, I honestly and truly didn't know what really had gone on between Diego and Ellie. Sure, Diego had denied anything serious between the two of them. But I wasn't stupid and neither was Ellie. Crazy mean maybe, but she was no dummy. Ellie didn't seem like the type who would have stuck around if she hadn't felt there was some *there* there.

I didn't trust that she would just walk away from Diego or from what she thought was going to be the life of an old lady. The way some women dreamt of a house, a husband, and a minivan full of kids, these biker chicks dreamt of wearing property patches and filling in the back seat of a Harley.

She was gone. For now. But I had *no* doubt. *Not one shred of doubt* that we hadn't seen the last of the train wreck that was Ellie. I just wanted to make sure I wasn't in her path.

I didn't talk about it, didn't feel the need to share, and tried not to think about it. The Winston sisters had survived a lot. *A lot.* Claire and I had barely survived what it took to grow up healthy and whole in a house headed by Jack Winston. Sitting here, now in our safe place, I was mad at myself for not seeking out Prosper earlier.

The years after my mother died hadn't been pretty. Not by a long stretch. Despite the promise that Prosper had made to my mother, he should not have brought us back to my father. Jack just didn't have it in him to be the sole caretaker of two little girls. Jack's version of doing what "the good daddies do" basically meant instead of going out to drink, he stayed at home to drink. Sometimes I had found myself furious with my mother. Had she really been that naive about the kind of man my father was? She never ever should have made Prosper promise not to separate us from Jack. In doing so, she had sentenced Claire and me to a life I couldn't imagine that she would have wanted for us.

Nobody had ever touched us. Jack had kept us safe in that way. Our house was a safe place to be in *that way*. Even when his friends came over. The rough, big, loud, shadow people. They stayed outside. "Not even to piss," I heard him say once. "You don't go in that house where Maggie's babies are, not even to piss."

Maggie's babies. Not his. Maggie's. Except for the fact that Claire and I had the exact shade of his deep violet-blue eyes and shared his long thin nose, I had often felt such a disconnect from our father that I doubted our parentage. I had spent a lot of time that summer at the lake house searching Prosper's face hoping to find some resemblance to us. It didn't escape me that Prosper was about as far as you could get from the perfect father figure, but he would have been better than Jack. By a lot. At eight years old, I knew that. *At eight.*

So because our father basically sucked, our only hope had been me. Sure I could have used that address that Prosper had given us years ago. But the straits never seemed dire enough. I was cooking and cleaning and getting Claire and myself off to school as far back as I remembered. Oddly though, there had always been enough money to get us through. Thank God.

Getting Jack to remember to pay the bills, however, that was another matter. After having the electricity shut off twice, I knew I had to step up. So at the tender age of ten years old, while other kids were playing with dolls and going to birthday parties, I was teaching myself how to manage the household finances. I would put together little envelopes once a month with the amount due on them. My dad would fill the envelopes with cash, and I would go to Petey's Variety where for an extra three dollars you could pay your utility and cable bills.

Our dad never once made me worry about not having enough money. Although he was gone sometimes, he never seemed to work at anything steady. We paid for everything in cash. Everything. Doctors, dentists, and one trip to the emergency room when I fell out of a tree and broke my arm. These were all paid for in cash.

My father also kept two guns in the house; they were both loaded. One he placed in the drawer by his bed, and the other was, of all places, taped behind the toilet. Claire and I knew never ever to touch them. Knowing they were there never made us feel safe. They made us feel the very opposite of safe.

You would think that with the men we had for role models in our young lives, Claire and I would have had the sense to look for something better. Neither one of us dated until much later. Just like with the friends thing, our situation hadn't exactly been conducive to dating the boy next door. We kept to ourselves. When we finally made that leap, we both picked men who abused drugs and then abused us. Yep, Baby Sister and I were not too smart when it came to choosing men.

Now here I was in the heart of Wrong Man City. The irony did not escape me. But here in that City Of All Wrong were also Pinky and Prosper. There was also the Viking God, who made the best home fries I ever tasted, and who winked at me when he thought I was sad.

And there was Diego. Who I was hoping wasn't Mr. Wrong at all. Who I was beginning to hope, with all my heart, was the man I could finally make a home with. I was hoping that, in the heart of the City Of All Wrong, I had finally found my Mr. Right. Maybe.

CHAPTER 43

R eport in."
Prosper had the gavel in his hand. He was seated at the head of the table behind closed doors. It was a few days after Lilah's funeral. Prosper had left the women behind to do whatever they had to do to clean up the rest of Pinky's family shit. And shit it had been. If it had been up to Prosper, he would have burnt that fuck house to the ground. He knew what had happened to Pinky behind those walls. But Dolly was there, and his Raine was there too. Pinky had been determined to try and make some green from that shit house. Maybe she was right. Maybe it was time that she got some back for the misery that had been her life. So he had left her to it.

Diego, Reno, Jules, Pipe, and Crow were at the table. Gunner, Ever, and Riker had driven up from Willows Point to sit in on this one too.

Diego and Crow, looking a little worse for the wear, were sitting opposite each other scowling. They both had swollen knuckles. Diego's lip was split, and although Crow was trying to hide it, he grimaced every time he moved.

Prosper knew it was coming and it had.

The minute Crow pulled up on his bike, Diego had gone for him at a full run.

At a full fucking run.

Then the two of them had gone at it like damn kids. Cocksuckers. Stupid brainless motherfucking dumbass sonsofbitches. Brother going after brother. Took Prosper and three members to pull them apart. Not gonna fucking happen. Never gonna fucking happen that his boys were gonna fight over a woman. Even if—no, especially if—that woman was Raine. Neither one of those shit heads was good enough for her anyway. After watching them almost kill each other, Prosper had booted them right in the ass and kicked them both all the way into a meet.

Prosper had known Diego and Crow for a long time. Too fucking long. He was too old to be playing referee like some kind of father to two horny sons. He told them that too. One of them as bad as the fucking next. Crow making his play for Raine knowing that D had made it clear she belonged to him. Although Prosper had to fucking give it to Crow. When that whore Ellie had given him that in by trying to lay claim to Diego, Crow had stepped right up to take it. Then he went ahead and let that bitch wife of his interfere in the way he always did. If there was ever a cunt, Crow's ex was one. That goddamn fucking wife of his had been playing him against the club for too long. You love the man, you love the life. Every brother and his woman knew that. Every woman but Crow's. Pain in the fucking ass.

Crow had been a wild child when Prosper found him. Dumpster diving and living on the street just outside a reservation in South Dakota, he had been a skinny, wiry kid, with hollow cheekbones and dirty black hair. He was Apache. But looking at him still had made him think of Maggie. Then again, Maggie had been gone by then, and most things came around to making him think about her.

Prosper had bought him a meal and got his story. Three meals to be exact. The kid had eaten three twelve-ounce steaks complete with three baked potatoes and three salads with blue cheese dressing. He had washed it down with six glasses of chocolate milk.

When they were leaving the steakhouse, Crow had made an excuse to go back to the table. Once there he had pocketed the tip. Sonofabitch. Prosper had never seen anything like it. He reminded him of that pickpocket in that fucking Dickens book that they had made him read in school. The kid had balls and he was hungry. Hungry in a way that all the steak and chocolate milk in the world couldn't fill. Prosper liked him right away and a lot.

After the meal, Prosper had had a sit-down with the Artful Dodger. Crow had been pretty much on his own after escaping a coked-up mother and the string of men who she fucked to keep her in booze and snort. He had run away after one of his mom's johns tried to get Crow to suck his dick. That's how he told it. Just like that.

He had been twelve years old and lived in a gutted-out apartment building. Ever mindful of bullshit, Prosper decided to assess the situation for himself. If it was as bad as the kid said it was, Prosper was gonna get him away from that. Prosper had Crow bring him around to where he was staying. The situation was not only as bad as Crow had said, it was a hell of a lot worse.

Prosper brought Crow back with him and gave him a job working around the club. Smart little fucker he was. Pinky got him enrolled in school and the little bastard got straight A's. Crow had been encouraged by some goddamn guidance counselor or do-good teacher to "realize his potential." He tried for college and got in. Prosper had been proud of the little shit.

He lasted two years and met that bitch Jaci during that time. Fancy fucking Jaci. Tiny tits, small mind, no heart. She looked down her nose at everyone and everything. Crow lasted a couple of years away from the MC. Then something happened and he was back. He had left school and he patched in. He lost Jaci in the process, but to Prosper it was no loss at all. Crow had married her in Vegas. Stupid, dumb fucking kid. Guess he was still married to her. At least, that's what Diego said when he charged after him.

Prosper ran his hands over his face at the thought of the big fucking mess. Diego had his own motherfucker of a fucked-up situation that Raine knew nothing about. No one did but Prosper. Jesus, he wasn't looking forward to that shit coming out. Maybe it wouldn't. That shit was pure pain for D.

Fucking MC wasn't anything but a big damn cocksucking soap opera lately.

But they had other business to discuss. The find that had brought Raine back to the fold had unveiled some very interesting shit. The MC was still dealing with the fallout from that. Drugs and gun running were something the Hells Saints stayed away from. Prostitution, money lending, adult entertainment was where the off-the-radar money came from. The legal enterprises were also pretty lucrative. Ruby Reds and the two other bars did really well. None of the brothers were hurting for green.

That whole Jamie mess had created a turf war that was threatening to cut into a neighborhood where the Saints had their biggest adult entertainment enterprise. Negotiations had to take place to stop that and quick. Prosper didn't want any of his girls getting hurt in some drive-by. Not to mention how bad that would be for business. His high-priced escorts had some pretty high-profile locals in their books. Town and city officials, cops, business owners, the fucking president of the Chamber of Commerce, and a few prominent physicians. Yeah, those in Willows Point and surrounding area had their predilections.

There was also the matter of the sonofabitch, Gino, the rapist and woman beater. The MC had gone in and tossed his house, but he had disappeared. Raine had said that he had dealings with Jamie through Claire. Once Jamie had been found dead, the guess was the bastard had gone into hiding.

Gino was a dead man walking.

That was for sure.

Diego wanted to be the one to pull the trigger but Prosper told him that he was going to have to wait in line. Prosper was gonna take his time killing that bastard. And he was going to enjoy it. But first they had to find him. Willows Point was Gunner's territory and a half day's drive from the south chapter.

It was also where Claire was in rehab. Claire's time was almost over and Raine was going to go to the Point for the family meeting soon. She also had to clear up some stuff with the house. Depending on where Claire stood with the rehab, Prosper was hoping both girls would decide to come back to Crownsmount and build a life. They could have the lake house. Raine could keep working at Reds, and they could find something for Claire. Or nothing. Prosper could afford to support his "girls" and Pinky was all for it. But one thing was for certain, as long as that cocksucker Gino was alive, Raine wouldn't be going anywhere near Willows Point without one of the brothers along.

As far as Crow and D were concerned, Prosper didn't give two shits if Raine took one over the other as her man. Or neither. As long as she was happy, it was all good with him.

"Where the fuck is he?" Prosper growled, looking at Gunner.

"No fucking idea." Gunner shook his head. "He houdinied himself right out of town. Vanished."

"Connected?" Prosper lifted his eyebrow. "How can it be that this little pussy ass disappeared if he ain't connected?"

Nods around the table.

"Shit going down with Claire and Raine being back in Willows Point for even a fucking day, and that cocksucker anywhere in that vicinity, ain't gonna happen, Brothers. I put his name out there, and Los Diablos became real fucking interested. Gino fucking Abbiati has some connection somewhere."

"I checked in with my guy, Gianni. He don't run with his crew," Riker added.

"Those goombahs stick together. You trust that dago to give it to you real, Riker?" Reno asked.

"Yeah. I hear ya, bro. But in this case, I know Gianni ain't lying. His sister got jumped a few years back. Gianni caught the asswipe and strung him up. Took him three days to kill the guy. Gianni takes rape real fucking serious. He offered to take him down himself if we ever got a hit on the motherfucker. So maybe those dagos do stick together, but goombah or not, Gianni's crew ain't protecting him."

"Raine know anything, Boss? She have any idea where the asshole could be hiding?" Crow asked.

"Leave Raine the fuck out of this," Diego snarled. "Don't even fucking mention her name at this table. As a matter of fucking fact, Breed, don't you fucking ever mention her name at all."

Crow's neck muscles stiffened, and the muscle in his jaw started clenching. He put his hand on the gun he wore inside his cut.

Gunner for the first time in his life actually did an eye roll.

"Not this shit again," Riker muttered underneath his breath.

"You stupid fucking spic. Your shit's so jealous that you have your head up your ass when it comes to keeping her safe. Raine. Raine. Raine. Raine." Crow leaned over the table.

"Not only am I gonna say it at this table, I'm gonna be calling it out when you fuck up and she's lying under me. 'Cause, Brother, you're just one stupid whore away from that happening. When was the last time you talked to that skank from hell Ellie, Brother? She been calling the fucking club nonstop. Jules was thinking about having the shit changed out of the phone number."

Diego roared and went charging around the table. Crow roared and charged to meet him halfway.

It took the rest of the brothers to pull them apart.

"ENOUGH!" Prosper roared. "You pissants settle this another fucking time. Diego, you fucking figure this Ellie shit out, so Raine doesn't get caught in the middle of some more fucked-up shit, or I'm going to string you up by your balls. I fucking mean it."

Then he pointed at Crow.

"Crow. Shut the fuck up. Just shut the fuck up and sit the fuck down." Prosper scrubbed his hand over his face and felt about eighty years old. Grown men acting like babies.

∼

Reno could not believe this. He was getting a mother of a headache. He had had enough.

Jesus Christ! Over pussy. Brothers fighting over snatch. Dis-fucking-gusting. Ever since she walked into the door of the MC, fucking hell had rained down on them. *Prosper going around blubbering like she was a long-lost daughter. Crow and D at each other's throats. Jules just about tripping over himself to make sure her every fucking need was met. You would think Raine Winston had a snatch of fucking gold.* Reno couldn't stand it. Couldn't fucking stand it. Even his own mother getting shitfaced on the plane and taking that fucking walk down memory lane. Some things better left alone. One good thing was that at least Diego had gotten rid of that crazy-eyed bitch, Ellie. There was something off about that one. Gone, but not fucking forgotten. Crow was right, bitch was calling the club nonstop. Fucking drama. This couldn't get any worse.

Then it did.

"Reno. Snap the fuck out of it," Prosper barked.

Reno looked around the table. All eyes on him.

"Yeah, Boss?" Reno answered.

"Raine's got to go to Willows Point and meet up with Claire. They got some shit to do at that house. Claire's gonna need some stuff. She left everything behind at that puke fest Jamie's house. Cops all over that shit. Raine's got to settle things at the grandmother's house. You gonna be with my girls. Fucking white-on-rice until they are done. You feel me?"

Yeah. I feel you. You want me to babysit the golden snatch and her junkie whore baby sister.

"I feel ya." Reno nodded.

"No fucking way. I'm handling this. No fucking way anybody but me is going to the Point with Raine," Diego butted in.

"SHUT THE FUCK UP. LAST TIME, D." Prosper was done with this shit.

Crow grinned and leaned back in his chair.

"Crow, I need you to go up to North Chapter. They are opening a new bar. Need your fucking expertise on that shit." Prosper looked at Crow.

"Got that." Crow nodded.

"D, need you to head east. Brothers up there might know something about Gino's connection to Los Diablos or whoever the fuck else that name rings a bell with. Gunner, you good to go with?" Gunner nodded and Diego relaxed visibly.

Gavel went down once more. Church was over.

CHAPTER 44

I was so excited I was squirming in my seat. I couldn't wait to see Claire. Couldn't wait. I had talked to her a couple of times over the phone, and she sounded good. Really, really good. We were going to have to go to some sort of family meeting before she was released; then she was coming home with me. Whatever we decided that home was to be. Claire and I, just like always. We would decide that together.

The only spot that threatened to block out the bright sun of my day was sitting next to me chain-smoking. Reno looked pissed. No, scratch that. Reno *was* pissed. My heart had fallen to my feet when Prosper talked to me about who my escort for the trip was going to be and why. They were worried about something going on with Gino. I didn't think I mattered enough to Gino for him to come after me, but Prosper didn't share my view on that. Plus Prosper said that Gino was involved in stuff that touched the club. Weird. Gino had no way of knowing my connection to the Saints when we met. I wasn't stupid. I knew that the club had criminal enterprises. There was no doubt in my mind now that Gino was criminal-minded. So I guessed like sought like. Something about water seeking its own level or some kind of crap like that. I wasn't surprised.

What did surprise me was the constant animosity I felt from Reno. He flat out didn't like me. He barely spoke to me unless he had to. A couple of times I caught him glaring at me for no reason other than that I existed at all. At first I had gone out of my way to be nice to him. Then I had gone out of my way to stay out of his way. Looked like he drew the short straw on this one. But I wasn't going to let him ruin my day. It was a half day's trip, and we had been driving for a couple of hours.

"Hey, Reno," I said lightly.

Nothing. Not a damn thing and I know he heard me. Sigh. Really?

"Reno?" A little louder this time.

Nada. Zip. Zilch. But I saw his foot push down just a fraction of an inch on the gas pedal.

"Reno, you have to pull over at the next stop." I leaned forward to turn down the radio.

"Not gonna happen," he grumbled.

"Reno, I've got to use the bathroom." I colored red.

"Should have gone before you left. You gonna have to wait till we get there now." He turned the radio back up.

This was ridiculous. We still had at least a few hours to go.

"Reno! I really have to go." I raised my voice.

"Raine! You're really going to have to fucking wait." He met my voice and raised me a decibel.

I felt tears form in the back of my eyes and a burst of anger flash along with them.

"Jesus, Reno, really?" My voice cracked just a little. My bladder was uncomfortably full and had been for about half an hour.

His face was hard. The wind from the open window blew his hair briefly in front of his eyes. He had a smoke dangling from his mouth and mirrored aviator sunglasses. I couldn't read his expression, but I had this nagging sense he was getting off on this power play. Prick.

"Reno, please stop at the next rest area so I can pee."

Asshole.

"What was that?" Oh he was so enjoying this.

"Please." I was going to find a way to make him eat dirt for this. I swore it.

"Magic fucking word, baby." He grinned and pulled into the next stop.

The whole time I was squatting in the woods, I was plotting my revenge. I continued plotting it until we reached Willows Point, where I promptly forgot my plot in the excitement of seeing Claire.

CHAPTER 45

Reno leaned with his back against the car, arms crossed, waiting for Raine to come out of the woods. He was being a real prick and he knew it. What he didn't know was why. Christ, she brought out the worst in him. The thing was, she was really an okay bitch when he thought about it. He had never heard her whine or complain. She didn't flash her tits around or hang all over the brothers. She seemed smart. She had a great smile, which she had flashed freely in his direction until she stopped looking at him completely.

Maybe it had something to do with Prosper. Maybe he didn't like sharing that father shit. Prosper had really stepped up for him and his mom. Reno had noticed and appreciated. They had a special bond, him and Prosper. Then Raine enters like a long-lost favorite daughter . . . Jesus, could that be it? Was he jealous? The thought pissed him off even more. When he saw her come out of the woods, he stomped out his cigarette. When Raine got in the car, she thanked him for stopping. Thanked him. After he had practically made her beg him to stop. Maybe the bitch wasn't so bad after all. Time would fucking tell.

CHAPTER 46

We pulled up to the rehab center where I was going to see my baby sister. It looked like a dormitory-type building made out of brick with no personality. It was a little depressing, honestly. I knew that there were literally thousands of rehab centers in the United States. Everything from boot-camp-style places to palatial settings on the beach. Claire was stuck with what our insurance paid for. Standard twenty-eight days in an insurance-approved institution. I squared my shoulders and poked my head out the car, searching the windows for some sign of life. There wasn't any. I really hoped for Claire's sake the inside wasn't as dismal as the outside. Willows Point Alcohol and Substance Abuse Center looked like it meant business.

I got out of the car and heard the driver's side slam shut as well. Oh no, he wasn't.

"Reno, you can't come in with me," I said to him.

Reno leaned against the car and folded his big arms across his chest.

"I'm waiting," he said.

"Waiting? This is not an 'I'm gonna run in for a minute so keep the car running' kind of deal here. I don't know how long this is supposed to take or even what to expect. This could be an all-day thing," I warned him.

"Still waiting," he answered.

"Suit yourself. But you might want to go get a coffee or a magazine or the newspaper or something. We just passed the center of town. I'm sure they have something you might want to read." But then again, I thought, probably he didn't read much.

He just kept leaning and staring.

"Jesus, you gonna sit there like that all day waiting?" I was exasperated and didn't like the thought of him just sitting there. It was unsettling. "I can call you when we're ready to go if you give me your cell number."

Still staring.

"So, you gonna just sit here for as long as it takes?" This was stupid.

"Order came down. White-on-rice. That's how it came down. That's how it's gonna be," Reno said.

I gave up and, shaking my head, I walked up the steps. Excitedly, I rang the buzzer by the side of the door. I couldn't resist one last peek at Reno, who except for lighting up his smoke, hadn't moved a muscle.

I gave my name at the front desk, and within minutes my little sister came walking through the frosted-glass doors. It took me a minute to recognize her.

I guess I hadn't realized how bad things had gotten for Claire in the year she was with Jamie. It had been such a slow and steady decline that I had somehow grown accustomed to the signs of desperation and addiction that had served to ravage my sweet sister. Seeing her now, I almost didn't know her. Gone was the stringy lanky hair, the dark hollows under her eyes, and thin body that had become skeletal under the throes of Jamie's abuse and her own addiction. The young woman that stood before me was healthy and whole. Her beautiful dark hair shone with luster and curl, her eyes were clear, and she had put on some weight. When she looked at me, her smile lit up the room. And my world. All my fears for Claire vanished. I had my sister back.

We hugged for a long time. She gave me a tour of the place and introduced me to some of her friends. The place was as gray on the inside as it was on the outside. But the staff was friendly, and there were little sprays of fresh flowers throughout the various halls and sitting rooms. Our family meeting wasn't scheduled for a couple of hours yet. I had arrived just in time for lunch, and I was able to join Claire in the dining room for a tuna salad plate, fruit cup, and unlimited soda, tea, or coffee. Guessing sugar and caffeine addictions were the least of the residents' problems, they let them have at it.

I filled Claire in as much as I could about what had been going on. She wanted to hear it all and said that we would be doing enough talking about her later. I tried not to leave out much. I told her about the MC and the brothers. I talked to her about Prosper and Pinky and filled her in on what my life had been like the past few weeks at the compound. I told her about Diego and Crow. I talked to her about the scene with Ellie. Then more about Diego. Then about my job at Ruby Reds. Then some more about Crow. Then a little more about Diego.

She understood. She understood everything. Not only did she understand, the student had now become the teacher. The hours of therapy hadn't been wasted. My little sister hadn't only acquired an inner peace, but a wisdom that rose above our circumstances. She started talking then. She talked about how scared she had been that night when it all went down. How sick she had been of the drugs and the lies and the beatings she had taken at Jamie's hands. How much effort it had cost her to keep most of it from me.

She told me about therapy. She had discovered that her recently acquired coke habit was a symptom of the real problem. That had come part and parcel with her nightmare relationship with Jamie.

She had a strong will to beat it. But her addiction to the wrong men was a lifetime pattern that had started real young. I got that. As much as I had tried to shield her and steer her away from bad boys, she had been raised knee-deep in it. Of course, that's something she would gravitate to! I got that and it scared the shit out of me for her.

When we sat down to the family meeting, I met Claire's therapist. Her name was Dolores. Dolores was in her late fifties. She was a large, dark-haired woman who had an easy smile and a no-bullshit attitude. She encouraged Claire to talk to me and she did. Boy, did she. And what she said made sense not only for her, but for me as well.

Dolores explained more clinically what Claire had already told me. Claire's underlying addiction was to Jamie and men like him. Those relationships would serve as gateways for her. Gateways to criminal activity or drug abuse or whatever else served the relationship. Thinking back, Claire's few boyfriends had been assholes. That was true. The whole bad-boy attraction thing.

Dolores explained that "bad boys" were men who acted like delinquent adolescents. They lied, cheated, and totally refused to take responsibility for any of it. They were not capable of intimacy. For them it was just the means to control and get their way. When they felt they had lost that control, they withdrew, looking for the next victim.

It was a toxic and addictive relationship. Toxic because it cost a woman her dignity and self-esteem. It was addictive because the good times were wound in with the bad times. Dolores went on to explain that these types of relationships perpetuated intermittent reinforcement, which research showed is the strongest kind of reinforcement there is. You were in it for the next happy time and would wait for it. Dolores said that women don't usually leave this kind of relationship. They get left. Claire found the strength to leave only when the one thing she loved most in this world was threatened. That one thing had been me. My heart swelled upon hearing this.

I didn't know if it was appropriate or not, but what the hell. This was family therapy after all. I shared my relationship with Gino, and how it had felt just like that. It didn't escape me that even though I left him, it was only after I caught him in bed with the underage neighbor. And honestly, if he had come back with his heart in his hand instead of his fist, who knows how long I would have repeated the cycle of taking abuse.

We talked about how we grew up and the kind of men that were our role models. Because I might be bringing Claire right back into the thick of all that, we talked about the Saints MC and the kind of men that made up that brotherhood. We talked about the roles of their women. We talked about our roles. We talked about Prosper and Jack and Maggie and Pinky.

We talked about cycles and how to break them.

Dolores then said something that really surprised me. She said that bad boys came in all shapes and sizes and from all walks of life. While the general consensus saw the bad boy as a James Dean or Marlon Brando type, that wasn't always the case.

She shared with us that she too had been an old lady back in the day. When Dolores's young husband came back from Vietnam, he joined the Renegades. I knew that MC by reputation, and they were pretty hardcore. Dolores told us that her man had done what he had to do to keep himself sane in the aftermath of the war. Joining the "Gades" is what had done it for him. Loving him, Dolores had supported that.

Dolores's young husband had worn the cut and had done everything his club asked of him. But he never let that touch her. He managed to keep his life in the club and his life with her separate. He didn't cheat, lie to her, or lay a hand on her. They had a love that had lasted through all of it. He had died of a heart attack a few years earlier. Dolores went back to college and got her degree in counseling. She worked with veterans a couple of days a week and addicts the other days. She said she had wanted to give back. I, for one, was glad she felt that way.

"So," Dolores was wrapping up the meeting, "what I guess I'm telling you is that you were born into a life and you might be going back to a life that is filled with what could be a host of triggers for you, Claire. However, you could also find those triggers in a college class or the local coffee shop. Use the tools you learned here to guide the rest of your life. I would and do recommend that you stay out of any kind of romantic entanglement for at least a year after treatment. As a matter of fact, I would say to run like hell from anything that even comes close to getting you laid in the next year."

I snuck a peek at Claire and she was colored a bright shade of crimson. Dolores waved her hand at Claire and continued, "Your drug of choice is the wrong men. But don't worry, lamb. I'm going to schedule you for some follow-up sessions, and you call me whenever you want. I know it may seem like we're cutting you loose, but we're always here for you. You're going to be just fine."

Dolores patted Claire on the knee and then we all grasped hands. We recited the "God Grant Me the Serenity" prayer and then we were free to go. Claire and I stopped at the desk and set up her next three appointments. Smiling, we strode arm in arm down the steps towards our new life.

Damn. I had forgotten about Reno. More importantly, I had forgotten to tell Claire about Reno.

Coming out of the meeting with Dolores, I looked at Reno through Claire's eyes, and I saw nothing but trouble. I felt her tense beside me and saw the smile leave her eyes.

For Reno's part, he had pulled away from the spot he was leaning against on the car. Otherwise he was nothing if not true to his word. He had stayed in the exact same spot that I had left him in hours earlier. A bunch of cigarette butts lay at his feet. He uncrossed his arms and stood with his hands on his hips.

He gave me a chin nod, then looked directly at Claire. She moved a slight step back and behind me.

"Claire, this is Reno," I said. "Reno, this is my sister."

Claire stood behind me frozen and Reno just stared at her. This was going well.

"Nice to meet you," my sister said softly from behind me.

"Likewise." Reno was looking at my sister like she was something to eat.

He looked at me. "Where to now?"

I explained to Claire, "I thought we would go check on Gram's house. Being there might help us to decide."

Claire nodded.

"Decide what?" Reno asked.

This was new. Reno taking an interest in anything that had to do with me. Those two words were two more than he had volunteered the whole ride down.

I thought about not answering him. But he still held the keys to the car, and I figured that no good would come out of building more animosity between us. If he was going to play nice for whatever reason, so would I. Maybe.

"Claire and I haven't decided what to do next," I said.

"Next?" Reno echoed.

"Yeah. Next. Our lives have been in sort of a holding pattern. We need to figure out where we're going to live, what we're going to do for money, where we're going to work. Things like that."

Things that haven't got a damn thing to do with you and are none of your business.

Reno was getting ready to light up again. He took his time, then pulled a long draw of nicotine before he continued.

194

"Seems a done deal to me. You and Claire stay at the lake house or at the kitchen house till the lake house is ready. That won't take me and the boys long. You keep working at Reds. Claire takes a minute to figure things out for herself. Club's got plenty of work. Legit work. Keep you two outta trouble." He squinted as a wave of smoke hit his eye.

Really? Really?

Claire stood stock-still behind me.

Reno leaned forward and craned to look behind me. At Claire.

"Sound like a plan, sugar?" he asked.

Oh no, he didn't. Before I had a chance to answer, Claire perked up behind me.

"I think Raine told you my name is Claire, and whatever the plan is, it's for me and my sister to decide," Claire said quietly. Then she added barely above a whisper, "But we thank you for your interest. Don't we, Raine?"

I was too busy eyeing Reno to answer. I felt Claire nudge the back of me. I answered promptly.

"Oh yeah. We thank you," I said with absolutely no conviction.

Reno smirked at my sister. "No problem, Sugar." Then he got into the car.

Claire and I moved together. When she whispered *asswipe,* I nodded in agreement.

We pulled in front of our grandmother's house. It seemed like much more than a month had passed. The plants in the window boxes were dead and even though I had stopped the mail, it seemed like it had come anyway. Whole house screamed *abandoned.* It made me a little sad seeing it because I knew exactly how that house felt. I had felt lonely and lost when I left it. Damn it if the little house didn't seem to project those feelings through its walls. I thought, maybe even was hoping, that if my grandmother's house would radiate anything to Claire and me when we returned to it, it would be a welcome.

That was how it had felt to me when I learned it had been willed to our father and then to us. Jack's mother had died when I was four. I had vague memories of a gray-haired woman in her seventies with a soft smile and a softer bosom. I had recollections of a cookie jar filled with Stella D'oro cookies and a refrigerator that held little bottles of 7UP in its door.

Our grandmother had loved to knit. I remember holding my hands out and apart so she could slip skeins of yarn around them. Then I would help her wrap that yarn into a ball to be used later. My father's laugh had been easy around her, and my mother smiled when she saw me sitting on Gram's lap.

Even though it would be another three or four years before my little life turned me into an official watcher, instinctively I had known at even that young age that my grandmother had secrets. And those secrets came from only good places. Secrets like how her house always smelled like warm vanilla, and how she had a magic closet that always contained an arrival gift for me. How when she put her hand on my mother's tummy, she knew that the baby was going to be a girl. She had been sure that the baby girl would have the exact same shade of blue eyes that the three of us had. Jack, Gram, and I all had those eyes.

I loved her and had never felt safer than when I was with her. I think we all felt that way. Being with Gram just made things better. She died of a stroke a month before my sister was born. Jack and Maggie named the new baby Claire after her.

I remembered walking into that house after Jack died. Everything just the way Gram had left it. I had felt the little house wrap its arms around me. I had. I really had. Despite the somewhat remote location, I always felt safe in the house at the end of a long dirt road, with its overgrown garden and creaky porch steps. I had loved the house and it had loved me back. I had never really felt the need to make it my own because, with Gram's things there, it had felt like a safe haven.

Until the day when it didn't. When nowhere seemed safe to me any longer. But that hadn't been the little house's fault. It had done its best. Now as crazy as I knew it would sound if I gave voice to it, the house didn't seem glad to see me back. If nothing else, with its overflowing mail and its dying flowers and its closed curtains, it seemed to be screaming, *Stay away.*

Something felt different about the house. Something *was* different. I couldn't place my finger on it, but it was something besides the dried flowers and the overflowing mail. Or maybe I was just overwhelmed and overwrought and paranoid. That could definitely be it. I let it go and searched in my purse to get the keys. Damn. Since I hadn't driven my own car in a while I hadn't remembered to bring my set of keys.

"Damn it," I said out loud.

"Problem?" Reno asked.

"Yeah, I forgot my keys."

"Good thing we drove six hours to get here then," he snickered.

Reno, the dickhead, was back. I was actually kind of relieved.

Claire leaned forward from the back seat and said, "We used to leave a key in the shed behind the house, remember?"

Reno turned around and winked at my sister. "Good girl." He smiled.

Holy shit. Reno was either trying to annoy me, or he had a hard-on for my little sister. I really hoped he was trying to annoy me.

Claire looked uncomfortable. Just then my cell rang. I looked at the number and it was Prosper. Smiling, I handed the phone to Claire.

"Hello?"

I watched as her eyes turned bright with tears and she whispered, "Been a long time, Prosper."

I decided to leave them to their conversation while I went to the backyard shed in search of the keys to the house.

"Be right back," I said to Reno. "I'll go around the back and open the front door. When Claire gets done talking to Prosper she can come in."

He took a look at the house. "What's up with the mail falling out all over the place? Didn't you put a stop on that shit?"

"Yeah, that is kind of weird. Maybe that's what came in before I put a stop on it. Anyway, no one ever comes down here. I'll be right back to open that door."

"I'll come with." Reno was moving to get out of the car.

"No. Why?" I was opening the car door.

"White-on-rice." Reno was moving to shut off the car.

I touched his hand to stop him from turning off the ignition. Then I pulled it back fast, realizing what I had done.

"Don't turn off the car. Let Claire relax in the air conditioning and finish her conversation," I said.

I turned to watch her. She was speaking in her quiet way with a small smile of wonder on her face. I knew that Prosper had put her on speaker and Pinky was joining the conversation. She saw me and raised her index finger to indicate that she would be just a moment longer. I shook my head to tell her to take her time and pointed to the house. She nodded her understanding. Then Claire was back to answering and asking questions.

∼

Reno took a minute to assess the situation. Things seemed cool with the house. When he looked in his rearview, Raine's little sister was smiling into the phone. It had been a long day waiting. That was for sure. Reno put his head back on the headrest. He closed his eyes for a moment, enjoying the quiet noise of Claire's soft voice talking into the phone.

After what seemed like half of a second, he felt someone lightly shake him.

"Reno?"

It was Claire. Reno jerked awake and looked at the dash clock. A little over twenty minutes had passed since he closed his eyes, and Raine had gone into the house.

"Yeah?" Reno was turning off the car.

"Where's Raine?" Claire asked.

"Went in the house when you were on the phone," Reno answered.

"Yeah, I know that. But I thought she said she would be out in a minute. Seems more than a minute. I've been on the phone a while," Claire said.

"What she said was she was gonna find the keys and open the front door for you."

He had his hand on the door and was getting ready to open it.

"Front door hasn't been opened." Claire had her hand on the door handle too.

Reno got out first. Claire looked at the house. As much as Raine had tried to keep things from her, Claire had grown up in the same exact environment. Actually, things had been harder for Claire in some ways because she had that much less time with their mother and the quasi-home-life stability having a mother had provided.

From an early age, Claire had watched Raine watch people. Raine seemed to have a natural instinct of knowing the good from the bad. Claire knew that and trusted Raine implicitly. Claire loved her with all her heart.

Claire had also grown up being terrified of losing Raine. *Terrified of losing her.* So while Raine was watching for secrets, Claire had been watching for anything in a situation that was out of place or looked like it didn't belong or could be a danger sign for Raine.

Claire had been the one to find both loaded guns that their father had hidden in the house.

Claire had been the one who had secretly gone to Prosper. She told him she was having nightmares when her mother was dying, even though she wasn't. She had done that because even at the age of four-and-a-half, she had known that their home was becoming a place that wasn't safe for her and Raine. Claire had also known that it had been important that somebody besides her small self knew that. After that, Prosper stayed at the house every night until their mother died. It was Claire who had done that. Claire had been looking after Raine in that way, almost as long as Raine had been looking after Claire. Only nobody knew it.

Raine had handed the cell to Claire at the same time they pulled up to the front of the house. Claire had felt instantly that something was off. But then her sister had given her the phone and Prosper was on it. Claire had been swept back to another time and place upon hearing his voice. She had stopped paying attention.

Now she did a full sweep of the house with her eyes.

It was the curtains.

They were never, ever closed. Gram had fitted the large front windows with three pieces of beautiful stained glass. Their grandfather had bought them at an auction. They filled up the front parlor window panes with jeweled shades of glittering crystal. When the sun shone through them, the colors danced like a soft kaleidoscope against the dark paneling on the walls. In the evening you couldn't see through them to the inside of the house even if the interior lights were on. The curtains on either end were really just to frame the stained glass and were never pulled.

They were pulled now.

Claire jerked open her door. She made a run past Reno towards the side gate that led to the back of the house.

Claire felt an iron band wrap itself around her waist, lift her off the ground, and toss her about five steps back. The iron band stayed on her until she regained balance.

"What's got you running like a bat out of hell towards the house, Sugar?"

Reno was standing too close to her. She stepped back. She pointed to the curtains.

"Those are never closed, ever."

Reno's eyes followed Claire's shaking arm to look at what she was pointing at.

"Never?" He raised a brow and was reaching for something in the waistband at the back of his pants.

"Never!" Claire said with all the urgency she felt.

"Get in the car." Reno had a gun in his hand and was turning towards the back of the house.

"I'm coming with." Claire started to move with him.

Reno turned on her, his face screwed up with frustration. Claire held her ground, but her face paled.

"Raine might be in trouble."

Exasperated, Reno reflexively raised his free hand to run it through his hair. When he did this, Claire knew he was going to hit her.

Claire recoiled. She moved her head back and out of the way quickly. But with great effort, she stood her ground.

What the fuck was that flinching shit all about? Reno wondered.

Claire colored, looked towards the house, and began walking quickly that way.

Reno started to grab her arm, then thought better of it. So he stood in front of her instead.

"You're wasting valuable time, little sister. If Raine's in trouble, I'm handling it. You being there, you'd just be in my way. Something else for me to worry about." Reno stood *his* ground. "If I'm not outta there in five, you get the fuck out of here and press four on the cell. That'll get you right to Prosper. You let him know what's going on. You know how to drive a stick?"

Claire nodded. Reno threw her the keys. "You feeling me, Claire? It goes bad, you get your little ass outta here."

Claire flushed but didn't move.

Jesus, her and her fucking sister. Never listened, neither of them.

"Now *move* and get in the fucking car, Claire, or I'm going to change my mind. Then I'm going to pick you up and lock you in the damn trunk."

Reno took a step towards her.

Claire moved quickly to the car. Reno threw the cell to her. Then he sprinted to the back of the house.

CHAPTER 47

I had left Claire and Reno in the car together, hoping it wasn't a bad idea. Not sure what Reno was up to or if he was really up to anything. It could be that he had just been in a bad mood for the past month, and the six-hour trip to pick up my pretty little sister had turned that all around for him. *Fat chance.*

Perhaps if I hadn't been concentrating so hard on the perils of leaving Claire with Reno alone together in the car for what I thought was going to be five minutes tops, I would have paid more attention. I moved through the backyard, past the overgrown garden that looked parched and needed weeding. A flash of guilt shot through me. I made a promise that I would spend some time before we left to harvest some of the crops that were dying on the vines. Then I would give the rest of the plants a good soaking.

I entered the cool, dark shed. It took me a few moments to locate the key. I knew it was hanging on a hook against one of the walls but there were several lines of shelves. They all held gardening trappings. There was potting soil and peat moss on the bottom shelves. The middle shelves contained seed starter flats, stakes, and spools of twine. The top shelves contained a variety of terracotta pots. Against the back wall hung a hose, a few spades, shovels of varying lengths, and two steel rakes. I checked quickly behind each of the tools in the back first and came up with nothing. Then

I found it. The key that was hanging on a rusty hook behind the terra-cotta pots.

I grabbed it and a pretty pot that I thought I would bring back to Pinky. I silently thanked Claire. It was uncanny, Claire always seemed to know where things were or if something was out of place. She was really observant about things like that. Someday I was going to ask her how she did it. For now I was going to get myself in the house and make some iced tea for Claire and me. And Reno, too, I supposed.

I walked towards the kitchen door with my head down, being careful not to step on any of the vegetables that were sitting heavy on the dirt. I pulled open the screen door, still deep in thought. When I went to put the key to the lock, the door swung open, and I was pulled inside. The pot I was holding crashed on the cement steps, and the door slammed shut behind me.

CHAPTER 48

Reno saw the broken pot on the steps as he rounded the corner. His gun was drawn, and he was holding it with both hands for a steady aim. If what was going down in that house was what he thought might be going down, he was going to shoot to kill.

~

"FUCKING WHORE!" Gino had grabbed me by the hair and was dragging me across the floor.

Sweet Jesus! That hurt. I clawed at his hands trying to stop him. He let up only to hit me hard across the face and then pulled harder. I was forced to raise my ass off the floor and do a bad imitation of a crab walk. I knew if he kept dragging my limp body by the hair he was going to rip my scalp apart.

Sweet Lord in heaven. How in the hell had I found myself in the hands of this madman again?

As he dragged me across the house, I reached with one hand into my pocket for my cell.

Nothing!

Damn it! I left my cell in the car with Claire. Gino picked me up under my armpits and threw me on the couch. Then he sat down heavy next to me. The room was unnaturally dark, and I noticed then that the curtains had been drawn. That was it. The damn curtains had been drawn. How had I missed that?

You dumbass!

"What the fuck did you tell them, Raine?" Gino sneered at me. He still had a tight hold on my hair, and I saw that he was clutching a gun in his free hand. He forced me to look at his face. He was a mess. He had a red, raw Frankenstein-stitched gash that ran from the top of his hairline diagonally across his face to the tip of his mouth. He also had two black eyes and his nose had been broken. Somebody had hurt Gino badly.

I heard something squeak in the corner. I turned to see the blonde who had been Gino's girl and who had stopped him from cracking my skull open. Seems he hadn't appreciated the gesture because she was trussed up like a Christmas ham. She had silver duct tape on her mouth, and her mascara was running down her face. Her hands were tied behind her back. Her legs were tied tight with some kind of cord at the ankles. She was bound to one of Gram's dining room chairs. A clump of hair was missing from the side of her head and one of her eyes was swollen shut. She was trying to say something.

"Shut up, cunt!" Gino screamed at her.

She shook her head and tried to talk through the tape.

He pulled me with him as he lunged towards her. He got close to her face and yanked the silver tape off her mouth. A thin layer of skin came off with it, and her lips began to bleed.

"What the fuck could you possibly have to say, bitch?" Gino's eyes were crazy and he kept wiping his nose. I noticed white powder stuck to his nostrils. Gino was higher than a kite. That and the adrenaline that had to be coursing through his veins made him one dangerous man.

"I keep telling you, Gino. Nobody told anybody anything. Why are you dragging her into this?" Her voice sounded raspy and weak.

Then her voice got softer. "You know I always look out for you, baby. Let her go. We don't need her coming between us. Me and you'll work this out. You know I know how to keep you safe. Let her go, honey. We'll get out of here and start all over again. You know how good I can make it between us, daddy."

Gino looked suspiciously at her. "I don't know."

The blonde squirmed in her seat and thrust out her chest.

"Come on, daddy. You know you want your baby girl," the blonde said huskily.

Ick. Ick. Ick.

"You fucking hit me with a fucking gun butt. Then I woke up and you and this bitch here was gone." Gino was oozing spittle from the side of his mouth, but his eyes were now on the blonde's boobs. Full on.

He pulled my hair harder to punctuate his point.

"You know how jealous I get, daddy." The blonde oozed sweetly, "I didn't mean to hurt you. I was just pissed seeing you with another woman."

"The bitch stole something from me." Gino's voice was getting whiny now.

"I know, baby. We'll get it back."

"Then some motherfucker trashed my house. Asswipes following me around. Parking their fucking bikes in front of my house. Asking Gianni about me. Now fucking Gianni wants me dead. Seems like *somebody* told him I beat women. Seems like *somebody* told him I rape women. They fucking broke my nose, cocksuckers. Then they fucking took a knife to me. Now they are looking to kill me."

He was saying this all in a sing-song voice. He was still holding on to my hair, but he seemed to have forgotten about me for a moment. His eyes hungry on the blonde's tits.

"They make me do it. Stupid fucking cunts make me hurt them. I don't want to. I didn't want to hurt you either, Glory." Tears were streaming down Gino's face now.

How creepy. Soooo creepy.

"No one understands you but me, daddy. No one." Glory was straining against the binds.

Gino held my hair tight with one hand and bent down to nuzzle Glory's boobs.

"That's it, daddy." Glory met my eyes over his head. "You let Glory take care of her man."

It's gonna be all right. I'm gonna get us out of this one. Just keep absolutely still. Glory's eyes were on mine.

I nodded once telling her that I understood.

"I never meant to hurt you," Gino was sobbing into Glory's chest.

"I know, daddy. I know. Untie me, honey. Let's get outta here before it's too late."

Gino nodded. His shoulders slumped, and I relaxed just a little bit. He started to untie Glory. Her eyes met mine over his head, and she tried to smile. I tried to smile back.

Then he put the gun to my temple.

I felt the bile rise in my throat, and the floor started spinning beneath me.

"NO!" Glory yelled.

"Why the fuck not?" Gino looked at her suspiciously. "What's she to you? Thought you were jealous of the bitch. I'm gonna prove to you once and for all, you the only woman for me. I'm gonna put her in the fucking ground"

"No, baby, let me do it. Untie me and let me do it. You owe me that. Let me kill the bitch. You can watch." Glory smiled up at Gino.

"Yeah. Yeah, sounds good, baby. Maybe I even fuck her one more time with you having eyes on that," Full-On Crazy said.

"I'm getting wet just thinking about it, daddy," Glory said, wiggling her assets at Gino.

He threw me to the couch and yelled, "Don't fucking move, bitch. Don't you fucking move, or I'll fucking shoot you right between the eyes."

Then with one eye on me and the other on Glory, he pulled a knife out with his free hand. Gino finished cutting away the ties at the back of her hands and her ankles. Glory took a minute to rub the blood back into her limbs, and I noticed she had deep bruises where Gino had tied her with some kind of wire. When she managed to stand, he trained the gun on both of us. Then Gino handed Glory the knife.

"I want you to start by cutting the bitch. Give her a taste of what I got from Gianni because of her lying fucking tongue."

"You know I will, daddy." Glory started unsteadily towards me with the knife in her hand pointing right at me.

As she passed by Gino, she elbowed him hard in the ribs. He grunted and almost went down. While he was doubled over, Glory kneed him in the chest and brought her elbows down hard on his kidneys.

I started forward to help. Before I could make it across the room, Gino had drop-kicked the gun across the room. He had flipped Glory on her back and was holding the knife high over his head. He was ready to plunge it into her throat.

I lunged forward, caught my knee on the side of the coffee table, and went down hard. When I heard the screaming, I wasn't sure if it was coming from Glory or me. I watched helplessly as Gino arched his back and got a strong hold on that knife. I saw him take a deep breath and heard him let out a roar.

Then it was over.

CHAPTER 49

Reno pushed open the door, careful not to make any noise. He heard them the minute he entered the house. A female voice that wasn't Raine's was "oh daddying" someone all over the place. Reno recognized the sound of desperation and whoever this chick was, was fucking desperate. Then he heard the whiny sick pitch of some seriously fucked-up dude.

In the thirty seconds that it took him to round the corner, Reno was hearing grunts and screams. Taking careful aim, he shot three holes in the sick bastard who was straddling the screaming chick and getting ready to thrust a nine-inch in her neck. Raine was on the floor holding her knee and grimacing in pain. The blond chick hadn't moved out from under the sick bastard who was slumped dead over her.

A whoosh came from the side of Reno. He turned just in time to see Claire dart past him and run to her sister. Damn her! Bitch was told to stay in the car. Fucking women. Never fucking listen.

Reno surveyed the scene before him and couldn't fucking believe it.

Couldn't fucking believe it.

He walked over to kick the dead, whiny guy off the blonde. He looked down at her to make sure she wasn't dead too. She wasn't moving. She had been beaten around her face badly, and the one eye that was not swollen shut was looking vacantly up at him. Shock. She was going into shock. Goddammit. *Goddammit.*

He looked over at Raine. She had her head nuzzled into her sister's neck and was cradling her knee in her hands. They were both sitting very still. Claire was whispering something soothingly into Raine's hair and rocking her in her arms. The front of Raine was riddled with splashes of the psycho's fucking brain.

JESUS.

The dead guy had bled all over the place. Pieces of the back of his head were blown apart. Reno had fired three shots from a powerful gun at close range. The house was pretty far away from anything he had seen driving up the hill. But shit, shots like that in a wooded area like this could resound for miles. He needed to get them all the fuck out of here. He also needed to get someone in here to clean up this mess. His prints were on the door handle, and God only knew where else.

And Reno's prints were on file. Definitely on file.

FUCK.

Reno looked at the three women. He had to give it to them. Not one of the women had gone hysterical on him. Of course, the bitch on the floor had definitely gone into full-blown shock by now. She had started shaking like a wet dog. But she had stopped screaming the minute he dropped the guy. Thank God for that.

Reno saw that Raine had left her sister's arms and, favoring her fucked-up knee, had crawled off the couch to grab an old knitted afghan. She had elevated the blonde's feet with pillows. Then she had pressed two fingers against her throat. Now she was covering her with a blanket. Claire had run to get the bitch some water.

"What are the chances that someone's gonna call about those shots?" Reno looked down at Raine.

Raine looked up at him. Jesus, her eyes were so dilated, they were fucking black. Then he looked at Claire. Her hands were shaking so hard that water was spilling out of the top of the damn glass. The three of them were way past being scared. They were terrified and still holding their shit together. Respect. Reno had to give it to them.

"No chance." Raine forced herself to focus on Reno.

"No chance?" Reno repeated.

"None. There's always been shots coming from the woods as long as I've been here. Kids target shooting. Hunting at times when it's in season and not in season. God only knows what else is going on, but no one pays attention. Plus we're miles away from the center of town. The police department has two units. One is always parked at Beth Zaminskies's house. So, yeah. No chance."

Reno nodded. Small-town justice. Either the locals were a big pain in the ass, pissing vigilantism in the guise of carrying out the law, or they were off banging the local widow and not giving a shit. Sounds like Willows Point had the "not giving a shit" kind. First thing that had gone right for him all day.

"Do what you have to do to get her on her feet. We gotta split. I'm gonna make a call. When I'm back we're gone. Feel me?"

Raine nodded.

"Addy?"

Raine stared at him blankly.

Claire spoke up. "Junction Route Three. There's an old lamp-post at the end of the driveway."

Reno nodded to her. Then stared hard at her. Claire looked away quickly.

"Told you to stay in the car, woman," Reno snarled.

Claire looked at him then. Her eyes violet in her dead-white face.

Jesus.

"Gonna leave it for another time, Sugar. But we're having that conversation," Reno said to her more gently than he wanted to.

Damn it all to hell. Claire wasn't at all what he had expected. The little piece was getting to him. He needed to get some air and figure this shit out.

Reno left the women to it and stepped outside to make the call. Sonofabitch! Prosper was going to be pissed. More than that, Reno was pissed at himself. He should not have listened to Raine. Bitch wasn't anything but trouble for him. Nothing but. Jesus, though. He had to hand it to them both. Those two had moved into action with barely a whimper between them. It wasn't lost on Reno that he had left them in there with a dead body. A dead body with two body shots and half his head blown out. A dead body with a nine-inch blade clutched in his hand.

Close range and messy.

Most chicks would have lost their shit. Even the blonde was going into *quiet* hysteria. Maybe it was what they called a delayed reaction. Post-traumatic shit. Gonna be a fun fucking drive home, if that was the case.

Reno had killed before. His hands were steady when he lit his Winston. He took a long pull and felt the sweet nicotine reach his system. He walked to the car and reached into the glove box for the cheap throwaway cell he always kept on hand. He flipped over the phone. The call was answered on the second ring.

"Hey, man. Junction Route Three. Lamppost at the end of the dirt drive. Need clean sweep."

After answering exactly two more questions, Reno was satisfied that things would be taken care of.

Now he had to go back inside and deal with the Powerpuff Girls.

CHAPTER 50

"If there's anything you want, take it now. Only one or two things. We need to be able to fit that shit in the trunk."

Reno braced himself, waiting for the questions and then the tears. The house had to fucking go. No matter how hard you try, there's no way to get rid of blood and bodily fluid shit. Dead men told tales, no doubt about it. And there was no way Reno was doing time over killing that piece of shit Gino. Executive fucking decision. Prosper would understand and if not, the hell with it. He would rather deal with Prosper than with Lady Fucking Injustice any day of the week. So Reno laid down the law and waited.

The three of them were huddled together. They had moved the blonde to the couch and changed her into some pink sweatsuit shit. There was still blood matted in her hair, but they had done their best to clean her up. She was cocooned in the afghan, and Claire was having her take little sips from the glass of water. Some of the color was back in her, but her eyes were scary blank. There was a clear plastic bag filled with bloody clothes sitting on the coffee table. Gino was lying stone-cold dead beside it.

"There's nothing we want here," Claire answered quietly when Raine didn't. Raine nodded in agreement.

"Wasn't this your grandmother's house? Sure there ain't any shit you want to take to remember her by?" Reno thought about

Pinky. How even though she had a lot of nasty memories of that house in Nevada, she had still wanted to take a piece of it with her. God only knew why. Reno wasn't good at figuring women shit out, but there it was.

The two of them just stared at him.

"Look, we're gonna have to torch it," Reno said harshly, making sure they got it.

"We understand that, Reno," Raine said quietly and wrapped her arms around herself tight.

Claire ignored him. She looked at the blonde and gently said, "Honey, we're going to have to leave now. Can you walk if we help you?"

Glory turned her head slowly to look at Claire. It took a while before the words made their way to Glory's dazed mind. Claire gave her that time. Holding Glory's eyes gently with her own, Claire nodded encouragement.

Glory nodded back.

Then Reno said, "Let's get the fuck outta here."

And they did.

CHAPTER 51

The ride back to the compound had been a long one, I guess. Honestly, most of it didn't register. Not for any of us.

Reno chain-smoked the first half hour. And he kept looking at us in the rearview, his eyes sharp, alternately taking in the three of us. The smoke had begun stinging my eyes, despite the fact that Reno had his window open. The cigarette was dangling from the hand he kept outside. When Claire went into a small coughing fit, he immediately dropped the smoke and didn't light up again. He asked us several times if we wanted to stop to "piss or anything."

We didn't.

The blonde. Glory sat rigid and still between Claire and me. Her eyes were blank pools of blue. I knew that look. That look meant one of two things. Either she had gone to a place where she could put aside the horror of what had happened to her until she could deal, or her mind lay imprisoned and shattered. I feared it was the latter. That place where I had once made a brief visit, a place that lay like a barren wasteland on the edge of sanity. A place that once summoned, a mind had little chance of escaping from. I was afraid for Glory.

And I stayed afraid. Afraid until that coughing jag of Claire's split the tense silence with just enough force to jar Glory's mind free. She reached out her hands to both Claire and me. Then she brought them close together to hold them on her lap. Her hands were ice cold and were eventually warmed by the heat of our own. I felt her relax just a fraction, and when I gently squeezed her hand, she squeezed back.

And then there was Claire. Poor Claire. Jesus, not even one day out of rehab and this. THIS. If today's events didn't send my sister headlong into a need for getting baked with some white gutter glitter, nothing would. Nothing.

And it wasn't only the dead guy who posed that threat to Claire's rehabilitative process. It was also the very much alive guy in the front seat. Talk about triggers. With his heavily inked huge biceps, the mirrored shades, the man bun, and the attitude, Reno screamed *beautiful bad boy*.

Screamed it.

Defined it.

Spelled it in capital letters and boldfaced it.

He was all the things Dolores had warned Claire to stay away from. He was all those things, and he was one more. He was the guy who could not seem to manage to keep his eyes off my sister. I met his eyes in the rearview more than once after I saw them skip over us, land, and then settle on Claire. After the last time, I caught his gaze and held it. And damn it all to hell, he did not back down. He not only returned my look, but he held it for so long I was afraid he was going to get us run off the road or worse. When my eyes left him to look down the highway, his did the same. But that stare-off, that silent battle of wills and warnings between us, that he had won.

Of course he had.

Then there was me. I was okay. That's what I told myself. My inner dialogue was a montage of self-affirming thoughts. I was okay, all right, just fine, good. I was good. Rainbows and flowers. Freaking raindrops on roses and whispers on kittens. Whispers? Jesus. I was at a point where I couldn't even quote the lyrics from my happy place old movie. *The Sound of Music* had never failed me before.

I felt a fleeting, but very real moment of complete and utter self-pity. And then I felt the shame of self-indulgence and had the grace to be disappointed in myself. Shit. I had caught the least of it. Glory had been shanghaied and held by Gino the madman for God-only-knew how long, while he plotted and executed his attack on me. And Claire. She did not need this after waging a war against her inner demons and winning that war. So yeah, I was golden compared to these two. I should have been in an all bright-copper-kettles-and-warm-woolen-mittens frame of mind.

Only I wasn't.

I glanced at Claire. She nodded slightly and tried a smile. Then as her eyes traveled the length of me, they widened just a little. Before Claire could hide the look of horror, I saw it. After my sister's eyes grew reassuringly soft on mine, she closed them. Claire rested her head back against the seat and took a deep breath.

I needed a minute. I took a deep breath and said a silent prayer.

I looked down fearfully. And yep, there it was. Multiple sprays of tiny red dots splattered across my shirt and on the skin at the top of my chest laid bare by my tee shirt. And bits of something else. There were bits of something else stuck to the specks of blood.

Holy Christ, did I have Gino's brain matter splattered on me?

Holy fuck. I fought down the urge to vomit and fought even harder the urge to scream.

Because I was not going to be the one to lose it.

That was not going to be me. Nah-uh.

I would not be the one to succumb to the gut-wrenching fear and nausea. Gino was the one who had spread that shit. He had spread that fear and that pain to these brave women. These women who had put on gloves and knocked the fuck out of the fear that Gino had rained on them.

So dead or not, Gino could still go fuck himself.

I felt Glory's head fall lightly to my shoulder and her hand give mine the lightest of squeezes. I laid my dark head on her blond one. Claire's head moved to Glory's shoulder. There we sat on that long ride home, drawing quiet strength from each other.

CHAPTER 52

I'm gonna fuckin' kill you!" Prosper had Reno up against the wall, his forearm a stranglehold on his neck.

Reno was starting to turn blue but made not one move to defend himself.

Then with another roar, Prosper grabbed him by his cut and threw him straight across the room. Straight across it. Reno felt himself flying and landed with a thump against the back wall.

"Get up! Get up you irresponsible, inept piece of shit!"

Reno got up.

Prosper was on him again.

BAM. Reno's head snapped back with the power of the punch. Then another vicious blow to his rib cage sent him right to his knees. Then another and another. Then an uppercut to the jaw.

Reno, moaning, made an attempt to get back up. He deserved the smackdown and was doing his best not to blow lunch.

"Stay down." Prosper had his foot on Reno's neck.

"Stay the FUCK down, Reno!" Prosper roared the warning. Damn it all to hell, his hand was killing him. He was gonna have to ice those knuckles. Another reason to want to kill Reno. Prosper hadn't been this fucking-insanely-crazy-mad since Jack Winston had left his girls alone. Twenty fucking years of holding his temper was fucking long enough.

"I fucking give you an order, you fucking obey that order! Maybe, just maybe, it avoids people getting killed! You hear me? YOU STU-PID MOTHERFUCKING IDIOT!"

Reno groaned from his place on the floor, "I hear ya, Boss. This shit's on me. All on me. I'm sorry, man. I really am."

Prosper looked at Reno. He rubbed the back of his neck hard with his hand and felt the sting of his knuckles beginning to swell. The kid had taken the beating like the man Prosper knew him to be. Came back to the MC. Told it straight, took full responsibility, and manned up for the smackdown.

His fucking fuck-up had almost cost all of their lives. Christ All Mighty. Dolly and Pinky would have gone out of their goddamn minds. Anything happen to that boy, might as well bury Dolly with him. Prosper loved Reno. Loved him like a son. Damn it. His girls, his son, he almost lost them all today because Reno decided to take a damn nap. Jesus. This father stuff was gonna be the death of him. If Prosper had lost any of them, he would have put a bullet to his own head.

Smackdown over. What's done was done. At least Reno had the brains to clean up the mess. That was something. And when it came down to it, he had driven three dazed and fucking traumatized women six hours in a car, all of them holding their shit together. All of them safe. There was that.

Prosper slapped Reno on the back and pulled him hard towards him. "Son, you and your sisters are gonna be the goddamn mother-fucking death of me."

~

Reno felt something inside him bleed open. Reno had always loved Prosper like that. Always. But he never knew for sure that Prosper felt the same way. Jesus, it felt good knowing it. He would have gone through a thousand smackdowns to hear Prosper say it.

His sisters? Well, Raine had kept her shit totally together all the way back to the MC with not one word of complaint. No hysterical bullshit from any of them. Bitches hadn't even asked to stop to pee, but Reno had offered. Little sister, Claire. Fucking beauty that one was. Looked just like her sister, but had this quiet about her that Reno liked to be around and for sure wanted to explore.

No, he definitely wasn't feeling brotherly towards Claire. He wondered how Prosper would take it. Reno going there, if and when that time came. Well. He sighed. He would cross the fucking bridge when he came to it. For now, he was gonna get fall-down, full-on, shit-faced drunk with his father.

CHAPTER 53

It had taken us four weeks to get on the other side of what the girls and I had come to refer to as *the event*.

It had been an uphill battle. But together, Glory, Claire, and I were making that climb. From some of my clinical work in nursing, I had learned all about the diagnosis, symptoms, and treatment of post-traumatic stress. I had learned the difference between the mind's normal response to traumatic events and when those responses become PTSD.

Post-traumatic stress disorder occurs when the victims of the traumatic events cannot get to the other side of it. When a poor soul does not get a little better every day, but gets a little worse and gets stuck in the horrible, terrible place of the traumatic event.

That was not us.

Thank God that was not us.

We were getting to the other side of it.

We were.

We definitely were.

All three of us.

Sure, we had the nightmares. We felt shattered and disconnected at times. There were periods when each of us still relived that horror in our minds until it numbed us.

But we were crawling out of it.

We had been through some shit, my girls and me. *The event* was proving to be a hard place to come back from, especially for Glory. Glory had suffered longer and more severely than we had guessed. Even a month later, we were still learning about the abduction and what she had suffered at Gino's hands.

But each day the memories were met headlong and then pushed aside. We did that for each other. Even if it meant being hypervigilant and stopping everything when those memories surfaced and fighting them together. We had that.

Our feelings of safety and trust had been shattered. The trauma we had experienced from seeing Gino killed in front of us hadn't left us. Seeing death close up like that changes you. You either find a place to reconcile and live with that change, or you relive and relive and relive the trauma in your mind until it kills the spirit.

Because my girls and I were survivors, we chose life. And we had to make that choice every day.

One step at a time.

And we hadn't done it alone. We had been surrounded by love and support. We had been made to feel safe.

When we had pulled up in front of the compound that night, Prosper had been waiting for us. It had been late and eerily quiet. No fire, no music, no shadow people tying one on in the fields. But the light had been on and Prosper had been in the driveway. He had opened the back door before we had come to a full stop, pulled me out of the car, held me tight and then looked me over from head to toe. His face dark and unreadable. Then he turned to Claire and did the same. He held her a long time and she wept into his neck.

Jules had come up behind me and pulled me against him hard. His big arms wrapped around my shoulders. My back up against his chest. Glory was still in the car, wrapped in Grandma's afghan. I gave Jules a tight squeeze back, freed myself, and moved to the car. Jules moved with me. When Glory saw him her eyes went wide, and she shrank into the back seat. I turned to look at Jules through her eyes, and I saw what she saw. A giant. A big blond warrior with sharp eyes and a grim, hard mouth. Assessing her, staring right back at her with shards of blue ice. I knew that look. I had been the recipient of that look, and it had scared the shit out of me then. *Now,* I knew it was the look of a trained Marine medic assessing for damage. *Then,* I had thought it was the look of a seriously pissed-off badass who might kill me.

I placed my hand gently on Jules's arm and said softly to Glory, "Honey, this is Jules. He is a friend of mine. A good friend and a good man. He has some medical training. If you want he can look at you and help you."

"Help me?" Glory croaked. Her voice cracked. And she licked her lips trying for moisture.

"When was the last time she had something to drink?" Jules said to me, his eyes on Glory.

"A few sips here and there. I was afraid to give her too much. Her pulse has been rapid and she's been sweating, then she gets the chills," I told him.

"Raine, get on the other side of the car so she can see you." Jules was leaning into the car, filling the space between the dark night and a barely holding-on Glory.

I ran to the other side and leaned into the car so Glory could see me.

"I'm right here, sweetheart," I whispered to her.

She turned her blank stare to me. Her hair was matted with blood and the side of her face where her hair had been pulled out was black and blue. Her one eye seemed even more swollen than before. The fist that had delivered that blow had been a strong one. I knew that fist. My heart bled for her.

"Honey, I am going to reach in and take your pulse. Is that okay with you?" Jules was saying softly.

Glory's eyes were on me—well, the one that was not swollen shut was, anyway. When I nodded, she turned to Jules and nodded too.

"That's good, honey." Jules reached for her limp hand and held it in his.

"Can you tell me your name?" Jules asked softly.

"Glory," she squeaked out.

"Glory, do you know what day it is?"

Glory's eyes filled with tears. She thought for a minute.

"He took me on Wednesday. I don't know. I don't know . . ." Her voice trailed off.

Jules's eyes grew hard for a moment, but he hid it. For Glory's sake, he hid it.

"Glory, honey, look at me." And she did.

Jules had a penlight in his hand and was looking at Glory's one open eye.

"That's good, sweetheart."

But Glory had retreated back to her safe place.

Jules brought his big body fully into the car then. He kept a light hold of her wrist and felt her heart race.

"Glory, baby, stay with me." He squeezed her hand lightly, and Glory made the effort to refocus.

"We need to get some fluids in you, and I want to give you something that will help you to relax. Will you let me do that for you?" Jules had moved closer to Glory and was kneeling on the seat beside her.

Glory seemed to be mesmerized by the soft voice and the close warmth of the big man next to her. Still, she turned to me again. Again I nodded to her.

"Okay," she whispered to him.

"Okay," Jules whispered back.

He helped her out of the car. When her legs buckled under her, he took her into his arms and carried her to the kitchen house.

The distant roar of something oncoming and fast was sounding up the road. I knew that sound. I wanted to run to that sound and keep running until the source of that sound enveloped me and covered me in the pure joy of it. I wanted to drown in that sound.

The roar grew louder and louder until it was upon me. Until that roar zoomed up the long drive and shattered the black of the night sky with light. Until that roar stopped two feet away from me, and he got off his bike, and wrapped me in his arms so tight I almost stopped breathing. I felt the warmth and safety of a love so deep that I knew if I let myself feel it and I lost it, it would shatter me. But tonight, I let myself take that risk. Tonight I laid myself bare and basked in the warmth of his arms and the strong beat of his heart. Tonight I opened to this man.

Diego held me close to him high off the ground as if he were trying to keep me away from anything except his touch. The minute my foot lightly hit the ground, I went down. Hard. I heard something pop and a blinding pain followed. I passed out in Diego's arms.

I woke to more blinding pain. Jules was standing over me and holding a leather strap in his hand. What was this? My mind could not wrap itself around it fast enough, and I opened my mouth to scream. Diego clamped his hand over my mouth and was saying something that I guessed was meant to be reassuring. I saw his face come into sharp focus above me. Past him, I saw the inky night filled with thousands of stars. He was saying something about my kneecap, and he used the word *dislocated*. Then he said something about *Jules* and *putting it back in place* and *biting down*. And *pain, just for an instant*. And *did I understand?*

He put a leather belt in my mouth between my teeth and told me to bite down hard. As I did, I felt something excruciating happen in my knee. The stars went out of the sky and I lost the night. I was out cold. Again.

Diego picked me up and brought me inside, and he didn't let me go. Not that night or the next day or the night after that.

Jules had given me some welcomed painkillers and a light sedative to help me sleep. My head hurt where that bastard Gino had dragged me by the hair, and I could not put weight on my knee. I was worried about Claire and Glory.

After he whisked me away to Prosper's rooms at the kitchen house, Diego had let no one but him near me. Claire had forced her way past the sentry once to assure herself that Diego didn't have me in some weird hostage situation. She was looking exhausted, and I know that she wasn't sleeping because she told me. Pinky and Prosper were keeping her at their house for the time being. She gave Diego a dirty look when he told her he "wanted Raine to rest now." She left, but not before she told him he had one more day of this protective bullshit. Then she was either coming to get me or bringing me to a real doctor to look at that knee. My little sister had some sass.

The third morning, Claire and I met for breakfast. I watched her for signs of drug use, and she watched me for signs of broken bones and concussion. After about fifteen minutes of that, we ate in relative comfortable silence. As was the case in the mornings, the brothers were off and it was quiet. Jules made us something light and we ate about a quarter of whatever it was. Neither one of us paid much attention to the food. But the coffee, that was heaven. We both refilled our cups of coffee, then went outside to sit in the sun and drink them.

We talked softly and for a long time. We speculated about Glory and her past. We wondered if there was someone we should be calling. Jules had her in the compound clinic, which was the infirmary for club members. Not *kind of* like, *was*, I corrected myself. He had everything in there. Syringes, vials, a defibrillator, a setup for IVs and the fluid to hang. He had crutches and slings and antibiotic ointments. He had three locked cabinets and two locked apartment-sized refrigerators. The place was amazing, and the club had begun to add on a small wing to it. I knew Jules had been a medic, but that didn't give him access to the stuff he had. Not by a long shot. For maybe the thousandth time I speculated about Jules, but this time I didn't have to speculate alone. Claire had some theories of her own about the Viking.

Claire had peeked in on Glory, just like she had on me. But every time she had done so, Glory had been asleep. She and I were going to try again today. I was still woozy from the painkillers and sleeping pills. Conversely, Claire was wired. She shared with me that she was afraid to take anything to ease her because she was desperately afraid of a drug relapse. So she was up most nights afraid of nightmares. My sweet sister told me that she replayed that awful feeling again in her mind when she realized that I hadn't come out of that damn house.

We didn't talk about seeing the back of Gino's head blow off. I couldn't think about that. I couldn't think about the bits of gray matter I felt crawling all over me sometimes when my world was still. Claire looked like hell. She hadn't slept at all in the past two days. Not closed her eyes once. I could see the dark smudges under her eyes and the hypervigilance on her face when she took in her surroundings. This was not good.

That's when I knew I had to get my shit together and help Claire work past this. While I had slept on peacefully in a drug-induced safe state in my man's arms, I had left Claire out there. Again. I had better compose myself and fast. No more painkillers or sleeping pills for me. My knee was feeling better, and if I couldn't sleep I would make myself some warm milk.

Diego was in my bed every night. Really nice. It was really nice. I had to be careful of my knee because in certain positions it hurt like hell. But I didn't want to sleep alone, and Diego hadn't wanted me to. So that first night we spent some time getting comfortable.

To keep the pressure off my back (which was still sore from being dragged across the floor), I settled on my side with my knee elevated by a pillow placed between it and the mattress. My knee was comfortable, but I wanted the warm assurance of Diego's body so I tried to wiggle in closer to him. He wrapped his steel arm around and whispered tightly against my hair.

"Babe, you got about half a second to stop pushing your ass against my dick. Then I'm gonna throw you on your back and bury myself deep in you, fucked-up knee or not. I really don't want to hurt you, Babe, but you gotta stop." Then he pulled his crotch away from me but held on with his arms tight.

Three days after we returned he had left me. He left on club business right after the sun came up. He kissed me hard and whispered that he would be back later.

I felt an emptiness that I did not want to feel when I woke up hours later to find him gone.

Claire and I continued getting better and so did Glory. She had been in pretty bad shape, and there was a lot she wasn't ready to talk about. A lot. And she looked bad. Her eye, when she could finally begin opening it, had been shot through with bloody lines. Her hair hadn't been pulled out in clumps like I had originally thought. That bastard Gino had taken a knife to her and had systematically hacked it off. About a week into her convalescence, Dolly and Pinky had come callin' on Glory. Dolly had a rolling suitcase with her that was filled with airbrush cosmetics and a variety of haircutting scissors, curling irons, straighteners, and other tools of a cosmetologist's trade.

Glory looked wary at the thought of anyone coming at her with scissors, so Claire and I volunteered. We each had our hair trimmed and layered and blow-dried. Dolly applied makeup to us expertly. It had been a really fun afternoon. Glory hadn't felt ready to leave the sanctum of the infirmary to meet the dynamic duo that was Pinky and Dolly, so they came to her. Glory's voice was still raspy from the strain of screaming in the days Gino had kept her imprisoned. She wasn't talking much, but she was smiling. And once she actually giggled at something that Pinky said about Dolly's choice of bright blue eye shadow back in the day.

Pinky and Dolly visited Glory with us every afternoon after that. Glory didn't say much. When we asked her if there was anyone we should call, she shook her head sadly.

Glory was a mystery that Claire, Pinky, Dolly, and I ruminated over, and not just a little bit. She was a beauty in the classic sense. Even in her battered state, Glory looked out of place at the MC. Glory had the silky blond hair, peaches-and-cream complexion, and pale blue eyes of a Ralph Lauren model. She reminded me of the photos I had seen of the ill-fated wife of John Kennedy, Jr. Her beauty was classic. We were all dying to know her story. But she contributed very little to any conversation that seemed to turn personal, and believe me, we shamelessly tried to steer that conversation towards the personal every chance we got.

Pondering the mystery that was Glory served to keep my mind occupied. It gave me something to think about. It was something I could call up like a talisman to steer my mind from the image of the back of Gino's head coming apart and landing in bits and pieces onto my bare skin.

Eventually things started to feel better. With the help of Diego's loving arms around me all night long, it was easier for me to face the day. He chased all my demons away and I loved him for that. *Loved him for that.* This could not be good for me on so many levels. I knew I would be taking a big chance if I gambled at love with a man like Diego. But I was beginning to think he might be worth that risk. I wanted to believe he was worth the risk. I wanted him. This man. This rough, tough, flawed, outlaw of a man. I wanted to be his woman.

The first few days after *the event*, he had been so worried and loving and attentive. And the attentive part was the best because we had talked. I was pretty sedated, but in that place between sleeping and awake, we had each other. We started off slowly, tentatively, but then we seemed to move along at a warp-speed rate.

Once those gates opened for me, I just didn't stop. I told Diego things that I had never shared with anyone, some of them not even with Claire. I told him about how hard I had worked to get into nursing school, and how one sad case then another then another had broken my heart. He got very quiet then and listened hard. At one point, the pain etched over his face was so deep I thought it might crack him in half, so I veered away from that subject quickly. I thought he was feeling that for me, that he didn't want me to relive those days of witnessing the interminable sadness of it all.

So because I was too self-involved, I didn't ask him about it. I didn't prod or question or gently lead him to full disclosure. I didn't ask and I should have. I really, really should have. Maybe it would have made a difference. Maybe not. But I wish I had asked.

Diego shared too. Not all of his story, not the whole of it. Not even the most important parts of it. But he shared. He told me that he had first patched in with the Nevada Chapter near Pinky's house, which is why he had known the brothers up there. He told me some funny stories about Prosper and Pinky's wedding day. I probably enjoyed it more than I should have when Diego told me about the hazing they had put Reno through before patching him in.

But it wasn't all about the MC.

Diego told me about places he had visited and places he still wanted to see. He talked about how much he loved being on the open road and his first bike. He said he missed the hot, dry heat of the desert and told me about a trip he took once through Mojave National Preserve.

I told him about my obsessive love of maps and all things geographical. How I had gotten a world globe one year for Christmas and had studied it and researched each country one by one until I could name all the countries in Africa and Asia.

Including their capitals.

In alphabetical order.

Then I named them for him. Diego smiled at that and just shook his head.

In between that place of sleeping and waking, when everyone else was dreaming, Diego and I became more than lovers. We became friends.

CHAPTER 54

Moving day. We were moving in to the mostly finished lake house.

While Claire, Glory, and I had spent the last few weeks recuperating, recovering, and regrouping, the brothers had been renovating. They had been clearing out and hammering and nailing and reinforcing and cutting and drilling and notching.

And they were good at it.

Glory had decided to stay. We still knew nothing about her. She never shared. She never slipped after a third glass of wine. She never blurted out a name or a place when she had her guard down. Maybe her guard was never down. I didn't know. I don't even know if she ever really even made a conscious decision or just rolled with it. There was no discussion. And on our part, we never questioned, we never asked, we never made it hard for her or uncomfortable for her to be with us.

So she just stayed.

Just her, with us.

With only the clothes on her back. She just stayed.

Like a whisper in the wind, sometimes she was barely there. Her voice hadn't completely come back yet and maybe never would. The raspy tone of it belied the pedigree that her light complexion and pale blue eyes spoke to. She had beautiful bone structure, and her new pixie cut showed it off even more. She was a beauty, our Glory. We were learning that her spirit was as lovely as her looks.

But Glory could also get down and dirty if she needed to. Like the way she stepped up to Gino and "oh daddied" him literally to death. Where that came from in her, God only knew. I looked up at her as I was handing her some painting tape and I wondered for the millionth time how she had ended up with Gino. But then again, she probably wondered the exact same thing about me.

We had each picked out a bedroom. The house had been fully furnished, but we still needed fresh bedding and some other stuff. Since none of us had felt like venturing out yet, we bought what we needed on the Internet and had it all shipped. The porch was filled with a litter of boxes from Amazon, Crate and Barrel, and several linen stores.

I felt someone grab me from behind and lift me off my feet.

"Babe." Diego was nuzzling my hair.

He turned me around in his arms, put his big hands on either side of my face, and laid one on me. God, I loved his kisses. But, Jesus, in front of everybody?

I laughed and tried to push him back, blushing.

"Going pink on me, Babe, is not gonna stop me. Makes me hard." He grinned against my ear.

He draped his hand around my shoulder and called out to Reno, who was on a ladder hammering.

"Gonna take Raine outta here for a bit. You got this?" It was not a question.

"No problem, Brother. Where ya going?" Reno whacked at a nail.

"Threw some sandwiches and shit together. Nice day. Thought we'd take the bike out an' stop somewhere to eat 'em."

"Yeah?" Reno was talking around some nails he had placed in his mouth as he hammered. "Go take your woman out on your damn picnic. I'll be sweating my balls off in here." He grinned.

"Ain't no fucking picnic, Brother. I don't do picnics," Diego grumbled.

"You got food. You got drinks. You taking that shit on the road." Reno was still hammering.

"Yeah, so what? We get off the bike, we grab some chow and eat it." Diego was frowning.

"You taking a blanket?" Reno hadn't broken his hammering stride.

"You got to have some shit to sit on," Diego explained.

"Then it's a fucking picnic, man." Reno still hammering.

"Ain't going on a fucking picnic; I don't do fucking picnics." Diego was looking wary.

"Hey, Ma," Reno called for Dolly.

"Yeah?" Dolly answered from the other room where she was hanging curtains.

"Diego's taking Raine out on the bike. He packed some food and shit. Is that what you call a picnic?"

"Is he taking a blanket?" Dolly yelled from the other room.

Reno stopped hammering and raised his eyebrows. Diego ran his hand through his hair.

"Fuck me," he said under his breath.

"You tell anybody about this shit, I am gonna kill you, Reno. You feel me?"

"Secret's safe with me." Reno was grinning wide open.

Diego grabbed my hand and said, "Come on, Babe. Let's go on a fucking picnic."

I laughed all the way to the bike.

CHAPTER 55

It was another perfect summer day. We rode under an indigo sky dotted with big, white, frothy clouds suspended in amazingly beautiful formations. The wind whipped through my hair, and I had my arms wrapped around my man. Tight.

After a while we pulled into a wooded area. There was a heavy chain across the dirt road and a sign that said "No trespassing." Diego pulled up next to it and reached in his pocket. He produced a key to the huge, heavy lock attached to the bulky chain.

I raised my eyebrows at him.

"My land, Babe," he said as explanation.

The road continued for about a quarter mile then turned into a path. After we had cleared the gate, the path pretty much was a slow and steady incline with a wooded area all around. After a short while we broke into a large clearing. It was beautiful. The land sat on the edge of a rolling hill in a pretty grassy knoll.

I just stood for a minute and took in all the wonder. On the edge of the natural clearing, someone had begun taking down trees. There was a chainsaw case and a felling ax sitting on a pile of freshly chopped wood. The smell of the timber joined with the pitchy smell of sticky pine trees. I could hear the rushing of water coming from somewhere. There was a flurry of startled birds fleeing from the trees.

I turned to Diego. He was pulling the blanket out from the bike.

"It's beautiful," I said to him.

"*You're* beautiful," he said to me.

Then he grabbed me by the hand and we walked in silence for a little while. I was in awe, taking in all the natural beauty and wondering again at this man beside me.

He stopped by a stream that was flowing fast with cold, clear water dancing over smooth river rock.

He spread out the blanket and turned to me. He began to pull my shirt over my head. Suddenly Diego was all hands and mouth.

Broad daylight and he wanted me naked.

He had never seen me buck naked in the blinding light of day. *Blinding light of day.*

I stood in front of him with my nipples pushing up past my demicup bra that was just a little too small for my semilarge breasts, but it was frothy white lace and I had loved it. Then I covered them.

"Diego . . ." I began.

"Babe, you gotta stop this shy shit with me. You're mine. I've been in you, had my mouth on you. I have tasted every single square inch of your beautiful fucking tits. I know what your ass looks like better than you do. I know that you have three freckles on the back of your left knee and I know that after I finger fuck you, it takes exactly five times of pulling on your clit with my mouth to make you cum. Then you spasm so hard all that sweetness sucks my tongue right in."

"Five times?" I croaked.

"Exactly." He held my gaze. "Now get your beautiful hands off those big tits that you know I love and come here." He stepped into me.

He stood before me and pulled his shirt at the back of the neck to yank it off. I never ever got tired of looking at his body. Diego seeing me in the bright light of day meant that I got to see him too. I drank him in. The way the muscles danced under his skin when he moved. The scars, the large intricate cross tattooed on his chest, the way his hip bones made a V pointing to the area of my greatest pleasure.

I took my hands away, reached back, and unhooked my bra. My breasts fell heavy against me, and Diego reached in and kneaded them with his beautiful, rough hands.

"Pretty bra, Babe. But you're not wearing that shit with me. I want easy access to your tits. I want to feel them soft against me when you're on the back of my bike. I want to be able to reach over and pull your shirt up and look at them. Lick them and touch them whenever I want. I want to be able to lay my hand on your skin and feel your heart beat."

How could you argue with that?

I reached down and unzipped him. I yanked off his jeans and boxers until they were a pool around his ankles. Then I did the same to myself.

And there we stood. Facing each other in the beautiful brilliant light of day. He dropped me to the blanket and when his body moved to cover mine, I flipped him on his back. He went down with a surprised grunt, and I smiled at him. Then I proceeded to cover every inch of his chest with my lips, my tongue, and my mouth. I licked and sucked and kissed him until his nipples were puckered and his cock was rock hard. Then I straddled him and grinded into him.

Totally uninhibited, I pushed away all thoughts of shyness or risk or fear. It was just him and me and sunshine and light and the perfect sound of clear, fresh, swiftly running water. I arched my back as I built. I felt myself tighten around him and moved faster. His hands on my hips guided me, pulling me back and forth and tighter to him. I pulled back just a little only to tunnel him deeper inside me. I did that again and again, feeling that sweet tension build. I loved feeling Diego's thighs rise on my ass and his muscles grow tighter. When I could not hold back any longer, I rose one more time and settled hard on his cock, stretching my body. I took all of him inside me then. I arched my back and raised my outstretched arms in welcome to the sun. The sky and the clouds and the love came radiating down from the heavens and fell in the space between us. And I gave thanks.

We lay totally naked in the warm sunshine wrapped up in each other. Diego was lying on his side with his legs draped over mine. He had one arm wrapped around my waist and the other cradled my head. I was still throbbing from the thrill of having him inside me.

Diego had stopped using protection right after the Ellie thing. He had gone for a blood test to make sure she hadn't "left him with any of her shit" and he had gotten the report he was clean. I hadn't asked him to do it but was glad he had. I had been on the pill and continued to be on it so we were protected. It was something I was pretty religious about. I may have forgotten a couple of days in between the chaos when the Gino stuff went down, but we weren't really active then anyway.

Diego was a little obsessive about making sure I took it. So obsessive that it kind of hurt my feelings a little bit. I guessed he just didn't think I was mother material or didn't want any kids with me. Or maybe any kids period. Or maybe any permanent me period.

And I went on like that sometimes.

Because honestly, my biological clock was beginning to tick. I was going to be twenty-nine my next birthday. I sometimes looked at mothers with babies, and I thought I would like that. But I wasn't sure Diego was the right baby daddy for that.

Actually, I would probably be crazy to think he would be the right baby daddy for that. He was a Hells Saint through and through. No denying that. He was an outlaw man. I knew that the things he did for the club were not legal or lawful or even moral. I grew up with two hidden loaded guns in my house for Christ's sake and my dad hadn't even been patched in. But I also knew that Diego was a good man in the way Prosper was a good man. Loyal, dedicated, raw, and flawed. After the Ellie thing, Diego only had eyes for me. He never came to me smelling of another woman, and he never came to me drunk or with a raised fist. Yet. Not yet. Time would tell.

So I took my birth control pills, and we fucked like rabbits and all was well. Until it wasn't.

CHAPTER 56

You're a fucking nurse! How fucking stupid can you be, Raine?"
He made a fist and slammed it hard, right through the sheetrock over my head.

Diego was breaking my heart. And he had been breaking it for the last twenty minutes.

Breaking my heart into tiny irreplaceable pieces. Humpty Dumpty and his great fall didn't have a thing on me. Nothing. All the king's horses and all the king's men stood not a chance at ever putting what was broken in me together again.

Me and Humpty. We were fucked.

He was still yelling at me. How could he still be yelling at me? Couldn't he see he was shredding me apart?

"You do this. You do this alone. I want no part of it. Nothing! You don't put my name on the fucking birth certificate. You don't send me fucking birthday pictures. I got nothing to give, want nothing in return. You Goddamn stupid little girl! How the fuck did you think this was gonna play out, Raine? You think we gonna buy a fucking minivan and get a house in the suburbs?"

I pulled myself so far in he started fading away. I stopped hearing him.

"Oh no, you fucking don't. You do not do that, Raine. You look at me and you listen and you listen good. You do not hide from this."

And he grabbed my chin and pulled me hard to meet his eyes. He was hurting me. I tried to focus. Tried to come back from that place because if I did, if I let him punish me enough, maybe he would go away, and I would never ever have to see the bastard again.

Yeah. I was back. Damn right, I was back.

I pulled my chin out of his hand and gave him what he wanted.

And because the screaming and yelling of his repetitive bullshit wasn't enough for the past half hour, he felt he had to say it one more time. I guess he must have been thinking that if I was stupid enough to get myself knocked up, I wasn't smart enough to understand the fact that he wanted out the *first five goddamn times he said it.*

"We are done. This is over. There is no hope for that fucking picket-fence-and-happy-family bullshit. It ain't gonna happen. Not with me! So you decide to do this, you do this alone. Doctor visits, that ultrasound shit, fucking childbirth classes. That guy ain't me. That guy ain't fucking me. You do this, you do it without me."

"You said that, Diego." I hated him.

"Yeah, I said it! I said a lot of things. Like 'Did you fucking remember to take your pills?' How many fucking times do you think I said that, Raine?"

"I did take them, you stupid jackass. How many times do I have to tell you? I TOOK THEM."

Glaring at him, I continued.

"Except for when I got a little messed up after the Gino thing. I was down for those few days. But we weren't doing it then. And you knew I didn't take them because you were with me every damn minute for three days."

I was exasperated and exhausted and heartsick and done. So the rest of it I said with a sense of resignation that I absolutely totally felt.

"Maybe it was the meds that Jules gave me. Maybe the stuff he gave me interacted with the pill. But I get it. My fault. My fuckup. You don't want a kid. You don't want a *pregnant me.* No name on the birth certificate. No birthday pictures. No happily-ever-after. I get it, Diego. I do this, I do this on my own. And the fact that you felt you had to say it *five* different times in *two* different languages helped me to get that you are pretty clear on that. So me and this baby. *My* baby. We are on our own."

I slumped against the wall. I was feeling dizzy. My vision blurred as I heard the sound of my own heart breaking. It was a clean, jagged sound, like the crackling of ice. I was afraid that when it stopped, I would fall straight through and drown in the sadness of it.

Or not.

I took a deep breath and I forced myself back.

And being back meant that I would not fall apart in front of him.

Oh no, I wouldn't. Not me. Not this time. Not now. Not in front of him. I would not give him that.

I caught my breath and pulled away from the door. I drew myself up to my full height. Instinctively putting my hands across a baby bump that was not there yet, I found the strength to go on.

"Now let *me* be clear. After tonight, you saying the things you said, and you throwing those words at me not once, not twice but over and over again . . . you backing me up against a wall, raising your fist and punching a hole in it just inches above my head two minutes after I tell you I am carrying your baby . . . those things, those words . . . *I will never ever forgive you for them. Ever.* You ever regret them, you crippled, you blind, you in a damn fucking old folks' home and you think about the kid you threw away, *you never, ever, ever* come knocking on our door. As of right now and for the rest of my life. No matter what. *No matter what.* You do not exist for me. So put your mind at ease, Diego, about this baby, about me, and about anything that has to do with us.

"Now get the fuck out of my house!" I walked to the door and threw it open.

He looked at me for a full minute. Eyes burning, nostrils flared.

"GET OUT," I screamed. "GET OUT. GET OUT. GET OUT!"

Diego turned from me then. He punched another hole through another wall. Then he got out.

Just as Diego was walking out, Claire and Glory walked in.

Claire rushed over to me, and Glory took a long hard, look at the massive holes in the walls.

"Well, I see that went well." Glory had her hands on her hips.

"Fucker." Claire took my hand in hers.

"Motherfucker," Glory agreed and flanked me on the other side.

"Motherfucking sonofabitch," I added, not to be outdone.

I almost started to cry. Almost. But I just couldn't bring myself to do it. As horrible and unexpected and as heartbreaking that scene with Diego had been, I *didn't want* to cry.

Because after years of watching for secrets, I had a secret of my own. And that secret came from a good place. That secret came from the best place of all. That secret was nestled within me, under my heart and deep in my core.

I was going to have a baby.

CHAPTER 57

Prosper woke to the sound of someone banging hard on his front door. He rolled away from Pinky and reached for the piece that he kept loaded on the bedside stand. Pinky got up quietly, threw on her robe, and stood beside her man.

Prosper had the gun out as a precaution. If someone had meant them harm they would not have come banging at the door. They would have shot out windows or crept in. Prosper would have woken up with a knife at his throat or not woken up at all.

No, this had to be a brother. It had happened before. Prosper's house was off-limits. He had made that clear long ago. Pinky's rule and he stood by it. Pinky had wanted Prosper to have a sanctuary. She had worked hard to make a home for him away from the brothers. In Pinky's eyes, the clubhouse was a Sodom and Gomorrah. A place of unrepentant sin.

She was not wrong.

Anything went and no one gave a shit. The drinking, the whores, the drugs, the guns, the sex, the bare-knuckled fights between brothers just for the hell of it. It was part of the life her man chose and a part of the life they led. But not all of it and not all the time.

So the house was out of bounds. Off-limits. Except for the most serious of shit storms, no one came to the house. That house sat on the side of a line that was not to be crossed. Crossing that line, knocking at that door, meant involvement. Heavy involvement in some deep personal shit. Knocking on that door meant that you were so up in your personal, that it was going to affect the club and you needed someone to know it. You needed help with that shit before it went to the table. Before it hit the brothers.

Knocking at that door any time of day meant counsel. That meant discussion, deliberation, advice, and help.

Knocking at that door in the middle of the night. That meant trouble.

Prosper moved to the door and pulled aside the curtain with the tip of his nine. Whoever was out there would see that he was holding. He was hoping with all his heart that it wouldn't be Diego at that door. Diego being at that door could not be good for Raine. Prosper had really been hoping that the happy the two of them seemed to be knee-deep in would last a while. God knew they both deserved it.

He sighed and placed his piece on the sideboard. He turned to Pinky, but she was already headed towards the kitchen to make a strong pot of coffee.

Diego stood under the glare of the porch light, leaning heavily on the cedar shingles. A light drizzle had begun to fall and the white tee shirt he was wearing was sticking to his skin in the places that weren't covered by his cut.

His cut.

With its worn leather patina, large broken-winged angel, and the rockers that circled it, the cut was Diego's talisman. The symbol of a brotherhood of men. The crest of his family. The family who had pulled a twelve-gauge out of Diego's mouth and knocked the fucking shit out of him for trying to blow his brains out.

These brothers were not them. Nevada had been Diego's home then. Twenty years ago when he was just nineteen and had been patched into the band of brothers.

A year later he had been married with a baby on the way.

He had buried them together. His beautiful young wife, the love of his life, and the child they had made together, forever in eternity. The tiny boy lying on his mother's chest. He had seen to all the arrangements. He had picked out the casket and the flowers. He had designed the headstone. The only thing that had been left was for him to join them. The day after he laid them to rest, he leaned against the gravestone of his wife and infant son with a shotgun shoved hard to the roof of his mouth. His finger on the trigger.

Her name had been Janey and Diego had loved her since they were both fourteen years old. Janey, who lived on the outskirts of the shit ghost town he grew up in and who was the one person Diego would turn to when things got bad. Janey, who never ever refused him, had opened her legs and her heart to him and had never asked for a damn thing in return except for him to love her back. Janey, who had left a rich bastard of a father to run off with him when they were both eighteen. Janey, who understood why he needed the club and stood by him when he made the decision to patch in. Janey, who never looked at him as anything less than a God-given gift to her. God how he had loved her.

For him, it had always been Janey.

And for Janey, it had always been him.

The day Diego married her was the happiest day of both their lives. They were young, but they were ready and excited to start their lives together. When she got pregnant a month later, that was cool, too. They were madly in love. Finally free to be together, to live the life they had planned. Diego was patched in and deep into the club by then. Janey liked being an old lady and fit right in. Life was good.

The pregnancy had gone well. Right up to the very end, things were great. Until Janey was six days past her due date. During the ultrasound, they couldn't find a heartbeat. When they induced her, they found out that the baby, Diego's son, had died in her womb. Janey had been forced to give birth to a stillborn baby.

Five hours later, Diego's wife stopped breathing. Her heart stopped beating and she died.

Janey, his beautiful wife and the mother of his baby boy, was nineteen years old and dead.

The doctors told him that she had died of a rare condition called amniotic fluid embolism. Something had caused the fluid from the baby to travel into her lungs and trigger a heart attack.

But Diego had known the truth. After holding their tiny dead baby in her arms, their perfect eight-pound boy, Janey had died of a broken heart. And Diego had wanted to follow. He hadn't even tried to live without them.

Prosper knew about Janey. But he was the only one in Crownsmount who did. The club had very strict rules about members trying to "off themselves."

Having to worry about the mental health of a brother was not on the laundry list of things outlaw bikers wanted to do with their time. There were too many business opportunities happening at any given moment. Stressful, unlawful, seriously criminal activity that could cost a brother a lot of years away should a member of the crew unravel.

But the brothers had loved Janey. Everyone had. They felt for Diego. He had lost so much. They couldn't deny him the relief of taking his own life and then make him patch out. Diego made the decision for them and went nomad for a while after that. Then some years ago he had asked Prosper if he could patch in to the East Coast division. The vote had been taken, the deed done. Diego had been a member of the Crownsmount MC ever since.

And Prosper had never been sorry. Never been sorry that he had supported Diego getting patched in.

Diego hoped—he really hoped—that what he had come for in the middle of the night was not going to change that. He really fucking hoped not.

CHAPTER 58

Diego sat at the table with his brothers. He was leaning forward with his elbows on the scarred wood. His hands tightly wrapped around each other in a fist. He talked to them. He told them everything. Janey, the baby, the suicide attempt. The years he spent going rogue and what brought him back in. It had been a long time ago. Diego had earned the respect of the brothers and more. Fuck, most of the guys at the table hadn't been in the brotherhood even half the time D had. But the shit had to come clean. Prosper had ordered it, and D knew it was the right thing to do.

Because Prosper claimed Raine as his family, and Diego had claimed Raine as his old lady, this was club shit. Too much emotion. Too much history. Too much that could make a man or a woman lose their loyalty and decide to act on some of the hurt they were feeling. The club could not risk that.

Prosper hadn't been happy when Diego told him what went down with Raine.

And Diego had told him everything.

He hadn't left anything out. He hadn't wanted to. It had been twelve hours after the blowup with Raine when D had knocked on Prosper's door. In that time, Diego had a chance to think. The panic had passed and regret hung like a noose around his neck in its place.

But even so, he couldn't go back to that place. That place of dead fucking wives and tiny blue sons. He could not even conceive of taking a chance of going back there. And when Raine told him she was pregnant, that's all he saw. Just that. Nothing else.

It was because he loved her. So fucking much. Diego loved Raine with everything he had left to give. He loved her with everything left that he was. And he had fucking knocked her up. Risked her life. Pinky had tried to tell him that it had been a lot of years since that shit had happened with Janey and that medicine had come a long way since then. But Prosper had put his hand gently on his wife's shoulder and she had stopped talking.

Because Prosper knew. Because Prosper had loved Maggie the way Diego had loved Janey, he knew. And Prosper knew that if there was a chance, even the slimmest of chances, that he would lose Pinky because of something he did, because of something that had come about as a result of the love he felt for her, he'd put a bullet in his head.

But first, God help him, he'd leave her. Because Prosper knew that he didn't have it in him to watch another woman who he loved die.

He would leave her.

But not forever and not for long. Prosper would never ever leave his woman to face whatever may come without him by her side. Because he was a flawed and reckless, rough, selfish sonofabitch, he would need a minute.

Prosper knew Diego would do right by Raine.

Eventually.

But in the meantime, the brothers needed to know what the fuck was going on when they saw D's baby growing inside of Raine and D acting like he didn't give a shit.

Complicated. Well, he had tried to warn him.

~

They didn't have much to say. The brothers just pretty much let D get it out. They had known Diego for years. None of those years together had been spent being choirboys. They considered this his personal business. No one was looking to put anyone to ground, no one was facing time, and no one was talking to the feds. So they considered this personal business.

The members knew Raine and they liked her. But she wasn't a brother, and that shit went deep with them. Were they all good with watching Raine grow big with Diego's baby inside of her and him not wanting any part of that? Most of them honestly didn't give a shit. As long as she kept her disappointment in her baby daddy reined in and did not threaten the club because of that disappointment, they were good. For most of them, it was domestic bullshit.

For most of them.

When Diego was done spilling his guts, he grabbed a bottle of tequila and went to stoke the fire in the pit.

"You gonna drink that all by yourself, Brother?" Diego turned to find Crow standing next to him throwing a couple more logs on the fire.

Diego handed the bottle over to Crow, who took a long pull of it.

"Sorry about that going down with your wife and your son, D." Crow sat back on one of the low wooden chairs and lit a joint. After a long toke, he handed it to Diego.

"Happened a long time ago, Brother." Diego took the joint between two fingers and inhaled deeply.

"Time don't matter the way it usually does when something that heavy goes down." Crow shot back a deep swallow of tequila.

"So this is you coming out here to hand me a fucking Hallmark?" Diego took the bottle Crow offered him.

"Nah, man. This is me coming out here to tell you that I'm sorry for that shit with Raine before. I saw an in and I took it. It was a dick move and I shouldn't a done it." Crow meant what he said. He had been wanting to man up for a while.

Diego squinted at him with one eye as he took another toke off the joint.

"S'okay, Brother. I should've been minding the store. Woman like that. Woman like Raine don't come around too often. Shit, situation reversed, I would've gone there myself." He handed the joint back to Crow and took another hit off the bottle.

"Yeah?" Crow asked.

"Fuck, yeah." Diego nodded.

"Guess you're right," Crow said around the mouth of the bottle.

Diego got up to throw another log on the fire. "Don't have to fucking guess, man. Best thing that could happen to a man is to find a woman like her."

"Yeah, she sweet and all, but a woman's a woman. All got tits. All got pussy. No disrespect, but after a while it's all the same shit. Day after day, same everyday crap." Crow was lighting another joint.

"Nah, man. Ain't true. Maybe true some of the time," he conceded. "Club band-aids like fucking Ellie and the rest. But a woman like Raine, Brother. Men like us, life we lead, the way the good citizens fucking cross the street when they see us coming, we don't get the chance at good women. Not too often anyway. And there's nothing sweeter in this world than being inside a good woman who really fucking and truly loves you." Diego was looking at the fire and continued.

"I was lucky to get that twice. First Janey, then Raine. A sorry no-good bastard like me. Lucky enough to have had two good women." Diego took the joint from Crow and inhaled deeply.

Crow moved towards him. He put his hand on Diego's shoulder and squeezed. "My point, Brother."

Diego didn't say anything for a while. They both sat there in silence, drinking and getting high.

"Sonofabitch. I fucked it all up, didn't I?" Diego passed the last of the tequila to Crow.

"Big time, my Brother." Then he put his arm around his friend, and they both staggered inside.

CHAPTER 59

Three months later, I hadn't seen him. Not once. I knew he was at the club. A lot. A lot more than he ever used to be. A lot more than he had to be, as far as I was concerned. I hated him being around. I hated it because that meant I could not go to the kitchen house and eat Jules's kickass French toast. I really wanted some of that French toast too.

The baby liked it. The first time that I had felt the flutter of the new life growing inside of me, I was eating that French toast. I smiled when I thought of it and put my hand on my growing baby belly. When I had told Diego, when all my hopes for a happily-ever-after were shattered once and for all, the little life inside me had barely begun. At eighteen weeks pregnant, I was beginning to feel the baby *move.*

I loved being pregnant. *I loved it.* I loved every single minute of it. I hadn't even minded the absolutely awful morning sickness. I just learned to avoid smells and kept crackers by my bedside to eat in the mornings before I put even one foot out of bed.

I was excited today for a few reasons. One was that I would be hearing the sound of my baby's heartbeat on my next doctor's visit. I couldn't stop thinking about that.

The other reason was that my girl posse and I had just come back from my first shopping trip for maternity clothes. My waist was getting thick and my breasts were getting bigger and heavier. I could no longer button my pants and my shirts were stretching across my chest. The first three months I had been so sick I had actually lost weight but that hadn't stopped my body from ripening in all those places. My belly was hard to the touch and I could see a slight bump when I stood naked in front of the mirror.

I had a small frame so I was able to still buy my favorite tee shirts. I bought lots of them in pretty, soft pastel colors. V-necks, scoop necks, capped-sleeved and long-sleeved in increasingly larger sizes. The jeans were maternity with thick, soft elastic waistbands that had me sighing as they stretched over my belly. Then because they were all so pretty and I couldn't resist, I got myself five sundresses. One matched the exact color of my eyes. I couldn't wait to wear it. I bought a couple of pairs of shoes that I could slip on rather than tie. Because I couldn't help myself, I bought a new pair of cowboy boots.

Dolly, Pinky, Claire, and Glory came with me. Between us, we had a trunkload of clothes, shoes, and accessories. I had never had friends to go shopping with. It had been such a fun day. I thought again of how many normal things that Claire and I had missed out on. I promised myself that this baby would have that. Boy or girl, my child would have all those normal growing-up experiences. I would make sure of it.

We were settling in. Claire and I and even Glory. We had the normal. It wasn't the peanut-butter-and-jelly-on-white, going-to-church-on-Sunday normal, but it was as close to normal as the three of us had ever had. It was our normal and we cherished it.

The lake house was a short drive away from Ruby Reds. I went in to work almost every day for a few hours. The club had really taken off. It was busy all the time, and Claire had begun to come in with me. She waitressed, bartended, and generally helped out wherever needed. Glory still stayed home unless it was absolutely necessary to go out. She was doing better, but I know that she had trouble sleeping because I did too. Sometimes we spent those sleepless nights drinking herbal tea together wrapped in the silence of understanding.

Life had taken on a rhythm. A regular pulsing life-affirming rhythm and mostly I was happy. Except for when I wasn't. Except for when the bone-crunching sadness sat so heavy on my chest that it had me wandering out to the edge of the dock in the stillness of the night. Sometimes Claire or Glory would join me and listen while I played long, mournful songs on my little harp.

The days kept me busy and helped me to push it all away, but the nights were different.

I missed him.

When I let myself, I missed him. I had learned to live with disappointment early on. I had learned to live with the heartbreak of loss, the worry of responsibility, and the ache of loneliness.

You would have thought that all those experiences would have prepared me, hardened me, and even helped me deal with the fact that Diego did not want this baby.

Or me.

Anymore.

He did not want me anymore.

But there is no way to prepare for heartache. There is just the aftermath. There is just the picking up the pieces. For me it was that way anyway. I always seemed to get blindsided. Gino, Diego, and even my own father.

Prosper had come to the lake house soon after Diego's fists had punched holes through my wall. Soon after his words had punched a hole through my heart. Prosper told me why he had felt it was important to share this very private and hurtful situation with the entire Hells Saints Crownsmount MC.

I told him that I felt humiliated and unhappy that he had done that.

Then he told me the rest of it.

Prosper told me what had happened to Diego's wife and tiny baby boy. As I sat with my hands around a hot cup of tea and my shoulders wrapped up in a warm quilt against the cool night air, Prosper talked for a long time and I listened. He told me not only about the death of Diego's wife and son, but what had happened to Diego as a result of it. He told me everything there was to tell. Prosper told me, he said, because he thought I deserved to know.

Prosper told me because he knew Diego would not tell me himself.

It was tragic.

It was sad and unfair and unbearably heartbreaking.

It was.

My heart bled for the young man who had lost his wife and new baby boy. It was a horrible, heart-wrenching ending to a beautiful love story. My cheeks were wet with tears for Janey. Now that I was carrying a child of my own, I knew the unbearable sadness she must have suffered at the loss of their child.

Going through that, going through the birth process knowing that you would deliver a stillborn baby, could take a woman to the edge of sanity.

Watching your woman go through that could push a man over that edge.

Then to lose both of them within hours of each other and to survive that was not a life worth living.

I would have tried to kill myself too.

Then having been prevented from doing that, I would have left.

I would have.

I would have gone off by myself in complete and utter desolation. I would do whatever I had to do and take as long as I had to take to find the will to go on.

I would have done all the things Diego had done to survive that.

Except for one.

Except for what he had done to me.

I would not have done that. I would not have left a pregnant me. Once I had found the promise of love again, I would have fought for it. I would have held it fast and protected it. I would have somehow found the strength to climb out of the crippling fear and build a life with that someone.

But he hadn't done that. He had left me. He had left me and the promise of what our life together could be.

Even if it had meant following Janey to the world beyond this one, Diego could not leave her.

That's the thought that haunted me. That's what kept me awake at night. It's what had me crying in the shower. It's what prevented me from calling out his name when I felt his baby flutter deep inside me.

Diego couldn't leave Janey.

But he could leave me.

It wasn't jealousy. I wasn't jealous of the love that Diego had felt for her. It was never that. The love between them, the love he felt for her stood as a testament to the kind of man he was. The love and commitment he was capable of.

The love he didn't feel for me. The commitment he didn't want to give to me.

Didn't feel. Didn't want. Not with me.

Not with me.

CHAPTER 60

Well, she had taken him at his word.

He had made his point.

He had made his fucking point alright.

Three months.

Twelve fucking weeks and she had not stepped foot on the compound. Not while he was there anyway. Not while he was in a fucking twenty-mile radius.

Had not even once called the kitchen house. Not even once. Diego knew because he took to answering the phone so much that he had started practically jumping across the bar when it rang.

"Jesus, man. Just fucking call her," Jules said.

"Don't know what you're fucking talking about." Diego scowled.

"Talking about you growing a pair and going to get your fucking woman." Jules was mopping up the bar.

"You don't know nothing about it, Brother."

Diego moved to the bar and handed Jules his empty coffee cup for a refill.

"Know you got a woman with a belly full of your baby. Good woman. Fucking beautiful woman and you here every night shooting the shit with me and the rest of your sorry-ass brothers. You and that fucking lovesick puppy, Reno. Enough to make me puke." Jules handed the coffee cup full and hot back to Diego.

"What's going on with Reno?"

Diego took a sip of his coffee.

"Got it bad for little sister, Brother."

Jules poured himself a fresh cup and put his forearms on the bar.

"Claire?" Diego's eyebrows were raised.

"One in the fucking same."

Jules sipped on his coffee and nodded at the brothers who had started streaming in.

"He up in that?" Diego nodded too.

"He wishes he was up in that. She won't fucking give him the time of day. She comes in and grabs some shit for the lake house. When he isn't fucking her with his eyes, he's fucking following her around. Kinda pathetic actually. She don't look at him or talk to him unless she has to." Jules shook his head.

"Jesus." Diego was smirking.

"Yeah." Jules was smirking back.

The phone rang and Diego leapt across the bar to answer it.

"Lovesick fucking puppies. Both of them," Jules muttered to himself then opened to the front page and finished his coffee.

CHAPTER 61

Pinky was flittering around the room.

"So send him on a bullshit trip or something."

Pinky cracked some eggs and whipped them into a frothy sea in the bowl.

"Nope." Prosper was reading his morning paper.

"Okay, then. Dolly told me the new club's central air is leaking all over the place. You know how much that contractor cost us and he hasn't returned her calls in two days. Put him on that."

"Weekend, honey. Fucking plumbers never return calls."

Prosper reached for the coffee that Pinky had poured for him.

"Send him up to Willows Point then. Check up on things."

She poured the mixture into a hot pan.

"Nothing to check on in Willows Point," Prosper replied. "Sweetheart, gimme some of that hard cheese and salami in those eggs." Prosper was looking over his half-moon glasses.

"Not gonna happen." Pinky was scrambling the eggs in the pan.

"Why the fuck not?" Prosper was not pleased.

"Because I don't want to see your sorry self hobbling around with the gout for the next week," Pinky flung back over her shoulder.

"Ain't the cheese, ain't the sausage," Prosper growled at her.

"No?" Pinky raised her eyebrows.

"And it ain't the fucking gout makes me hobble around like that." Prosper had a glint in his eye.

Pinky had finished dishing up the eggs and was walking towards Prosper.

"What is it then?" she asked, exasperated.

"Just like the attention it gets me from my old lady. Like leaning on you when I walk and like you buying me black cherries and waitin' on me." Prosper was grinning.

"Crazy old man."

Pinky smiled at him. Then worry took the smile's place in that pretty face of hers. The face that Prosper loved.

Pinky stood over him while he put a forkful of eggs in his mouth.

"Service is due on the new utility van. Diego can go up to Elmswood tonight and stay there. Then tomorrow he can get the van serviced and come home."

"Reno got an appointment for that on Thursday." Prosper was chewing.

Pinky let out a deep sigh and moved to cross the room. Prosper grabbed a hold of her hand and pulled her on his lap. He put his big hand on the side of her face and forced her against him until he felt her relax.

"Honey, we gotta let them sort it out," Prosper said to the top of her head.

"I'm afraid she won't come if she knows he's gonna be there." Pinky sighed.

"Did she say that?" Prosper asked gently.

"No, honey. You know she wouldn't say that. Raine wouldn't miss your birthday for the world. She loves you," Pinky answered and sunk deeper into Prosper. Feeling the relief of him taking her worries, knowing that he would stew on them, mix them all around, and give them back in a way that made her feel better. In a way that would make everything better.

"Honey, it's all gonna be okay." Prosper smoothed her hair.

Pinky hoped with all her heart that he was right.

CHAPTER 62

No. Over there." Claire was pointing to a branch to the left of Reno.

"Here?" Reno asked.

"No. We need a little more of them to the left," Claire answered him. She stretched to hand him another string of lights.

"Here?" Reno threw a few lights on a lower branch.

"Reno. Is that your left?" Claire asked him, exasperated.

"Honest to Christ, woman. I don't know where you are looking." Reno feigned innocence.

"Geez. Get down. Get out of my way. You hand me the lights and I will put them up."

Claire positioned herself near the bottom of the ladder.

"Okee dokee." Reno jumped.

As soon as Claire worked her way to the top of the tall stepladder, Reno was on it. Behind her. Very close behind her. His hard chest and long muscled thighs pushed against her back and ass. His arms outstretched, biceps bulging reaching past her long, thin, graceful ones.

"I got it," Reno said against Claire's ear.

Claire went very still. When she pulled her arm away, Reno caught the string of lights before they fell and reached past her to string them precisely where he knew Claire wanted them.

"Reno," Claire whispered.

"Claire," Reno whispered back.

Then he put his hands on either side of her waist.

"Step back, Reno."

"Not this time, Claire," Reno said against her ear.

"This ladder is unsteady. I'm afraid," Claire said breathlessly.

"My arms are here, baby. Tight around you. You take a minute and feel that. Feel how strong I am. Ain't gonna let nothing happen to you, Claire. You're safe with me. I fucking swear it. "

It took a moment, but then Claire relaxed into him. With his hands still on her waist, he gently guided her down.

CHAPTER 63

"Well, this is new." Glory was looking out the window of the lake house.

I went to stand behind Glory. We both stood at the window watching Claire ride up to the house on the back of Reno's bike.

"Yep, that's new alright." I nodded in agreement.

I put the palm of my hand on the small of my back and stretched. Glory and I turned as a very flushed, windblown sister came bouncing through the door. And she was smiling. As a matter of fact, she was all smiles. She was smiling and bouncy.

This was not good.

Glory and I looked at each other. Then we looked at Claire. I opened my mouth to say something, and the words were stopped just short of coming out.

"I know. I know. I know. I know. I KNOW!" Claire made the stop sign with her hand.

She ran upstairs and came down with the rest of the twinkling lights we had bought for the party.

She bounced back out the door, only pausing once to look at us and throw another "I KNOW!" at us as she scurried past.

Glory and I turned to each other.

"Well, I guess it could be worse," Glory said.

"How?" I answered.

Glory just smiled.

We went back to putting the finishing touches on Prosper's cake. Pinky had planned a big blowout for Prosper's sixtieth. We had been cooking mountains of food for days and the boys had dug out three deep pits at the compound where pigs would be roasting. Brothers were coming in from Nevada and Willows Point to join the festivities. All available space at the compound was taken. I knew there would be a small but impressive show of federal and local police enforcement lining the street going up to the private driveway tomorrow. They always did that when there was a large gathering of the MC.

While I loved Prosper, I was not looking forward to this party. I knew Diego had stuck to the compound lately like white-on-rice. No brother wanted to miss the opportunity of raising a glass to Prosper on his birthday. The boys had been arriving all day and it was to be a weekend-long celebration. My plan was to go over early to the ranch house to deliver the cake and food. I thought this would be the best way of contributing to the festivities without actually having to take part in them.

Claire, Glory, Dolly, Jules, Reno, and I had chipped in and bought Prosper and Pinky VIP tickets to the NASCAR Sprint Cup Series and the plane tickets that went along with them. That gift would be presented to them at the party.

But I had another gift for him.

A little something special that I wanted to deliver myself. Weeks before, I had made an appointment with a jewelry designer in town. We had worked together to come up with a necklace for Prosper. A tiny sterling silver harmonica hung from a soft leather cord. On the same jump ring as the harp hung a teeny roughly hewn angel wing set with two diamonds. One for me and one for Claire. It was perfect. I knew he would love it.

The MC womenfolk had been cooking up a storm all week. I knew the kitchen house had been a sea of activity because Jules had taken to showing up at the lake house early in the morning for coffee and spending a good part of the day with us complaining about it. It was kind of funny really. Big bad Jules, six-foot-five inches of muscle-bound mountain. This scarred, tattooed warrior was sitting in our kitchen kvetching about women taking over his pots and pans. Glory complained to me every night about Jules "barging in" and prayed that the preparations for the party would be over soon.

On the fourth day of Jules's unsolicited visits, Glory read in the local paper that the lake had been stocked for the season. When he arrived, she was waiting for him on the front porch. Glory handed Jules a tackle box, a fishing pole, and a cooler containing a six-pack and three liverwurst sandwiches. Then she sent him out to the dock. He came back hours later smiling with a bucket full of bass. The next day when he caught a large trout, we took a picture of him holding it up in his massive paw and smiling.

A fisherman had been born.

Jules's love of fishing continued long after the disruption of his kitchen ended. He would show up several times a week to drop a line. Glory took to having sandwiches ready for him and she seemed to delight in thinking up different combinations. Even months after *the event,* Glory still stayed pretty much at home. The first time she would venture out completely on her own would be to go to a delicatessen fifteen miles away to stock up on various condiments, meats, and cheeses she thought Jules might like.

A couple of weeks after that, I noticed two fishing poles instead of one leaning against the shed door.

CHAPTER 64

I'll go if you go." Glory was standing in the door of my bedroom. "Go where?" I was putting away my laundry.

"Prosper's party," Glory said nonchalantly, moving to help me with the clothes.

"Prosper's party?" I stopped what I was doing and looked at her.

"Yeah." Glory was moving to hang up my shirts.

"You would consider going to Prosper's party?" I felt like an idiot, but the question bore repeating.

"I dunno. Maybe just for a few minutes." Glory was hanging another shirt.

"You would go to Prosper's party?" I asked again.

"Raine." Glory stopped what she was doing and looked at me. "Yes. I would consider going to Prosper's party."

"You . . ." I began.

"Stop that," Glory said.

"Jesus, Glory, forgive me. But it's not like you've been exactly jumping to go anywhere and now you tell me the one event you think you may want to attend is an outlaw-biker birthday party with a greeting party of federal law enforcement?"

"Well, if you put it that way . . ." Her voice trailed off.

I immediately felt guilty. Who was I to discourage Glory from going to the first thing she had felt any interest in attending in months? Shame on me. Glory was my friend and I should support her in this first valiant attempt at venturing forth.

"Well, I'm not going," I said.

"You can't hide from him forever, Raine," Glory said softly.

"I'm not hiding," I said softly back.

But she was not wrong.

I *was* hiding and it couldn't keep going on. I was tired of it. Tired of looking over my shoulder, tired of having to call Pinky to call Prosper to call me because he was old school and refused to get a cell for anything other than club business. It had been months since I had dialed the number to the compound. Months since I had stepped foot on club property. I missed it. I missed dropping in on Prosper and taking walks with him on the wooded paths. I missed the French toast that Jules insisted could only be made properly in his own kitchen. I missed dropping off outrageously expensive, rich, creamy French pastries for the brothers and watching them gobble them up, leaving mustaches of Bavarian cream and powdered sugar on their scruffy, hard faces. I missed all of it.

I sighed heavily and looked at Glory with careworn eyes.

"The things he said, Glory. I hear them. *I still hear them*. And I don't know how to look at the man who said them to me," I said, sitting down heavily on the bed.

Glory sat down next to me. "You don't have to see him, honey."

"But he'll be there. Not just today or tomorrow. He'll be *there*. This club is his family, and now we've made it ours. He will always be *there*. I'll always have to see him." My shoulders were slumped.

"There's a way of looking at a man without seeing him, Raine. You can look right through him." Glory took my hand. "I've been doing it for years."

I looked down at our clasped hands and looked sadly up at Glory. This time the sadness was for her and not for me. I had watched Glory. I knew, like Pinky, her darkest secrets were about things that had been done to her. I also knew that, unlike Pinky, some of Glory's secrets were about things she had done to herself.

I squeezed her hand and held her eyes.

"Raine," Glory began uncomfortably, "it hasn't been lost on me what you and Claire and everyone else have done for me. The things you don't say, the questions you don't ask, and the scars you pretend not to see. I thank God every night that when I finally fell, I landed here."

"You saved my life, honey." I held on tight to her hand and then added, "More than once."

Glory's eyes were wet. "And in doing that, Raine, I saved my own. You've taken me in and treated me like a sister. You've never asked. You've done for me what I couldn't do for myself. You have given me back me."

She smiled a little then.

"I was a dancer. Yeah, *that* kind. Not always. Not in the beginning. But eventually, yeah, it came to that. *All nude. All the time.* That was me. It wasn't something that I planned on, Raine. It wasn't supposed to happen that way. But it did and I was."

She searched my eyes before going on. I was careful to keep them open and clear.

"Sometimes the shame of it almost killed me. Every time I went out there, I felt the humiliation grow and grow until I thought it would swallow me whole."

"There's no disgrace in doing what we need to do to survive, Glory." I moved in closer to her so our bodies were touching from knee to shoulder. I would not leave her alone in the telling.

"You might think it strange, but the naked part didn't bother me that much. My parents were throwbacks, left over from the days of free love and clothing-optional solstice celebrations." She smiled a little at that and I smiled a little back.

"It was the hunger in the eyes of the men when they looked at me that made me sick inside." She held my gaze.

"It was an exclusive club," she added quickly.

Then she laughed derisively. "What does that even mean? I used to wonder that. We danced buck naked for men just like any other stripper. They leered at us just the same, went home and jerked off to us just the same. Guess it meant no lap dances, no fat, sweaty hands putting money in a G-string. The dark and the stage separated us from them. We wore golden headpieces and body jewelry and a strategically placed sparkle now and again. But really, we were just naked dancers like the rest."

Glory went on, "I didn't escort but some of the girls did. There was a private lounge too. This area had its own private setting. Private stage, private bar, private cocktail waitress, and private dancers. I worked that room a lot. *A lot*. Good money. Great money. Unbelievably fantastic money. There was that. The money part of it. I did it for the money, Raine."

I nodded understandingly. That made sense but I wondered why Glory felt she needed all that money. If she felt so debased doing what she did, why did she need the money? But I had learned long ago not to cast judgment. Someday we would know the whys of Glory's sad story.

For now I would listen while Glory talked.

"I performed on stage while those disgusting men jerked off or got hard while the escorts wiggled in their laps getting them ready for the 'later on.' And I could see them. They were right there. On the public stage downstairs, we usually performed together parading in and out with ridiculous synchronized acts. The stage was so brightly lit you couldn't really see the customers. This was in Vegas. Did I tell you that? Did I remember to tell you that?" Glory's eyes were looking at me, bright with tears.

"No, honey, you didn't," I answered.

She nodded and continued, "Well, it was. When I danced downstairs it wasn't as bad. But then after the act, they would often request a private show and the deal was we had to go. Had to dance privately. But anything else, that was up to us. They were real good about that. It was up to us. I never did any of the other stuff, but the private dancing was bad enough. I could see them. I could see their faces. I could hear their thoughts. It was revolting. But I had to do it. It was something that I had to do at the time. So I learned how to hide my revulsion. Revulsion was bad for business. So I taught myself to look right through them, see right past them. I learned to be where they were but have them disappear.

"That's how I know you can do it too." Glory focused on me and was back.

Then she looked horrified. "Oh God, Raine. I know it's not the same. Diego isn't that guy. He isn't that leering, disgusting guy. I didn't mean it that way. Not at all. Not at all."

"I know that, honey. I know you didn't mean that." I was quick to reassure my panicked friend.

"I only meant that there is a way of avoiding seeing him when he is where you need or want to be. Doing that may make it easier for you until you are ready to deal with him again."

I doubted if that would ever happen. If I ever would be ready to deal with him again. If I could ever look at Diego without hearing the words he threw at me. If I could ever see him without revisiting the fury in his eyes at the news I was carrying his child. Maybe there would come a time when I could look at him and not feel that pain. That absolute total pain that presented itself like anger. Maybe that time would come.

But until then I had to find a way to be where he might be. To stand where he might stand and not be affected. I needed to not see him. I needed to have him hidden from me when he was in plain sight.

"Teach me how. Teach me how to make him disappear," I said to Glory.

And she did.

CHAPTER 65

After Glory and I talked I felt better. And I think she did too. We were both afraid and that made us both braver in the long run. Strength in numbers or something like that.

Like the misbegotten princesses in some old forgotten fairy tale, Glory and I were going to the ball.

And it was time to get dressed.

It was fun actually. Glory did my hair and I did her makeup. We both chose sundresses. Hers was a beautiful soft cotton blue that was long and stopped midway on her pretty, toned calves. It had a strapless bandeau top that crossed tightly over her breasts and fell into soft drapes around her. She wore thin, flat, white sandals on her feet. The look was sexy without being trashy and the cotton made the dress casual enough for the party. Honestly, with that cute little pixie cut of hers, when she didn't sex it up just a fraction, she looked to be about twelve years old. A fact we lovingly teased her about often, but Glory didn't seem to mind. Once she told me the newly shorn hair felt like it gave her a chance on a newly shorn life.

Nothing wrong with that.

My dress was a flirty little thing. It was black rayon with tiny little pink flowers sprinkled liberally throughout the fabric. It was one of my new maternity dresses so the waistband was set empire and it flowed nicely over my little round tummy. It had an eyelet trim peeking out from the hem and a bodice that gave it a country look. It stopped just at my knees. I was going to wear a thin pair of strappy sandals but then thought about the unevenness of the field and dirt road of the compound and decided on my new cowboy boots. They had been expensive and were beautifully stitched with pretty designs. They were feminine without being clunky. I kept my hair loose but tied it with a pretty pink ribbon.

When I looked in the mirror, I thought I looked beautiful. My skin had deepened to a golden tan, and the prenatal vitamins had added luster to my hair. At this stage of the pregnancy I had lost the chubby no-waist look, and it had been replaced by a definite baby bump. Thankfully most of the weight had gone there. So far there had been no puffing out of my ankles or face. I still looked like me, only a better me. A prettier, healthier, happier me. A braver me. A mommy me.

Claire was behind the food tables when we got there. They had gathered the half-dozen or so picnic tables and set them up end to end. The tables were covered with cloths and those heated disposable foil trays. In between the trays of ziti and meatballs and sausage stood mountains of desserts. I counted four kegs of beer already set up, and there were three pigs roasting in the three pits. A band had set up farther out in the field and they were tuning and doing sound checks. I chuckled to myself as I thought that this was the bikers' version of wine, women, and song. It was men, music, and meat.

The afternoon had been progressing pretty well. Mostly Claire, Glory, and I hung back and stayed behind the food tables. We were serving it up to the masses, keeping things hot, getting rid of the cold stuff and bringing out the fresh stuff. We knew we didn't have to do it, but it was where we all were most comfortable. We fit in but we didn't. You would think that a biker club like this one that had such disregard for the law or anything mainstream would not give two damns about labels and where folks belonged. But they did. There was a definite pecking order and hierarchy of the way things went down.

Glory, Claire, and I fell under Prosper's umbrella. Everyone knew at this point that the baby I was carrying was Diego's, but that I was not his anymore. They knew Glory belonged to no one and what was happening between Claire and Reno was anybody's guess. And the knowing of this stuff mattered to them. It mattered to the women who were interested in being owned by Diego or Reno, and it mattered to the men who were interested in laying claim to one of us.

So while we got the respect of belonging to Prosper's family (and that respect went a long way), we didn't get the entitlement of being hands-off either. Plainly speaking, the three of us were fair game. So we stood where the tables would separate us from the wolves.

And we stayed together. For the most part we stayed together.

But the first time I saw him again, I was alone.

I was moving towards the door with two handfuls of cold cut trays. I was thinking about how I was going to manage opening it with both hands full. I laughed at myself for being so dumb as to fill both my hands knowing I was going to have to open the damn door. I was almost upon it when it opened for me.

I knew it was him. I smelled the clean scent of soap wafting through the screen. I knew the muscled shoulder and the tattooed bicep that held that door open. I almost lost my lunch when squeezing past him caused my protruding belly to brush against his in a long motion, while I tried to navigate the door, my balance, and the two trays on my hands.

I knew it was him.

But I didn't look up.

Not once.

My eyes never moved out of my line of vision. I heard him call my name softly as I passed him. Then as my eyes lowered to fasten on those trays, I muttered a quiet thank-you and walked on.

I walked right past him.

I busied myself in the refrigerator and felt him leave.

Only when I heard the screen door snap closed did I breathe again, putting my palm on my belly and a hand to my head.

Glory was right, my eyes had rendered Diego invisible.

But my heart . . . well, that was another story. My heart had known he was there.

My heart had known. It had shown me it had known by skipping a few beats and sending a drumming to my ears and a sweat to my palms. But it had also shown me that it had recovered. That the pain from being near Diego had not stopped my heart from beating.

The pain of seeing him had not and would not kill me.

I rested a little easier after that. Glory, Claire, and I were spelled from our duties and we grabbed something to eat and went to sit closer to the music and Prosper.

"Hey, Grandpa." I leaned down and kissed his cheek.

"Hey, Little Darlin'." Prosper patted the side of my face as I leaned in to him.

"How's that grandbaby of mine doing?" he asked.

I smiled at him, patted my tummy the way pregnant women do, and I said, "Baby is loving him some meatballs and reggae."

"Him?" Pinky leaned in.

I laughed at that. "Just a pronoun, Pinky. Not an indication."

"So you still don't want to know what my grandbaby is gonna be?" Prosper asked with just a slight slur beginning to form around his words. The day had turned into dusk, and he had been nursing his brews all afternoon, pacing himself. The empties in front of him were being constantly replaced.

"Don't know, don't care . . ."

"Don't matter!" Pinky, Prosper, Claire, and Glory finished the sentence in unison for me. We had had this conversation a few times before.

I laughed good-naturedly.

Suddenly I felt the air change and a shadow stand next to me. His big arm reached around me to put another in front of Prosper.

"Happy birthday, Boss." Diego did the man arm-shake thing with Prosper. Crow was behind him and did the man arm thing too.

"Thank ya, Brotha." Prosper's slur was a little more pronounced now and he staggered on his first attempt to stand up.

"Sit down, old man. And drink the fuck up." Crow set down a sterling engraved flask with the Saints insignia on it, Prosper's name, and the date he founded the MC.

"What the fuck is this?" Prosper roared.

"It's your goddamn birthday present, you ungrateful sonofabitch," Crow rejoined.

"Jesus, look at that date." He was holding the flask in his somewhat unsteady hand. "Been doing this a long time. Guess I don't look too bad for an old fuck."

"Oh yeah, you're one pretty bastard, Prosper," Crow said. Then he put a bottle of Johnnie Walker Blue Label in front of him.

"Whoaaa hooo hooo hooo! What we got here?" Prosper's bleary eyes were focused.

"Just a little something to put in the flask from my man D and me," Crow said.

"Thank ye, boys. Thank ya vewwy muxh." Prosper was slurring steadily now.

"Jesus." Pinky pushed the bottles away from him and shoved her cup of hot coffee in front of him. "If you don't want me to have the boys bring you home and tuck your drunken birthday ass into bed, you better drink up."

"S'okay," Prosper said with a grin and reached for the coffee cup.

Crow looked at me and caught my eye. "How's it going, Raine?"

I nodded at him.

"Glory, Claire." Crow nodded at them.

They nodded back.

I turned to go and Diego was in my path. I did what Glory told me to do and did not look up past his chest. Did not look into his eyes.

"How are you, Raine?" he asked me.

I felt my heart race and the baby move.

"I'm okay," I responded.

"Good. Glad to hear it. You look okay," he said.

Okay? I looked okay?

I glanced up at him then. Big mistake. Big stupid mistake.

Because he didn't look so good. Oh, he looked *good*. He always looked good. Diego was a big badass good-looking guy. No getting around that. So it wasn't that he didn't look good. He looked damn good, but he also looked worried. He looked sick with worry. He looked like a man who hadn't slept in a long time. Stubble filled his hollowed cheeks, and he had fine lines around his eyes that I didn't remember seeing before.

Well, join the club, I thought. *Join the goddamn club.*

I raised my eyebrows.

"I mean you look okay, but better than okay. You look uhhh . . . you look uhhh . . ." Diego was looking at me from head to toe, his eyes lingering on my rounded belly.

"You look uhhh . . ." Diego was still stuck.

"Pregnant. Diego. I look pregnant." I thought I would help the idiot out.

Then I walked past him. Again straight past him.

Then my girls got up and walked straight past him too.

∽

281

Crow scrubbed his hand over his face, slapped D hard on the shoulder, and said, "Jesus, D. *You look . . . uhhh?* What the fuck was that?"

"I was gonna say beautiful," Diego said, watching Raine walk away.

"Yeah, well that probably would have been a fuckload better." Crow was watching Raine walk away too.

CHAPTER 66

Yup, and do you know how much a good car seat costs?" I was sitting at the kitchen house with Jules, munching on my third piece of French toast. I was looking through a baby-store sale pamphlet and was circling my wish list.

"No fucking idea, honey." Jules was rigging his fishing pole. Crimping the leads, choosing the lures, tying the hook.

"Another piece, please." I pushed the syrupy plate towards him.

"Coming up, fatty pants." Jules moved towards the stove.

"Twenty pounds so far. And all of them due to your French toast, Jules," I said, rubbing my baby belly.

"So maybe gonna have to name the kid after me. Jules if it's a boy." Jules was dipping the bread in the egg wash.

"And if the baby is a girl?" I asked smiling.

"Julia. Julie. Jewel. Something along those fucking lines," he said totally seriously.

"I'll consider it," I said laughing. "Just keep that French toast coming."

Just then the door opened and Crow, Reno, and Diego walked in. Shit.

I had been doing pretty well at the "looking through him" stuff. I had been where he was several times since the party. I was becoming very good at letting my eyes dance on the heads of the brothers without ever quite landing on Diego. But every time it took a little more out of me. Every time I saw him, every chance he got, Diego would find a way to be near me. He would comment on the weather or tell me a little about his day. Where he was going, what he was doing.

The weather. Really. Like I gave two shits whether or not it looked like rain.

I had no idea what he thought he was doing.

So I would nod politely and get away from him as soon as possible.

He never asked about the baby. After that first embarrassing encounter, he never blatantly looked at my baby belly. But a couple of times out of the corner of my eye, I would see him watching me, and his eyes seemed to be fixed on my stomach.

There were days I could deal and days I just didn't want to have to. Today was one of the days I didn't want to have to.

So I grabbed my purse, regrettably leaving the fourth piece of French toast on the counter. I nodded to the boys and walked past them out the door. I was at the car when I heard my name called. Diego was coming at me at a run. I turned and tried to put the key in the lock fast but he was faster.

"Hey, Raine." He was standing right behind me.

"Hey." I was still fumbling with the keys so much that I dropped them. When I went to bend down to grab them, I got a sharp pain in my belly that took my breath away.

"Hey, baby, you okay?" Diego had bent down to retrieve the keys.

Oh no, he didn't.

"Yeah, I'm fine. But I really have to get going." I put my hands out for the keys.

Diego palmed them.

"Yeah, well maybe you shouldn't be driving if you don't feel so uhhh . . . if you are . . ."

Jesus. He was stammering again.

"Baby. Diego. It's the baby. B . . . A . . . B . . . Y."

Maybe if I spelled it out for him . . .

"Sometimes he kicks and surprises me, that's all." I was exasperated.

"He?" Diego was looking down at my belly.

"No, not he, or maybe he. I don't know yet is what I mean." I was getting flustered.

"You don't know yet?" he repeated.

"The baby. I don't know the gender of the baby." I took a breath and let it out in a whoosh.

"Don't want to know." Diego was looking at me.

Pain clouded my eyes and I said, "Yeah, I got that a few months back."

Diego looked confused, then rubbed the back of his neck. "Shit, no, honey. No. That was a question. As in, you don't want to know?"

"Oh," I said uncomfortably.

I held out my hands for the keys. Diego looked at my hand as though he was confused.

"Keys?" I said to him.

"Why don't you want to know, Raine?" His voice was strained and those worry lines were creasing his eyes.

"Why?" I was looking at those new creases of worry.

"Yeah, the uhhh . . . the uhhh . . ." Damn if his voice didn't trail off again.

"The baby. Why don't I want to know the sex of the baby?" I asked.

Jesus. We had been reduced to the verbal communication of third graders.

"Yeah. Is something wrong? Are you worried?" Diego stepped in closer.

"Worried?" I backed up into the car.

"Yeah, are you worried the baby won't make it? Is that why you don't want to know?" His voice cracked when it stopped on the words *won't make it.*

Oh, my God.

"Jesus, Diego, of course not. No. No. Everything is fine. Everything is fine."

I put my hand on his arm to emphasize my point. Then when I realized what I had done, I went to pull it away.

His big hand covered mine.

"So you are okay? The . . . the . . . the . . . *baby* is okay?" He put pressure on my hand.

"Yeah, everything is okay." Right then the baby kicked hard.

I made a pained face and rubbed my belly where the little foot had kicked hard at his mamma.

"Ouch," I said and despite myself, smiled reassuringly at my archenemy and the father of my baby.

Diego grabbed my elbow and tried to steer me towards the picnic tables.

"Are you okay? Come on over here and sit, Raine." He was leading me away from my getaway car.

"Stop it, Diego, I am fi . . ." and I felt the whoosh of a hard kick again.

I put my hand over my stomach and rubbed again.

"Raine, you are freaking me the fuck out." Diego was by my side looking pale.

"Oh, for Christ's sake. Here." I grabbed his hand and put it on my stomach. "It's the baby kicking."

I realized what I had done too late. The baby kicked his daddy again hard. Diego's hand jumped as the baby pushed against the warmth of his big hand. Diego had such a look of pure wonder and joy on his face, for a moment I forgot all the horrible, terrible heartwrenching things he had said to me.

But just for a moment.

"Wow. Strong little ass-kicker." Diego was smiling down at me.

At that minute I really wanted to be anywhere else but here.

Because that smile made me realize everything I could have with him and this baby and everything I wouldn't have. Everything he didn't want. I wasn't sure what this momentary lapse was, but I was pretty sure he hadn't changed his mind about wanting us. And even if he had, I wasn't sure I could ever want him back.

"Yeah, well . . ." I said eloquently.

"That stuff in the paper you circled. You need that stuff?" He was standing close again.

"What stuff?" I was walking back towards the car again.

"That baby seat and shit." Diego had caught up with me.

"Yeah."

Damn it.

"I mean no." *I mean not from you.*

Then I had had enough. I stopped dead in my tracks and turned to him.

"What are you doing, Diego?" I asked him.

"Trying to figure out what you need, Raine," he answered heavily.

"I'm going to get what I need for the baby. I have a job and the money I still have left from savings. Glory, Claire, and I all pitch in for the rent at the lake house even though Prosper doesn't want to take it . . ." I trailed off, not really understanding why I was telling him any of it.

"I'm trying to figure out what *you* need, Raine." He moved his big body closer to me. "I'm trying to figure out what I need to do to get you to the place where we can at least talk. I am trying to figure out what you need to get to that place where you stop looking right fucking through me."

"Why?" I demanded.

"Why what?"

"Why does it matter? Why do you care?" I heard the crackle of my heart breaking.

He looked at me like I was crazy. "You're carrying my baby, Raine."

"Are you kidding me right now, Diego? Are you fucking kidding me?" I could not believe this. "*Now?* Now I am carrying your baby?" I was not going to cry. "What happened to *not happening?* What happened to *you do this, you do this alone?*" I threw his words back at him.

"Well, I made a mistake," Diego growled. His eyes hard. His arms bulging tight against his chest. Standing there in front of me like he had every right to.

Oh, no. Oh, no he was not.

"A mistake?" I was fuming. "Diego, have you really no clue? Really? A mistake?"

His arms crossed tighter and he widened his legs. A muscle clenched in his cheek.

"Yeah, baby. I made a mistake." His eyes on me.

"A mistake? Is that what we are calling it now? A mistake?" I hissed.

"Forgetting to pick up the clothes from the cleaners is a *mistake*, Diego. Paying too much for milk is a *mistake*. Picking the wrong shoes to go with the wrong goddamn dress is a *mistake*. What you said to me? What you made me hear coming out of the mouth of my baby's father? That was more than a *mistake*. That was a blunder of epic, *epic* proportions, Diego. It was mean. It was hurtful. It was unforgiveable. *Un-fucking-forgiveable!*"

And there it was. I was crying.

"Raine." Diego moved his hand to the car and his body to the left of it, boxing me up against the hot fiberglass.

"Jesus. No. No. No. No. You hurt me, Diego. You threw me and this baby away. You stood in my house and punched two holes in the wall to emphasize your point. And you left them there. You left those holes there. Just like the holes you left in my heart." I was wiping the wet off my cheeks.

"You broke my heart." I was heaving. "Look what you've done to me."

I moved my hand to my left breast. "You have broken my heart."

Then I started to really sob.

"Raine." I heard his voice through my heaving.

Goddammit. I had not wanted to do this in front of him.

"Diego, give me the keys. Just give me the keys." I was beside myself.

"Crow, follow me up to the lake house? I'm gonna need a ride back."

Through the blur of my tears, I saw that Crow was now standing near the kitchen house door. Just what I needed, another witness to my shame. Could this day get any worse?

"Got that, Brother," Crow called out, his voice ladened with concern.

"Get in the car, baby. No way am I letting you drive this upset." Diego was evidently back to bossing me around.

I got in the car. Not because I was back to letting him, but because he was right. I was too upset to drive.

CHAPTER 67

It wouldn't start. Her goddamn piece of fifteen-year-old shit of a car would not start. Jesus.

Then on the third try it turned over. Goddammit.

Diego heaved a sigh and counted to fucking ten before he put the ancient tin can in gear.

Was there anything that worked in his life right now? Anything?

Raine was sitting next to him holding a tissue in her tiny hands trying to stop crying, but the wet kept coming down her cheeks, and she was doing this little hiccup thing. Her face was towards the window, but he knew she was still fighting those tears. And his beautiful woman was losing the battle.

When had he become such a prick?

He had lost his shit when she had told him about the baby. Lost. His. Shit.

When had he become such a fucking coward?

Janey and the baby. That was bad. That was earth-shattering, tear-your-guts-out, lose-the-will-to-go-on sad shit.

But he had gone on. He had moved on. He had chosen to go on. After that first attempt at blowing his brains out, he could have tried again. He could have walked away from his brothers, from his life, and in the privacy of his own home, done the deed.

But he hadn't.

And it had taken a long time. A very fucking long time. But he was glad he hadn't.

The unbelievable true love he had for Janey was that of a boy on the brink of manhood. When they fell in love they had been just kids. When it ended he had barely begun to shave.

The love he felt for Raine. That was all man. That was the love a man felt for his woman.

He was no kid anymore. He was a big, hard, tattooed outlaw. Afraid of nothing, game for anything. He was a tough sonofabitch who had seen it all, done most of it, and regretted none of it. He had balls of steel and a backbone to match.

Except when it came to her.

This little black-haired, blue-eyed beauty sitting next to him. When it came to Raine, Diego came undone. It had started when she walked into that filthy little kitchen and put herself between her sister and that loaded gun, and it had never stopped. Everything about her fascinated him. Her courage, her sense of humor, her loyalty to friends and devotion to family.

She would have taken a bullet to save her sister, of that he had no doubt. That kind of courage was something the brothers knew and respected. Jules had seen it when Raine walked into the clubhouse. Prosper . . . well, he had seen it when she was a little tiny bit of a thing. Crow had seen it too, and he had been willing to go up against his brother for a chance at owning that.

And the rest of them. He lost count of how many fucking times he had to lay claim to her in Nevada. Jesus, the brothers may be a bunch of dumb fucking badasses who had made more than a few bad choices in their lives, but they all fucking knew quality women when they saw them.

And Raine wasn't the only one they were sniffing to get a chance at. Jesus, if Claire and Glory knew how many of his brothers were lying in bed jerking off at the thought of getting them in their bed, on the back of their bikes, and under their hard bodies, they would have gone running towards the hills.

Come to think of it, maybe they did know. You never saw one of those chicks without the other. Never caught them alone. Now that he thought of it, Claire and Glory didn't even fucking really talk to anyone but Dolly, Pinky, or Prosper. They weren't snotty bitches, no noses-up-in-the-air kind of thing. They just didn't make themselves available for the smooth rap of the boys. Reno and Jules were the exception. Where that shit would lead was anyone's guess.

But nah, these three women, Raine, Claire, and Glory, they were different. Definitely different from the pieces that hung around the club. They looked different. They weren't half-dressed all the time, for one thing. It was a rare occasion when you would see one of them without a pair of jeans and a tee shirt on. Their skin was smooth and unmarked. No tramp stamps on any of them. Most of the bitches who hung around the club smelled like tobacco and cheap perfume. The two sisters and Glory smelled like flowers or vanilla.

And they were natural fucking beauties.

Raine and Claire.

Copper-skinned, dark-haired, blue-eyed beauties. Claire had a small smattering of brown freckles across her nose. Her hair was wavy where Raine's was straight, and Claire wore it a little shorter. But the resemblance to each other was amazing.

Glory.

She looked like a fucking angel.

Her eyes were a light glacier-blue that Diego knew could turn to ice in a split second. Her hair was silky and almost white. It was beginning to grow out a little from the rad short hair that Gino's fucking actions had caused. She had a long, thin neck and was taller than both the Winston sisters. She had long legs and, by the looks of it, perfectly formed tits. Her vocal chords had been permanently damaged from the beating they had taken when Glory had tried to scream her way out of the clutches of that dago lunatic. So her voice was low and raspy and throaty. She always sounded like she was just getting up out of bed.

And she was wide-eyed. Glory looked lost and scared most of the time. It drove the brothers crazy. At the party, a couple of the brothers from Nevada told the boys that they had seen Glory or someone that looked a hell of a lot like her dancing in a titty bar. When the brothers heard that, they all had looked in Glory's direction where she was dishing out mac and cheese and instantly got wood.

Glory was a puzzle that had the brothers standing in line to solve. Claire was a challenge that more than a few brothers were up to taking.

But aside from how it affected his woman, Diego didn't really give two fucks about all of that.

What he cared about, who he cared about, was the woman sitting crying in the seat next to him.

He was going to make this right. He had to. Had to make it right for her. For himself. And for the baby they were going to have.

And he would.

But first he had to figure out how.

Then he had to convince Raine to give him another chance.

To give them another chance.

How was he going to do that when she hadn't looked at him in months? That was going to take some doing.

Somehow Raine had made him invisible to her. Even when he was standing in front of her practically waving a fucking white flag, she looked past him.

He had to find a way to make her see him again. Goddammit. Most of the things he had done and said that night were a blur for him.

But evidently not for her. Apparently Raine remembered every single thing he had said. Every fucking hurtful word he threw at her, she had caught and used to form a barricade around her heart.

He had done this and he had to fix it. But for the life of him he didn't know how.

Fucking complicated. Prosper had been right.

CHAPTER 68

Over the next week, after my run-in with Diego, virtually all the items on my wish list showed up at the lake house door marked *rush shipment*. Even though I was pretty sure I knew who the gifts were from, I did my best to investigate. I tried the tracking slips, but to no avail. I even put Pinky on snoop detail. She turned up nothing. If I knew for sure that Diego had sent them, I would have returned them. But I knew he would deny it. Without proof, I would just look like a dramatic pregnant woman causing a scene.

Besides, the stuff was kickass, and they were all the items on my list except they were the highest end in their category. I received a car seat, a stroller, a baby bassinet, a baby sling, a carrier, and some soft receiving blankets in neutral colors. I couldn't help but be delighted when I opened them.

I hadn't picked out the crib or the other baby furniture. There were two small spare rooms in the lake house. They were both too far away from my own bedroom to be appropriate and would require me switching rooms with Claire or Glory so I had waited on that for now. Both of the rooms would require some work anyway. A fresh coat of paint and some carpeting at the least. Prosper wanted to help with that, but he had been away a lot since the party, presumably on club business. Pinky wasn't saying much and the small bit of info she was willing to part with made me think whatever it was, it was serious.

The holes in the wall that Mr. "Don't want anything to do with the baby" had put his fist through had been fixed. Diego had actually showed up himself to do it. But Glory, who was the only one there at the time, wouldn't let him in. So Claire and I had come home to find two Hells Saints prospects sheetrocking over the holes in the walls that Diego's fist had left.

I guess having those holes sealed up was supposed to make me feel better. I would have felt better if they had been sealed up months ago. I would have felt a whole lot better if they had never been left at all.

But no use crying over spilled milk. Diego was trying to make those words up to me. I knew he was. I knew he regretted saying them.

I knew he wasn't that guy.

I knew it.

I knew the things he said probably kept him up nights with self-recrimination *because he was not that guy*. The guy who did and said those things was an utter and complete asshole. I knew Diego was not him.

But he also was not the guy who wanted a baby. He was also not that guy.

CHAPTER 69

I was buttoning up my blouse after my eight-month checkup. Everything was great. My visits were now every two weeks. I could hardly believe that I was at that point.

My blood pressure was still good, urine was fine, and I added another three pounds to the growing number on the scale. At thirty-two weeks I had a weight gain of thirty pounds. I had been eating a healthy diet and exercising faithfully, so whatever pounds my body was putting on, it evidently needed. My uterine growth was right where it should be. All in all, the pregnancy was progressing just perfectly.

And I loved my doctor. He was old school. He was in his mid-seventies and although he was no longer taking new patients, he had made an exception for me. He practiced gynecology as well as obstetrics. Pinky and Dolly were not only patients of his, they were also friends. Reno had been delivered by Dr. Gideon. His practice was small and he liked it that way. I was never kept waiting more than half an hour in the waiting room. Once I had an appointment and he had been called into the delivery room; I was told of the situation and rescheduled for the next day.

The man took his time. He spent as much time with each of his patients as he needed to. He didn't nag me about my weight, and he didn't order any tests that he felt were unnecessary. Yet he was thorough. The one thing that did bother him was that I had filled in nothing about the medical history of the baby's father. He was not pleased with that and had no qualms about telling me how he felt.

My poor baby. I knew very little of the medical history of our family. I knew a little about my father's side. But my mother's side I knew nothing about. I had filled in the sections as best as I could. The part of the health questionnaire that asked about the baby daddy's history, I had left totally blank. It bothered me. It did. I spent more than one night lying in bed thinking about Janey and her baby, and wondered what had caused the baby to die in her womb and if the baby had been healthy otherwise. If not, did that have something to do with Diego's DNA?

I knew it was important. I knew I should find a way to ask him, but I just couldn't. So I crossed my fingers and toes and hoped for the best.

"Okay, Raine, everything looks good. Get dressed and meet me in my office." Then the doctor was out the door.

Well, this was new. Except for the initial meeting, we had always had all our discussions in the examination room. I had a moment of panic, but quickly squashed it down. Everything had looked good during the exam so I figured we would just be talking about what was to come in the next few weeks. I finished getting dressed and went to Dr. Gideon's office.

When I walked in, he had his back to me. He was pouring himself a cup of coffee from the sideboard table in the corner of his room near his desk. Dr. Gideon turned when he saw me and instead of going around to the other side of his desk, he walked in front of it and he leaned against it. He took a sip of his coffee and sighed deeply.

"Nectar of the gods," he said and winked at me. "Can I get you some water or juice, Raine?"

"No thanks, Doctor." I smiled back. Then, because I was nervous, I asked him if everything was okay.

"Oh, yeah," he nodded. "Absolutely, no worries. It all looks fine."

"Then why . . . ?" I started.

Just then the door opened. I knew it before I saw him. The way you know who is going to be on the phone when it rings or that the next card pulled from the deck is going to be the ace of hearts. I knew it was Diego entering the room.

"Dr. Gideon." Diego extended his hand.

"Diego." Dr. Gideon took his hand and shook it.

"Hey, Raine." Diego ignored my astonished face and sat down in the chair next to me. I was speechless and probably in shock. No, *definitely* in shock.

"So I brought that family history in for you." Diego was handing over a form to the good doctor.

"Dr. Gideon?" I managed to croak out. Had he really gone behind my back and asked Diego for the medical history? How had he even known Diego was the father? We had never had that talk. I had carefully avoided that particular discussion.

Dr. Gideon took in my flushed face and shaky voice and raised an eyebrow. "Raine?"

"It's okay, Babe. I called the Doc here and came in and grabbed the forms." Diego said it like it was the most natural thing in the world.

I looked at him then. It occurred to me that I had never really seen him much outside of his "element." When we had been outside the compound, we had been on the bike or alone or with people we had known. I had never really looked at him from the perspective of what other folks saw.

He looked so big in the small office. His forearms hung over the armrests of the chair he was sitting in. He was hunched forward, the worn cut, his long dark hair, and his biceps straining against the sleeves of his white tee shirt screamed *outlaw biker*. His jeans were clean and worn and fit him like a glove.

He was beautiful.

He was a beautiful, dangerous man who had stolen my heart. Then broken it.

I put my hand protectively over my stomach. Diego was talking. He was talking to the doctor in earnest. And he was talking about Janey and the baby. He was talking about the stillbirth and he was handing him two pieces of paper. I was sitting in a daze and was trying hard to listen, I really was. But the voices sounded so far away.

"Doc," Diego was explaining, "I think these might help you. Janey's father ordered them and because Janey had a sister who might be having babies someday, I agreed. I knew she would want to spare her sister the pain she went through if the baby's death could be avoided with some sort of testing . . ." His voice trailed off.

The papers in Diego's hand were the autopsy reports from Janey and their son.

My heart broke again. But this time for him.

Then Diego looked at me. "I'm sorry, Babe. I should have thought of this sooner."

The doctor was looking through the papers. Intently. And he was frowning.

"I know these are old. I don't know if they will help or not . . ." Diego was wringing his hands.

I looked at them sitting in his big lap and thought dully that he was lucky he could still feel his limbs. I had stopped feeling anything the minute he had walked into the room.

Then the doctor looked up. He refocused on us and what he saw written on Diego's face scared him into looking at mine. He hurriedly spoke up.

"No, no. Everything looks fine. There's a lot of medical terminology here that I could put in layman's terms for you. Basically there's nothing here to indicate that the baby Raine is carrying would be at risk." He smiled at us then.

Then because Dr. Gideon was who he was, he looked at Diego. He saw past the outlaw cut, the hard eyes, and the inked biceps. He looked past all that and saw the worried look of a father for his baby. Of a man for his pregnant woman. And when he saw it, he did his best to ease it.

"Son, I can see you're worried. I'm sorry for your loss. Twenty years ago or yesterday, a loss is still a loss." He reached in and put his hand on Diego's shoulder.

He leaned back to take the both of us in.

"Can genetics play a factor in stillbirths? They sure can. Would this information have been helpful a little sooner? Maybe. But only to relieve you both of any worry that you're experiencing. Worry that I wish you had shared with me." Now the good doctor was looking pointedly at me with an arched brow. I blushed uncomfortably.

"Because this"—he waved the paper in front of us—"is not that." He gestured towards my baby belly.

"Now, stillbirths can happen. I don't want to force statistics down your throat but they do happen and not too infrequently. Childbirth is a risky business with chromosomes and pre-genetic dispositions and a host of other factors. In many ways it's a crapshoot really." Then he smiled. "I guess that's why they call it a miracle. But the two of you . . . err . . . the three of you are in good shape."

He stood up. "So if that's all, I'll see you in another couple of weeks."

He shook Diego's outstretched hand and smiled warmly at me.

I could hear my heartbeat but I could not feel my feet, which made it hard to stand when it was finally time to go. So I gripped the rails of the chair and, like pregnant women everywhere, led with my belly. I held on tight for a few minutes, letting the blood flow back into my limbs.

"Doc, I know this is your office and shit, but you mind giving me a minute alone with my woman?" Diego had stood up. I don't know if he meant to be intimidating, but he towered over the doctor. He was practically stepping on his toes in the small office.

To Dr. Gideon's credit, he did not seem to be the least bit intimidated.

He clapped Diego on the arm and said, "Alarm is set. I got my own woman to get home to. Take your time. Just make sure the door is locked when you're done." And off he went, closing the door behind him.

Diego turned to me then. "That was me taking care of shit."

"Taking care of shit?" I stammered.

"Damn. I ain't good with words, Raine, and you know it. I mean to say that was me stepping up. Reaching into the past to take care of you and the baby. My baby. Our baby." Diego was looking at me.

I was still standing, but I thought I should probably sit.

"Prosper told me about Janey and the baby, Diego." I don't know why, but I felt it was important to say her name.

"Yeah, I know that, Babe." Diego's dark eyes narrowed like a cornered jungle cat.

"I'm sorry that happened. I'm sorry. I get why maybe me springing a baby on you out of the blue was a lot, *a lot*, to handle. But I was . . ." My voice trailed off.

"You were what, Raine?" Diego asked warily.

"I was happy, Diego." And there it was.

He was hardly breathing and I couldn't look at him and find the courage to go on. So I looked at my folded hands instead.

"I was *happy*, Diego. I wanted this baby. From the minute I thought it was the smallest possibility that I was pregnant, I was filled with *utter and complete happiness.*"

And because at this point I really had nothing left to lose, I decided to tell him exactly, *exactly* how I felt about him and the baby and well, everything.

I was done being angry.

I was done being hurt.

I was done playing the "He is invisible to me" game. Because that was not me. I was not her. And I just didn't want to pretend any longer.

"Diego, I was happy not only because this baby was *mine*, but because it was *yours*. I was happy because us being *together* had created something beautiful and miraculous and wonderful."

Then because I didn't want him to misunderstand, I looked at him and added quickly, "I was careful about taking the birth control every day. It's important to me for you to know that I never ever set out to get pregnant. I want you to know that I would never knowingly put you in a position of being the father of a child that you had no intention of having. I know it sounds stupid, but I'm still not really sure how it happened." I took a breath.

"It was those pills that Jules gave to me to give to you, to calm you down after the shit with Gino." Diego was looking at me. "Jules, the fucking idiot, never thought to tell me they could interfere with the birth control, and me, the fucking idiot, never thought to ask." He reached out and covered my hands with his.

Then he went on.

"Yeah, I was shocked. I was fucking out of my mind when you told me you were pregnant. But despite what I said to you, Raine, despite those horrible fucked-up words that I threw at you like a fucking grenade, it was never about not wanting it, Babe. It was never about not wanting you. Fuck, I hadn't even gotten that far in the processing before I lost my shit." Diego let go of my hands, leaned back in the chair, and scrubbed his hand over his face.

"When you told me, all I could see was a *dead you*. I didn't want to lose you, Raine. Fuck, Babe, I still don't want to lose you. I want you. I want the baby. I want it all. I want the white picket fence and the tire swing in the yard. Cookouts on Sunday and fucking family vacations. I want this baby and a few more like it if you're game." He looked at me then, straight in the eye with his heart on his sleeve.

I couldn't move. I couldn't think. I just knew I wanted and needed to feel myself in the arms of this big, beautiful, bad man. I made my eyes meet his and in them I saw the love that I was looking for. I knew by the way he smiled down at me that he saw that same love reflected in my own. Everything was gonna be alright.

It was all going to work out.

I was going to get my happily-ever-after.

Diego and me and baby makes three.

I stretched up to him as he reached down to me.

I was singing that happy tune in my head right up until the time I saw my man do this weird little full-body-dance then crumble down in front of me.

I was singing that happy tune right up until I felt something hard hit me on the back of my head.

Fall back. Fall back. Protect the baby, I thought to myself just before it all went black.

CHAPTER 70

I'VE BEEN FUCKING TASERED!" Diego was shouting into the phone.

"At the fucking doctor's office!"

"They took Raine. They fucking took her!"

"Yeah, it took three fucking times to get me the fuck down but the motherfucking cocksuckers fucking succeeded."

Then louder.

"NO FUCKING IDEA."

Then at a pitch that could be heard two towns away.

"Do not. Do not fucking tell me to calm the fuck down. I need you to get here now. Fucking yesterday. Motherfuckers blew out my tires!"

Diego was gonna fucking kill his brother if he asked him one more fucking question.

"Ninety-eight fucking Liberty Street, you fucking moron. I just fucking said it!"

He hadn't said it. He knew he hadn't said it.

"You fucking tell me to calm the fuck down one more goddamn time I am gonna rip off your balls and shove them down your fucking throat."

He took a deep breath because Jules was right.

He had to calm the fuck down and figure out what the hell had just happened. His hands were shaking and he felt like he was going to be sick. He put his hands on his knees and took three deep breaths.

"Jules?" he croaked out.

"Yeah, Brother. I'm with you. Right here, man. Right here." Jules was working hard to keep his voice steady. Because if they had any hope of finding Raine, they had a very short window of time and they had to keep their shit straight up and fucking *think*. The club had to start putting it out, calling in favors, taking out marks, doing whatever the fuck they had to do to get D's woman and baby back to him.

Everyone in the club had a job to do and when it worked, it worked like a fine-tuned clock. Jules had no doubt, no doubt that they would find out who did this. Finding out in time, well, that was another story.

And they all knew it.

Diego was losing his shit. *Losing his shit.* Jules could hear it in his voice.

"Stay with me, Brother. Look around, you see anything? Doc have cameras up? You got anything?" Jules had a pencil in his hand.

"Yeah, Brother. He has cameras up. Lights fucking flashing." Then with a little hope in his voice, "Looks like they are recording and trained right on the lot."

"Good, man, that's great. I'm calling the doctor right now. We're gonna get him over there with that tape. Now, anything else? Look at the ground. You got anything?" Jules was already on the other line to Dolly getting Gideon's number.

Diego heard the calm in Jules's voice and it brought him back to where he needed to be. He could not, could not, could not fucking fall apart right now. Everything. Everything depended on him not fucking falling apart.

Diego was looking at the contents of the spilled purse lying next to the open door of Raine's car.

Then he said with deadly calm, "Brother?"

"Yeah, D. Right here."

"You better call Reno. Looks like they got Claire too." Then Diego turned off the cell and waited.

CHAPTER 71

The doctor showed up not fifteen minutes later, his black Mercedes escorted by four of Prosper's crew. He was out of the car before the bikers had pulled their bikes back to park.

Dr. Gideon went quickly to Diego and, putting his hand on his shoulder, forced him to look him in the eye.

"You okay, son?" Dr. Gideon's concerned face came into focus.

"Yeah, yeah . . . They must have hit her . . . I don't know. I think they hit her. On the head. The baby? Raine . . . I don't know." Diego was looking into the doctor's eyes.

Dr. Gideon had been dealing with Prosper's crew for years. He had delivered half the babies born into the MC. He had done his homework. He knew not one of those kids had ever wound up in an emergency room with any unexplained bumps or broken bones. None of them had ever ended up in foster care. While he knew all that, he also was not naive enough to think that most of them would end up to be pillars of the community either. However, the way he figured it, the grown-up part was not his concern. He knew Prosper made sure his crew treated those kids right, and that was enough for him.

He also knew that having a waiting room filled with the hard women and their hard men from a disreputable motorcycle "club" would be cause for most doctors to turn their heads the other way at accepting these new patients. This was one of the reasons Gideon had stayed in practice for so long. And one of the reasons he worried about getting out. But his wife had laid down the law, and he grudgingly had decided she was right. Forty years was long enough.

He had dealt with many a hard man in his days, but the look of fear and panic on the face of a man like Diego scared the hell out of him.

"Okay. I'm going in to get that tape for you. But first I want you to listen. I doubt very much whoever did this was would hit Raine hard enough to do any permanent damage. My guess is if they had wanted her dead, she would have been killed on the spot. You know better than I do, but I think it is safe to say that for now Raine is okay."

The doctor held Diego's eyes.

"Now for the baby."

He took a breath and went on.

"A fetus needs adequate oxygen and nutrition. A blow to the head is not going to interfere with these vital necessities. Not even to a small degree. Nature has provided a very well-protected environment for fetuses, otherwise the whole race would be too fragile to survive." Dr. Gideon smiled faintly, hoping he had gotten through to Diego.

Diego looked into the doctor's eyes and took a deep breath. He had heard him. Raine and their child were okay for now. While it made him sick inside to think of Raine being hit like that, Diego agreed that if whoever did this had wanted Raine dead, she would have been. If Raine had been dead from that blow, they wouldn't have taken her. No. They hit her just hard enough to knock her out, he was sure of it. But he hadn't known if Raine being unconscious for even a short time would hurt the baby. He felt only a little better at the news. But he would take it.

"Let's go get that tape, Doc." Diego was back.

Because Dr. Gideon was not only a good doctor but a good God-fearing man, he looked into the blackness that reflected back to him from Diego's eyes and said a silent prayer for whoever it was who had abducted Raine. Because no matter what the outcome, Diego was not only going to kill that someone, he was going to make him suffer unbearably first.

CHAPTER 72

The next few hours served to prove why Prosper was one of the most influential and feared men on the eastern seaboard.

Within twenty minutes of hearing of the girls' kidnapping, Prosper had made contact with three federal agents and four congressmen, all of whom were in his pocket. They were all on standby waiting for information that they could use their extensive influence to act upon.

Twenty-five minutes after viewing the tape, Prosper had ordered a sit-down with the heads of three of the most feared crews in the outlaw nation.

He had been spending a good deal of his time in the last few months putting together a very lucrative deal involving the crews of Los Diablos, the Mob, and the Aces. The Mexicans, Italians, and blacks all coming together was unheard of. But Prosper was getting on in years and was a very smart guy. He had worked hard on this deal and, while being extremely profitable, it would not work without the cooperation of the heads of the other crews.

It had taken him months to get them all at a table. Months. Once there, he had laid out his plan. If properly executed, there would be little risk involved. But only if done right. Each organization was a cog in the wheel of the plan, with the Saints being the beginning and ending cog, therefore taking on most of the risk.

That and the promise of all the green made the other head members of their crews want in.

Prosper had spent many hours finessing the deal. Easing tensions, soothing egos, and dancing the fucking dance. No one wanted to see it go down the toilet.

But that was exactly where it would be if both his girls weren't found safely and fast.

Prosper sat at the table. Jules to his right. Diego to his left.

Prosper had just finished showing the tape of Raine and Claire's abduction. He was looking straight at the head of Los Diablos.

"So this fucking shit your play, Ese?" Prosper's eyes were shark black.

"No, man." Lucius was shaking his head. "No fucking way this falls back on us."

"Fucking member of your crew did the deed." Gianni was pissed. Who the fuck took a pregnant woman?

Lucius was looking around the table. He was thinking he was pretty well screwed. Either he was going to look like he couldn't handle his crew or he was going to look like he put a hit out on Prosper's family. Either way this was bad. And Lucius did not like looking bad under the best of circumstances. This shit was epic. This shit was so incredibly fucked that unless he handled this right, Lucius had little hope of coming out of it alive.

"Yeah, my crew. But not my order, friend. The stupid motherfucker acted on his own. He's a dead man. That I promise you." Lucius was looking around the table.

Prosper looked at Lucius. "I really hope that's true, motherfucker. Because as of right now, I have two men at your house pointing .45s at your woman and your three fucking kids."

Lucius's face showed no emotion, but he chin-nodded to his man to make the call to his house. When Lucius's second came back to the table, he nodded once at Lucius.

Lucius said nothing.

Prosper's face was grim. He looked at the bosses.

"This tape shows a prospect from Lucius's crew taking my girls. He acted against my man to do it. With no provocation."

Prosper delivered those words with dead calm.

Then he slammed his hand on the table so hard it sent a splinter through the wood that ran half the length of the slab before it stopped.

Prosper's eyes flashed red. His gravelly voice delivered a message straight from hell.

"With no fucking provocation. My girls. Raine is eight months pregnant. Her sister Claire, sweetest girl on the planet. Hit on the head. Pushed into a van. My man tasered. Nothing. Nothing makes this right except blood. Nothing!"

He looked around the table. He was shouting at the top of his lungs.

"Everything is on hold. If my daughters are not found within the next few hours, you pay, Lucius. And you pay with blood.

"I am going to start with your kids first. I am going to make you watch while I put a bullet in their heads. You feel me, Ese?

"Then your woman. You are going to fucking watch them all die. I don't give a shit! Everybody you ever loved is going to die fucking slowly.

"If my girls get hurt . . . NO ONE IS SAFE." Prosper was leaning in and pointing his big thick finger in the face of Lucius.

Then with dead calm.

"Raine and Claire are returned safely first. That's first. Past that, I want that fucking piece of shit who could be swayed by that crazy snatch dead. And I want that snatch dead. Anyone got a problem with that, you can fucking get up now and leave. I want a bullet through that bitch's throat. I am going to kill that prospect myself."

He continued, "Any man at this table not seeing this my way, leave now and know I take that personal."

"Ain't got no problem," Demetrius said. "Shit's fucked up. I got a woman carrying a baby myself. No way I'm gonna want to worry about her when she goes to the goddamn doctor's office because some bitch who was blowing me gets a bug up her ass."

Then he added nodding around the table, "Bitch has got to go."

Gianni leaned in. "Lucius, you better contain this now. Bring in your prospect and find out what the fuck. Family, we don't touch. You know it. I know it. Everybody around this table knows it."

Gianni paused to nods all around. Then he continued.

"I'm telling you right now. My boys ain't got no beef with Los Diablos, never have. You and me, we don't dabble in the same pond. But this shit goes down with Prosper's family and I am with him. Nowhere to hide, man. You need to contain this. For a lot of fucking reasons. Word gets out you can't control a prospect, you lose your cred. You lose your cred, we don't want to go into business with you, *capisce?*" Gianni finished.

"Yeah, I understand." Lucius was rubbing the back of his neck. "Manny's my sister's kid. Took him on as a prospect as a favor to her. Kid addicted to bad snatch. Just like some women addicted to bad men. Manny did time for his love of pussy. Bitch fingered him for a deal few years back. He just got out. Hooked up with this gash. Crazy chick. But my nephew, he loves that shit. I'll find him. Got his mother on it now."

"His mother? You got his fucking mother on it?" Diego had been quiet up until this point. Following protocol, giving Prosper respect, knowing he would handle it. But now he spoke up.

"Yeah, man, my sister." Lucius was looking at Diego. "Raised four brothers when our mother died. Then had a man and raised four more while he did time. She's one tough mamma. Her boy hoping right about now that you find him first before his mother does. She threatened to rip off his dick if he pulled this shit again because of pussy and she is good to her word."

314

"Okay then. We're fucking done. You all know what's at stake. I suggest strongly, Lucius, that you call in every favor owed you and take as many markers as you can to find this piece of shit family member of yours before I put them all to ground looking for him. You hear me, Ese?" Prosper was sick of dicking around with these assholes. He needed to get out there and find his girls.

"You sitting here threatening my boss's family, man? Los Diablos don't take kindly to that." Lucius's first hand sitting to his left spoke up.

"Shut the fuck up," Lucius said to him.

"Yeah, that's a threat and a promise." Diego spoke quietly but not one man mistook his tone.

Prosper brought down the gavel three times and it was done.

~

Reno had been leaning against the bar watching the door for the past hour. The ashtray next to him was full, but the shot glass next to that had stayed empty. He wanted to be clear when he heard what had gone down in the meet. He wanted to be clear to do what needed to be done to get Claire back.

Because he loved her.

Yeah, he fucking did.

He loved her.

He loved the way she laughed and how her smile made the freckles across her nose dance. He loved how she twirled her hair when she was tired and how her clothes always seemed to be one size too big for her, as though she was hiding in them. He loved how she avoided being too close to him. But how, when she thought he wasn't looking, she would stare at him with a sort of wonder and longing in her eyes that even she was not aware of. He loved, fucking loved, that she did not look at any other man that way.

315

He loved how shy she was.

He loved how brave she was.

He loved the way she teased Prosper, easily the biggest, baddest dude in a club of very big, bad dudes and made him laugh at himself in ways nobody else, even Pinky, dared to do.

He loved that he hadn't kissed her yet. Because that was worth waiting for.

Yeah, he fucking loved her. And the thought of her out there with some psycho bitch and love-crazy prospect spic was making him crazy.

Crazy enough to kill.

The meet was over and Reno pulled himself away from the bar, watching the heads of three gangs and their seconds walk out. The faces were grim but they were all moving to the bar, as was custom, to raise a glass in solidarity.

Well, that was something.

Diego and Prosper flanked each side of Reno. They drank their shots down quickly and let the men see themselves out.

Then Diego and Prosper took Reno, Jules, and the rest of the executive branch of the Saints and filled them in.

Lucius's second was allowed to go. But Lucius was being held in one of the rooms on the compound. His life and the life of his woman and children were hanging in the balance.

CHAPTER 73

Claire had seen it in a movie. With that and her well-honed instinct for noticing her surroundings, she was keeping track of the turns they were taking and things she was hearing. Trying to get a fix on their location if at all possible. Not sure why, but she thought if she could somehow control this she could keep it from happening.

But the moment she felt Raine waking up from where she had her head cushioned on her lap, all that went right out the window. Thank God, she was beginning to moan and toss her head from side to side. Claire had had her hand over her sister's stomach partly instinctually and partly to make sure the baby was moving.

It was. Thank heavens.

Reno had dropped Claire off at Dr. Gideon's office. Raine had booked the last appointment of the day and Claire had plans to meet her there to go out afterwards for a leisurely dinner and some baby shopping. She had used the spare key to open the door to Raine's car and was going to sit in it and wait. It had been a long day waitressing at Reds and she was bone tired. Just as she was about to hop into the car, she was dragged from behind, hit over the head, and pushed into a van. When a woman had turned Claire over, she screamed at the Hispanic man with her.

~

"I don't know who the fuck this is, Manny, but it ain't that fucking bitch!" Ellie had foam at the corners of her mouth.

"Well, what the fuck, Ellie? She fits the description. She was getting in the car and at the doctor's office," Manny sniveled. Jesus, he was Lucius Rieldo's nephew. A prospect of one of the most feared MC clubs in the country and the son of Luisa Sievas, and this bitch had him sniveling. What was wrong with him?

Manny had seen Ellie when she had walked into Los Diablos clubhouse. Wearing practically nothing but a big bright smile, she honed right in on him. Made him feel special, like he was not just a prospect but the president, vice president, and sergeant at arms rolled into one. She was on her knees for him a half hour after they met and had been ever since. She let him do anything he wanted to her and even had a couple of suggestions. She had a mouth like a pro and sucked him off like nothing he had ever had.

She told him the story of how this chick named Raine had double-crossed her only brother. He was a veteran from Iraq who shot himself after learning she was knocked up by his best friend. He knew he had to help her get vengeance. He agreed to take the chick and give her a good talking-to, put a good scare into her. Much as he loved Ellie, Manny could never hurt a pregnant woman. Not so it mattered anyway.

"Does this bitch look fucking pregnant to you?" Ellie had hissed.

"Jesus, you didn't say how pregnant. Look the fuck where we are, Ellie. Doctor's office, fits your goddamn description, and getting into the shit heap of a car you described." Manny was getting pissed.

Ellie knew she needed to be careful. Manny was dumb, really dumb, but maybe not that dumb. And he had a trigger temper. She had better be careful and play this right until the end. If Ellie wanted to end up with Diego, she needed to play this right.

"Alright, alright. I'll stay in the back of the van with her. Must be a sister or something. Jesus, they look so much alike. Cunt must still be in the office. Go in there and see." Ellie was furious but maybe this could be salvaged. She was just getting ready to tie the chick up when Manny came running out with a very pregnant knocked-out woman in his arms. He practically threw her in the service van and yelled to Ellie to get in the front.

"What the fuck was Diego Montesalto doing in that office, Ellie?" Manny was barrel-assing it out of the parking lot.

"Who?" Ellie's voice did not reflect the fear she felt in her heart. Only for a minute. She felt that fear only for a second. Then thought to herself: *Good! Let him know what it feels like to lose someone like I lost him. He wants that half breed over me? Well, he's not getting her now. Soon as we put her to ground, he'll see what a mistake he made and then he'll come crawling back to me. We can pick up right where we left off. And Manny? Well, I'll just have to make that look good. He'll be dead. She'll be dead. No one will ever know. It will look like some old vendetta crap. Bikers are big on that.*

"Montesalto, Prosper's boy. One of the kingpins of the Saints. You know he was gonna be there, El?" Manny was driving fast and freaking out.

"Aw, baby, of course not. Breed whore must be playing him like she played my brother. That must be it." Ellie rubbed one of her tits on his arm and Manny immediately got hard. Seeing that, Ellie decided that it might be a good time to show Manny again just how grateful she was.

When they heard the moaning and hushed voices behind the metal mesh in the cargo van, neither one of them bothered to look back.

CHAPTER 74

Claire was feeling nauseous but didn't think she had gotten hit as hard as Raine did. She didn't think she was out that long. She was trying to listen to the conversation in the front but things were too muffled. God help her, she saw that skank, whoever she was, go down in the guy's lap face first. Van careened a little after that. Gross. Yuck. Yuck. Claire wondered for the millionth time who they were and what they wanted with Raine and her.

Claire was looking at Raine. She was pale but her pupils looked okay. Claire was no nurse though. And she was scared, more scared than she had ever been in her life. Claire hushed Raine as her moans became louder, and her eyes became more focused. She didn't know why, but instinct told her that it would be better for Raine if the two fellatio-enjoying fools in the front were not aware that her sister had regained consciousness. She tried to keep Raine as comfortable as possible while trying to keep the terrifying numbness from taking over her body, and her mind. Claire had to *think*. Raine had always been the hero in Claire's story; now it was time for Claire to step up and save the day.

Save the day.

Yep. She just hoped she was up to it.

They stopped much later and the door to the van opened. A small wiry Mexican wearing the prospect cut of an MC called Los Diablos Rojos stood there with a gun pointed at them. Next to him was a skanky-looking white girl. Young. Could have been pretty once, but the life she had chosen had put hard lines around her mouth and eyes. Her hair was a brash, bottle blond, and her red fingernail polish was all chipped and the nails under the polish were dirty.

The two were obviously together. But what didn't make sense was what they wanted with the two of them. Claire had no idea.

"Get her on her feet," yelled the crazy white chick.

"You realize my sister is eight months pregnant?" Claire was still cradling Raine's head in her lap.

"Eight months?" The prospect was looking at the skank. "I thought you said . . ."

"Never mind that," the white bitch said. "Get her the fuck up."

Claire was looking at the prospect. "You realize who we are?"

"Don't know who *you* are. Don't give a shit either. But your sister here, she's got blood on her hands. My girl's brother fucking offed himself because your sis got knocked up by his best friend," Manny replied.

"What? What? What are you talking about? My name is Claire Win . . ."

Claire heard the blast before she saw it. The skank had grabbed the gun out of the prospect's hand and fired a shot right near Claire's head. It pinged off the side of the metal wall and Claire moved quickly over her sister to protect her from what might be a ricochet.

"JESUS CHRIST!" Claire screamed.

"Shut the fuck up. Just shut the fuck up, bitch." Ellie was pushing the gun at them.

Then she looked at her man. "You gonna listen to these skanks trying to talk their way out of this, Manny?"

"Get her up and get her in that car over there," Ellie was saying.

Every instinct, *every instinct* Claire had told her to stall. To keep her and Raine from getting in that car at all costs. She didn't know why, but she knew if they allowed themselves to be taken into that car, they were going to die much sooner than later. Claire needed time. Most of all, she needed time. Prosper and the brothers must be going balls to the wall looking for them right about now.

She just needed to figure out how to separate these two fuck buddies and to wind up with the prospect instead of the crazy whore. They stood absolutely no chance of getting out of this once alone in the hands of Crazy Pants. Of that Claire had no doubt.

In the few minutes since the two amigos opened the van door, she figured that for whatever reason, either mistaken or for some personal vendetta, the blonde was feeding the outlaw-in-training a boatload of shit. When she had tried to make it clear, the bitch had almost blown Claire's head off. So she figured the deception was intentional. But what did this have to do with Raine?

Unless . . . there were few things in this world that would cause a woman's eyes to go crazy like that. And one was the loss of a man to another woman. Jealousy. Jesus. Were their lives at risk because this skank wanted Diego? Back when Raine had come to get her from rehab, she mentioned a run-in with some club whore. The girl had not only called Raine out, but her sister had said that there was something crazy, something wild and irrational going on behind the eyes of the woman. Claire was thinking hard. She seemed to remember that Raine said Diego had run her off. But Raine had been sure that they had not seen the last of her.

Oh, my God.

Was this her?

Jesus, what was her name? Eileen? Ellen? Shit. Not that it mattered. Was this what this was?

A random car pulled into the rest area and the door was shut quickly again, keeping the two sisters out of sight. Claire thought about screaming but before the door closed, she caught sight of a baby car seat and two small children in the back. She didn't want to put the family's life at risk.

Putting her ear to the door, she heard the two bastards arguing in muffled voices. Then she heard a car door slam. Claire prayed it was the crazy one getting in the car, and that the prospect would be driving the van. Not sure why, but Claire felt sure she might have a better chance talking the duped fool into reason.

Claire felt Raine stir and saw that her focus had become clearer. Raine looked at Claire with fright-filled eyes. "It's *Ellie*," she whispered to me. "This is about Diego."

Really? Over a man? They had been kidnapped and hit over the head and a life that had not even had a chance to begin yet had been put at risk? Over a man?

Once they were on the road again, Claire eased Raine into a sitting position and grabbed some blankets that were in the van to support her back against the cold, hard fiberglass interior. Claire took a minute to assess her situation. The van looked like it might be a carpenter's or mason's rig. There were some tools bungee-corded on peg-board. A claw hammer and a nail gun stood out like beacons of light against a few other items that were of no interest to the girls.

Claire looked at them, then at Raine and nodded. Claire got up and plastered herself against the mesh barrier and began trying to talk to Manny. He turned up the radio to drown her out. Asshole move on his part, but the sisters used the noise to shield the sound of them prying the tools from the peg-board.

Claire slipped the hammer in the back of the waistband of her jeans, and Raine hid the nail gun up the elastic sleeve band of her voluminous shirt. She felt momentarily for the baby moving and gave Claire a thumbs-up.

They were armed.

Once she had Raine comfortably wedged against the van wall, Claire took advantage of her small stature and crawled over to right under the mesh rigging. She was trying to hear what Manny was saying to whoever he was talking to on his cell.

He had turned the radio back down and seemed to be trying to talk his way out of the trouble he had gotten himself in. Whoever was on the other end of the phone was not pleased.

Claire started shouting from the back, "Let Prosper Worthington of the Hells Saints know where we are. Tell him Claire and Raine are with this asswipe."

Manny elbowed the mesh and caught Claire on the lip through it. "SHUT UP, BITCH."

Then he was back on the phone. He shouted something back to whoever was shouting at him. He shut off the cell and threw it on the seat next to him.

"Who the fuck are you?" Manny yelled back into the compartment at Claire.

Now they were getting somewhere.

"I'm Claire and that's my sister, Raine. We are Prosper's family. Raine is Diego Montesalto's woman, and that's his baby she's carrying. That woman you have been banging is cat-lady crazy. Diego sent her packing months ago. This is about her getting him back." Claire was talking with her mouth back up against the metal mesh.

"She told me—" Manny began.

"Yeah, I heard what she told you. It's not true. You know it's not true. Whoever was on that phone knows it's not true. You take us wherever you're taking us, that bat-shit crazy bitch is going to kill us and then probably kill you too. And if she doesn't kill you, after what you have done here, there will be no place, no place you will be able to hide. Prosper will never ever let you get away with this. If we die, you die. Ellie dies. Your family, they all die. You know it." Claire knew every word she said was true, and Manny knew it too.

"Motherfucker!" Manny screamed.

Then he swerved the van hard to the side of the road and shut off the engine.

Claire looked at Raine and whispered, "It's now or never. You ready?"

Raine nodded.

Manny pulled the van door open. He was waving his gun at them and shouting.

"Get out! Get the fuck out of the van right now." He was sweating and his eyes were black. The hand that held the gun was shaking. He had powder residue on his nose and on the side of his mouth.

Shit. He was jacked to his core. Claire hadn't counted on him being coked up.

Claire looked at Raine.

Raine nodded. "Yeah, I see it."

The two of them were cool as cucumbers. Years of self-preservation and instinct took right over.

Claire moved in front of Raine and once again shielded her sister and her baby from the madman.

Manny moved aside as the girls got down from the van.

As Raine passed in front of Manny, she bent over and held her belly, groaning. Pretending to lean against him for support, she moved into him and reached for the nail gun under her sleeve. Not being at all careful where she aimed, she pumped three nails into Manny's groin area.

His face spasmed in unbearable pain and he let go of the gun. Then a rush of adrenaline coursed through his veins and he roared.

Claire felt a rush of adrenaline of her own and hit Manny over the head with the hammer. Hard.

The two women looked at Manny slumped unconscious on the ground, a stain of blood beginning to pool the front of his pants.

Raine looked at Claire and grinned. "Ouch."

"Yeah." Claire grinned back.

CHAPTER 75

The state trooper was reporting in to Prosper. "Interstate 7. Yeah, family called it in a few minutes ago. Seems they pulled into a rest area and noted some suspicious activity. Looked like two women, one pregnant, were being held in the back of a van. Guy was standing in front of the plate, but it was a gray service van. Family wanted to get out of there quick. Guy was wearing a cut, but they couldn't make it out. Young woman with him, early twenties, skinny, blond hair. Sound about right?"

"Yeah. Thanks, man." Prosper hung up.

Diego and Reno were looking at the map.

"Runs north," Diego was saying, "Turns off here. And here."

Prosper was on the phone again.

"Get guys up on North 7 up near junction 29. Gray utility van," Prosper ordered.

Pinky and Dolly walked through the Hells Saints door and put out a pot of fresh coffee, sandwiches, and several new packs of smokes on the table. They also brought in four shots of brandy but didn't leave the bottle. Jules was in the other room getting a bag of medical supplies ready. Just in case.

CHAPTER 76

It's different being scared for yourself. When you're scared for yourself, that's bad. Really bad. But being scared for a life you are responsible for, that brings scared to a whole different level. *A whole different level.*

Crazy goddamn Ellie. I knew it. I knew from the moment I saw her watching Diego and me from the woods that first night that she was going to do me harm. I felt it. I felt it in my bones the way you feel the winds of an impending storm or the drizzle of rain before it turns into torrents.

I knew she would try to hurt me.

But I never thought she would go after a pregnant me. I had underestimated her baseline of crazy. I had seen the mean, but I had not recognized it as the pure evil it was.

And because of that, I had put two of the things I loved most in this world in harm's way: my sister and my unborn child. I was filled with self-recrimination.

I was also filled with anger and a sense of protective instincts that sent adrenaline coursing through my veins. The disappointment that I felt in myself would have to wait. I had better use for my fury.

Claire and I left Mr. Shit for Brains in a pool of his own blood. By the tearing sound I heard when he tried to straighten himself up, my guess is that I had nailed his nut sack to his thigh.

Good for me.

Claire and I had scurried into the van and found the keys in the ignition. Not knowing the whereabouts of Miss Crazy Pants scared us and upped our sense of urgency to get off the side of the road and fast.

Neither of us had any idea where we were going, and it was a damn good thing that Claire knew how to drive a stick shift. We decided our best bet was just to turn the van around until we figured out where we were.

I grabbed the cell on the seat and said a prayer that it was a smart one. But no, just like its owner, this phone had limited capability. Actually it was locked on two numbers. One said "Clubhouse" and the other said "Lucius." This was not uncommon. Prospects usually carried a throwaway. Throwaways could not be traced. This prospect could receive any calls coming in, but calls he made out were only to his president or his clubhouse. Other access was earned.

Figuring what the hell, Claire and I decided to press the "Lucius" button.

"Manny, where the fuck are you?" someone roared into the phone.

Claire and I looked at each other, and I almost lost my nerve.

Claire nodded and I swallowed hard.

"This is not Manny. Manny is on the ground somewhere with his nuts nailed to his leg and his head bashed in. I'm Raine."

"Jesus," Lucius answered. "You okay, chica? Your sister okay?" Lucius's voice sounded anxious.

They had been right. Prosper had put the word out.

"Yeah, we're okay for now," I answered.

"Where the fuck are you?" Lucius wanted to know.

"Just have Prosper call this phone," I answered, then I hung up.

Claire and I looked at each other and barely stopped ourselves from high-fiving.

It seemed a little too soon to be that optimistic, but for now, we figured we were out of the woods.

The phone rang and we felt the bump come from behind us at the same time.

"Hello?" I answered.

"Thank God." It was Prosper.

Our smiles of relief turned to something else instantly.

"Ouch," I said into the phone as the seatbelt strained against my swollen abdomen. I leaned forward to put my hand on the dash and release some of the pressure.

Then I felt it again. Whack.

We were being plowed into from behind

"Ouch? What the fuck is ouch, Raine?" Prosper worried into the phone. I looked at Claire. I wanted my hand free to cover my stomach so I handed her the phone.

"We're in the van. Something is hitting us from behind!" Claire yelled into the phone.

Then.

"I don't know!" My sister's hands on the wheel were shaking.

The whole contents of the van were propelled forward. We could hear the tools come loose and clang against the metal mesh of the divider. Claire's chest hit hard against the steering wheel.

I looked in the rearview on my side and there she was. Like some crazy phoenix rising from the ashes, Ellie was ramming us hard from behind.

"Claire, look." I adjusted the interior mirror for her. "It's Ellie." BAM.

"I don't know. I don't know, Prosper." Tears were threatening my sister's voice.

She was desperately looking out the windows.

"There's nothing around here to look at, Prosper." She was full-on crying now.

"Stop yelling at me!" Claire sobbed into the phone. "That crazy bitch is ramming us from behind.

"I don't know which fucking direction. I can't tell." She was running out of brave and fast. I knew exactly, exactly how she felt.

Claire looked at me helplessly. Ellie crashed into us again. Hard. The seatbelt retracted against my belly, but I held the slack in my hand. My arm outstretched against the dash.

I wanted to help, but I sucked at directions too. I looked around desperately.

Then I saw the little compass bobble thing on the dash. I pointed to it for Claire.

She took a deep breath and nodded.

"North and there's a marker. We are traveling north on Interstate 7," Claire breathed out.

~

"FUCKING BITCH!" Ellie had pulled up beside us in a black Jeep and took a sharp turn into us.

"CRAZY PSYHO!" Claire yelled back.

I screamed. I couldn't help it.

Claire dropped the phone.

She looked at me and yelled, "Raine. Hold on. I'm going to have to force some road rage on this LUNATIC"—she spared a glance in Ellie's direction—"or she is going to run us straight off the damn road!"

I braced myself with my feet and hands. Then I thought again and reached for the blanket and put it between my pregnant belly and the dash. Damn old heap did not have air bags. That was a good thing for my baby, I thought. But I still wanted to provide as much protection as I could if things went bad.

"Ready?" Claire glanced at me.

"Yeah," I answered. I put my hand to Claire's briefly. Our eyes met and misted over.

"I love you," we both said at the same time.

Then Claire swerved violently to the left, catching Ellie off guard on a sharp corner. The Jeep veered on two wheels, throwing sparks as the muffler dragged on the ground. I looked in the rearview mirror and saw the damn SUV right itself.

She was coming at us again.

Claire looked at me and said, "I don't think I can outrun her."

I looked back at the SUV and at the road ahead. "Look, there's a steep embankment to the right up there."

"Yeah, I see it." Claire was looking ahead.

"She can't see past this van. If you stay in front of her, just enough so she doesn't ram us, and then swerve to the left at the last minute, she won't have time to corner the turn and will drop off the cliff."

"Yeah, or she'll lock on to us with her fucking bumper and we'll both get pulled over." Claire looked at me.

Then the bitch bumped us again. Really hard.

"We have to try it. Claire, I think we have to try." I was crying too by then.

Claire took her eyes off the road long enough to search mine for a moment.

I could see the terror in her eyes.

"It's our only chance, honey. You can do it. I know you can." I smiled at her through the tears and took my hand off the dash just long enough to clasp hers in mine.

Claire squeezed my hand and nodded once.

"Damn right I can do this." Claire sat up straighter in the seat.

She swerved the wheel and looked into the rearview. She positioned the van right in front of Crazy Ellie. I looked in the mirror and helped Claire navigate to stay in front of her. Claire had the pedal pushed to the floor.

"Ready?" Claire's hands were white-knuckled on the steering wheel.

I just nodded.

"RAINE?" Claire had the pedal to the metal.

"READY!" I yelled over the roar of two engines.

Claire veered sharply to the left then, and the whole van careened and squealed on two wheels for what must have been a mile before it finally landed upright then halted to a dead stop.

We looked behind us just in time to see the Jeep miss the turn and fly high over the embankment. We listened for it and heard it land heavy in a sea of bent metal. The sound of thick tree trunks being broken in half filled our ears before the raging bull finally succumbed to broken glass and torn gas lines.

It went up in a roar of deep crimson flames.

Claire and I got out of the van and walked towards the edge of the cliff. Even though the crash was well beyond the steep ledge, we could hear the hiss and pop of explosions going on around the vehicle. The heat was so intense I could feel it on my face.

I suddenly felt Claire clap her hands tight against my ears.

I looked at her face and her eyes were bright. Tears were streaming down her cheeks.

Then I heard them.

The sounds that my sister met full-on in her attempt to spare me from them.

Through the warmth of her hands I heard them.

The tortured screams of Ellie being burned alive.

CHAPTER 77

A roar of engines sounded towards us. We listened to them approach. The pavement reverberated with the sound. The welcome vibration ran through our bodies. *We could feel them.* A fleet of steel horses ridden by dark knights charging to our rescue. We knew before we saw them. Our men had come to take us home.

Our family would be waiting for us.

Our outlaw father and brothers and lovers. And their women.

The shadow people. The brotherhood. The ones I had hidden Claire and myself from so long ago when their dark images had given way to my every childhood nightmare.

They had now become the heroes in our story. Our dark avengers.

They were now our hope.

They were now our loved ones.

Loved ones.

This not-so-merry band of outlaws had taken us in. Had made us feel warm and welcome.

Had made us feel *wanted.*

They had opened up their own careworn, damaged, hard hearts and saw what had been broken in ours.

And they had fixed them.

They had held our hearts in their hands. They had glued and stitched and hammered and nailed until we were whole again.

Our outlaw family had succeeded where even royalty had failed.

They had done what all the king's horses and all the king's men could not do.

They had put us back together again.

Putting my hand on the life growing inside me, I knew that someday the shadow people would cast firelit images on the walls of my own child's bedroom. My silhouette would merge with theirs as they formed the dancing shapes.

And my child would feel warm and safe and secure in the seeing of it.

My child would not be afraid.

CHAPTER 78

Claire and I stood on the edge of the road and waited for them. Holding on tight to each other like we always had.

It was going to be okay. We were safe. We were together and help was on its way. We were golden.

I looked at Claire and started laughing. "Little sister, I am so relieved I think I just peed my pants."

She looked at me smiling too.

"Seriously?"

Then I felt a deep pain in my belly that doubled me over.

"Raine, you okay?" Claire was holding on to me.

"Yeah, I'm fine. Except I don't think that was pee." I was trying not to panic.

"That's okay. It'll be okay." Claire was looking at me.

Then she really looked at me.

"Oh, my God, Raine! Do you think your water just broke?" I could hear the rising panic in my sister's voice.

I nodded.

"But it's too early." Claire was really scared now.

I looked at her, feeling that panic too.

Because she was not wrong. The baby was coming and it was too early.

And for the first time in a long time, I started to pray.

CHAPTER 79

They were waiting. They were pacing. They were waiting and pacing and filling up the small room with their big bodies. Their inked biceps flexing as they brought cups filled with strong coffee and splashes of a little somethin'-somethin' from the flasks they kept hidden on the insides of their worn leather cuts.

And they were scared. Prosper could see it in their faces, could feel it in the way they moved. They were frightened for Raine.

He looked around him. His boys. They were like caged jungle cats. Revved up on strong coffee and hard liquor, trying to keep themselves checked and on their best behavior waiting on the arrival of Raine and Diego's baby.

Raine's first baby.

Maggie would have been proud. Prosper couldn't help but think of her. She would have been so proud of Raine.

And of Claire. That one had turned out to be a little firebrand. She sure had. Still waters . . . yeah, in Claire's case, they sure as hell ran deep.

The first thing she had done, the very first thing she had done, after they had gotten Raine safely to the hospital, had been to move towards Diego and hit him.

Hard.

Claire had walked up to Diego and without a word had slapped him so hard that the sound had echoed against the cold tiles of the hospital waiting room.

Dolly had gasped and Reno made a move to stand in front of Claire. Diego put his hand out to halt him.

She had let them have their reunion. Had let them have their hugs and kisses and had allowed Diego to show Raine how worried he had been.

Claire had kept herself in check for hours.

Little sister had stepped aside while Diego had pushed past her to ride in the ambulance with Raine.

She had listened respectfully and intently with him while Dr. Gideon had explained the risks of delivering the baby a month early.

Then when she was sure it was all said and done, when she was sure that everything was stable and in place and working towards the good, she had walked up to Diego and slugged him.

Without a damn word, the little bit of a thing had let him have it, and she had to stand on tiptoes to do it.

She cracked him so hard that Prosper, sitting across the room, had felt it.

Everyone had held their breath.

"That's for— " Claire began.

"I know what that's for, Claire, and I fucking deserve it. Have at it. You might as well get it all out because I ain't going anywhere and when Raine and my baby get on the other side of this, I don't want anything getting in the way of us being a family. And I get that you being okay with this is a big part of her being happy. I get that my woman, my baby . . . you come with that."

"Damn right!" She spat at him.

Then she looked at him hard. "You in this?"

"All the way," Diego replied.

"You know, Diego, what's gonna happen in that room? That baby being born, that's just the beginning of it. I know what happened to you before, and I'm sorry for it. But it's done. It's over. I pray to God it never happens again to you or to anyone you love. But the truth is, Diego, it could. Getting past this day, that's the first part. Babies, they get sick. They puke, get ear infections and have been known to cry at ear-splitting decibels for hours at a time. You showed up today. That's one day. *One day. Being a father, that means showing up every day.*"

The whole room held their breath. Reno placed his feet wide apart, getting ready to lunge between D and Claire if it came to that. Claire was going for it, and after what D had been through in the past few hours, Reno wasn't sure how he was going to react. But then, his girl had been through some crap too. D was right; better she get it out.

Prosper folded his arms over his big chest. *Shit had to be said*, he thought to himself. So he let Claire continue.

Claire continued. "Diego, you cannot, *cannot* fall apart on them every time something happens because of letting those old memories get in the way. Later on when the kid falls off a swing or a bike or a goddamn high chair, you gonna be there to catch that fall, Diego? You gonna be able to get past that old grief and *man up*?"

At *man up* half the brothers in the room unwound their crossed arms and legs and stood straight up.

Prosper raised an eyebrow. Reno tensed.

"Because, Diego, Raine and I, we were raised by a man who could not get past his grief. And I cannot even begin to count the many, the very many ways that it sucked. This baby does not deserve that. If you don't think you have it in you, if you have one shred of doubt of what you feel for my sister and this baby, it's better for everyone that you leave right now. Because if you stay, I am going to be there every step of the way making sure you do *what the good daddies do*." At that she looked at Prosper.

Then back again at Diego. "I need you to be what we never had. I need you to be that for Raine. I need you to be that for the baby. And I need you to be that for me. Because I have got to tell you, Diego, I am getting really fucking exhausted."

Then she slumped forward just a little bit.

Reno was all over that, but Prosper put out his hand and stopped him.

Diego's eyes went soft when he saw Claire finally let herself feel the tired. When he answered her, he did it from his heart.

"I love her, Claire. I love that baby. And even though you are a little pain in the ass, I love you too, Little Sister. So yeah, I am here. For the puking and the falls and the infections. For the croup and the nightmares. I am here for the first day of kindergarten and the first day of college. I am here on Sundays, Saturdays, and every day in between. I am here every night and every fucking morning. I am here."

"That good enough for you, Little Sister?" Diego was looking at her.

Claire looked at Diego long and hard.

Well, finally.

Yeah, that was good enough for her.

Dr. Gideon came bursting through the swinging doors.

"Ready to come help me deliver that baby, son?" The good doctor twinkled.

And he was. Oh hell, yeah. Diego was.

EPILOGUE

It was Willow's second birthday. We had decided to celebrate it together with the housewarming of our newly built home up on the grassy knoll beside the little stream. Crow and Diego had begun drawing up the plans right after Willow's birth. The house was made of stone and timber. It was beautifully rustic and filled with large windows that let in lots of natural light.

The house sat in the middle of the meadow where I had made love to Diego and had thanked the heavens for sending him to me. And I still gave thanks for him. My beautiful bad man had given me this perfect little dark-haired, blue-eyed baby girl. Willow Magaskawee Montesalto was a happy, chubby imp and the apple of her father's eye.

We had gotten married as soon as our whole little family had been up to it. The birth of the baby had gone quickly, but Willow had been small and had needed some extra time in the hospital. Diego and I had kept a constant vigil. I honestly believed that I heard the entire nursing staff heave a collective sigh of relief when little Willow had been released.

Diego kept his word to Claire. He did what *the good daddies do* and he did it all the time. He left us only once and that was to go to Nevada. He had stopped at the florist and brought Janey and his son a beautiful bouquet of flowers. He also brought the ring that was now too small for him, the one he had kept in his wallet under the only picture he had left of Janey. He took the picture and the wedding ring, buried them deep in the soil below the gravestone, placed the flowers lovingly on top, and said his good-byes. He had explained to me that it was not the memory of them he was saying good-bye to, but the crippling fear that had risen from their ashes and had almost destroyed him.

Then he had come home to Willow and me. That night he'd planted the seed of our next child deep within me. I rubbed my round little belly lovingly. Willow would have a baby brother or sister in the fall. I could not be happier.

It had been a good couple of years for the brotherhood. The deal that Prosper had been working on came through and had proven as lucrative as he had known it would be. Apparently the Italians had been instrumental in seeing it through. Gianni's crew had worked alongside the Saints on a couple of deals since then. In an odd turn of events, I had met Gianni's family and I had liked them.

The MC had used the money to move towards more legitimate enterprises and they were all taking off. The brothers were rolling deep in green. Life was good.

Gradually, Glory began to open up to us more and more. And although she stayed on at the lake house, she eventually found the courage to step back out into the world.

Claire, secure in the knowledge that Diego was going continue to do right by Willow and me, finally felt free to follow her dreams. And some of those dreams included Reno.

Dolly and Pinky remained as thick as thieves and spent a whole lot of time spoiling Willow.

～

Dusk was setting in and the boys had begun to stoke the fire in the pit. Prosper was playing Seger on his harp. Reno and Jules were setting up the deck table for a poker game. The women were beginning to clean up from the cake and presents.

Willow was rubbing her sleepy little eyes with her chubby fist. I picked her up from the middle of her cache of new toys. She held on to me sleepily until she saw her daddy. Then she wiggled out of my arms and into his. Together we walked with her into the house. I watched as Diego washed her little hands and face, changed her diaper, and put her into her little pajamas. It always amazed me to see how much he loved doing both the "mommy and daddy" things for her. I settled into the rocking chair and he handed her to me. I snuggled her little body against me. Softly singing, I rocked her. Diego kissed me, then her, and moved to the door.

I stayed with Willow, holding her in my arms long after she had fallen asleep. I rocked her lovingly, watching the light of the shadow people dancing on the warm wood patina of the light pine.

I watched as the silhouettes caught in the firelight, casting long shadows on my daughter's walls.

I looked at her sleeping peacefully under the dancing images, satisfied that she had nothing to fear.

I kissed her softly, placed her in her warm, safe crib, and gently closed the door.

Then I went to find my husband.

ACKNOWLEDGMENTS

I would like to thank my husband, Pasquale, for being the hero in my story. Thank you for everything you are, and for everything I am when I am with you. This would not have been possible without your love guiding me.

I would like to thank my son, Jake, who helped me to navigate through the choppy waters and gave me the courage to put myself and my words out there. Thank you for your patience; I know I wasn't easy.

I would like to thank my daughter, Leah, who is currently teaching English two continents away from me. Your fearlessness, sense of adventure, wit, and talent inspire me. You are the bravest person I know.

I would like to thank my sister, Linda. Thank you for your enthusiasm, encouragement, and technical support. Who would have thought that those long, sad days at Kaplan House would turn into something wonderful and lasting?

My girl posse . . . Laurie and Angie. What would I do without the laughs? I am so blessed to be sharing this wonderful new adventure with you.

To Donna . . . Thanks for the times you have had to be the both of us. I know it is exhausting. You are my bestie forever. xxoo

To my Allendale and Crosby friends. I am honored to stand among you. Thank you for taking time away from evaluations, grades, lesson plans, and the rest of the growing list of academic craziness to support me. Where you find the time to read I will never know, but I thank you for it!

My Goodreads girls . . . Chaddy and Diana. Your encouragement, support, and friendship have meant so much. Thank you from the bottom of my heart.

And last but not ever, ever least, thanks to all the readers who took a chance on a new author. I thank you for your fearlessness! And for your support, and your encouragement. I look forward to continuing this journey with you.

ABOUT THE AUTHOR

Photo by Pasquale Marinaro, 2014

Paula Marinaro was born and raised on the North Shore of Boston. She lives with her husband, Pasquale, in the beautiful Berkshires of Western Massachusetts. She is the proud mother of two children, Jake and Leah.

She enjoys creating worlds and stories for others to enjoy.